BEIRUT

AN EXPLOSIVE THRILLER

Alexander McNabb

Also by Alexander McNabb

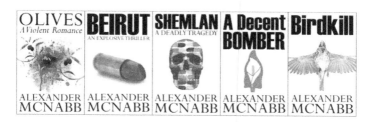

Olives – A Violent Romance

Shemlan – A Deadly Tragedy

A Decent Bomber

Birdkill

You can sign up to Alexander's newsletter, find out more about new releases, giveaways and other updates from

www.alexandermcnabb.com

My mother has put up with an awful lot from me over the years. This is for her.

Chapter One

The smell of death was everywhere. Gerald Lynch wrinkled his nose, his eyes adjusting to the darkness inside the villa. He picked his way through the rubbish, shaking his head at Palmer's blundering outside. The small washroom off the entrance hall had overflowed.

Shit and death.

Lynch tiptoed across the hallway and gingerly opened a door, yanking it shut against the buzzing cloud of flies. The next entrance led to the kitchen, the floor strewn with empty cans and water bottles, plastic cups, rotting food and, oddly, a number of dried teabags stuck to the ceiling, flicked up there when they had been hot and wet, their little yellow and red printed tags dangling from tea-stained strings.

He winced as Palmer stumbled into the building.

'Lynch?'

Moving back into the hallway, Lynch found Palmer smoking in his white, open-necked shirt. The younger man had a linen jacket slung over his shoulder and a look of disgust on his reddened face. Lynch grabbed the fat arm, digging his fingers in. He hissed, 'Shut up, would you?'

Palmer barked. 'What, you think they're here, do you? You reckon they're hiding in the bog waiting for us? We wouldn't have got within a mile of this place if they were still around.'

Lynch shoved the young man away. 'Shut up. And don't touch anything.'

Shaken by Lynch's violence, he whined. 'Okay. Anything for a quiet life. I wouldn't have to be here at all if the Embassy hadn't taken that call.'

Lynch stole into the living room. The furniture was scattered; the terrazzo-tiled floor littered with clumps of stuffing from the destroyed sofa. He searched for the TV remote, gave up and walked over to the set. He pulled a pack of tissues from his pocket and wrapped one around his finger to switch the set on. The sound was almost deafening in the hot gloom: urgent Arabic, Hezbolla's *Al Manar* channel. Snapping it off, he turned to speak to Palmer, but the Embassy man had left. Whispering a curse, Lynch followed him to the bedroom doorway.

'Christ,' said Palmer.

Lynch pushed past. The rich stench was appalling. The overturned bucket in the corner of the room spilled waste onto the burn-pocked carpet. Rusty streaks arced across the walls. Something darker, likely more shit, completed the artwork. Eyehooks were set into the wall at the opposite corner to the bucket, a long tangle of Day-Glo yellow rope coiled on the floor below them. The bed sheets were streaked with filth.

Lynch flicked the newspaper on the floor with his foot: *The Beirut Times*, 22nd March. Five days old. He reached towards the piece of expensive-looking paper folded on the bed, halted by the sound of Palmer puking. Lynch wheeled, the rebuke dying on his lips as he took in the opened cupboard and the thing, once human, slumped inside. Pulling the paper tissue over his face, he shoved the retching man's bulk aside and stared into the cupboard. The corpse stank, even through the scented tissue. Fat bluebottles crawled over sightless eyes. Dark rivulets crazed the marble white flesh. The slashed throat, an obscene second mouth, grinned blackly at them.

Palmer stumbled from the room. Lynch stared at the body, his mind and heart racing, his stomach knotted. The shock numbed him, his lips drawn tight and an unpleasant pricking sensation in his eyes. He tensed against his stomach's impulse. Unlike Palmer, he had done this before. Bending to pat down the pockets, he ran his fingers against the distended flesh and checked for documents. He turned to the bed and picked up the fold of paper. Opening it revealed the name 'Paul Stokes' in calligraphic script on the textured surface.

The note was familiar, the parchment placed beside the victim of every murder ordered by Raymond Freij. The old man had inscribed dozens of them throughout the long Lebanese civil war, before cancer had written its own note in fine tendrils to crush his wracked body until he could breathe no more. Raymond was said to have had a teak Indian clerk's desk he liked to sit at cross-legged to as he wrote each death warrant with a fine quill pen. The calculated flamboyance added to the fear and legendary status the warlord had courted. The humility of a *babu*'s desk, each death so ordered reduced perhaps, then, to a clerical error.

'I'm sorry, Lynch. Truly.' Palmer's bulk framed in the doorway, his face turned away from the cupboard. His voice faltered. 'I know Stokes was your agent.'

Lynch reviewed the pathetic earthly remains of Paul Stokes, journalist and latterly spy, and smiled despite the lump in his throat. At least Paul was reunited with Aisha, the girl he had loved and lost so completely. Anger welled up in Lynch as he ran his thumb down the rough edge of the vellum in his hand.

Freij. Like father, like son.

Michel must have done this. Michel Freij, the joint head of the biggest defence technology company in the Arab world and Raymond Freij's pride and joy. When cancer carried Raymond the great warlord away, it brought his son Michel the loyalty of countless Lebanese Christian mountain villages and towns. Michel also inherited his father's sprawling business empire and the keys to a political career Michel had lost no time in developing. Stokes had been rattling Michel's cage, a little job for Lynch on the side. And Michel had rattled back. Hard.

Lynch strode outside, stooping to inhale the clean air. Palmer burst from the house a few seconds later, gasping. 'So that's it, is it? You just walk... walk away now?'

Lynch stared into the hills dotted with gnarled trees, the sky bright blue above. He breathed in the warm Mediterranean spring air.

Palmer manoeuvred to face him down. 'Is that it? Job done, Gerry? Write off your joe and piss off back to your nice, comfy flat in Beirut? What was there to smile about back there? Stokes was a fucking human being. He was a good man, dammit.'

'Don't call me Gerry. It's Gerald.' Lynch handed the boy a tissue and watched him blow his nose. Tears welled up in the washed-out blue eyes set deep in the puppyfat features. Every man has the face he deserves by forty, thought Lynch. *Oscar Wilde.* At this rate, Palmer would look like a Vietnamese pot-bellied pig.

'Th-thanks.'

'Come on. Time to head back home. The Lebboes can clear this lot up.'

Palmer pocketed his tissue. 'Does Stokes' death truly mean nothing to you, man? Are you intelligence people all so cold?'

Lynch spoke gently, but his fists were clenched. 'We all have different ways of dealing with events.' He strode across the dusty roadway to the car and wrenched open the door. He waited for Palmer to move. The boy supported himself against the concrete wall, great dark

patches under the arms and spine of his jacket. Palmer
staggered towards the car as Lynch started the engine.

In the dark quiet of the villa, a mouse started to move,
scurrying across the warm tiles at the very moment Lynch,
racing up the track onto the Batroun Road with Palmer
huddled damply beside him, decided to pay Michel Freij
a personal visit.

Lynch left the car with Palmer and jumped up the steps
fronting the Freij Building. He shoved the glass doors
open and strode across the echoing marble hall to the lifts.
A woman got into the lift with him. She seemed nervous.
He turned his glare back to the stainless steel doors as the
robotic voice announced, 'Executive Offices. Doors
opening.'

Lynch stormed through the open-plan office, ignoring
the insistent flunkies asking him if they could help him.
The brass placard glittered on the double doors to the
'Executive Suite'. He slammed them behind him. The
picture windows looked out over Beirut harbour, the
cobalt sky reflected in the polished, minimalist office
furniture. Lynch whirled to face the secretary standing
behind her desk, a file pressed to her breasts. The desktop
hosted a single hyper-thin screen and matte black keypad.

'Where's Michel Freij?'

She snapped him a clinical smile, perfect teeth framed
by pumped lips. 'I'm sorry, Mr Freij is not in the office
right now. Who can I tell him called?'

Lynch snarled. 'I will ask you one more time nicely.
Where is Michel?'

'I'm sorry, Mr?' She stepped back, her smile faded. 'I

think you had better leave.'

She raised her head to call but Lynch moved fast around the desk and grabbed her throat. He pushed her hard against the shelving unit. The file flew from her hands, her face coloured under the pressure of his grip. Her painted nails scrabbled at his strong wrist.

'Where the fuck is he?'

He relaxed his grip enough for her to breathe, her voice gurgling. 'G—Germany.'

'Where in Germany?'

'Berlin.'

'Why?'

'A meeting.'

Lynch squeezed again, her creamy skin rucking under his hard fingers. 'Who with?'

'H—Hoffmann. That's all I know. At the Landsee.'

A man's voice called. 'What's going on here?'

Lynch let go of the woman. He turned to face the black-uniformed security guard, the badge glinting on his chest.

'Fuck off,' Lynch snarled, prowling.

The guard blocked the exit, slapping a black nightstick in his hand and smiling grimly. 'You're going nowhere.'

Lynch kicked him hard in the crotch and scythed his fist down into the guard's face, driving him to the floor. Lynch ground his foot into the writhing man's stomach and stepped over him.

Outside the smoked-glass building, Lynch caught his breath and scanned the busy street either side of him. The traffic jostled, cars honking in the hot sun.

His knuckles were raw, but he was feeling better about Stokes' death already.

Chapter Two

It was late in the afternoon as Gerald Lynch hopped along the uneven paving lining Gouraud Street, the heart of Beirut's bustling Gemayze area. He wore jeans and a leather jacket against the chill spring air, his hands in his pockets as he squeezed between the parked cars.

Gouraud's bars, as ever, welcomed those who wanted to party and forget the woes of a world where violence and conflict were a distant memory but a constant worry. Orphaned by Belfast's troubles, Lynch appreciated Beirut's fragile peace and sectarian divides, the hot embers under the white ash on the surface of a fire that looked, to the casual observer, as if it had gone out. Lynch scowled as he passed a poster emblazoned with Michel Freij's grinning face, encircled in strong black script: 'One Leader. One Lebanon.'

The sky was fading to the dull aubergine of dusk; the bars lining the street glowed a welcome. He glanced around, crossed a side street then peeled left off Gouraud to slip into the entrance of an ancient Ottoman building. The rusting iron railings on the ornate stone balconies wept streaks down the lichen-tinged walls. Bullet holes still peppered the stucco. Brick showed through where shell bursts and, in places, time had peeled off the tired facade.

Lynch stole up the stone stairs to the first floor and paused by a battered red door, holding his ear to it for a second. He crouched to pick the lock with quiet efficiency. He rose a few seconds later, pushed into Paul Stokes' flat and closed the door softly behind him. Like many apartments in Beirut, the drabness of the exterior belied the opulence inside. Stokes had rented the place from a Lebanese family living in the Gulf and it was decked out to their taste, packed with ornate furnishings, cut glass and deep-pile carpets. Tapestries lined the walls and gold statuary decorated the green marble fireplace.

Stokes' writing table stood against the window overlooking Gouraud's busy throng. His laptop was still open and switched on, the screensaver drawing neon swoops. Lynch picked up the voice recorder by the laptop and pressed 'play'. The memory of the dead thing in the cupboard rushed back as Stokes' voice rang out and Lynch hit the stop button. He composed himself before pressing 'play' again to hear Stokes say, 'Interview with Michel Freij. March fifteenth.' The volume varied, Lynch guessed, as the recorder was moved to face the interviewee.

Lynch placed the recorder on the inlaid rosewood coffee table in front of the sofa. He had sent Stokes to conduct this interview and prepared him with the information to use. It had been the young man's death warrant. As the voices from the recorder played out their encounter, Lynch wandered over to the cabinet by the fireplace and poured himself a stiff scotch. He returned to the sofa as Freij was halfway through answering a question. Lynch folded himself into the sofa, the whisky burning in his throat as he listened.

'My partnership with Selim Hussein started when we were at university. Selim is an unusually talented engineer and we quickly established Falcon Dynamics as a key contractor to the Lebanese military, particularly in the field of RVs. We have expanded that to a broad portfolio of advanced defence and homeland security systems, both hardware and software. The success of our partnership together is precisely why I believe we, as a nation, can come together and join hands across any sectarian divide.'

Stokes' voice was measured. 'Falcon Dynamics has been phenomenally successful, and now you have services and hardware contracts with the Saudis, the Bahrainis and the Egyptians. Will you target other markets, such as Europe?'

'Yes, why not?' Freij's rich voice was expansive. 'Our aim is to build the company. As you say, we have business in services, but also in security analysis and threat response procedures. We have major interests in software systems together with key partners in America and Germany and now we are growing our capabilities in tactical delivery systems. In all of these, we are at the forefront of developments and we can compete with European companies if we have a level playing field. Imagine, other Lebanese companies could follow this example, if provided with a government that would support innovation and entrepreneurialism.'

Stokes shifted gear a little, his eagerness apparent. 'But you already have at least two European subsidiaries, don't you?'

There was a long silence. Freij's voice was low. Lynch imagined the man's frosty smile and quizzical expression. 'I am sorry, I do not understand.'

Stokes' voice in the recording was louder, Lynch guessed as the journalist leaned towards Freij. 'Two years ago, you acquired the successful German online retail operation, kaufsmartz.com.' Again, silence. Stokes pressed. 'Did you not?'

'What has this to do with our defence business, Mr Stokes?'

Stokes' voice was airy now as he moved in for the kill. They had rehearsed the question together and Lynch winced as he acknowledged ownership of the words that had resulted in the brutal death of the young journalist and, yes, Lynch's agent. 'Over the past two weeks, millions of transactions have taken place from customers in the Middle East ordering one product from Kaufsmartz, a door alarm device costing nine dollars ninety-five cents. That device is ostensibly manufactured by a Falcon Dynamics subsidiary based in Greece.'

Stokes paused and Freij shifted, a chair creaking. Lynch imagined him pushing the call button. Stokes became urgent. 'Over eighty million dollars of orders took place in that period. It was a successful marketing campaign by any standard, wasn't it? Mr Freij?'

Michel Freij's chair scraped back, his hands banged on the desktop as he shouted. 'This interview is terminated.'

Stokes was relentless. 'Except there was no marketing campaign was there, Mr Freij? Every single transaction took place from one of twenty IP addresses in Beirut, every one of them owned by Falcon. Not one product has been shipped, has it Mr Freij? Because this was no online marketing success, it was *hawala* taken to the Internet age. You transferred eighty million dollars to yourselves in a flood of micro-transactions that bypassed all of the conventional financial controls and regulations you would normally be expected to comply with for a transfer of this size.'

'Enough. This is finished.'

Lynch grinned at the phrase. *Hawala taken to the Internet age*. It was the ability to turn a phrase like that which made Stokes a good journalist. *Hawala*, the ancient trust-based Arab system of transferring money from location to location remained a highly effective international funds transfer network. Once untraceable, *hawala* transactions now came under intense scrutiny by security agencies, particularly the US, precisely because it made money movements so hard to trace. Freij's ingenious method of moving funds was just as effective. The listeners at Government Communications Headquarters in Cheltenham had been lucky to catch the fleeting flood of transactions as eighty million dollars bypassed the conventional banking system on its way from Beirut to Germany, transferred and laundered in microsecond bursts of Internet traffic. But catch it they had.

Lynch focused on the recording, the sound of the door bursting open and the ugly voices and scuffles, the violent crackle as Stokes grabbed his voice recorder.

Freij's voice was furious. 'Get him the fuck out of here.'

Stokes was shouting as he was manhandled from the office, the sound quality patchy as the recorder bounced in his pocket. 'Why did you need eighty million dollars sent secretly to Germany, Mr Freij? What were you buying with this illegal money?'

More scuffles and the echo of voices shouting in a corridor, Stokes' muffled 'Get your hands off me,' before the sound died out. Lynch looked at the red LED blinking on the little silver voice recorder for a long time. He leaned forward and switched it off.

Lynch was puzzled. Freij's thugs must have let Stokes go, then. The recorder showed he had time to get back to his apartment, yet he hadn't had time to call Lynch. There was no sign of a struggle and certainly Freij's people hadn't come and lifted Stokes' laptop or the record of the interview that had been so incendiary it had forced Freij to call in his security to terminate it.

Lynch pushed himself up from the sofa and peered out of the window across Gouraud Street, the drink in his hand. Dusk had deepened to night as he was listening to a dead man goading a living one. Did they know where Stokes lived? How had they picked him up in the first place?

The streetlight picked out two men striding across the street towards Stokes' apartment building. Lynch recognised the type, both men burly, one wearing a forage cap and camouflage trousers and the other sporting a crew cut. Militia. He dodged back as one of them paused and stared up at the window. Lynch grabbed Stokes' laptop and slid it into the bag lying on the floor. He drained the tumbler and slipped the voice recorder into his pocket, leaving the apartment with the laptop bag on his shoulder. He just made the corner. The men's hobnailed footsteps rang on the stairwell. They were making no effort to be quiet. He held his breath and listened to them unlock the door and enter the apartment. The door banged shut.

They had a key. There had been no key on the corpse. Had it taken them this long to figure out where Stokes lived? Lynch reached instinctively for the Walther P99 nestled under his armpit, the lightweight grip smooth in his hand. The urge to action gave way to rational thought. Lynch waited and, when they left the apartment a few minutes later, followed them into the darkness.

Lynch tailed the two men down Gouraud Street, dancing on and off the pavement to avoid groups of early revellers. He used the parked cars as cover. Many of the bars and restaurants were already busy with the evening shift, office workers clustered along the counters. The traffic was ponderous down the narrow street, the ebb of rush hour a press of cars, scooters and tatty vans.

The man in the forage cap bunched his fists as the pair barged their way down Gouraud. Lynch guessed they hadn't found what they'd gone to Stokes' apartment for. Sure they hadn't. It was hanging on his shoulder. He loped after them.

The pair flagged down a *servees*, the broken-down shared taxis which ply Beirut's streets, cheaper than regular private cabs because they'd stop for any other passenger going in your direction. Lynch strode past them as they got into the car, tempted to hop in and join them. Another *servees* drew up a few cars behind to set down a balding man and his pretty companion. Lynch slid into the back. 'See that *servees* in front of us?'

'What of it?' The man's yellowed fingers tapped on the wheel, his voice a low rasp.

'Follow it.'

The driver chuckled, a wheezy rumble. The engine whined as they pulled away and he wrestled with the juddering steering wheel. 'So we are in ze movies?'

Lynch glanced at the grubby jumper and the wisps of yellow-grey hair escaping from his woollen hat. 'You could say that. I'll pay you twenty dollars to be a movie star. How about that?'

The driver chuckled again. 'Sure. Suit me.'

The *servees* in front turned right, picking up speed in the thinner traffic. The driver fought with the gear lever, the ancient engine screeching in protest as he tried to keep up, muttering imprecations in throaty Arabic. The smell of exhaust was becoming overpowering – Lynch turned to wind down the window but there was a ragged gap in the door panel where the handle should be. The far-side door handle swung uselessly. Lynch gave up and focused on the car drawing away ahead of them on the long, straight road through the city. As Lynch craned to catch sight of it, they were plunged into darkness.

The driver laughed. 'Power cut. *Khara.*'

They were coming into Ashrafieh, the smart Christian area. The shop fronts, usually lavishly illuminated, were looming shadows. The car ahead slowed, Lynch caught its taillights turning right.

He raised his voice above the engine noise. 'Right here.'

'Sure, *meester*. No problem. Twenty dollar, I turn left, right, any way.'

The other car stopped just beyond the turn. Lynch cursed quietly. 'Carry on past him.'

'As you like.'

Lynch turned away from the other car as they passed it. He waited a few seconds. 'Okay, right here. Stop. *Khalas*.' He held out a note. 'Thanks.'

The driver was still thanking the *khawaja* as Lynch shut the door. He took a deep breath of clean air before he padded back down the dark side street to the corner. The *servees* they had followed drove past empty. Lynch peered round the corner. The two men crossed the street towards him. Lynch pressed himself back against the wall.

Forage Cap was angry, his voice carrying in the chill evening air. Lynch eased away from the shadows and followed the two men at a healthy distance, the unwieldy laptop bag annoying on his shoulder. He adjusted it to hang the strap across his chest, right to left so he could still reach the P99 in its shoulder holster. He didn't fancy his chances against two of them without it.

They turned left across a patch of waste ground. Lynch waited in the shadow until they reached the other side of the open space. They rounded the corner, lost behind an apartment block. Lynch crossed the uneven ground, picking his way through patches of broken-up asphalt.

The street lights flickered back on. Lynch muttered a quiet 'Fuck' as he scuttled for the safety of the periphery, feeling like an East Berlin escapee caught in the floodlights. He turned the corner into the street leading away from the open waste ground. The little blue enamel plaque: *Rue Abdul Wahab El Inglezi*. The two men mounted the steps of a smart-looking office block on the other side of the street a hundred metres or so ahead. Lynch paused by the corner, shadowed by a faded shop awning.

Forage Cap halted on the steps, touching his companion on the shoulder to stop him. He turned and stared at Lynch. Barking a command at the other man, he started down the steps again. Lynch turned and ran, breaking across the open ground. He turned his ankle on a lump of concrete. His arms flailed wildly to try to regain his balance and maintain his forward momentum. The pain from his twisted ankle forced him to hobble. A shout rang out behind him and Lynch glanced back as the two men broke into the square. He reached the other side of the open space, the laptop smacking against him.

Lynch halted, his ankle jarring pain. He turned and crouched on his knee, drawing the P99 in a fluid motion. The two men's faces registered the danger a second before Lynch's shot placed a red rose on Forage Cap's upper leg and dropped him to roll and squirm on the rough ground. The other scrambled to a halt, his hands held towards Lynch, palms up.

Lynch backed away, leaving the man to tend to Forage Cap's roaring. He jogged across to Ashrafieh Street, where he flagged down a *servees*.

Early the next morning, when Lynch returned to get the address of the building the two men were entering, there was a large, rusty patch in the middle of the waste ground. His original intention had been to go into the building and discover more about it, but just in time he noticed one, two then more tiny CCTV cameras mounted on top the of the buildings lining the street. He told the driver to move on.

The big 'One Lebanon' sign on the building was clear enough, anyway.

Chapter Three

Charles Duggan's shoulder ached, the bulky dressing rubbing against his heavy leather jacket as he walked. The chill Hamburg fog deadened his steps in the dark street as he passed a restaurant, beery smells escaping in a gust of warm air from the doorway as a couple entered. Even hunched against the cold, Duggan was a big man, his breaths puffing little trails as he forged ahead.

He reached the crossroads and was waiting for the lights when her soft call came in German and, when he didn't respond, in English.

'Would you like some company, sir?'

Duggan glanced at the young woman stepping from the shadows. Pretty, wearing a white leather jacket, red and white cropped tights and carrying a patent leather handbag. Snub nose, small breasts, shapely legs. Her hair, bleached white, was cut short and layered. She smiled uncertainly, her red lipstick striking against her pale skin. The lights changed and he crossed. Her high heels clattered as she kept up with his long stride.

'Perhaps to be warm in the arms of a woman? This is not such a bad thing to want.'

Duggan's jaw tightened. He replied in German. 'No. Leave me alone.'

She stopped and he walked on.

'Please?'

The desperation in her voice made Duggan turn to face

her. The crossing lights behind her changed. The car speeding towards them had its headlights off. Duggan dived at her. She span to face the danger reflected in his eyes. The car mounted the pavement. Chrome-work flashed. He shouted at her to move but she froze. He hit her hard. He span her away from the car. The wing mirror smashed into his thigh.

They slammed against the wall as the car screeched and crabbed to a halt. Duggan's wounded shoulder screamed pain. A dark figure unfolded itself from the car, raising clenched hands. Duggan waited a split second, imagined the tightening knuckle. He pulled the girl with him to the ground. They rolled on the wet flagstones to the spit of a silenced gun and a stinging hail of stone chips. Held together by Duggan's strong arms, they slumped off the pavement onto tarmac.

A truck's horn blared. The massive wheels on the wet road spattered dirty gutter-water into their faces. The heavy vehicle jack-knifed to a halt, engine pulsing. The airbrakes released with a whistle and hiss. Duggan raised his head, but car and gunman had gone.

The truck driver barked at them. 'Are you fucking mad?'

Duggan waved him away.

'You two are okay?'

Duggan slurred his voice, replying in German, a thick Bavarian accent. 'Never better, my friend. Never better.'

'Well, get out of the fucking road, then.'

Duggan beamed stupidly up at the truck driver's pale

face, hamming up the drunken reveller act. 'Thanks. For the advice. And for stopping. It was good of you.'

The trucker spat and slammed the lorry back in gear. 'Jesus. Hamburg. Fucking drunks.'

Duggan propped the girl up, weaving and waving at the departing truck. Dirt streaked her leather jacket. A small cut on her right temple fed a tendril of blood down into her dark eyebrow. She leaned against him, breathing in small gulps, her scared eyes searching his face.

He helped her away from the road and she slumped against the wall. He ran his fingers along the two pale bullet marks in the stone.

She smiled shakily. 'Thank you. That was good of you. But they will come again.'

'They?'

'Those men.'

Duggan brushed the gritty dirt from his jacket sleeve, the movement triggering a dart of pain from his shoulder. 'I only saw one. How do you know they'll come back?'

She fought for control. 'They are working for my father. He is trying to finish me.'

'To kill you?'

She searched his face, wringing her hands. She dropped her gaze. 'Yes.'

A customs officer by trade, Duggan had seen desperate people before. Trained in reading the tiny signals of body language, he had spent years scrutinising nervous travellers in airports as they walked through the customs channels. He had waited by lorry drivers as his officers had pulled little plastic bags of white powder from the prised-open boxes and had felt the heat they radiated as they tried to look calm. He was a specialist in fear, he reflected.

Just the ticket for this girl, a man who understood frightened people. He weighed her up, took her unresisting arm. 'Come on. I think I had better buy you a drink.'

Duggan guided her back past the crossroads and into the warm fug of the bar. He led her, unresisting, to the toilets at the back. 'Here. You can freshen up. I'll have a wash myself and meet you at the bar.'

Duggan washed the dirt from his hands and wiped his face clean, peering into the mirror. He went back into the bar, pulled up two stools and called for two double brandies. He wondered if the girl would slip through the back door. Looking back, he saw her returning and relaxed. She scanned the room and struck out towards him through the throng, her face pale and serious. She reached the bar and drained her glass in a gulp. Her nose was slightly off-centre, the imperfection lending her a quirky prettiness. The cut above her eye no longer wept blood now she had cleaned it up, but the nasty graze on her cheek burned crimson.

It seemed as if they were the only people in the bar not chattering animatedly to each other. The long room resounded with constant outbursts of bright laughter, the bitter reek of beer mixed with rich food smells.

'So. We have not yet been introduced,' he said in

German, smiling. 'I'm Charles.'

'Elli. Elli Hoffmann.' Her eyes were on her hands cupping the small brandy balloon.

'You certainly know how to make a first impression, Elli.'

She grimaced at her torn sleeve. 'My jacket is ruined.'

He acknowledged this with a wry dip of his glass at her. 'You could have lost more than your jacket out there.'

She glared up at him. 'It would perhaps have been better.'

'Oh come, on. You're being melodramatic,' Duggan said, signalling the barman for more drinks. 'You could have died. A jacket's a small price most people would be glad to pay.'

'Maybe I am not most people.' She ran her hand through her short hair. 'So, thank you for trying to help me. This was very nice of you. But now I think I would be better to leave.'

He signalled to the two glasses on the bar. 'I bought you another drink. You're still very shaken.'

She paused for a second, resettling herself on the stool. 'And then I leave.'

'As you like,' he said. 'It is after all a free world.' He felt her eyes on him. 'You know, you're not a very good prostitute.'

Her laughter softened her fierce glare. 'Is this a compliment, I wonder?'

'Why do you do it?'

'This is my business, Charles with no family name who

speaks German like a Bavarian but who is not, I think, German.'

Duggan inclined his head, accepting the compliment. She talked to the glass again. 'I am, as you say, not very experienced as a prostitute. You would have been my second customer. I washed myself so hard after the first one that I have been not able to work for the past week.' Her small smile was a private mourning. She was fierce again. 'I hurt myself.' Tears brimmed in her eyes. 'Thank you. You looked kind. You are kind.'

Duggan hadn't expected her to be so vulnerable. Her eyes were dark under the makeup. He shook his head. 'There are other ways to make money.'

'Really? This was the only one that came to mind,' she snapped. She raised her eyes to the roof, took a breath and held her palms up at him. 'Sorry. Sorry, Charles with no name. I shall call you Charles English, I think. You are English, aren't you? You speak very good German.'

'British. And my family name is Duggan.'

'So, Charles Duggan. I am running away from my home because it is dangerous for me. I cannot do any decent job because this requires identity and I cannot afford to have this identity because they will find me. And now I have no money, I must eat while I try to survive from these murderers.'

'Your father?'

'You say I am melodramatic, so you will not believe me, but yes, my father.'

'Why would your father want to kill you, Elli?'

'He is breaking the law for money. I know what he is doing. The bitch's brother helps him.'

'The bitch being?'

'His wife. Not my mother. His second wife. His business is doing badly and the bitch is bleeding him dry with her dresses and handbags, her surgeries and diamonds. They are selling bombs to the Arabs.'

Duggan kept his face neutral but his movements slowed. 'Does he often do that?'

'Sell to Arabs? Yes, but usually he sells them boats. Not bombs. This is first time. It will make him lot of money. They do not belong to him. He found them.' Elli glanced up at him. 'I am telling truth, Charles.'

He left money on the bar. 'I believe you,' he said, taking her arm. 'Let's go somewhere quieter and safer and perhaps get cleaned up properly.'

She pulled free. 'And what if I don't want to go with you?'

Duggan grinned. 'Then I will arrest you. Come.'

They sat in the coffee shop of Duggan's hotel, Elli jittery and Duggan intrigued. It was late and they were alone. The red upholstered chairs and dark wood fittings marked a hotel overdue for a refit. He ordered coffees and a club sandwich to share. When the food arrived, Elli grabbed a tranche of sandwich. She held it in one hand, trying to cover her over-large mouthful with the other. Duggan was grateful for his fluency in German. 'It's been tough, then.'

She nodded, reaching for a napkin, then her coffee. He waited for her to wash down the food. 'Yes. I am trying to be polite for you.'

He pushed the plate at her. 'Don't bother. Eat.'

'Alone?'

He smiled, picked up a fry and dipped it in ketchup. 'I think your need is perhaps greater than mine.'

She paused, uncertain, the food held up to her mouth. He looked away, beckoned the waiter and ordered a bottle of sparkling water, fussing over the brands the hotel offered precisely so she could have some time to eat. Finally she leaned back and wiped her mouth. 'Thank you.'

'It is nothing.'

She appraised him, the corner of her mouth turned up a little. She wiped her hands, checked her chipped nails and frowned. She leaned forwards, her chin on her clasped hands. Her blue eyes caught the light. 'So who is Charles, the gallant knight who rescues fallen women and threatens to arrest them?'

'I work for British Customs and Excise.' He felt pompous, the formality at odds with her amused interest in him. 'I had some business in Hamburg.' He leaned forward. 'Now, tell me about your father.'

Her gaze darted around the reception and the revolving door to the street. It was quiet, the night staff on reception murmuring. She pressed her hands together and rocked as she talked. 'My father owns a business, he is an entrepreneur. The business makes luxury boats for rich people. He has built this business from nothing by working hard. He and my mother lived in a caravan at the boatyard. That was where I was born, in a caravan. I am a gypsy, you see?'

He nodded. 'I see.'

'Five years ago my mother walked out. My father was having an affair with a woman he met during an inquest into an accident at the boatyard. This woman was married but she was very attractive and much younger than her husband. She was younger than my father, too. Her name is Hilde. Her husband died, which was very convenient for her, because she was free then to put her claws further into my father. He carried on the affair with Hilde for two years before my mother found out. When she did, my father told her to live with this affair. He started to invite this Hilde to visit even when my mother was still in the house. She could not stand it. After she left, Hilde moved in. Am I boring you?'

He shook his head. 'No. Where is your mother now?'

Duggan regretted the question the second it escaped his lips. Elli looked as if she had been slapped. She stared at him, wide-eyed before looking down at her hands. When she looked up again, her eyes were bright. 'She never came back. I do not know where she went.'

Duggan nodded. 'I am sorry. It must have been tough.'

Elli glanced up at the ceiling and bit her lip. 'Tough. Yes, I suppose it was.' She drew a deep breath, her hands clamped together. 'She was fast, this Hilde. She liked eating in fancy places and she loved to buy horses and diamonds and she paid surgeons to make herself perfect for her "little Gerty". I hated to hear my father called this. I hated her. She gambled. His business suffered, all the time with her wanting this and wanting that, this expensive holiday, that expensive car. They gambled together. He gave her everything until Luxe Marine was rotten and there was debt. The market had changed but my father wasn't looking. The orders stopped coming. He owed millions. He was desperate. He needed money and the bank would not help him anymore. He knew where there was a store of guns and bombs left from the cold war, from when he played as a child. He decided to try and sell this store and the bitch's brother helped him to find a buyer, because he is involved in such things and he has a taste for fine things like she does.'

She was talking to herself now, Duggan forgotten. Her anger or perhaps the warmth of the lobby brought red spots to her pale cheeks, her full lips moistened by her flicking tongue. 'The night Meier came to the house with the news he had found a buyer in Beirut, I was listening at the door. I didn't like the smell of him and wanted to know what he was getting up to. He opened the door and discovered me. He hit me in the face. My father did nothing to protect me. He joined Meier in shouting at me. They locked me in my room, but I escaped across the roof.'

'Meier is Hilde's brother?'

She blinked. 'Yes, yes he is.'

'So how do you know your father is trying to kill you?'

Elli sighed. 'I stayed in a hotel that night and went to

work the next day, as usual. I didn't think to be scared, but there were men there who tried to make me get into their car when I left the office. I ran away, but there were more men at the hotel waiting for me, in the car park. One of them had a gun and this is how I finally realised my life is in danger.'

Duggan shifted in his chair. 'Why did you stay in Hamburg? Why not flee to, oh, I don't know, Berlin?'

'They are planning to move these bombs in one of my father's boats, the ones he makes. They are big yachts for the luxury market, thirty metres and more. I have a friend in the ports department here who will tell me when this boat comes downstream through Hamburg. When it does, I will recognise it and tell the police. Until then, I have to live. So I sell myself.'

It was said so simply he almost missed it. In these four words, she gave up everything that was hers to keep and award for love. Duggan felt old-fashioned and stupid. He ran his hand across his forehead to clear his conflicting thoughts. How could someone throw away so much with so little consideration?

'Could you not have borrowed from your friend?'

'No. I cannot even meet him. It is too dangerous. I call him every day from a different place.'

'Why did you not go straight to the authorities?'

She looked up at him with such simple candour, he wanted to reach out to her. 'I am scared, Charles. I can't trust them. Meier has connections. I have no proof. Only with proof will they listen to me.'

'I understand. I think.' He rubbed his face. 'Look, it is late. We shall go to the authorities in the morning, I will talk to my liaison here. We can start to discover what's going on and make sure you're safe. For now, I think it best you stay here with me. Nothing funny. I shall sleep on the sofa, you can take the bedroom.'

He rose and offered his hand, which she took, turning it to examine it closely. Elli squeezed and let go, following him to the lift. She dropped her gaze as they rose silently, following Duggan out of the lift and down the corridor. He opened the door for her and followed her into the room.

She turned to him. 'You have been very kind. Thank you.'

'It's nothing. This is the bedroom. Is there anything you would like?'

'Do you mind if I wash? I still feel dirty from the road.'
'Please.'

As the shower started, he pulled the winter over-blanket and spare pillow from the cupboard and made up the sofa as best he could. He took his mobile charger from the bedroom. Coming back with it, he met her, wrapped in a towel and wearing hotel slippers, her clothes held against her in a bundle. She smelled of lemons. Her short hair was damp and she laughed at him.

'You look like you have seen a ghost.'

He smiled. 'Good night, Elli.'

'Good night, Charles.'

She walked to the bedroom and he watched her slim

legs and the slow swing of the towel on her shapely body, silhouetted against the bedroom lights for a second. The door closed behind her and he sighed, wondering how much of Elli Hoffmann's wild story he could believe. He washed and turned in, fidgeting as he tried to fit his long frame onto the short sofa.

Elli lay on the bed shivering, the fluffy hotel duvet clutched around her. She hated the dark, especially now she had no home and nowhere to hide. Except Charles, she reflected. He might as well have been riding a white charger. Her knight.

The pain snuck up on her as it always did, her fear making her whole body tauten and suddenly too-bright memories crashing into her mind like shots from a gun. The bitch shouting at her, yellowed mare's teeth in a carmine maw. Everyone shouting at her. Voices beat down on her from every side and she quailed before their assault. Gasping, she slid across the bed to reach for her handbag on the bedside table. It still had mud splashes on it. She delved inside and found the little strip of pills. Shaking, she pushed one from its blister and swallowed it.

She lay back and let the drug take effect, the cacophony receding and leaving her at peace in the darkness.

Chapter Four

Lynch sipped his beer, screwing up his face as he surveyed the minimalist surfaces around him. The purple mood lighting highlighted the bottles in alcoves across the back wall. The bar was quiet, but Lynch knew it would soon fill up with the eager, loud voices of young bucks competing for the attention of scantily clad girls with pumped tits and lips.

'Why do you drink in these places, Tony?'

Tony Chalhoub sighed as he leaned on the bar. His voice was gravelly, his accent spiced by a curl of French. 'I'm Lebanese, Gerald. I suffer from the inherent need to celebrate life with each passing moment. You should take the glass rod out of your British ass and try it sometime.'

Chalhoub, the deputy head of Lebanon's police intelligence division, raised his bottle to clink against Lynch's. Lynch laughed and shook his head at his friend's taunting. Over the years, the two had shared good times, information, cases and even on one occasion, long ago, women.

'That's a filthy habit.'

Chalhoub lit the cigarette, blowing smoke high into the air. 'What the fuck happened at Michel Freij's place, Gerald? His office manager has lodged a formal complaint. I had to burn valuable markers to get the case dropped.'

'GCHQ in Cheltenham picked up a number of Internet

microbursts which turned out to be a stream of small payments to a company in Germany about ten days ago. Looking at it from the German side, it would have seemed like ordinary international e-commerce traffic, but we tracked the payments back to a tiny range of IP addresses, all here in Beirut. Each of the bank accounts they used had received transfers from a British Virgin Islands company. It was clever stuff, virtually undetectable unless you are looking very hard for it. The BVI company is Falcon Finance, a subsidiary of Falcon Dynamics.'

Chalhoub whistled. 'Michel Freij.'

'Yup. Freij. And his fat friend.'

'How much money we talking about?'

'Eighty million US.'

'And the German company?'

'An e-commerce website, sells home security stuff and gadgets. And it's a Falcon subsidiary.'

'So what's the problem? It's their money, isn't it?'

'Come on, Tony. Don't be bloody daft. They laundered offshore money to Germany using a complex Internet scam. Why? To avoid regulators? Us?'

Chalhoub shook his head, his hand raised in negation, the smoke trailing from his cigarette. 'No way, José. These people are legit, Gerald. They don't need to launder money. Falcon Dynamics is a highly respected company and close to the government here as well as the Americans. Michel Freij and Selim Hussein are heroes. They're the successful business partnership that transcended sectarianism and outdid the Israelis at their own game, the defence business. Christ, Freij is running for president. And he'll do it, too. This One Lebanon party of his is already strong in the coalition and they're likely going to piss the elections next year. He's untouchable.'

'I don't care. They're fucking crooks. My masters want to know why Falcon sneaked eighty million dollars into Europe through the back door. And I want to know why they'd kill to protect that reason.'

Chalhoub paused. 'Kill?' He peered at Lynch across the frosted green neck of the bottle he had been about to drink from, understanding dawning on his baggy-eyed features. 'This dead journalist. Stokes. He's one of yours.'

Lynch drank, nodding. 'The dead journalist is one of mine.'

'Now I get it,' Chalhoub drew on his cigarette. 'Finally. You must think I'm slow, yes?'

'No. I don't.'

'*Kazab.* Liar. You were trying to flush them out, but they bit you on the ass.'

Lynch signalled the barman for another Almaza. 'Whatever.'

'This Stokes guy. He was close to you?'

Lynch studied the label on his beer bottle intently. 'Yes, yes he was. Move on, Tony.'

'How are you so sure it was Freij?'

'They left a little note with his name on. A little vellum note in fine calligraphy.'

Chalhoub whistled. 'That was Raymond Freij's thing, wasn't it? The little notes? You think Michel's started doing the same his father used to? That's crazy, Gerald. It just points the way straight back to him. Why would he do that?'

'I went to Stokes' apartment yesterday. Two militia thugs let themselves in just after me. They had a key. I followed them up into Ashrafieh. To Freij's party headquarters.'

'So what next?'

'Frankly, Tony? I don't know. I'll file a nice, neat report and let my masters rule on what to do next.'

Chalhoub took a pull of beer. 'Okay. I've got your little white Irish butt covered for now, but you can't go around beating up security guards in billionaire presidential candidates' offices. Not even in Beirut. I got the case dropped, but we'll still be lodging a formal protest with H.E.'

Lynch winced. H.E. was His Excellency, the British Ambassador to Beirut, Sir St John Winterton. He raised his bottle in a tight-lipped toast to the last crusty old cold war era twit left in the diplomatic service and drew a deep breath. 'Fine, Tony. We all do what we have to do. Sorry for the trouble.'

'I understand. Anything I can do to help, let me know. I'll have a man put on the party HQ and let you know if anything interesting happens.' Chalhoub patted Lynch on the arm. 'Don't go near General Security with this. Anything to do with Freij and Falcon is off limits and loaded with a cocktail of sectarianism, *wasta*, bribery, and vested interests. They'll just fuck you around, pass any information onto Michel and Selim and then shaft you. The Yanks will stamp on your ass, too. Those boys are way off limits. Way, way off.'

Lynch scraped his hand over the stubble on his chin. He gazed into the mirror behind the stacked bottles. He was pale, the dark patches either side of his nose circling down to underpin the fleshy bags padding the bottom of his eyes. His open shirt was a washed-out blue and his collar was worn.

Chalhoub slid off his bar stool. 'Come on, Gerald. You should get some rest.'

Lynch nodded, drained his bottle and banged it down on the bar top. 'You're right, Tony. I'm beat. Thanks for the shoulder and the hint about Michel and company. I'll back off a bit until we have formal guidance from London. I was just pissed off they killed my boy.'

Lynch patted his friend's shoulder, palm-slapping Chalhoub's bodyguard on his way into the night with its cicadas and the smell of apple *shisha* smoke on the breeze carried along with snatches of conversation and the clink of glasses.

Lynch flagged down a *servees*, the ancient Mercedes taxi squeaking and groaning its way across the busy traffic until they reached *Ain Mreisse*. Force of habit had him pay off the grubby old driver ten minutes' walk from his apartment and take to the streets alone and watchful.

Lynch froze at his apartment door. A sliver of light shone under it. He had switched the lights off before he left. He paused to catch his breath and slipped open the door. He crept down the hallway lined with books, framed photographs and Bedouin artefacts, his hand ready under his jacket, the butt of the P99 cool against his fingers. The muted notes of violin music sounded. He glanced at the black iPhone in the cradle of the Bose speaker and relaxed.

She was reading, curled up on the rattan chair by the open door to the balcony, her poetry notebook at her side. She glanced up, her faraway eyes focusing on the present and her full lips smiling.

'Lynch. You're done snooping for the day?'

Leila Medawar, student activist, dissident, blogger and poet to the leftist anti-sectarian intelligentsia. Born into wealth and privilege, she was heart-rendingly idealistic. Lynch sighed at the sight of her; beautiful dark-haired Leila, lover of freedom, equality and British spies. *Well, spy.*

Six months back, Lynch was looking into a student protest that threatened to march against the British Embassy, a boring little job he was only taking half-seriously. Leila was one of the ringleaders. Her defiant eyes had caught his across the student bar and held them. A week later they were lying together in his bed, her hair a tumble of brown curls across the pillow, and sweat glistening on her full breasts. The memory made him randy for her. He kissed her, a brief touch of the lips then a second, lingering, open-mouthed melting. She laughed and ran her hand back through her hair.

'You are dirty minded always, Lynch.'

He caressed her cheek. 'Thanks for washing up. Sure,

you didn't have to do that.'

'An Arab girl, Lynch. It's what you wanted, no?'

Lynch regarded her seriously. 'Just let me know, Leila, before you come round. We discussed that before. Anyway, I thought you were studying.'

'I got bored. Beside, you live like a pig, so I thought at least I would clean the sty. Why don't you get a cleaner?'

Lynch snorted as he poured a whisky. 'It's not very secure, is it, hiring cleaners?'

'You fuck activists, so why not have a decent hard working *Sri Lanki* in the house too?'

He acknowledged her point with a sardonic tilt of his glass, the ice clinking. In truth, most of what he did would trigger an outbreak of kittens back in London. Gerald Lynch was quite aware he wasn't a textbook intelligence operator. Then again, the Levant was hardly a textbook market.

He pulled a Siglo IV from his beloved walnut humidor and clipped it. She gestured to him to bring her a drink and he did so, heavy on the ice the way she liked it, and in the Orrefors tumbler she had brought to his flat the evening after they first made love, pulling it from her silver-studded handbag and plonking it down on the side table with a diffident, 'This is what I drink my scotch from.'

Lynch never asked her why. Questions weren't part of the deal between them. Sitting down at Stokes' laptop, he searched the recent documents and pulled up a file of the contacts Paul had made chasing after Michel Freij, the little job he had been doing for Lynch that had cost him his life. The last entries were in bold text, 'Spike' and 'Deir Na'ee'.

Lynch called across to Leila. 'Where's Deir Na'ee?'

She uncurled and came to him, looking over his shoulder at the screen, her blouse opening to show the warm brown mound of her breast. 'Deir Na'ee? The lonely home? Sounds like something up in the Bekaa. Never heard of it. Try Googling it. Might be a village somewhere.'

'And "Spike"?'

She paused, then turned to regain her place on the sofa. 'No idea, *habibi*. I'm not a phone book.'

Lynch chuckled, the search phrase 'Deir Na'ee' for some reason returning the Irish poem *A bhonnán bhuí*, The Yellow Bittern. He read it out loud, the Irish words coming back to him from the mists of distant childhood, the disinfectant reek of the Sisters of Charity's classroom. '*A bhonnán bhuí, is é mo léan do luí, Is do chnámha sínte tar éis do ghrinn, Is chan easba bidh ach díobháil dí, a d'fhág i do luí thú ar chúl do chinn.*'

Leila was laughing at him. 'What are you *saying*?'

'It's Irish. Deir Na'ee gets that in Google. Christ alone knows why.'

'That is not a language. It sounds like dogs fighting.'

'*Póg mo thóin.*'

Maps drew a blank for Deir Na'ee. Lynch decided to move on. Leila picked up her book again as Lynch opened the next file in the computer's 'recent files' list, a Word document with the filename *Olives.* The smile left his face as he read the document with dawning horror.

To be honest with you, this was not one of my finest moments. I waited for something to happen, picking flakes of paint off the wall and cracking them between my fingernails before dropping them. The only sound in the cell was the ambient roar of emptiness; the occasional dry snap of paint.

It was Stokes' memoir of his time in Jordan. Lynch felt sick. He flicked to the end of the document, 267 pages down.

And in sorrowful envy he outran me and took you apart into his quietness.

They were Paul's last words to his lover Aisha, the words taken from TE Lawrence's dedication. Lynch's breathing was harsh as he read the preceding paragraph, Paul's description of the moment when he lost her to the brutality of Jordanian special forces. Lynch had arranged the raid himself. He hadn't reckoned on them to be so heavy-handed, so keen to clean up the loose ends.

They had killed the girl.

His attempt to resettle Paul in Beirut had been his way of making amends, giving the young man a new life after Lynch had ruined his old one. He had, of course, concealed that he had been the architect of the raid. Bitterly, Lynch reflected he'd made the same mistake twice, underestimating the amount of force his actions would bring to bear on Paul Stokes' life.

Lynch had recruited Stokes in Amman, blackmailing the young journalist into providing information on Jordanian government contracts as well as on Aisha's family as part of a joint operation with Israeli intelligence. Now he had Paul's side of the story at his fingertips. He went back to the beginning and read, flicking the pages until he reached Stokes' description of their first meeting together at the British Embassy.

Lynch was sweating and I caught a hint of stale alcohol under the supermarket aftershave. His accent was Northern Irish softened, I guessed, by years away from home.

He stared at the black text on the screen, his heart pounding in his chest. *Yeah, thanks for that, Paul.* He couldn't read any more of the dead man's words. He closed the file and slumped back, his forehead dotted with perspiration.

Lynch had a long and rich past and he didn't like it catching up with him, any of it. He gouged his fingers into his eyes to drive away the thoughts with physical sensation and assert his sense of self in the wash of encroaching memories.

'Christ, I'm sorry. I didn't know. I'll nail the bastard, Paul. I won't rest until I do, I swear.' He didn't realise he was talking out loud until Leila moved over to him, her long, tanned legs catching the light. 'What's wrong, Lynch?'

He forced a smile. 'Nothing, nothing. A ghost.' He pulled the lid of the computer down. 'I need a light.'

She handed him a lighter and curled up on her chair, catlike. She was reading Proust. He went onto the balcony to feel the cool evening air on his damp face, lit the clipped cigar and watched the red glow tremble as he forced himself to stop thinking of the blackened gash in Paul's neck.

Lynch gazed down from the balcony to the street and the sea beyond where the last of the day's light still shimmered red on the distant waves. The *azan* sounded, the *maghrib* prayer. Lynch listened, enjoying the sweetness of the *muezzin*'s voice carried over the sound of traffic on the streets below as the man repeated his affirmations: *Allahu akbar*, the rhythm calming and familiar. God is great.

The doorbell sounded. Lynch paused, puzzled, the cigar halfway to his lips. Leila uncurled from her chair and escaped into the bedroom, part of their unwritten agreement to lead separate lives in public. He left his cigar balanced on the green plastic Heineken ashtray and went inside.

Palmer stood at the door. The embassy man was freshly laundered; Lynch could even smell the soap and toothpaste. Palmer simpered. 'Can I come in?'

'Sure.'

Lynch kicked the door shut with his heel and followed the young man down the hallway, catching the flash of Palmer's forehead passing the mirror.

'Drink?'

'Um, no thanks.'

'Suit yourself. What gives, then?'

Palmer pulled an envelope from his jacket pocket. 'You're to accompany Paul Stokes' body to London. The funeral's on Monday. H.E. is not terribly happy about the complaints from the Lebanese and the local press have been giving Chancery quite a hard time about his death.'

Lynch took the envelope. At least it was a business-class flight. His eyes narrowed. This was a hospital pass. 'How much media interest, exactly?'

Palmer snorted. 'You know what they're like, journalists. Stokes was one of their own, all that.'

'And pre-fucking-cisely what does that do for my cover, Nigel? You remember *cover* don't you? The quaint, old-fashioned notion that intelligence is a covert activity? Like, you know, *secret*?'

'You're supposed to be the deputy commercial attaché, it's not totally unprecedented. You won't be asked to act as spokesperson or anything. But Chancery needs to send someone to accompany the body and so on.'

Lynch read the booking slip printout stapled to the ticket, *Accompanying deceased: Paul Stokes*. He noticed Palmer staring at the Orrefors glass on the table and the volume of Proust lying next to it.

'Thanks, Palmer. Door's right there behind ye.'

Palmer actually shuffled backwards before turning to leave. Lynch waited for the snap of the front door lock and took his whisky back outside where he finished his cigar in the growing darkness, listening to the honking traffic on Beirut's twilit streets. He remembered Stokes unmanned and crying at Aisha Dajani's funeral in Amman. Her mother, Nour, standing by Stokes' side and comforting him as her daughter lay in the ground that had accepted her two sons and her husband. Nour led away from the grave by the police who had brought her to the funeral, a humanitarian concession.

Lynch flicked the butt of his cigar into the bushes below, watching its pinprick of light spin into the darkness. He was going to England to bury Paul Stokes. The cold thought crystallised. Fair enough, but then he would come back to Beirut and bury Michel Freij.

He slipped inside to the bathroom where, after a while, Leila came and helped him wash.

Chapter Five

Gerhardt Hoffmann fiddled with his blue and silver Bulgari cufflink, feeling the smooth cabochon stone as he gazed over the immaculate rolling greens. The players wore heavy sweaters and jackets against the spring cold. Their breath formed tiny clouds.

The waiter laid down a long porcelain dish of canapés. 'Chef's compliments, Herr Hoffmann.'

He started, his eyes devouring the colourful line of delicacies arrayed on the white china, and smiled. 'Thank you, Hans. And please convey my gratitude to Chef.'

Grunting, Hoffmann took an artful pile of salmon and roe on black bread and popped it into his mouth. After months of avoiding the Landsee Golf Club, he was now able to enjoy, once more, the privilege of dining in its immaculate clubhouse. Life was good again. He sipped the excellent Gewürztraminer and swallowed luxuriantly.

The distant cry of a golfer and the warm sun streaming through the glass bore him back to his childhood, the cry of young voices in the trees and the sun breaking through the woodland in blades of light. They played simply back then, hide and seek and war games. Bigger than his friends, Hoffmann had never won at hide and seek until the day he stumbled across his Great Hiding Place, the heavy metal door in the undergrowth. A clever child, he used a branch to lever the door open and had the presence of mind to leave the lump of mossy wood as a wedge in case it slammed shut and trapped him inside.

He remembered the cold gloom, the sound of dripping water and the looming shapes in the darkness beyond the finger of light the gap in the door let in. Days after, he had returned with a torch and his two closest friends for safety in numbers. They fought over who went first, almost dropping the torch in their fear. Emboldened by the silence, fearful of the echoes, they crept farther down the iron staircase and onto the wide concrete floor, huge doors to their left and right. One of the nearest doors was open, marginally, and they sidled in to prise open one of the stacks of crates. What they found scared them so much they ran out, removed the prop and let the door slam shut. They covered the whole thing up with undergrowth again. As they stood in the clearing, shivering with the cold and fear, they nicked their hands with Hoffmann's knife and took a blood oath never again to mention the dark cavern to anyone except each other.

The distant click of a teed-off golf ball and then, a few seconds later, distand clapping brought Hoffmann back to the Landsee. He scooped up another canapé, a sesame toast of red tuna topped with a delicate green wasabi rose. Michel Freij was late, Hoffmann noted as he let the tastes mingle in his mouth. They were really rather good, but then one had certain expectations of the best golf club in Berlin, arguably in Germany. Perhaps, Hoffmann speculated mildly, in all of Europe.

Hoffmann watched as the slim, dapper figure wove through the green and cream striped chairs towards him. He pushed back his chair and got to his feet to receive his guest with an outstretched hand and a smile.

'Mr Freij.'

Freij bowed slightly. 'Herr Hoffmann. A pleasure, finally, to meet in person.'

Hoffmann was struck by the man's forceful charisma. Peter Meier, a man who moved amongst the rich and powerful and so not easily impressed, had said Michel Freij was the most powerful man in Lebanon. He certainly carried himself as such. Hoffmann gestured to the chair facing him. 'Please.'

Freij lowered his tall frame into the chair, placing his mobile onto the linen and taking his napkin before the waiter could reach him. 'A beer please. Staropramen.'

The waiter stuttered. 'We do not have this beer, sir.'

Freij flicked a glance at Hoffmann, sharing his disappointment with his host. 'Oh. A shame. Then a wine. You have wine?'

'Certainly, sir.'

Hoffmann gestured at his frosted glass. 'The Gewürztraminer is excellent, Mr Freij.'

'I am sure it is.' Freij turned to the waiter. 'You have Pouilly Fumé?'

'Of course, sir.' The man flipped open the wine list and flourished it. Freij nodded approval. 'Excellent. The Asteroïde, then.'

The waiter retired backwards. Freij plucked a canapé, to Hoffmann's horror. He had been looking forward to the smoked chicken breast topped with aubergine mash and pomegranate seeds.

Hoffmann cleared his throat. 'The shipment has cleared Hamburg. We will be delivering as per our agreement. I take it this is still convenient to you?'

Peter Meier had drilled him on the details until he had dreamed about them. Hoffmann was briefed and word-perfect.

'That's good,' said Freij, wiping his fingers on the napkin as he chewed. 'We have made the deposit, of course. As per our agreement.'

'So I understand. Excellent. Can I recommend the business lunch menu? It is pleasingly fast and yet delicious.'

Freij ordered á la carte. He waited for the waiter to

depart. 'We are slightly concerned regarding the delivery of the consignment. We... appreciate our partnership, but think it prudent to seek further guarantees.'

Hoffmann beamed. 'We have already foreseen this eventuality. It is appropriate, given the value of the cargo.'

The sommelier arrived carrying an ice bucket. He pulled the bottle from the ice, displaying it nestled in a white linen napkin. Freij waved his approval and the man opened the wine, laying the cork on the linen tablecloth. He poured a taste. Freij sniffed the wine briefly, nodded and waited for his glass to be filled. He raised it to Hoffmann, who returned the salute with a gracious smile that disguised his dismay at the cost.

Facing almost certain financial ruin had forced Hoffmann into a true appreciation of the value of money and he had slipped into being a mean man, an attribute Hilde had remarked upon with increasing bitterness in recent months. Having teetered on the precipice, Hoffmann did not intend to look into the abyss again, not even for Hilde.

When the manager of Deutsche Bank Hamburg had finally called to deliver the intention to foreclose, Hoffmann was terror-stricken. He drove into the night, stayed in a cheap motel in Frankfurt and drank himself to sleep. The next morning, hung over and exhausted, desperation drove him to see Hilde's brother, Peter Meier. An influential man whose business dealings were, Hoffmann knew, more colourful than his own, Meier was rich as Croesus and infinitely resourceful, worldlier than Hoffmann, and harder, too. A man you would want with you in a fight to the finish. Hoffmann had reached the finish.

Freij leaned back as the waiter delivered his pan-fried foie gras. Hoffmann took a green salad.

'Is Herr Meier not joining us?' asked Freij, placing a wobbling pink lump on a slice of toasted brioche. Hoffmann watched as the manicured fingers pushed it into the red-lipped maw framed by trimmed goatee beard. The Hollywood perfect white teeth sliced into the warm liver and left crumbs on the moist lips. He shuddered. 'Hoffmann?'

'Sorry, sorry. No, he has been called away on an urgent matter. He asked me to convey his sincere apologies, but to tell you he was looking forward to meeting when we make the delivery.'

Freij laid down his knife and fork. 'I see. We were talking about additional guarantees.'

Hoffmann had reached Meier's house in tears, begging for money. Ignoring his pleas, Meier had painstakingly walked the desperate man through his assets, sources of potential income and expectations of remuneration. The cupboard was, as Meier had said when twisting the knife, quite bare. Finally, crying like a child, Hoffmann had remembered the game in the woods on what had been the East German border all those years ago and the macabre contents of the bunker they had found. He tossed it into the conversation as a joke, as a desperate gambit to entertain Meier and buy some sort of consideration: 'Unless Soviet missiles have a value.'

Meier froze, his voice chill. 'Soviet missiles, you say?'

Hoffmann, feeling foolish, told Meier of the bunker they had found as children, their fearful pact made in the woods near Hřensko. The great looming shapes in their cradles.

Meier was ferocious. He grabbed Hoffmann's arm. 'Your troubles could well be far behind you. Take me there. Now.'

Pleased to finally engage Meier's interest, Hoffmann

was taken aback by the man's sudden passion, protesting, 'Please, Peter, it is late. The morning, surely?'

Meier arranged the early morning drive into the forests of Hoffmann's childhood. Hoffmann had never imagined the sleek green missiles in their stacked wooden crates would still be there, let alone could be worth so much money, but Meier had been dismissive of them. He had taken them as what he called the cherry on the cake. Meier's cake had been behind two huge blast doors. He had surveyed the doors, gone out to the car and returned with an aluminium suitcase which opened up to reveal a complex computer screen. He had hooked it up to the doors' electronic locking mechanisms. After a few minutes, the lock clicked open. Meier unhooked the cables from the lock and heaved open the door to reveal the hangar and the looming, fearful shapes lying on their massive oiled chassis'. Two of the brutal missiles had detachable warheads, a three-meter cone of green. Meier stared, his breath coming in little gasps. 'My God.'

Hoffmann had wondered quite who Meier's God was.

The clamour of his mobile tore Hoffmann back to the present. He excused himself to take what he assured Freij would undoubtedly be a short call and strolled across the restaurant floor. Nodding and grinning, he cut the line and swaggered back to the table. He placed his handset on the white linen, smiling at Freij with a renewed confidence. 'I am so sorry. We were talking about guarantees, were we not?'

Freij nodded. His slicked-back hair was receding at the temples. Together with his goatee, it gave the man what Hoffmann rather thought of as a vaguely Mephistophelean air.

Hoffmann beamed and leaned back. 'My own daughter Elli will be on board the *Arabian Princess* personally. It is an exceptional guarantee, but then she is an exceptional yacht, I think we can both agree.' Hoffmann's slow, conspiratorial wink was accompanied by the broadest of grins. 'I think you could hardly wish for more assurance than that.'

Hoffmann basked in Freij's appreciative little smile, marvelling once again at Peter Meier's exceptional ingenuity. Elli had gone against him, and Hoffmann found her betrayal, like her mother's before her, hard to forgive.

Lynch shivered as he passed the tumbles of purple hydrangeas up to the door of the imposing Edwardian house. He pressed the doorbell and waited, hunched against London's damp fog. He had arrived that morning, the five-hour Middle East Airlines flight to Heathrow was overbooked and the staff bad-tempered. He missed Beirut already. It was cold there this time of year, the Lebanese skiing season was in full flow, but at least it was a clean cold with sunshine brightening the days. London, on the other hand, was sheer misery, the leaden moisture permeated his clothes, invading his every breath. The trees dripped.

'Hello, sir. What a surprise seeing you here.' Yates, ancient and bowed, the faithful family retainer of an intelligence service which had long ago discarded faith and family.

Lynch squeezed the old man's shoulder as he passed. 'Still here, old friend?'

Yates had never been a friend, but he chuckled like a fond father welcoming the prodigal as he led Lynch to the sitting room. Brian Channing was seated by the unlit fireplace. He gestured to the chair opposite, a genial expression on his face that didn't reach his analytical eyes.

'Welcome back to Blighty, Lynch. Well, well. The youngest son gone to the colonies. What can we get you? Tea? Too early for a *chota peg*, really.'

Chota peg. Christ. Channing still thought it was trendy to be a young crusty. Mind you, he was putting on the years now, good-looking for all that. 'Scotch. On the rocks.'

Channing turned the unreliable lighthouse of his smile on Yates. 'Can Mrs Bryson rustle up a pot of tea, do you think, Yates?'

Yates backed out of the room. 'Course, sir.'

Brian Bloody Channing, thought Lynch as he stared into the cold fireplace. Dapper deputy director for security and public affairs, consummate politician and the most genial host ever to slide a knife into his guests' backs and twist it even as he smiled and served them more drinks and dips.

Lynch had as little as he could do with Channing. Most of their conversations revolved around some form of rebuke or another, one more rule Lynch had broken or petty bureaucrat he'd pissed off. Their relationship was often stormy, but Lynch had once met Channing's secretary out on the town with the girls and she had later confided in Lynch, as he lay by her side, that Channing thought the world of him. The knowledge sustained him through the darker days.

Channing settled into his high-backed chair. 'His Excellency the Ambassador not too pleased with you right now, Gerald, truth be told. Seems to think the Secret Intelligence Service should be secret and, well, *intelligent,* apparently. Not thrashing around beating up billionaire presidential hopefuls' secretaries. That sort of thing.'

Lynch opened his mouth to reply but Channing held up his hand. 'Old-fashioned, is our St John, I know. But perhaps you might take his ability to cause an almighty stink in Whitehall into account next time you decide to tase yourself in a china shop or whatever it is you thought you were doing.'

Lynch frowned. 'A good man flew back here with me, Brian. He was lying in a box in the hold of the plane. And Michel Freij killed him.'

'Gerald, I understand your feelings. It's never easy to lose an agent. But Freij has complained formally and my minister has officially instructed me to, and I quote here, Gerald, "Get my dogs off Freij". Lynch leaned forward, but Channing's hand was still up. 'No, Gerald. I won't hear it. We don't have a great deal of time. Down the corridor, a meeting is taking place, which you will join in due course. It is a meeting of EJIC, the European Joint Intelligence Committee. It's our newest toy and it represents a quite unprecedented step forwards in European cooperation. In my personal opinion, it also represents the surrender of the last shred of our sovereignty, but then I suppose I am out of sync with the times on that one.'

Lynch grinned. 'Jesus and me Irish? I could care less about your sovereignty.'

'You're a British bloody subject and public servant, Lynch.'

Lynch sat back. 'So is this about the Falcon Dynamics transfer?'

'Go to the top of the class, Gerald. The committee's current chair is French, a certain Yves Dubois. He's heavyweight. The French have few if any active assets in Lebanon at this moment following the Lévesques debacle. That whole network being exposed by Al Jazeera has blown their Levantine operations sky high. It's remarkable. Apparently the French embassy in Beirut is almost empty without its usual complement of watchers and hoods. We can expect European Joint Intelligence to use its ownership of this operation to include some form of attempt to rebuild French operations there. You will be offered "resources". Kindly accept the offer graciously.'

'You mean I'll get a French shadow?'

'Precisely. And you are, of course, to cooperate fully and *report* fully on what he gets up to.'

'Does it matter? I mean, Beirut's not exactly the jewel in SIS' crown, is it? I'm a one-man show most of the time. It's a far cry from back in the days when we had the language school in Shemlan and all that carry on. You know yourself, you've mothballed pretty much every source I've come up with since the Jordanian water affair blew up.'

'Don't be bitter. It doesn't suit you.' Channing leaned forward. 'Another thing. Dubois is on the warpath. Watch the bastard. He's empire building and I won't have it.'

The door opened and Yates pushed a small, creaking trolley into the room. Channing rose, brushing imaginary dust from his trouser. 'I'm going down the corridor. Join us after your cup of tea, twenty minutes or so. Be pleased to see me. I know you're a natural actor, so it shouldn't be too onerous.'

Lynch glared at Channing's back as he left. He grimaced at the teapot on the trolley and winked at Yates. 'Yates, can you fix that scotch?'

'Course, sir.'

'Good man, yeself.'

Chapter Six

Lynch barged into the meeting room. The faux-Georgian table hosted a collection of ghost-faced waiters and watchers. Brian Channing was halfway to his feet, surprised by the speed of Lynch's entry, his mouth half open. To his right, frozen in immortal tableau was Jefferson from customs and excise. Lynch had met him once, some shitty security conference in a tatty Northern hotel, an internal affair. Next to Jefferson was a big, sandy man wearing a beige jacket. Lynch guessed he was another customs type and a stranger to the rest of the group, his big hands cupped the cheap porcelain coffee cup in front of him.

'Top of the morning to ye,' Lynch said, thickening his Northern accent.

Channing's smile took in the room. 'Everybody, I'd like you to meet our head man in Beirut, Gerald Lynch. Gerald, I shall make the introductions. You know Nigel Jefferson from Customs and Excise, to his right is Charles Duggan. This is Yves Dubois, the chair of the European Joint Intelligence Committee and to his right is Nathalie Durand. Nathalie represents the technical directorate of the *Direction Générale de la Sécurité Extérieure*. Herr Dieter Schmidt represents the *Bundesnachrichtendienst*.'

Lynch took his place, stretching to help himself to sulky spurts of coffee from the battered canteen.

'Shall I summarise our discussion and bring Gerald up to date? Gerald, I think I can speak for us all when I offer my condolences on the death of your colleague. It was really most unfortunate.' Channing picked up a pencil as a baton for his exposition. Lynch settled in for the long haul, a glance round the table confirming a similar air of resignation among the listeners and earning him a tight-lipped smile from Durand. Her lipstick was carmine, offsetting her alabaster skin, her hair shoulder length and jet black apart from a single red streak. A little badge of individuality there, thought Lynch as he idly wondered why she was in the room. Channing extended his hand. 'So, for Gerald's sake, Mr Duggan here is a customs officer involved in high-risk operations against organised criminals in cross-border situations. Whilst on leave following an injury sustained during an unfortunately concluded operation in Hamburg, he encountered a young lady who claimed to be the daughter of a certain Gerhardt Hoffmann, a German businessman who is the CEO and sole shareholder of Luxe Marine, a manufacturer of high-end luxury yachts. The young lady claimed her father was trying to kill her after she discovered he was in the process of selling illegal arms to Arab buyers and shipping them using one of Luxe Marine's yachts. The arms in question, she claimed, were looted from a cold war arms cache near the Czech border. She has subsequently been reported as missing, believed abducted. Dieter?'

'We have preliminary results from electronic surveillance of Hoffmann's personal finances as well as his business interests. Both were a problem until before two weeks. At this time a deposit counting eighty million US dollars was made to the Luxe Marine business account from Bankhaus Löbbecke. The payment was justified as an eighty million dollar order from a pair of Middle Eastern businessmen, Michel Freij and his partner Selim Hussein, for a fifty-metre yacht. The price of almost two million dollars per metre is very high – significantly in excess of two, even three times the market rate, I am informed.' He smiled. 'Although I am, sadly, no expert in luxury yachts.'

Lynch joined in the dutiful rustle of amusement that passed around the table. 'The Bankhaus Löbbecke payment originated from a German dot com company, Kaufsmartz.com. You know this company I think, Mr Lynch.'

'Sure and I do. Kaufsmartz is owned by Falcon Holdings, an offshore investment vehicle owned by Falcon Dynamics, which belongs to Freij and Hussein. We tracked the transfer they made to top up Kaufsmartz' account – they were using a stream of micropayments to make the transfers surreptitiously.'

'Quite so. We also have tracked a payment of forty million dollars made almost immediately afterwards by Luxe Marine to a certain Peter Meier, Hoffmann's brother-in-law. Meier has long been known to us in connection with a number of cases involving the shipment of arms. We have found no trace of the girl.'

Lynch glanced around the people in the room, his attention drawn to the big customs man, Duggan, who was running his hand distractedly through his ginger-blond hair and looking like he might explode at any second. A physical man, a man of action cooped up with dull talkers, Lynch conjectured. Duggan caught his eye and glanced away.

Channing brandished his pencil. 'Thank you, Dieter. Now, while investigating Luxe Marine, Mr Duggan also made brief contact with a person who identified himself as Gonsalves. There is a known associate of Peter Meier's, a Joel Gonsalves. He is an experienced ship's captain and a man with, let us say, a chequered past. We believe on this basis he is commanding the yacht, which is called the *Arabian Princess*. It is obviously early to draw any concrete conclusion from what is, at this stage, highly circumstantial evidence. We have an unusual transfer of money that is not, as far as I am aware, strictly illegal, from Beirut to Germany. We have an order for an overpriced luxury yacht. But we also have a missing girl who claims her father has become an arms smuggler. She was, incidentally, a prostitute.'

Duggan was on his feet, Jefferson pulling at his sleeve. He shook Jefferson off. 'What the hell does that change?'

'Nothing, Mr Duggan. Please, be seated.' Dubois' voice was a surprise. Insidious and smooth, it flowed like mercury into the room. His accent was faint, but Lynch reckoned women would find it attractive. He wondered if Nathalie of the night-black hair and green eyes had heard Dubois talking dirty in those low, musical tones.

Dubois waited for the big man to settle. 'You are suggesting we proceed in monitoring only, Brian? The man you employed to investigate this matter in Beirut was killed, is it not so Mr Lynch?'

Lynch glanced at Channing. 'May I speak openly?'

'Of course, Gerald. We're with friends, *partners*, here.'

'Yes, he was killed. His throat was slashed. Paul Stokes evidently struck a nerve when he interviewed Freij. I obviously had no idea of the ferocity of the reaction it would trigger. I have a transcript of the interview. Stokes rattled Freij when he started to talk about the money transfer from Falcon to its German subsidiary Kaufsmartz, but Freij terminated the interview the second Stokes brought up the micropayments. His reaction was mad altogether. I believe Michel Freij had Stokes abducted and killed.'

'Michel Freij is a significant public figure, Mr Lynch.' Dubois' voice was no less smooth but he leaned forwards, his eyebrow raised. 'As well as being a successful businessman, he is a high-profile political player. You are laying a very serious charge.'

Political player my arse, thought Lynch. Tony Chalhoub had called Lynch's mobile as he waited for his flight that morning. Apparently there had been a shooting near the headquarters of the One Lebanon party the evening before, Chalhoub had continued. The building Lynch had mentioned. Did Lynch know anything about it? If he heard anything, he'd be sure to call Tony first, wouldn't he?

Lynch shifted in his chair. 'Michel is the son of Raymond Freij, one of the most feared Christian warlords during the Lebanese civil war. He was a prominent Phalangist.' Lynch turned to the others in the room. 'The Phalange is a far-right Lebanese political movement, supported by the Christians. Its militia has long been notorious for its brutality.'

Dubois' voice was sharp, 'I am aware of that. What of it?'

Lynch gazed at Dubois. He pulled a folded piece of textured vellum from his inside pocket and slid it across. 'This was next to Stokes' corpse.'

Brian Channing was on his feet, craning his head to catch sight of the document. 'What the hell is it?'

'It is a death warrant.' Dubois sat back and examined the elegant calligraphy. 'The type Michel's father used to write. Raymond died over ten years ago of cancer. He was a cruel man and fond of grand gestures. This has the name Paul Stokes written on it.'

Lynch wondered how Dubois had known about Raymond Freij's odd habit of writing out his enemies' death warrants with a quill pen on vellum.

'This isn't conclusive,' said Dubois, waving the paper at Lynch.

'Isn't it? I suppose the two thugs from Freij's One

Lebanon militia who entered Stokes' flat didn't steal the key to his front door from his dead body then, did they?'

A dip of Dubois' head acknowledged the point. 'And yet Michel Freij would surely not link himself to the crime by leaving a *billet-doux* behind.'

'His father did. Freij is probably more powerful than his father. And arrogant. He's virtually untouchable in Lebanon and he knows it.'

Channing's gaze flicked round the room, taking the temperature. His hands layered in front of him, catlike, he turned to Dubois. 'We *have* to be reasonable. We can't *surely* start intercepting international shipping on the basis of some Hamburger whore's sad luck story and mount a major operation against international terrorism because an Arab businessman buys a yacht with a bit of hooky cash? We need a *deal* more evidence than this before we can justify allocating resources.'

Lynch glanced sourly at Channing. *Your bloody minister's pulling your strings there, Brian.* He pushed back his chair and wandered to the window. There was a rustle in the room behind him as they reacted to his sudden movement. 'The trouble is, it isn't just any old Arab businessman, is it? It's Michel bloody Freij and he killed Stokes because he was pushed about that money transfer. Freij is in Berlin right now. He has a meeting at the Landsee. It's a golf club, right?'

'Ja. Hoffmann is known to be a member.' Schmidt answered.

Lynch turned, framed darkly against the dull daylight behind him. 'So let's just conjecture Michel Freij is meeting with Hoffmann at his golf club. Hoffmann the bankrupt who has just come into forty million dollars in the nick of time and straight away paid half of it over to a known arms dealer. The same Hoffmann whose daughter says he's selling bombs to Arabs?'

'And what arms are we talking about here, precisely?' Channing challenged. 'Conventional? Chemical? What is this shipment that's worth the price of two superyachts?'

The viscous voice seeped into the room again as Dubois placed his hand on the small pile of papers in front of him and leaned forwards. 'Mr Channing is perfectly right in this. We know too little about this affair. But I would suggest there is enough here for us to investigate. We must place Hoffmann under surveillance. Meier, too. We need to find what, if any, weapons were sold, on what basis and to whom. We also have to substantiate this story of a luxury yacht being used to transfer them. This is an ideal operation for European Joint Intelligence as it touches so many of our stakeholders. Surveillance will be handled by the *Bundesnachrichtendienst* who would oversee the domestic service, the *Bundesamt für Verfassungsschutz*. Does this work for you, Herr Schmidt?'

Schmidt nodded, his head lowered. Lynch's lips tightened. *Jesus, would ye look at him? He's only fucking delighted.*

Dubois continued to deliver his judgement. 'Mr Jefferson, could British customs coordinate with our European partners in the marine search for the boat and lead the liaison with the International Marine Organisation? I think this is urgent. Ms Durand and her digital intelligence team will work closely with Mr Lynch in Beirut on this. I would like to prioritise an assessment of the security dangers posed by any plan to import arms into Lebanon – and particularly why a respected Lebanese defence company with known American affiliations would want to become involved in the black market for weapons. Brian, as Mr Lynch is already with us here in Europe, perhaps he might care to coordinate our efforts to discover precisely what has happened at Luxe Marine? We are, as you know, very stretched for resources.'

You wily old Froggie bugger, Lynch marvelled, you were going to do this all along. It was all mapped out ages before I came into this room. You've given gifts to everyone and Channing's outgunned.

'Agreed,' said Channing, a politician conceding the battle. Lynch had worked for Channing for years, knew the man well and had rarely seen him politically bettered. This one went to Dubois. Lynch shook his head. The politics of intelligence had always revolted him. He relished Channing's brittle smile.

Channing sighed. 'Well, that's settled. It will be at least good to have some professional help for Mr Lynch when he gets back to Beirut.'

Brian Channing had just let his pain show and Lynch's black Irish heart sang for joy.

Duggan sat staring from the window, a lonely figure picked out in the dull daylight. Lynch closed the door behind him and sipped his whisky. Yates had fixed him a second on his way upstairs to meet the customs man after the EJIC meeting had broken up and the guests had left the safe house.

'So you're the MI6 man on the case?'

'So they tell me. What was it you were doing in Hamburg again?'

Duggan turned to regard Lynch. 'Isn't that in my file? A drugs bust, went wrong and I copped a bullet in my shoulder. I was recuperating for a couple of days before I flew back.'

'Did you believe her story?'

'Not at first, it seemed pretty far-fetched to be honest.'

Duggan stood and peered out of the window. 'But there was no doubt she was scared. I thought she was safe enough in the hotel, took a trip to the Luxe boatyard to have a look myself. That was where I came across Gonsalves. When I got back the hotel, the room was empty. They had taken her.'

'Who's "they"?'

Duggan grimaced. 'I don't know. Meier's people. Where can I get one of those?'

'Hang on,' said Lynch. He opened the door and called down to Yates. He grinned at Duggan. 'There's a bloke makes them here. Very civilised, I must say.'

The big man sat down again at the window, his hands clenched in his lap. Lynch pulled a chair over to join him. 'What did you find at the boatyard?'

'The men were on strike. They hadn't been paid in months. This last refit was meant to be their big payoff. It was a Luxe 500, rebadged the *Arabian Princess* under a Monaco flag. They fitted extra stowage under the pool deck. The boat was floated off at night, went upriver according to the shop steward there, guy called Jan Wolfe. One of the workers saw it come back downriver again ten days later. That was two days ago.' Duggan gestured at the last car leaving the drive to the front of the house. 'These idiots have burned valuable time waffling.'

'What was in the arms dump? There's nothing about it in the report you filed.'

'That's because she didn't know anything about it. She was listening in and heard it mentioned, that it was across the Czech border. The *Arabian Princess* sailed up the Elbe for ten days.' Duggan shrugged. 'You sort of put two and two together.'

And get twenty, Lynch thought.

Yates poked his head around the door. 'Here we are,

sir. Mister Channing says it's to be your last.'

'It's not for me, Yates. It's for him. Tell Channing to fuck himself.'

'Right you are, sir.'

Duggan took the glass. His face was drawn. 'Will she be all right?'

'Did you sleep with her?'

Duggan froze, the glass to his lips. He drained it and stared into the mist.

Chapter Seven

Lynch pulled off the main road into the cemetery. The rain had died back to a light drizzle. Fat droplets slapped the car as he passed under the Victorian gateway. The air smelt of leaves and moist earth. His shoes crunched on the path across the green. He passed a great oak and headed for the small group huddled around a freshly dug grave.

He recognised Paul Stokes' mother, her face crushed by grief, holding onto the arm of a strong-chinned man in a greatcoat. Dark hair, smooth features – Stokes' brother Charles. The earth-smell was stronger here. The droning of the priest ended, an abrupt silence. The flat tattoo of wet soil on wood interrupted the little sounds of grief.

Paul in the damp of a South London cemetery. Paul crying in the smashed remains of his house in Jordan, Lynch helping him to his feet after the *Mukhabarrat* raid that killed the woman he loved. Paul coming to terms with Aisha's death, slowly healing after Lynch arranged his relocation to Beirut. Paul drunk, hammering his fists against Lynch's chest and screaming abuse. Paul in a cupboard, fat flies crawling on his eyes.

Lynch watched his clouded breath, felt his warm body inside his rustling jacket, his barrier against the dank air. He offered up a silent prayer for the gift of life. He noticed the lone watcher standing by the oak. Crossing himself like a good Irishman, Lynch turned away from the grave and struck out across the silvered grass to meet Michel Freij.

Freij wore a Crombie. Underneath the heavy jacket, his striped tie was held in place with a golden pin that reflected like a little buttercup on his crisp shirt. Droplets from the grass glistened on his black shoes. He smiled and held out his hand as Lynch strode up. 'Mr Lynch, isn't it? How pleasant to see you.'

'What are you bloody doing here?' Lynch ignored the hand.

Freij tilted his precisely clipped chin upwards towards the little group of people breaking up. 'I was in London for meetings with your foreign office. I came to pay my respects. It was,' Freij smiled humourlessly, 'unfortunate Mr Stokes died in this way.'

Freij turned to the path, stamping his feet on the asphalt to dry his shoes. Lynch, following, kept his hands in his pockets with an effort. 'Unfortunate? It was pretty fucking disproportionate.'

'Disproportionate to what, Mr Lynch? I am not aware of the circumstances surrounding his death. But I had never considered death to be a matter of...' he paused and turned to Lynch with a half-smile, 'proportion. It always seemed to me to be a matter rather of finality.'

Lynch scanned the horizon. 'I should have you nicked right now. You're well aware of why he died.'

'That's as may be, Mr Lynch. But I am unaware of *how* he died.'

'He—'

Freij held up his hand. 'Please, I'd rather not know. You assaulted my secretary and security guard on an assumption, Mr Lynch, which you cannot prove. You have a specious motivation, Mr Stokes' interview with me. Mr Stokes was not respectful, I had him removed from my office. That is scarcely a motivation to murder.'

Lynch halted. 'You cheeky fucker. Your thugs were all over Stokes' apartment.'

'You shot one of them, Mr Lynch. They were overzealous and have been reprimanded. What consequences have you faced for the shooting precisely?'

'So what about the note on Stokes' body? The Freij family trademark?'

'Mr Lynch,' Freij frowned and arched his hand across his temples. 'Please credit me with at least a basic level of intelligence and believe that if I were to embark on a series of murders, I would not scatter them with clues that directly implicated me.'

'Why not? Your father did.' Lynch rounded on Freij, his hand freed from the voluntary constraint of his coat. 'You can well afford to drop the act, Michel. Your whole fucking family is steeped in blood and you've killed more than most men could even imagine.'

Freij's eyes narrowed. 'My family has survived in Lebanon since the Crusades and we have done so by being strong in the face of our many enemies. I do not make a habit of snuffing out the lives of every annoying Brit I meet, Mr Lynch, *even* when the provocation is severe.'

'How do you explain the payments to Germany?'

Freij paused and gazed obliquely at Lynch. 'I do not propose to explain them. There is no reason why I should be called to do so. It is not illegal to transfer money under Lebanese law, Mr Lynch. My lawyers inform me that it is similarly not illegal to transfer money into a German company. And it is most certainly not illegal to buy a luxury yacht. My partner Selim and I have worked very hard, Mr Lynch. We are successful men and we believe we deserve to enjoy the fruits of our success. Luxe Marine makes very good yachts indeed.'

Lynch struggled to keep his face neutral and mask his growing confusion.

Freij offered a silver cigarette case. 'Do you smoke, Mr Lynch?'

'I gave up.' He felt the little adrenaline kick, the desire

to take one and give in to the momentary urge.

'Congratulations.' Freij's glance was sardonic as he lit up. 'Mr Lynch, I have a proposal to make to you. As you likely know, I am launching a significant political campaign and I have no particular desire to be under constant surveillance by the British or any other intelligence organisations. I will ask my people to try and trace Paul Stokes' murderers and place the resources of my family and company behind the search for justice. But please, no more bursting into offices or wild accusations.'

'Political? Like your father? The Phalange?' Lynch inhaled the sweet smoke from Freij's cigarette, feeling like a Bisto kid.

Freij stopped in his tracks, stabbing the cigarette at Lynch. 'No. Not the Phalange. A new way, a centrist way. A voice against sectarianism. Selim and I built Falcon Dynamics together. Selim was the technical genius. I provided the resources, marketing and sales. He is a Shia Muslim. I am a Maronite Christian. Together we have shown by casting aside sectarianism we Lebanese can forge true success. I want to give that opportunity to our nation. A new Lebanon. One Lebanon.'

Lynch couldn't keep the surprise from his face. He hadn't expected idealism, not from this polished son of privilege. Leila's Lebanon was idealism and activism – Freij's Lebanon was power, control and rapacity.

Freij grunted. 'You see? We mean change and a new hope for the future. There are many men who would like to see us fail. I will not let that happen. Do not join their ranks, Mr Lynch.'

Lynch followed as Freij turned and made his way back towards the car park, leaving a fine tendril of blue-grey smoke rising from his cigarette, slow-moving in the still air. 'Not that it is any of your business, you understand, but part of the funds we transferred to Germany were used to pay for a new corporate identity and communications campaign for the One Lebanon Party. I am going to win, Mr Lynch. I am going to cure the greatest ill that has ripped our nation apart. A strong government that truly represents the people and welcomes them regardless of belief or origin. A strong Lebanon that can stand up to its neighbours and can rebuff Israel and Syria alike. One people brought together under one nation, not divided by sectarianism.' Freij flicked the butt onto the grass, his Rolex rattling. 'I did not, and do not, want our opponents knowing how we are disbursing funds to support my campaign.'

The large Mercedes was waiting in the car park, the driver standing by his open door.

'I am going to win, Mr Lynch. And I am not going to let this,' Freij gestured at the cemetery, 'get in the way of winning.'

Freij offered his hand. Lynch took it, automatically, his mind revolting too late at the gesture.

'Goodbye, Mr Lynch. My people will be in touch.'

Footsteps approached from behind, turning as the bulky figure passed and got into the front of the car. The big guard pulled the door shut as Lynch glimpsed the unmistakeable bulge of a shoulder holster. He hadn't spotted the security and was glad he hadn't given in to his initial urge to give Freij a slap.

Lynch watched Freij's car leave. He paused by his own, shook his head and fetched the wheel a savage kick.

Chapter Eight

Peter Meier liked to drive down Unter Den Linden; it gave him a sense of history and perspective. Berlin could be a fine city, he reflected. A lady of rare taste and breeding. She could also be a harlot. Meier could deal with either quite happily, his expensive lifestyle masking a life born into poverty and grown up on theft.

Meier thought of fat, stupid Hoffmann and the fortune the man had made him. He settled into the soft leather seat and imagined the sound of hooves and iron wheels, the creak and clatter of the tack as Germany's beau monde took the air in Europe's first and finest boulevard, whiskered gentlemen upright in their smart uniforms as their women smiled and waved with grace and sensibility. Turning right with a sigh, he found himself once again back in modern East Berlin, the glass and steel architecture a rude awakening from his period daydream. A young couple necked passionately on the street corner.

Meier guided the Mercedes into the narrow street at the rear of the prestigious building that housed his elegant offices. He raised the remote control for the basement car park, but paused in the act of pressing the button as he noticed the back of a police car tucked into the parking area of the apartment block opposite.

Men are usually born of instinct or logic. Meier was unusual in that he embraced both. An accountant's eye for detail and a constant need for order sat alongside a predator's ability to distinguish opportunity from danger. He dropped the remote and drove on. He turned at the end of the alley into the main road and parked a short distance away in front of a row of shops. Walking back, he sniffed the air: fresh springtime tainted with exhaust fumes, a strong whiff of coffee as he passed a busy café and turned into the sunlight and the wide pedestrian area to the front of his offices. He strode past the boutiques and restaurants, then peered into the smoked glass frontage of his office building. He stepped through the sliding door into the atrium.

Meier veered away from the marble reception desk and the two men talking to the uniformed security guard. His purposeful stride took him to the lifts and he waited impatiently, watching the numbers on the display counting down. He controlled the strong urge to flee. The lift door opened.

'Herr Meier! Herr Meier!'

It was the security guard. Meier entered the lift, turning to catch the man's idiot face and his raised arm. The two suited men talking to the guard turned. One started to run. The other, unsure, was swept along by his colleague's momentum. Meier punched at the fifth floor button. The lift doors closed on the sound of skittering feet. A body thumped against the door. Meier watched the display count up, tapping his fingers on the wall as the impersonal female voice announced the fifth floor and the doors opened. He crossed the corridor to the opposite bank of lifts, slammed the down button and waited, shifting his case from hand to hand and biting his lip. The doors opened to reveal a woman in a suit. Meier lunged inside and shoved her out. She screamed, flailing at him with her bag as his thrust sent her flying backwards to smack against the steel doors opposite. He slapped the basement button, hammering G twice to cancel the woman's request. The door shut out her shocked face.

Meier cursed his stupidity in trying to reach the office when he had sensed something wasn't right. Caution in everything, care above everything. Now, with so much at stake, he had let himself down.

The door opened and Meier peered out, scanning the basement. He turned left along the wall, following the carefully planned route that avoided the CCTV cameras his own company had installed at a sizeable discount for the building owner.

Emerging from the ramp up to the street, he squeezed past the car scanner and number plate camera. Meier ignored the two men in the police car. He turned left down the street, walking at a harried businessman's pace and checking his watch. A car door opened behind him. He walked on. The cry he dreaded didn't come and Meier rounded the corner, his own car in sight along the busy main road where he had parked.

It had been too close. Meier never took risks like that. He threw his case onto the front seat and pulled out into the traffic. He dug at the call button on the centre console. The line answered after three rings.

'We leave tonight at six.'

The dusty voice on the line was factual. 'The paint won't be dry.'

'I don't care. It can dry as we drive. Tonight at six. Tell them all.'

'You're the boss.'

Yes, thought Meier as he cut the line. *I most certainly am.*

Lynch woke up with his tongue stuck to the roof of his mouth. He spent a full thirty minutes in the shower, letting the jet massage his neck and shoulders. He packed and went downstairs to check out at the hotel's functional front desk. He had a last job to do before he travelled to Hamburg. Lynch never went back to the UK without going over to Belfast, his home town. He left Nathalie a note at reception before he headed for the airport: *Thanks for last night. See you in Beirut.*

Alone and the master of an entire row of empty seats on the plane to Belfast, Lynch stared at the grey clouds below him and thought about her. They had eaten together at the hotel, a nondescript Sofitel near Vauxhall after they had met for a few drinks at the bar. 'We might as well get to know each other,' Lynch had told her. 'We're going to be in each others' pockets for a while.'

She had agreed. He drank pints while she drank gin and tonic. She pronounced it 'jeene', which delighted him.

She lifted her drink. 'So you must not be pleased to work with me, I think.'

Lynch bobbed his glass at her and took a deep pull. 'I have absolutely no problem with that at all. Sure, and this game can be lonely at times. I respect the way the DGSE trains its people. I've worked with your guys before in Beirut. I'm sorry about the Levesques scandal. I understand you've had to virtually start your Beirut operations again from scratch.'

Nathalie Durand inclined her head in acknowledgement. 'However, I am not like the DGSE people you have worked with before, I think. I work in network intelligence, online security, digital networks. It's an office job. I do not really become involved in knocking down doors and these things. My team just knocks down computers. Like skittles.' She sipped from her glass with an impish peek at him over the rim. She wiped the condensation from her slim fingers on her jeans.

No rings, Lynch noted. She wore a long black leather jacket, a plain t-shirt and black cowboy boots. She pulled a stray curve of hair back from her mouth.

'What about you, Mr Lynch? You knock down doors,

is it not?'

He nodded. 'Yes,' he said. 'Yes, I do.'

They had dinner at the hotel's 'international restaurant', drinking too much to compensate for the appalling food. They said their goodbyes on the doorstep of the hotel, Nathalie to prepare for her trip to Beirut and Lynch headed for Hamburg. He hadn't mentioned his Belfast detour to her. That was private.

After they parted, Lynch stayed up in his room, popping miniatures from his mini-bar and channel-hopping. He had finally settled on the 'premium entertainment' channel.

The plane approached the runway in drizzle, streaks on the rounded windows. Vapour streamed over the wing as they came down. A little over two hours after he had dropped his hire car at Heathrow, Lynch carried a set of keys from the Hertz office in Belfast and headed for the car park, an unusual cash customer.

Driving under the surly sky with his lights on, Lynch left the drab city behind him. The road was slick, the sparse drizzle intermittent. The wipers squeaked across the windscreen and he switched them off. He left the motorway, turning by the outskirts of the town into the long driveway up to the sprawling red brick building. He shivered as he passed the gates.

His shoes crunched on the loose stones as he reached the steps to the front doors of the convent. He paused at the bottom to take a deep breath. The memories threatened to engulf him. His chest tight, his hand flew involuntarily to his open shirt as he cleared his throat to speak to the big, cow-eyed nun at reception.

'Sister Helena Mary, please.'

The smell of wood polish and frankincense and a vague hint of institutional cookery brought the sound of hushed children's voices back to him, echoing in the corridors down the years. He took the seat she offered, steadying himself as he pushed back the tide of memory, as he always did.

A nurse appeared. 'This way, please Mr—?'

Lynch followed her in silence, the light shining off the wooden floor polished by a million childish feet. The room was airy, the walls a cornflower blue. The tiny woman in the hospital bed twisted her sparsely haired head to see him enter. Her skin was lined and yellow.

'Ah, I wondered what all the noise was. Gerald Lynch, you always did sound like a herd of elephants in a terrible tear.'

Her voice was reedy and her breath came in gasps after she spoke, but the strength in her eyes was astonishing. He sat on the bed and took her emaciated little hand. *Like a monkey's paw.*

'How are ye keepin', Sister?'

'Sure, ye know yerself. The days are gettin' shorter as me life's gettin' longer.'

He picked at the blanket, pulling it up over her chest. 'I brought you some Kendal Mint Cake,' he said, laying the white plastic-wrapped bars out on the side table.

'Are ye married yet?'

He shook his head, smiling at her. 'Ah no, Sister. Sure, amn't I busy enough in Beirut?'

'Is that where you are now?' She noticed the nurse hovering by the door. 'Thank you, Simone.'

Lynch unwrapped the mint cake and broke off a corner. 'Yes, Sister, Beirut's nice, a very old city. It's a lively place, all right. I was there before, you know, during the war.'

She took the white triangle and popped it into her mouth. 'Well, as long as you're staying in trouble.'

Lynch laughed at that, her little brown eyes in the wrinkled, moist lids dancing in response.

'I am so, Sister.' He frowned, stroking her hand. 'The old place seems quiet now. Where have the children gone?'

'They'd close it down, Gerry, if they could. Sure, they'd have shut it already if it weren't for me and Darina and a few other throwbacks the likes of which they'd rather not be dealing with. This place is too likely to go *telling stories*.'

She grabbed him, squeezing hard, the coughs bursting from her. She turned to wipe her mouth and fell back on her pillows, her breathing laboured and her eyes closed. He remembered the younger Helena, brown-haired and laughing, the nursing Sister who had befriended him: Gerry Lynch, the scared toddler they had brought in after the bomb whipped away his family. Sister Helena brought him up when everyone had decided this rebellious child of a mixed marriage belonged to the devil. She had been there for him, even when the foster parents had returned him to the Sisters as unsuitable material, their son dead from a drug overdose and Gerry blamed for leading the lad astray. Gerry Lynch who had never taken a drug in his life.

Her breathing softened and Lynch waited as she slipped asleep. Gently, he slid his hand from under hers. He crossed himself and leaned over to kiss her on the forehead.

Darina was looking old, too, thought Lynch. She had suckled him as a child, her own baby torn away from her. He recalled with awful clarity the warmth of her breasts and the smell of washing powder that clung to her until one day he was judged too old to sleep with the fallen woman from Derry who worked in the laundry.

'You're looking good, Darina.'

'I'm fine, Gerry, I am. I'm leaving here soon. I've a man, you know.'

He knew the game. He spun, taking her shoulders and laughing, her own eyes laughing back at him. 'Never. That's fine news altogether. What's he like?'

She twirled and counted on her fingers. 'He's handsome, well-spoken, darkish, a little like Mr Darcy, and he has his own money.'

'What does he do?'

'He's a blacksmith. His name's George.'

There never was a man. Lynch always wanted to cry when he walked with Darina, her mind shattered by a lifetime of injustice and cruelty. She took his hand and they gazed across the park together. The clouds, heavy with rain, blotted out the last of the watery sunshine.

'She's going to die, isn't she, Gerry?'

The clarity of Darina's question halted him. 'Yes, Darina, one day. Not quite yet, now.'

'No. Sooner than that. I feel it. I'm not always stupid, you know.'

'You're not stupid, Darina.'

'She killed him. I heard her, so an' I did.'

Lynch was still. 'Killed who?'

Darina searched his face. 'Come on. Let's go back. I'm cold.'

He caught up with her. 'Killed who?'

She twirled again, a little dance. Coquettish. 'Who?'

'You said she killed him. Who did she kill?'

The words tumbled out of her. 'Father McLaughlin. She killed him. She kept it secret all these years. They thought she was going to die last week and she had a last confession from Father Didier, the new priest at the cathedral in town. I listened. I know I'm not supposed to, but I did.'

When Lynch got back to the cornflower room, Sister Helena was still asleep. He kissed her forehead, gave Darina a final hug and left.

On the flight from Belfast to Hamburg, Lynch dreamed of Father Eammon McLaughlin's hot breath on his shoulder, the man's weight on his back. He had to be woken by the flight attendant; his shouting was disturbing the other passengers.

Chapter Nine

Hamburg was cold and the sky bore down on the humans huddled below. Gerhardt Hoffmann pressed his bulk into the seat as he drove through the huddle of men outside the boatyard gates. Their shouting, reddened faces pressed against the glass and fists pummelled the bodywork. Hoffmann reached the point of just hitting the accelerator and ploughing through the press of bodies when he made it through the gates, the security guards stopping the men trying to follow him in. The shouts died away behind him and the car drew to a smooth halt outside the office.

Hoffmann stood panting by the car as Bayer, the uniformed head of the security team, strode up.

'Herr Hoffmann.'

Hoffman had brought in the private security contractor the second he had confirmed the Beirut transfer had arrived. Bayer's team of six burly men had secured the premises well.

'Herr Bayer. Thank you for your assistance. These men are very ... unruly.'

Bayer frowned. 'They have a grievance. It is perhaps understandable.'

'Perhaps.' Hoffmann turned to the office steps.

'The guard on the gate reports a journalist came yesterday, but he did not stay. He said he had an appointment with you. I tried to call you, but your mobile was switched off.'

Hoffmann stopped in his tracks. 'A journalist?'

'Yes, from *Der Spiegel*. Philip Grossman, his name.' Bayer smiled nervously at Hoffmann's outraged stare. 'A

Bavarian from his accent.'

Hoffmann frowned at the incongruous detail. 'I set no meeting with a journalist, Herr Bayer. Who met with him?'

Bayer stuttered. 'Nobody, apparently. The guard said he waited for you and then left. Nobody came here otherwise. None of the management or office team have come to work since last Friday.'

Hoffmann started up the steps. 'Thank you, Bayer. Thank you.'

A very particular man, Hoffmann noticed a number of small things in his office had moved. He pulled open the filing cabinet and immediately noticed the position of his Inmarsat file had changed. He called Peter Meier on the mobile, but there was no answer. Hoffmann gazed from his window over the deserted sheds to the great dull expanse of the Elbe. It started to rain, the droplets on the glass gathering and running down in glittering streams.

Hoffmann sighed and turned to go home, patting the case that housed his beloved Enigma machine, the absurdly generous gift from Joseph Scerri, the Maltese Enigma expert and his old friend. The two men shared a fascination for Enigma and the world of wartime encryption and intelligence. They had long corresponded, meeting at occasional Enigma symposia like long-lost brothers. Hoffmann's father had helped to develop Enigma, Scerri had lost his parents to the Luftwaffe air raids the British had allowed to take place over Malta rather than reveal they had broken the Enigma code. Hoffmann and Scerri had long ago buried the hatchet over a bottle of good malt. Soon he'd see old Scerri again and they'd have a glass and a laugh in the Mediterranean sunshine. The thought cheered him. Whoever had been snooping in his office could go to hell.

Hoffmann's residence in the country outside Hamburg was large, white and set in formal gardens bordered by pretty woodland. His apartment in Berlin was similarly sumptuous, decorated with fine art. Some of the more expensive items had recently been repurchased. Many remained to be located or replaced with similar fineries. It was here, though, in his Hamburg house he kept his second wife, Hilde.

Hoffmann's first marriage had started as a stormy, sexy and fulfilling adventure then slowly degenerated into merely stormy. Hoffmann, frustrated, had discovered Hilde and promptly fallen head over heels for her. He found himself less motivated to spend time with his wife and more energised by the company of his younger paramour. Hoffmann's wife had walked out one night, curtailing the pretence of marriage and leaving behind their daughter Elli. Hoffmann had always spoiled Elli, who had repaid his love and dutiful affection by rejecting Hilde, the partner he had chosen to replace her mother.

Hoffmann could not understand how the girl he had given so much could betray him like this. To his intense annoyance, Elli's rows with Hilde had eventually become untenable and the rebellious child was packed off to boarding school. This made Hoffmann sad, but, as he often told the chaps at the Landsee where he would go to relax on a weekday evening, Elli had clearly made her choice and it wasn't as if she hadn't been warned. Hoffmann didn't appreciate disobedience.

Weekends and the first two or three days of the working week were, of course, spent with Hilde at his Hamburg residence. Hoffmann had at first regretted being dragged away from his new love by the exigencies of business, although recently his regret had diminished to the point where he would habitually spend the entire working week in Berlin. As the money started to run out, Hilde had started taking out her many frustrations on those nearest to her – particularly Hoffmann. His growing inability to react properly to her needs had been an especially painful chapter in their short but expensive time together.

Hoffmann drew up to the grand front porch, flanked with its square pillars. The thud of the Mercedes door sounded flat in the damp air. He pulled his jacket around him. He knocked on the red wood panelling and waited, eventually snatching his keys from his deep greatcoat pocket and opening it himself.

Hoffmann called out, 'Hilde?'

The house was warm but silent. Hoffmann found her in the living room, asleep, an empty glass on the coffee table and her hand draped over the arm of the chair. He scanned the room, its expensive furnishings and the great colourful vase of flowers exuberantly cresting the Ormolu sideboard he had bought at auction in Bremen. He grimaced. It was two in the afternoon and Hilde was already dead drunk, her head lolling back on the sofa. He didn't bother going to face her.

Hoffmann sighed and went to the kitchen, dropping his attaché case, gloves and keys on the worktop. Filling the kettle, he became aware of another presence in the room. He placed the stainless steel cordless jug on its base and flicked it on as he turned to face his visitor, an expression of friendly puzzlement on his broad face.

'Peter? What on earth are you doing here?'

'I am sorry, Hoffmann.' Meier wore a beige greatcoat tied tight at the waist. Tall and lean, he was clean-cut, with peppery temples. His hand, raised to Hoffmann, carried a mean-looking, long-barrelled gun.

'Sorry? Sorry for what—' said Hoffmann as the bullet from the silenced Glock pistol entered his chest, knocking him back against the sideboard. Blood sprayed the wall behind as the bullet exited. His mouth worked spastically as his hand scrabbled on the worktop, the strength gone out of him and all the world's sounds reduced to the pumping hiss of blood in his ears.

With a disappointed groan, Gerhardt Hoffmann fell to the floor, bringing the kettle crashing down with him, the water gushing to mix with the blood on the floor in a viscid wave across the white tiles.

Meier picked his way past the spreading tide and walked into the living room, where the crash from the kitchen had woken Hilde from her torpor. Her makeup had smeared on the white arm of the chair. She blinked at him, an uncertain half-smile on her face and her hand flying to her messy hair.

'Oh. I didn't realise you—' Once again the gun spat. This time Meier didn't apologise.

He detached the silencer from the still-warm Glock and fitted both into the charcoal foam lining of the small suitcase on the kitchen table. He left the house quickly and strode down the driveway to the road.

Precisely three minutes later, Meier reached his car. He drove quickly but within the speed limit, heading for the outskirts of Hamburg, where he pulled over in the middle of a busy little neighbourhood and swiftly completed a transaction on his notebook computer, crediting a forwarding account in Liechtenstein with the balance of almost twenty million dollars from the Luxe Marine holding account. He smiled, grimly. It wasn't as if Hoffmann needed the money anymore.

It was not often the countryside outside the sleepy Schleswig-Holstein town of Wedel, a quiet suburb of the great city of Hamburg, played host to major crime scene investigations. Officers deployed on the taped-off roads around the Hoffmann house turned back curious locals and news crews alike. Inside the house, the forensics teams were at work. In the driveway, standing by Lynch's hire car, Dieter Schmidt was placatory.

'Look, Gerald, we can't act on the instant. We had no reason to suspect Hoffmann's life was in danger. You don't get judges out of bed on a Sunday here without a very good reason.'

'You weren't taking this seriously, Dieter. Dubois took the decision to act on the information on Friday. You had time to get your order, even from a provincial judge in Bad fucking Bramstedt.'

Schmidt sighed. 'Dubois also agreed that we weren't going to make arrests until we had performed at least some basic investigations. We needed time to plan and assign responsibilities in this operation, particularly considering the resource limitations we all face. But I'm not going to argue about it, Gerald. We can't roll back the clock. If you don't like it, complain to Dubois.'

Lynch's frustration found expression in his physicality, shifting his body weight from heel to heel and tapping the roof of the car. Schmidt handed a plastic folder across the roof.

'Here. GSG 9 helped us interview the workers and the office staff at the Luxe Marine boatyard. The customs man Duggan was right. The boat they converted was a Luxe 500, a fifty-metre luxury cruiser. We have a copy of the general arrangement before the refit, but there is no copy of the new layout. The boat left the yard at night and crossed the Czech border, coming back ten days later. We've now confirmed it passed the Kiel Canal on the twenty-eighth. Its reported destination was Southampton.'

'Three days ago.'

Schmidt nodded. 'There has been no Luxe 500 reported entering Southampton. We have requested air patrols from the British and the French, but this boat could be almost anywhere.'

Lynch whistled. 'Amazing. They floated the whole fucking lot down the Elbe in a luxury yacht. Have they located the bunker?'

Schmidt was cautious, his hand held out to slow Lynch down. 'Whatever 'the lot' was. We still don't know what this is all about, Gerald. The Czechs are still searching for it. All we have is the girl's word there was something illegal on that boat.'

'Have they brought Meier in?' Lynch flicked through the folder.

'No, it appears they just missed him at his office. He gave them the slip. He hasn't been near his apartment. We have circulated his car details and photograph to all stations.'

'Have you alerted the border people, at least?'

Schmidt shook his head. 'That would be a serious escalation. We would need to have made some sort of charge. There is no charge against Meier—'

Lynch slammed his hand down on the car roof. 'For fuck's sakes, Dieter, why aren't you guys taking this seriously? You want a charge? Try two counts of fucking murder for a start!'

Schmidt had been leaning against the car. He straightened up to face Lynch. 'You think *Meier* did this?'

He gestured back to the house with his thumb.

Lynch reached into the car and tossed the folder onto the passenger seat. He spoke slowly, controlling himself with an obvious effort. 'Hoffmann didn't struggle at all. He didn't run, the shot was clean in the chest. He just stood and took it. So did she, sitting up on her sofa. She sat there while he levelled a gun at her head without even uncrossing her legs or putting up her hands to protect herself precisely because he was her brother.'

'That's one possible scenario. There is any number of others.'

Lynch's fists clenched and his jaw tightened. 'I don't care. That's the one I'm going with. That and the one involving a shitload of arms from a cold war dump that's heading for a city which really does not need supplied with any more bloody guns and rockets. You're not taking this seriously, Dieter, any of you. But if that girl was right, God help her, Meier is a major fucking hood, and if I'm right, he's a murderer as well. So why don't you people get off your arses and prove me wrong? Or do you want to wait for more people to get killed?'

Lynch waited for an answer but Schmidt merely looked down at the roof of the car. The slate sky reflected on the paintwork. Lynch tore the door open and got in. He wrenched the key in the ignition. Schmidt leaned in the passenger window.

'Okay, Gerald, we'll play it your way. But we'll need time to alert the border police.'

Lynch gripped the wheel. 'Time? I'm not sure we've got much of that left.'

His mobile rang and he grabbed the secure handset. Dubois.

'What happened at the Hoffmann house, Gerald?'

'Both shot at close range. I'd swear it was Meier, but

Dieter and his boys aren't convinced.'

Dubois' voice was silky. 'A transfer was made from Luxe Marine's account to a private bank in Liechtenstein four hours ago. Just under twenty million dollars.'

'Meier. They haven't blocked his passport yet, you know. Dieter's onto it now.'

'Shit.' Lynch was impressed. Dubois was far too smooth to swear. The silky voice paused, then gained an edge. 'Gerald, I have a favour to ask. The Czechs have located the arms cache. It is close to the border in an area of heavy woodland. I need someone there.'

'Sure, no problem. But Michel Freij is in Beirut, not in Czecho.'

'Time enough for him, Gerald. Let's see what Meier's sold to him first. Let's see how much trouble is stored on that boat.'

Lynch gripped the handset. 'Sure. Let's.'

Chapter Ten

Lynch ran doubled over until he was well clear of the rotors. He straightened up to shake hands with Branko Liberec, his liaison in Czech Security Intelligence. Liberec was tall with square hands, and prematurely grey cropped hair. Lynch put him in his early fifties. Dressed in a heavy greatcoat, Liberec shouted above the roar of the helicopter, his face screwed up against the wind and the hail of wet leaves whipped up by the rotors. 'Welcome to the Czech Republic. You have brought light to our week, you know?'

'I can imagine,' Lynch laughed as they strode together away from the helipad. 'Dubois said your guys have found the facility.'

Liberec opened the passenger door of his black Skoda with a flourish. 'We have found it, indeed. It is ten minutes from here. We shall go there first, yes?'

A silver squad car followed them as they pulled away, its lights flashing but no siren breaking the calm of the brown-flecked, sodden countryside.

'We had some witnesses to this boat of yours. It is not always we see this type of vessel on the Elbe, you know. We get mainly cargo or pleasure cruisers. Not so much the luxury yachts.'

'Do you inspect shipping at the border?'

Liberec winced. 'We are all Europeans, Mr Lynch. Our customs wave through ninety-nine point nine percent of traffic. The Elbe has been an open river for over a hundred years.' He chuckled. 'With occasional periods of disruption, obviously.'

They motored through the increasingly hard rain, the wipers whipping as Liberec slowed in the face of the onslaught, the lorries on the motorway lashing spray. Lynch settled deep into his jacket. Liberec glanced across. 'They said you're based in Beirut.'

'Yup.'

'Is that where this materiel is headed, then?'

Lynch nodded. 'We think so. We're sort of keen to define what "this materiel" actually means.'

Liberec glanced across at Lynch. 'We have many very expensive specialists here finding that out just for you, Mr Lynch.'

Lynch liked Liberec's sardonic grin. 'I am honoured, Branko. Deeply honoured.'

They took a number of branches into the muddy bronchioles of the wooded hillside, eventually halting in a clearing packed with pulsing blue lights and silver Skodas, vans with rear doors open, revealing banks of equipment and figures bustling in white boilersuits. After a short, squelching walk down a muddy track, Lynch halted by the concrete doorway set into a long barrow in the woods, Liberec panting by his side. Wooden sheeting led away from the opening, long lines of tape cordons floated lazily.

'So this is it?'

'Come,' said Liberec. 'It's still being dusted, so hands off please.'

Lynch followed Liberec down the steep steel stairway, the handrail glowing with the reflection of the strip lighting. At the bottom was a wide corridor with six great steel bulkhead doors leading off.

Lynch was open-mouthed. 'Christ. An honest-to-goodness cold war museum piece.'

Liberec signalled to one of the boiler-suited figures, who bustled towards them. 'As you say. One we had forgotten about. We are officially embarrassed.' He grinned at Lynch. 'Unofficially, we are barely surprised. This was a messy time and our record keeping is not as good as we would like. Many records were kept in Moscow, not in Prague. Certainly not here in Děčín.'

A woman in a rustling Tyvek suit gave her hand to Liberec and then to Lynch. She was blonde, with wide-set blue eyes. She looked, Lynch thought, typically Slavic, as if she had escaped from a propaganda poster exhorting the people to farm the happy collective.

'I am Milena.'

'Gerald. Nice to meet you.'

She smiled, her speech halting. 'I am sorry, I not speak very good English.'

'Better than my Czech. Do you know what was taken from here yet?'

She nodded. 'This is big facility. We have some record now but some Moscow claim it is lose. We are ask again. Mostly we guess because of gap in stacking.'

Liberec led the way through one of the great bulkhead doors. The poorly lit storeroom stretched back into gloom. Clear spaces were apparent in the phalanxes of stacked boxes. He gestured at the piles of crates. 'High explosive 122mm warheads. These are designed for the RM70 launcher. We think they took something like two thousand of these. The RM70 launches up to forty at a time.' He grimaced.

Milena cut in. 'We think two hundred they took are early Trnovnik.'

Lynch shook his head. 'Sorry, Trnovnik?'

Milena turned to him. 'Yes. They are ban from Czech army now. They are HEAT warhead. You know this, cluster bomb.'

Lynch whistled. 'Nice.'

She read from her clipboard. 'The rest is Soviet 9M22

type Grad warhead. HE fragmentation. This is ordinary shit.'

Liberec led the way into the gloom, his hands shoved deep into his pockets against the cold of the concrete and steel bunker. He turned towards Lynch. 'So, a mixture of tactical short-range missiles. Maybe forty of these are chemicals grade.'

'Go on.'

Milena tapped down the list with her pen. 'These are perhaps two tonnes of explosive in these warhead. There is plastic also. This we are not sure is good.'

'Why not?'

Liberec cut in. 'It's Semtex, pre-1991, so it hasn't had a tagging vapour added to it. Semtex has a nominal ten-year shelf life, so this explosive could be useless. But conditions here are good – if it is well packed, it perhaps is viable.'

Lynch pulled a black notebook from his inner pocket and started to catch up.

Milena's voice was matter of fact. 'We are still count. Perhaps 250 Russian Vampir launchers and projectile, maybe two thousand in total.'

Lynch felt the cold sweat on his back. 'Headed for Lebanon? This is enough to start a small war. Question is, whose war is it?' Lynch wandered along the central corridor, marvelling at the sheer weight of the huge, open doors and at the stacks of crates behind them. He called back to Liberec. 'They took only a fraction of what's stored here.'

'Yes. We think they were planning to come back for more but for some reason were interrupted.'

Lynch stopped by the last door. 'This one's still shut.'

Milena and Liberec caught up with him. Milena held her clipboard to her chest. Lynch could see the faint mist of her breath escaping her full lips and smelled mint.

'We have not access code for this door. We think it is Russian access only.'

Lynch scanned the door. 'Russian access? I don't understand.'

Liberec spoke slowly. 'These facilities are many in Czech Republic and other countries around us. The Russians controlled them even if they nominally belonged to the host country. Sometimes the Russians keep access to areas only for Russian personnel. At that time we Czechs had to allow this.'

'And you have no records of what is stored here?'

'No. The records are in Moscow and we have requested them, but we have no idea of what they kept. We are little bit concerned because obviously they would only use access codes for highly controlled materiel. It does appear as if your friends had access to this area. There are some scrape marks here showing recent activity.'

Lynch reached for the door. 'So how did they get in?'

Liberec shrugged. 'There are sophisticated systems that can manage this type of lock. It is over thirty years old, please remember, although it was very advanced for its time. We have asked for electronics specialists, they will take perhaps a few more hours to arrive. Come.'

Liberec nodded his thanks to Milena and led Lynch up to the door. 'The thieves used the lift, over there at the end of the corridor. We have lorry tracks up to the exit. They did not bother to hide their traces. They used one lorry. This has been found abandoned. The tracks confirm it performed many trips. We think perhaps ten men or more were involved in this. We have found no significant fingerprints but we are still dusting. Sorry.'

Sorry for what, thought Lynch. For the lack of prints or the certain evidence they were now chasing the biggest shipment of illegal munitions he had ever heard of since the Libyans had sent their heavily laden ships across to the IRA? Sorry for the destruction these crates of metal and plastic were going to cause when they got to the Middle East to be lifted out by eager hands? Lynch breathed deeply as they emerged from the bunker, clearing his head of the musty premonition of death.

'What next?' Liberec asked.

'Report back to Dubois and then I have to get back to Beirut. I guess they're going to start looking for this boat, but the Germans are all tied up in red tape. Me, I want to find out what the Lebanese hoods that bought this lot from Meier and Hoffmann want to use it for. Did you get descriptions of the boat?'

Liberec turned. 'Yes. They matched those you sent us from Hamburg. We even had one witness who confirmed the name. It's the *Arabian Princess,* surely. She must have been low in the water on the journey back down the Elbe, though.'

'And she just sailed through the border.'

'I'm sorry,' said Liberec. 'Today is my day to be sorry to you, no?'

Lynch waved Liberec's protestations down. 'Sure, ye can buy me a drink to say sorry properly when we get back to Prague.'

Liberec surveyed the hotel reception area appreciatively as Lynch led the way to the bar. The sumptuous art deco room buzzed to the low chatter of well-heeled tourists preparing for their concerts and dinners in the bustling heart of Prague. 'This place is expensive. They treat you well at EJIC, no?'

'I'm not EJIC,' said Lynch. 'That whole thing's a crock of shit as far as I'm concerned. They can take European cooperation in intelligence and shove it. What do you fancy?'

'Beer, thanks.'

Lynch called to the barmaid. 'Two draught beers, please.' He settled on the wooden bar stool, turning to face Liberec. They were alone at the long wooden counter, at the opposite end of the bustling service area. The tables in the bar were packed with revellers, a chattering throng. People wandered past on the street outside, couples and groups looking in from the cold night air through the bar's wide glass frontage.

The beers came and they clinked glasses. Lynch licked the foam from his upper lip. 'I'm with SIS, British intelligence. EJIC's running this operation, and I got caught up in it. As far as I can see, EJIC is just more European bureaucracy getting in the way of good people's hard work. As usual.'

Liberec raised his glass. 'Amen to that. We already have liaison committees and European intelligence coordinators on our staff. Soon they will be running our service.' He drank. 'Let's not worry about them now. We have full hands, no? How do you get caught up in something like this, my friend?'

'Dunno, you just do. Like you say, there's a lot of "joint European cooperation" going on these days. I should be back in Beirut. I just got mixed up in this end of it.'

Liberec laughed, a short bark. 'Get unmixed. Our people are having huge row with the Russians already. This whole mess is toxic. That is one hell of boat those boys are sailing around in, Gerald. Enough to blow them to kingdom come and back again.'

Lynch ran his finger down the frosted glass. 'A row with the Russians?'

'It is a Russian installation. We are asking them for a

full inventory. Before, they started to cooperate, but something has changed. Now they are denying it ever existed. It brings back some long memories, this kind of thing. We all wish it had stayed buried.'

They were silenced by a group of young men who arrived and clung to the bar nearby. Lynch shared small talk about Prague and the glories of tourism for a few drinks more. By the time the noisy group moved on, Liberec had introduced Lynch to Becherovka and they had started to chase their beers with schnapps as Liberec embarked on an alcoholic tour of Czech culture.

Lynch held his hand up at the third shot. 'I need to eat something.'

'Good, so I order some *bramboráky*. This is good drinking food.'

As Liberec turned to the barmaid and negotiated in Czech, Lynch thought of Leila and the waves along Beirut corniche, a sense of alienation washing over him. He was feeling out of his depth, playing the freelance plod for Dubois in a territory he knew nothing about. Where were the specialists, he wondered. Why was this operation being run as a one-man show? Now they knew the boat was loaded with hundreds of rockets and cluster munitions, surely it was up to the defence boys?

Liberec mistook his preoccupation, gripping his elbow. 'Gerald, you are sad.'

Lynch drained his glass. 'No, not really, Branko. A passing cloud.' He gestured to the barmaid. 'Two more, please.'

Lynch scanned the room. He leant towards Liberec. 'So when was it last in use, this arms dump?'

Liberec blinked, understanding dawning on his face. 'Ah, this place. Bad place. Long time, I think. We had Velvet Revolution in 1989, but the Russians did not all leave until 1993. Is hard to tell. How this guy Hoffmann ever found this is beyond us, really.'

'His daughter says he found it by accident when he was a kid. He lived by the border and must have played in the woods with his friends. It seems odd, because that's probably back in the seventies?'

Liberec's face was a picture of wonderment. 'This is impossible. How could they let kids into this place? No, I cannot accept this. Before Velvet Revolution, it would have been guarded heavy.'

'Unless it was abandoned and then recommissioned.'

Liberec was silent, his hands on his head as he considered Lynch's point. He gazed around the bar as if searching for an answer. He pushed his forefinger into Lynch's chest. 'Yes. Yes. My God. This is why the bastards won't tell us about the place. Because they stock it up ready to put down the Czech independence movement – will they, won't they? They think doing it again to us, another invasion, another Jan Palak. Sure, bastards. Russian tanks on the Charles Bridge once more and we Czechs learn another lesson in how to suck Russian dick. Thank you for stop Velvet Revolution, Commissar bastard. Thank you for rescue this poor whore from Europe and freedom. Hoffmann found old dump, we found new dump. Always these bastards dump, no, Gerald? Always on us.'

Lynch slipped off his bar stool, patting Liberec's shoulder. 'Toilet.' He wove through the increasingly busy bar.

When he returned there was food on the counter and more beer. The potato fritters were crisp and hot, the pickled sausage piquant. There was cheese, too. Lynch hadn't eaten properly since Belfast airport's overpriced stodge, beans and chips.

Liberec waved his finger owlishly as Lynch ate. 'That boat of yours, she full of ammunition meant for Czechs, Gerald. That dump, she Russian last gift to the Czech people, but it was lost in post.'

'We don't know for sure. It's just something you made up.'

Liberec was bright-eyed, gripping the bar to steady himself. 'Consider careful and you find is only answer. Your German loot Soviet dump was part of build-up against Czech independence.' He breathed heavily, waving his beer glass at Lynch. 'Now we toast Czech men and women who are still alive because the bastards not have guts to use this weapons.'

Lynch spread his hands. 'But new bastards have them.'

'You will find them. I trust you. Come, we drink for Czech people!'

Liberec's mobile rang and he fished in his pockets for the handset, cursing and flailing at the folds of cloth. Lynch couldn't help grinning at the performance.

Liberec listened, blinked, frowned and started to interrupt. The blood drained from his face. The mobile dropped onto the counter from his limp hand.

'What the fuck is it?' Lynch demanded.

'Wait. Not in here. We pay bill.' Liberec called the barmaid and settled with her. He led the way unevenly through the massed tables to the street door. Lynch followed him, mystified. They walked together in the cold air, the orange streetlights reflecting off the cobbles.

Liberec held onto Lynch's shoulder as they made their way together up the street, just two more drunks in Prague. Liberec's voice slurred as he struggled to sober up. He enunciated slowly. 'The closed door, remember? They have opened this door. This is store for twenty Russian missiles, Oka missiles. Two of these have warhead you can remove. Two, you hear? Both are remove now. They have take them. Leave missile body, take warhead.'

Lynch massaged his cheeks to clear his head. 'So what? What are two more warheads in a bunker full of them? You said already they took hundreds of missiles.'

Liberec's expression was desperate as he struggled against the drink to speak in English. 'No, not this warhead. They are tell me that only warhead you can remove from Oka missile like this is nuclear warhead. Czech government destroy these missile when we part with Slovakia. But this Russian facility. Forgotten. Russia is denying. There is now trouble between Czech Republic and Russia. Big trouble.'

'And?'

Liberec's drink-reddened face was haggard as he turned in the street and pinioned Lynch's shoulders. 'You not *understand,* Gerald? These are *nuclear* warhead they have take. This is on your boat, these Oka warhead. Going to your Beirut.'

My Beirut. Lynch struggled to grasp the facts, trying to work out what Michel Freij would want with nuclear warheads. 'So how big is an Oka warhead?'

Liberec swayed, speaking with an incredulous, open-mouthed expression. 'How big? Warhead only is maybe less than three metres.'

'No, I meant how big in terms of power.'

Holding on to Lynch's shoulder, Liberec was crying. 'Oka is tactical warhead. One hundred kiloton. Each. You understand, Gerald? Two hundred thousand ton of dynamite total. Dirty dynamite. Each one can destroy city. Poison whole country. Your country.'

They're not headed for Ireland flashed through Lynch's mind before he realised Liberec meant Lebanon.

Chapter Eleven

Elli woke up in pain. Her head was fuzzy as if packed with cotton wool and her dry taste buds felt rough. She moaned, the room's motion powerfully emetic. She flailed around, trying to gain some sense of where she was. She pulled back the duvet and stumbled towards the crack of light in the round-cornered door. It was a boat. She was on a boat. Elli knew boats. She blinked in the unaccustomed brightness and lunged for the toilet, where she voided her stomach in acid heaves.

She cupped her hands under the cold tap to drink and washed her face. Walking unsteadily back into the cabin, she tried the door and then hammered on it. Eventually tiring, she lowered herself onto the bed and listened to the slow swell of the waves, dreading each descent into the sickening troughs. She whispered his name, 'Charles' as a comfort. He was supposed to protect her; she had trusted him. Yet he hadn't been there when she needed him, when they came for her. It wasn't his fault, she told herself. It wasn't his fault.

Dozing, Elli was jerked awake by the snap of the door's lock. A frowning, thickset man in jeans and a white t-shirt filled the doorway, his muscular arms crossed.

'Get up.'

'Where am I? What's going on?'

'No questions. Get up.' His accent was foreign to Elli. Perhaps Italian. She slid across the bed, letting her feet drop to the floor. The man grabbed her arm, urging her. 'Come on. You're going for a walk. Exercise.'

Was this the plank or freedom? Elli tried to hold back but he was relentless and strong. She stumbled in his grip as they marched up the corridor. They passed a short man, a hard, incurious face that seemed to look past her. Her captor shouldered a bulkhead door open. Elli blinked in the warm sunlight, the salty air lashing her face. She breathed deeply, trying to shake his grip from her upper arm.

'Come, exercise,' he growled, herding her along the walkway. The brass railing to her right separated her from the expanse of blue-green waves glistening into the far horizon. They promenaded along the warm decking, Elli pausing by the elegant prow as it carved its way through the azure waves. She could barely see the thin, misty line of land to her left. She grasped the railing to steady herself, her legs weak and tired. Elli took in the spaces and shapes around her, a luxury yacht. A big one, familiar to her. It was one of her father's, a Luxe Marine yacht. The man waited by her, leaving her to regain her strength. Elli pointed to the strip of land.

'Where is that?'

'Nowhere. Come. You need to eat now.'

She licked the salt from her lips, feeling as if she had woken from a coma. They went back inside, down the passageway and Elli realised she was going back to her cabin. She turned, pleading, but he pushed her in and slammed the door shut.

Breakfast was laid out on a tray by the bed and the smell of coffee filled the room. She lifted the plastic cover, bacon and scrambled eggs. She took in the sachets of tomato ketchup, butter and jam. There was toast.

Elli ate.

Joel Gonsalves surveyed the glittering sea, the Spanish sun warming the big cruiser's decks. His Rolex Mariner told him they were on course to make the port of La Coruna in twenty minutes. He flicked a cigarette from the soft pack and lit it, his dark eyes flashing gold for a second as he dipped his head to the lighter. Watching the girl walk around the deck, Gonsalves stiffened, his eyes tracing the curve of her legs as Boutros herded her back inside. He adjusted himself with a grunt. He would have to find himself some entertainment soon or go mad. A sculpted, slim-waisted man, Gonsalves' Latin looks and high-roller lifestyle came together with an insatiable urge for conquest. Some men climbed mountains, some hunted game. Gonsalves' sport of choice was the pursuit of beautiful women.

He licked his lips. They wouldn't be in La Coruna long enough for him to chase tail – he was going to have to wait until Valetta, maybe even longer. Checking the mobile confirmed they were close enough to land to pick up the network. He made the call.

'Meier.'

'We're coming into Coruna. No problems so far.' Gonsalves crossed himself. 'I've unhooked the Inmarsat like you said.'

'Good. We have to assume it's compromised, so continue using the mobile. Buy another line in La Coruna as well so we have a backup. Cash, obviously. I will send you an alternative number for me, in the format we discussed. When do you expect to reach Valetta?'

'Four days at our current rate of going. Forecast's good.'

'Excellent. The girl?'

'She's awake now. Boutros took her for a walk up on deck.'

'It will be better if she stays sedated. Our plans have changed, Gonsalves. She needs to go to sleep again.'

Gonsalves glanced around him, although the sea protected him from eavesdroppers and onlookers, its green-blue expanse stretched to the horizon. This sedation business made him nervous. He was no doctor and had been scared Boutros got the dosage wrong the first time around. The girl had gone down deeper and longer than he thought possible. He fidgeted nervously with the cigarette packet.

'How long for?'

'Forever, Gonsalves. Before you get to Tangier and the Straits. Do you understand me?'

Gonsalves' fingers reached blindly behind him to find the edge of the swivel chair. He sat. 'That's a big ask, boss.'

'It's worth an extra hundred thousand if it's done neatly.'

Gonsalves halted, his cigarette halfway to his lips. His hesitant voice seemed to come to him from far away, from the fog they had left behind in Hamburg.

'Okay. Deal. It's done.'

Gonsalves took a deep drag and flicked the butt out to sea. His looks, free way with money and Midwestern accent spoke of a successful American adventurer. Only the small scar above his right eye talked of the child living rough in Lisbon. The boy who never missed an opportunity to make money, not even a couple of coins for carrying backbreaking loads off the ships and onto the quayside. Not even to turn over an old American tourist who had shown off a wallet too fat to miss in a bar near the docks. It wasn't his fault the old fool had a weak heart, after all.

Gonsalves cut the line and gazed unhappily at the blue line thickening on the horizon. After a few minutes' listening to the thrum of the engines and feeling the regular roll and splash of the big boat's motion, light dawned on Joel Gonsalves' face and he grinned, clapping his hands together delightedly. Elli Hoffmann was attractive, female and on his boat. As far as the world was concerned, she was missing and even Meier would think she was dead. Fate had delivered a pretty plaything into Gonsalves' capable hands.

He felt himself stiffen again. After Coruna, he promised himself.

Night was falling. Gonsalves concentrated on steering out of La Coruna past the Hercules Tower. They had been as fast as possible refuelling the boat at the little Spanish port and Gonsalves had ensured the harbour master was rewarded for his help in speeding their progress. One curse of the *Arabian Princess'* refit was the cargo space below the pool reduced the fuel tanks, cutting her range. He grinned. But Christ, she was fast.

Gonsalves gazed incuriously at the Hercules Tower as they passed. Floodlights picked out the magnificent sandy stone monument against the aubergine dusk, shadows filling the cracks and crevices between the buildings packed along the shoreline. The spice of the hot land mingled with the brine of the sea. Lights from another boat danced on the water behind, a constant presence slowly gaining on the big yacht. Gonsalves kept his speed steady as he felt the pricking of sweat. The lights grew larger, resolving into a grey, functional vessel. He slowed the engines as the coast guard boat came into clear view and punched the intercom panel.

'We've got company. Business as usual, repeat business as usual.' He punched another button. 'Boutros, give the girl a jab and leave her cabin door unlocked for now. Use the Fentanyl, half the dose this time, *kapisch*?

And do it fast.'

Gonsalves lit a cigarette and waited for the customs boat to draw level, watching his crew throw the pilot ladder over. Two men in plain clothes boarded, followed by a couple of gun-toting uniforms. He stubbed out his cigarette and danced down the spiral staircase to meet them on the main deck.

'Welcome on board, gentlemen. We filed our papers at Coruna. Is there a problem?'

The larger and older of the two spoke, puffing from the climb. 'Benemérita. I'm Garcia, this is Galván. Just routine. You were very fast out of Coruna, no?'

'She's a fast boat,' said Gonsalves. He led them into the bar deck and watched with pleasure as both men took in the eight leather high chairs at the curved, black glass bar, the big leather sofa, the armchairs and walnut-topped tables, the glittering mirrors and the huge video screen.

Gonsalves called out, 'Pedro, you lazy son of a bitch, where are you?' Getting no answer, he took up station behind the bar, signalling to the two men to sit.

'Beer?' Both men nodded, still darting glances around them. Gonsalves spoke in Spanish, his American accent masking the Portuguese guttersnipe. He cracked the tops off three frosted bottles, sliding two over the bar. 'What do you want to know? Owner's a billionaire, Lebanese guy. Industrialist. He's just bought this, so I'm taking us to Monte Carlo where he'll fly in with his mistress to inspect his new toy. They'll pick up a bunch of friends and party across to Nice and then party right on back again. If I'm lucky, next year it'll be St. Lucia.'

Garcia finished unbuttoning his coat and swigged his beer. 'It's a nice boat, all right. A Luxe Marine 500, right?'

'That's it,' said Gonsalves. 'She's upgraded. We've the twin MTU engines, almost five thousand horsepower in total. This baby can easily cruise at twenty knots. The boss wanted the very best money can buy and this is it. You know what? When he got it, it wasn't good enough and he had to have it made even better.'

Gonsalves lit a cigarette and offered the pack, but the two men declined. 'So what are you guys looking for?'

Garcia reached into his jacket and pulled out a notebook, flicking through the lined pages. Gonsalves' instant thought was a flash of contempt: *plod*.

'Nothing. This is purely routine, like I said. Where did you come from?'

Gonsalves tapped his cigarette, held one arm crooked in the other, the cigarette held aloft. 'They should have told you back in Coruna, saved your time – they went through the paperwork with me there. We embarked Hamburg.'

Galván was sharper and leaner than his colleague, with a spiv's moustache and darting, hamster-like eyes. He licked his lips. 'Hamburg? When did you leave there?'

'Six days ago. We've been in no hurry. We've been checking in and out like good boys. Like I said, your people at Coruna went through the paperwork with me.'

Galván licked his lips again. 'Funny time to leave Hamburg for Monte Carlo, April, isn't it? Not really the start of the season.'

Gonsalves chuckled easily. 'Like I said, she's a new toy. She had a refit. Job ran over. Can't say the boss was happy about it. Glad it wasn't my ass on the line. He wanted it ready for the summer season. At least he's got his new toy for spring. But he was real pissed at the boatyard guys. I'm being very careful not to remind him about the overrun fiasco, you know?'

Gonsalves laughed and Galván joined him, raising his bottle to clink against Gonsalves', a commoner's conspiracy against The Man. Garcia took laborious notes, his balding head still beaded with sweat from the exertion of climbing the pilot ladder, his tongue poking out from between his moist lips.

Galván slipped off his bar stool and wandered aft to stand by the eight-seat round table. 'This the dining table?'

Gonsalves snorted. 'Dining? That's just a casual table. The dining saloon's upstairs. Look, why don't I show you boys around her? We're in no hurry anyways.'

'Sure,' drawled Garcia. 'That'd be interesting.'

They waited on the deck as the coast guard vessel drew alongside again, Gonsalves smoking and holding his beer. 'So you see, she's pretty well kitted out.'

'And what's this, here?' said Galván, gesturing at the covered-over pool with his angular chin.

Gonsalves chuckled. 'That's the swimming pool. We've fitted the winter cover, the boss won't be using it, so it doubles as a dance floor. Want to take a peek in there too?'

Garcia's mouth was open when Galván spoke. 'No, thank you, Captain. We've enjoyed having a look around, but we're not conducting a formal inspection. You have been very kind.'

'A pleasure.'

They shook hands and the two men descended the pilot ladder, Garcia first. Gonsalves' smile was hurting his cheeks as Garcia paused at the top of the ladder and stared across at him for what felt like a lifetime. Garcia nodded, then his pig's head disappeared. Waving them off, Gonsalves ached for another drink, the tension leaving him in a rush of exultation. He returned to the bar and poured himself a large single malt. The sick feeling in his stomach dissipated as the spirit burned through him. He poured another, appreciating the sherry cask nose of the fine Macallan that he'd blindly pulled from the selection of bottles lining the bar.

Gonsalves felt good. Very good. He wandered back to the aft deck and watched the lights of the coast guard vessel twinkle their merry way back to La Coruna, past the ancient lighthouse floodlit from the ground. He looked forward to spending some quality time alone with Elli Hoffmann in her cabin once she woke up.

Although, thinking about it, he wasn't really fussed about that. He just needed to get some.

It wasn't until past ten the next morning Benemérita captain Alonso Garcia opened the urgent email to all stations. He had stopped off at the little bakery with the blue shuttered windows on the way in and was still wiping sugar crumbs from his chin as he bustled into the office. The email made him physically stagger. With an awful feeling in his stomach, he checked his mobile, which he had set to silent the afternoon before as he had settled for a nap before the evening shift.

Six missed calls. Four in the early evening. Two later at night, from Madrid. He re-read the email. *Cristo*. They'd sack him. He was too old to retrain. He had a wife. Children.

He hadn't logged the uneventful and routine boarding of the big yacht. He checked that Galván hadn't come in early and done so himself. He hadn't.

Alonso Garcia made a decision. He scrolled through the movement log and located the entry from yesterday afternoon and the boat's evening departure. His finger hesitated over the 'Del' key. He was sweating.

A second later, he picked up his mobile to call Galván and let him know they had never seen a yacht called the *Arabian Princess*.

Chapter Twelve

Gerald Lynch waited in the reception area in the upper reaches of the European Commission's Berlaymont building in Brussels, lulled by the quiet hum of office activity. His eyes started to close. A pretty blonde wearing a black skirt and green blouse arrived.

'Mr Lynch?' She smiled down at him. Lynch rubbed his hands over his face. 'He'll see you now. This way.'

Lynch followed her down the corridor and into the big room, the long oval table scattered with the detritus of a recent meeting, a clutter of coffee cups, pens and notepads with doodles and jottings. The panoramic window looked out onto the Boulevard de Charlemagne.

Yves Dubois rose to greet him.

'Gerald. Good to see you and thank you for the excellent work you have done.' He turned to the secretary. 'Anna, could you please ask housekeeping to get this table cleared? And could we get some coffee for Mr Lynch? He look like he could use it.'

Lynch sloughed off his jacket and draped it over the back of the chair. Dubois peered at him.

'Are you okay, Gerald?'

'Fine, sure I am.' Lynch grimaced. 'I was having a few drinks with Liberec last night when we got the news.'

'A few is it? Well, there's little enough time for that sort of thing now. I cannot stress how important this affair has now become. Brian Channing has briefed your prime minister. I have briefed mine. We have agreed this will remain essentially an Anglo-French operation carried out in the strictest secrecy, but under the coordination of EJIC at the highest level only. We cannot afford to widen the briefing to other European heads of state. The Czechs and Russians are both embarrassed and have agreed to cooperate fully with us and also to keep this news confidential until we have better evaluated the location of these devices. If the news that two nuclear warheads have been stolen gets out, we will face widespread panic at the very least. The Czechs have moved quickly, thank God, and told their media that a cold war arms cache has been uncovered and is being catalogued prior to its safe destruction by the United Nations under existing treaties.'

Lynch pushed his hands back through his hair. 'So what's next?'

'The British Navy has deployed several patrol boats from Gibraltar to search for the *Arabian Princess*. They have turned off their Inmarsat, otherwise we could have located them in a second. We have also requested US satellite imaging, using the excuse that this is a narcotics-related investigation. We are hoping to intercept the boat in the Straits of Gibraltar. A blockade, if you like, although we haven't got enough resources available to make it as effective as I would like. We need to find the boat before it gets into the Mediterranean and is lost to us.' Dubois brightened. 'Ah, here's your coffee.'

'Lost to us?'

'The Mediterranean is packed with large, expensive yachts, Gerald. One more won't really stand out. It would be searching for your needle in the haystack.'

Lynch sugared his coffee and sipped. It was piping hot, strong and good. Dubois was still talking, his fingers picking at papers. He slid a file across to Lynch.

'Peter Heinrich Meier was born in Frankfurt July 7th, 1962, the son of a steelyard worker. His first criminal records date back to when he was eleven, when he was cautioned for shoplifting. A ward of court at fourteen and then six months in a young offenders' institution at fifteen. After this, we have nothing until he was thirty. Nothing. He went to school, did his homework and obtain his examinations. His results academically were excellent. He worked for a shipping company and rose quickly. His colleagues mention he kept long hours and was exceptionally committed and talented. He was popular. He left to found his own company in 1990 and quickly won contracts to ship materials to Kuwait from the armed forces stationed in Germany. In 1992, there was an investigation into some of these shipments, but the paperwork exonerated Meier from the charge of shipping materiel stolen from British Forces Germany. Since this time, there have been several report of illegal arms shipments linked to Meier and two full-scale investigations, but he has not been found guilty of any misdemeanour.'

Starting to drowse, Lynch jerked as Dubois slapped the desktop. The Frenchman jumped to his feet, fists clenched. 'We've known Meier's rotten for twenty years and yet we've got nothing on him. Nothing. Now he is gone so bad on us that we lust for him like a bitch in heat, but we are blind. We have nothing to go on at all. We don't even know where he is, the bastard.'

Lynch regarded Dubois over the rim of his coffee cup. 'What about the Enigma machine? The customs guy, Duggan said Hoffmann had an Enigma machine.'

Dubois pulled another paper from the pile in front of him. 'We talked to the man who presented the machine to Hoffmann, a Maltese called Joseph Scerri. He is one of the world leading experts on Enigma and the wartime work of SOE, especially the X and Y section radio teams. To stop the Germans knowing the Allies had cracked the Enigma code, Churchill allowed them to bomb Malta. Scerri's parents were killed in the attacks. He is eighty-two. Scerri corresponded extensively with Hoffmann. Hoffmann's father was involved in the development of Enigma. They had arranged to meet next week.'

Lynch's tired muscles tautened. 'Where?'

'Valetta, Malta. There is a team interviewing Luxe Marine's staff. Hoffmann's secretary told our people Hoffmann was planning to visit Scerri in Valetta.'

'That's where they're going to refuel the *Arabian Princess*. The boat's range was reduced when they added the extra storage. Hoffmann planned to be on that boat.'

Dubois nodded. 'This is what we think. We're going to set up a welcoming committee. You're flying back to Beirut today, are you not?'

'Sure am. I have a score to settle with a Lebanese businessman with a taste for nuclear warheads.'

'Nathalie Durand will fly back with you. It is probably best she stays with you in Beirut.'

Stays with me? Lynch tried to keep the shock from his face but he was too tired to play act. 'I'd rather not, actually.' *Christ*, he sounded English.

The apartment in Beirut was his bolthole, a private life away from the prying — his rebellious retreat. The little world where he was himself. Where he was with *her*. No. *Not there.*

Dubois' smile was tight. 'Believe me, Mr Lynch, I share your feelings regarding the arrangement, perhaps more than any other man alive would. However, given the absolute secrecy this operation necessitates, it is crucial you minimise any communication across public networks. This is the only viable way to proceed.'

Lynch staggered from Dubois' office, trying to work out how he was going to break the news that a French woman was moving in with him to Leila Medawar.

*

The immigration official handed back Nathalie's passport and took notes in a ledger. In all his years of travelling in and out of Beirut, Lynch could never fathom why this system remained manual. He caught the look of surprise on Nathalie's face as she waited for the man to finish fussing with her papers. Here was a network her team wasn't going to knock down in a hurry.

They waited for Nathalie's bag and waited again as the bored customs official opened it and pawed through her clothes. Lynch noticed she liked expensive lingerie. He caught the customs man's eye and held it until the man looked away and dismissed Nathalie and her underwear with a flick of the wrist.

It was cool outside the terminal, the afternoon sun washing the shabby airport in mild orange light. A car pulled up, the driver grinning. 'Welcome back, *seer*.'

Lynch reached in through the window and slapped the man's shoulder. 'Hassan. Good to see you.'

Lynch opened the back door for Nathalie and took the front seat himself. They pulled away, Lynch and Hassan sharing pleasantries. Lynch turned to Nathalie, caught her preoccupied air. 'You okay?'

Her voice was distant as if Lynch had somehow intruded and she gazed out of the window as she spoke. 'Yes. Sorry, it's all a little fresh for me. I'm sure I'll get used to it quickly enough.'

Lynch snorted. 'Beirut takes more than getting used to. It's a complicated old place at the best of times. You'd want it in your blood, so you would.'

She turned, her hair swinging. 'That is lucky, is it not? I was born here.' She held his gaze, her lips tight. He felt the challenge rising in the silence between them. He hadn't seen the fire in her before and retreated, amused, from her glare, his hand held up in supplication.

'Sure, how was I to know that? Welcome home, then, petal. Welcome home.'

Concrete blocks lined the way to the airport, listless red-capped soldiers dotted the roadside, occasional pedestrians in leather jackets and heavy winter coats meandered, chatted or just stood incuriously watching the traffic jostle past.

Lynch's neck prickled, an uneasy frisson that he knew meant trouble. Born to good Irish stock, he was a great believer in the sixth sense. His finely honed feeling for danger had saved his bacon on many an occasion. He checked the side mirror. The white car behind them had pulled out at the airport but hadn't picked up any passengers, the two men in it had sat smoking with the windows open. Something about them caught his eye. They hung back now, but he noted they always moved to keep the taxi in sight.

'Hassan, we've got company. Step on the gas, would ye? Big time.'

The white car inched closer. Hassan glanced in the mirror, grinned and gunned the engine. They swerved through the cars on the Al Assad Highway, Hassan's eyes flickering between the road ahead and the mirror.

Nathalie steadied herself against the car's swaying. 'What the hell's going on?'

'We were picked up at the airport.' Lynch watched the white car gain on them, then its bonnet as it started to pull abreast of them. 'Jesus, Hassan, can't you get this thing to go any faster?'

Lynch caught Hassan's eye in the mirror. The white car was almost alongside, its passenger trying to hold a gun steady with both hands, a forage cap jammed on his head.

The man grimaced and Lynch hoped it was from the wound in the bastard's leg. He swore softly. Unarmed, he felt naked.

He barked at Nathalie. 'Get down.' He lunged back to pull her down across the back seat.

The impact of the white car against the rear of Hassan's Mercedes sent them crabbing across the carriageway, narrowly missing the big container lorry to their left. Hassan was deft, bringing the car under control. Lynch jerked at the thunk of a bullet impacting the bodywork to his right.

He caught Hassan's pained grimace. 'It's okay, I'll pay.'

Hassan nodded, his mouth set in a line. 'If we live, *seer*.'

The screech of metal against metal and another impact, this time smashing the car against a battered bread van in the slow lane. All three vehicles locked together for a suspended moment. Nathalie screamed. Hassan dropped a gear and wrenched the wheel. He stamped on the throttle and released them from the grip of the van. The move sent the white car careening across the highway to the right.

Lynch punched Hassan's shoulder and pointed. 'Keep right here, at the stadium. Into Chatila.'

'Chatila?' Hassan was incredulous.

'Just do it.'

The screaming of the engine masked the gunshot, but the crack of the bullet exploding the rear windscreen was deafening. It collapsed, tiny shards of glass falling into the back seat and a starred crack appearing on the passenger's side front windscreen. Hassan barked in fear; the car swerved as he jerked in reaction. They cut across the path of the white car, another impact as they clipped its bumper. Hassan tried to edge past a slow-moving water bowser exiting in front of them. They scraped along the grimy concrete wall of the exit, the sound of rending metal piercing the air, a coruscating shower of sparks flying behind them. They cleared the bowser and were free into the slip road, swerving to pass the cars ahead of them, jinking first left and then right to roar past the slow traffic. They burst onto the roundabout. The tyres screeched as Hassan fought the curve and flung the car right towards the exit. They narrowly missed a blue BMW, its driver stood on the brakes to avoid them. The car span to a halt by the roundabout exit. The driver leant on his horn, red-faced and gesticulating from the window. The white car chasing them hit the BMW hard and swerved out of control. The driver fought to reign in its bucking slide, righted it and came after them again. Nathalie sobbed, a low constant moan. She hunched in on herself, her hands tightly wrapped around her head.

The white car fell behind as they slowed for the crossroads to the Chatila refugee camp. Caught in the slow moving traffic, they were enfolded in a new world of dirty-faced children and sullen-eyed men gazing at them. Lynch watched the white car pause in the traffic behind them, then peel away back towards the airport road. He grinned.

'Lost the bastards.'

Nathalie uncurled, her ashen face streaked with tears and her makeup smeared. She stared about as if at a new dawn. 'How did that happen?'

Lynch gestured. 'This is Chatila, the Palestinian refugee camp, where the Israelis stood by as their Christian militia allies massacred thousands of innocent people during the civil war. I didn't think Michel's Christian thugs would be too keen to come in here firing off their guns. They'd never have got out alive.' He patted the driver on the shoulder. 'Thanks, Hassan. You did a good job. I was serious, I'll pay for the damage. Next time you meet me flying in, bring a gun in the glovebox.'

Hassan smacked the steering wheel, wheezing laughter. 'It was like driving during the war, huh? Shit, those guys were crazy.'

Lynch brushed shards of glass from the armrest between him and Hassan. He glanced at Nathalie, who was trying to repair some of the damage to her makeup and dignity. 'Now, there's a proper greeting committee for you. Welcome back to your homeplace, Miss Durand.'

Her brief smile in response was tight-lipped.

Chapter Thirteen

The strollers along Beirut's paved corniche hunched against the buffeting cold, the watery late afternoon sunlight tempered by the looming shadows across the railings and sea wall. On the roadside by the silvery thrust of the Manara lighthouse, a street vendor handed steaming sweetcorn to a group of young men who tossed the cobs from hand to hand, laughing. Above the city's swathes of buildings and the green hills rising up from the rich blue Mediterranean, the snowy peaks of Mount Sannine gleamed.

Lynch and Leila waited together for their double espressos at Uncle Deek's roadside coffee shop, the two coffees handed over in brown plastic cups with wooden stirrers thrown in with surly panache by the coffee man. They crossed the corniche road, wary of the speeding cars. Leila was warm in his arm, nestled against him as they promenaded along the seafront, her hair tumbling over her shoulder. Her pale, fine skin reddened in the chill, the cold making her sniffle. Lynch's smile faltered, his happiness tempered by the necessity of breaking their idyll.

He stopped at a railing overlooking a tumble of barnacle-encrusted concrete slabs, remnants of one of Lebanon's many conflicts. Leila hooked the hair blowing in her face back behind her ear, uncertain as she gauged his expression.

'What is it, Lynch? You've been funny since we met today.'

Lynch spoke to the sea, the clouds reflected in his green eyes. 'You have to stop coming to the flat. I've arranged a place for you nearby, you can stay there and I can come and see you there. I have a big job on and you can't stay with me or come to the apartment for now. Apart from anything else, it's dangerous.'

Lynch knew she'd be unhappy, but this was worse. She was shocked, searching his face. He focused resolutely on the sea, the breakers smashing against the rust-streaked concrete.

Her voice was low. 'You have someone staying with you.'

'Yes.'

'From intelligence.'

'Yes.'

'A woman.'

Lynch glanced down at the little brown plastic cup in his hand. *Damn her intuition.* 'Yes.'

'Fine.'

He reached for her. 'Leila, come back.'

He followed her, striding to catch up until they were both almost running down the corniche. He caught her, spun them both around and held her pinioned against the cold metal as she pummelled his chest, the tears streaming down her cheeks.

'Fuck off, Lynch.'

'It's not personal. It's what I do – we're part of a big operation against,' God help him, but Lynch the practised liar faltered for a split second, 'drug smugglers and they need her to be here. She's an expert in electronic surveillance and online security stuff. She's nothing to me, just a colleague from another intelligence service.'

'Which one?'

'Oh come on, you hardly expect me to ...'

'To what? To tell me?' Leila broke away, stepping back from him. 'To let me into your private world? The secret garden, where all you little boys play your dirty little games with the destinies of decent people?'

'Look, here's the key to the flat. It's in Hamra, it's close by. The fob has the address and everything on it. It's furnished. I'll call you.'

'I don't want it, Lynch.'

'Here. Just take it.'

He took her unresisting hand and placed the key there, closing her limp fingers on it.

'I will not wait for you, Lynch. Not while you play with your Bond girl.'

'I'll be in touch.'

He reached for her, but she turned her head away, leaving his unfulfilled kiss a brief contact against her cold, salty cheek.

Lynch watched her walk away up the corniche, the urge to smoke a cigarette clawing at his frayed nerves. When she had gone, he turned to the sea. He wandered along the seafront until darkness fell, flagging down a *servees* to take him home to his apartment with the stranger who'd moved in.

He drew on his cigar and sat back in the chair, settling down to enjoy the dusk bringing the streets to life. The umber sunset tinged the waters of the Mediterranean, the sea at the end of the street. Church bells rang out far away across the city, answered a few seconds later by the sweet tones of a nearer bell. One by one, the *azan* sounded from the mosques, joining the bells.

Nathalie stepped onto the balcony, held the railing and surveyed the street below. 'It is a very beautiful city, no?'

Lynch puffed smoke. 'It has its upsides.'

Nathalie raised an eyebrow. 'Are you sure it is no

problem I stay here?'

Lynch shook his head and tapped the cigar on the rim of the faded green plastic ashtray he kept outside for cigar nights, stolen from a pub somewhere in Monot a million years ago.

'Not at all,' he lied, Leila's teary face remembered, 'it's a pleasure to have you here.'

Nathalie had settled into the spare room and sat gazing at her laptop on the coffee table in the living room when Lynch returned from his awful confrontation with Leila. He had called her mobile but she hadn't picked up. He found himself constantly resisting the temptation to go across to the flat in Hamra, torn between wanting to give her space and his dread of her threat to pass him by. Lynch knew her too well to shrug off Leila's fiery revenge. He abhorred the thought of a tousle-headed girl answering the door in the oversized shirt she liked, some swarthy ape calling from the bedroom, 'Who is it, *Lei-Lei*?'

Lynch shuddered as his imagination ran amok.

Nathalie turned from the railing, her voice breaking his bleak reverie. 'There are two nuclear warheads on this yacht. What do you think Freij intends with them when he brings them here?'

Fuck. Shop. Lynch drew on his Cohiba. 'That's the big question, isn't it? Freij is a spoilt billionaire brat who holds huge political power and wants to be president on a unity ticket. He never disbanded his father's militia, just folded it up into his political party. Yet his business partner is a respected figure in the Shia community, someone you'd have thought would be violently opposed to Freij's Christian militia thugs. It's hard to call. I just know they're not safe hands to put those warheads in. Actually, come to think of it, there are no hands here I'd put them in.'

'Our analysts have found this question hard, too. They

have compiled a list of known assets of Falcon Dynamics. It owns many companies. Falcon has major holdings in Germany, Albania, Greece and Lebanon, and offices in several more countries. They are obviously very close to the Americans. We do not know how close.'

Lynch drew on the cigar again, sending blue smoke into the encroaching darkness. 'And that'll be the tip of the iceberg. Freij and his fat friend have a whole network of offshore companies.'

'Fat friend?'

'His partner, Selim Hussein. He's a big lad, got more chins than fingers. They founded Falcon together. It's built on Freij's money and Hussein's engineering skill. Freij is a Maronite Christian, Hussein is a Shia Muslim. As I said, it's an odd pairing to find here in Beirut.'

Lynch finished his cigar, flicking the stub over the balcony. He pulled himself to his feet wearily. 'Have your people had any luck getting past their security systems?'

Nathalie shook her head. She was wearing an elegantly understated evening dress and burgundy lipstick.

Lynch paused by the sliding door. 'Are you going out?'

'We have gone as far as we can with remote hacks and surveillance. Their systems are very good, and we are worried if we try any harder over networks, we will be identified. We are setting up a team here at the French Embassy but we need a physical intervention. And yes, I am going out for dinner. So are you, if you would like to clean up a little and come.'

Lynch crossed his arms behind his head, stretching. 'Where?'

'Chez Madame Chalabi. She worked for my father during the civil war. She has long been a great ally for France here in Beirut. I thought she might help us with some links to people associated with Falcon. She knows everybody.'

'Your father? Here?'

Nathalie laughed at Lynch's evident confusion. 'Yves Dubois. My father is Yves Dubois, *non*? He was our head of intelligence here throughout the war. Do your British *intelligence* people not brief you anything?'

'No,' Lynch growled kicking the door to his bedroom open. 'They bloody don't.'

Nathalie and Lynch tramped together past the flashy boutiques and designer frontages of Beirut's Hamra district. The dummies pouted and preened in lifeless tableaux of scant cloth and revealed flesh. Owl-eyed at the richness around them, cars honking and jostling to their left, a feeling of sadness washed over Nathalie and she hooked her arm into Lynch's.

'You know I said I was born here? My mother was Lebanese. I suppose they didn't tell you that, either. This is the first time I have come back here since I was a child. It feels very strange to be here. Familiar, even safe.'

She caught the surprise in Lynch's glance down at her. He was gruff. 'It can be, sure. It can be vicious, too. When did you leave?'

'Eighty-eight. My father came out here at the start of the civil war. He met my mother here and they worked together.'

'For French intelligence.'

Nathalie nodded, hopping up onto the uneven pavement to avoid a blaring *servees* as it squeezed past. 'Yes.'

Nathalie forgot Hamra for a second and was back in the airy kitchen in Dijon, bees buzzing around the lavender outside the window. 'You can blame Damour,' her mother told her, laughing and still beautiful in middle age, despite the illness eating away at her. 'We first became lovers after Damour. The massacres made everyone scared and many people found comfort in each other, then and in the years to come.'

Lynch's voice broke in on her reverie. 'So how come the name change?'

She blinked to clear her head. 'The same way all women change their names, *non*? I was married. I think it is here if I understood the directions correctly. It has been a long time since I was here before.'

They passed a tatty shop front. Lynch pushed open the creaking iron gate to its side that led into a musky alleyway lit by a dirty glass carriage lamp. Leaves and rubbish littered the concrete path. Nathalie rang the doorbell as Lynch gazed up blinking at the arches and decorations of the fine Ottoman house looming into the darkness above them, the brass ornamentation on the mahogany door dull in the baleful light. She thought him attractive in a brutal sort of way but, really, not her type. Catching her eye, he smiled. Old enough to be her father, for a start. She smiled back.

Madame Chalabi answered the door herself, dressed in black and wearing a string of remarkably large, round pearls. She smiled regally.

'Goodness, you must be Nathalie. Good evening, my dear. It has been so very many years. And welcome, Monsieur ...'

Distracted by setting up her team of hackers and online watchers, Nathalie had neglected to mention Lynch would be with her. She cringed inwardly at the crass oversight. Madame was far too genteel to make a fuss, which made it feel worse. 'Lynch. Gerald Lynch. He is working with me. He is English.'

'Well, welcome to Cedars. Come in now, both of you, don't stand there in the cold.' She led the way across the small, elegant courtyard, a small Moroccan-tiled fountain at its centre. Her accent was a riot of influences, a strong hint of French and perhaps a touch of Arab but above all public school English. 'The drawing room, dear. Do you remember where it is?'

'I do,' Nathalie laughed. 'How can I ever forget?'

Cedars hadn't changed at all. The delight died on her lips as the memories flooded back and Nathalie gripped the wooden doorframe for support. She surveyed the room, transported back to her childhood. She had often played here when her parents had gone away. She had always been confused by the brittle hilarity that accompanied their return, a reaction she now recognised as laughter born of fear.

Vivienne Chalabi had worked tirelessly to aid the victims of the bloody war that had consumed Lebanon for some fifteen years, extending her protection and assistance to anyone in need, Christian or Druze, Shia or Sunni, like a polytheist Daniel. In the end, *Tante Vivienne* had survived the war in order to live without the one thing she had wished above all else to preserve – her beloved husband Maurice, hit by an Israeli phosphor shell. Vivienne had watched him burn to death in front of her. She was horrified to see his body catch fire again after each attempt to douse the persistent flames. Vivienne stayed until she could bear to watch no more and ran home to avoid the vision of her beloved husband in hell, bursting into a blaze each time his remains were unwrapped.

Nathalie's father had wept with *Tante Vivienne* in the mortuary, returning to Cedars where his little girl played in the living room with Beauchamps the butler.

Nathalie stared into the room, her hand on the cool,

white paint of the heavy door, hearing her own, girlish voice singing out, 'Where's Uncle Maurice?' Her father scooping her up and whispering urgently, 'He has gone to a better place than this, *Nino*. Hush now.'

Lost in the past, Nathalie started at the movement of the large-framed man as he rose from the sofa, leaning on a silver-topped black cane to move towards her. He was dressed formally, grey-haired and balding and sporting a bushy, white moustache which he brushed with the back of a finger as he took her hand, touching it to his lips. She found the gesture, like his tuxedo, old-fashioned and yet delightfully gracious. She recognised the subtle little red thread on his lapel that signified he held the Légion d'honneur. The man unsettled Nathalie, a familiarity about his features and demeanour at once comforting and worrying. Catching her eye, he smiled at her. She dropped her gaze.

Madame Chalabi fussed. 'I am so sorry, I have not made the introductions properly. Nathalie is the daughter of Monsieur Yves Dubois.'

'Is she? Remarkable.' The man said with a throaty chuckle. He beamed at her with tobacco-stained teeth. '*Enchanté.* I am Ghassan Maalouf.'

Nathalie fancied something dark passed across Maalouf's face as Lynch walked into the room behind her. Madame Chalabi's arm embraced the air around Lynch. 'And this is Monsieur Lynch, who is working with Nathalie.'

'Good evening, Monsieur Lynch,' Maalouf rumbled. 'Vivienne had not mentioned we would find ourselves in such distinguished company.'

Madame Chalabi stood poised by the white marble fireplace, framed by the heavy gold decorated mirror. 'Ghassan is a very old friend of the family. He was *most* keen to meet you, my dear. Please, Monsieur Lynch, take a seat. Nathalie, I must say, you have grown up to be a very beautiful young woman.'

Nathalie curtseyed playfully. She sat, accepting a glass of sherry from the maid's silver tray. Lynch's eyes were on her. She was conscious of the moisture in her own.

Madame Chalabi sipped at her sherry. 'Tell me, my dear, how is your mother?'

Nathalie winced and wished desperately they were alone. Shooting an apologetic glance at Lynch, she spoke in French, her eyes on the ornate carpet. 'I thought Father had kept in touch, I am sorry.'

She looked up to see the old lady's hand fly to her mouth, her eyes widening with a survivor's prescience.

'*Maman* died six years ago. Of breast cancer. I still miss her every day.'

'My dear, I am so sorry. I was deeply fond of Helene. She was a light in our darkness. Excuse me, I think I shall sit. I am too frail these days to bear loss as well as perhaps I might have done in times past.'

Maalouf moved to help her, supporting her from his own sitting position. She handed him her sherry glass to bend elegantly into the settee beside him. Maalouf turned to Nathalie, his deep voice trembling. 'I knew your mother well. I am sorry to hear she is no longer lighting the world.'

She waited for him to say more, but he looked down, his face sad and far away, lost in reflection. She leaned forwards to place her hand comfortingly on Madame Chalabi's. 'It was quick, in the end.'

Nathalie glanced over at Lynch who was sitting forward, his blue eyes fixed on Maalouf. There was something feral in there. The pent-up violence was a constant tension in the man.

Madame Chalabi sat back and sipped. 'Is your father

well, at least, dear?'

'Yes, thank you. He sends his regards, of course. He is very busy these days. He travels a lot, mostly within Europe. There are so many seminars and conferences, meetings and so on.'

'So tell me, Monsieur Maalouf,' Lynch sat back in his chair and drained his glass, 'how is life in Lebanese intelligence?'

Nathalie watched Ghassan Maalouf's hooded eyes move slowly to meet Lynch's, his face totally devoid of expression. 'Well, thank you, Lynch. Well.'

'Shall we go through to dinner?' chirped Madame Chalabi. They rose and followed the butler through to the dining room.

Lynch sipped truffled consommé, lifting the Christofle spoon carefully from the Versace bowl. The silver and crystal glittered in the candlelight. Vivienne Chalabi was talking, her food untouched but her sherry glass replenished regularly by the attentive waiter.

Lynch's eyes were on Maalouf. The old man kept stealing glances at Nathalie. It was unusual to see him so unguarded. The few times Lynch had seen the feared intelligence head in public, he had been stiff and formal, giving away nothing. Lynch knew Maalouf better by reputation than he did in person. A career forged in the blood and sawdust of the *mukhabbarat*, the Lebanese secret police, Maalouf's talents were recognised and he was sent to join the General Directorate for General Security. There was a rumour at the time that Maalouf had gone too far and killed someone linked to a powerful family. His career had faltered then risen again. Now he was the head of the directorate and a powerful man in his own right. Lynch wondered what had brought him here tonight.

She had.

It hit him hard. Maalouf had come on her account. Nathalie hadn't expected him to be there and was blithely unaware of his interest in her. Maalouf was here for Nathalie.

The waiter removed Lynch's soup dish with an almost imperceptible flick of the wrist, breaking his reverie.

Lynch turned to Madame Chalabi. 'Does the name *Deir Na'ee* mean anything to you? Perhaps in connection with Michel Freij?'

Maalouf's expression was politely disinterested but Lynch glimpsed a momentary quickening. He turned back to Madame as she considered the question, her head held a little to one side. 'No, no it doesn't. *Deir* is a homeplace. *Na'ee* means lonely.' She smiled and sipped her sherry. 'Perhaps in the mountains, to the north? It sounds remote. The Freij family comes from the mountains, you know. They have lived around the village of Beit Hamza for hundreds of years. It is a beautiful village in the mountains.'

In an instant, Madame Chalabi was in another world, bright-eyed and talking to the chandelier with a beatific smile. Lynch marvelled at her histrionic talent.

'You ask about the Freij family, Monsieur Lynch? They are a very great family, a powerful lineage. Michel's grandfather helped to found the Phalange, you know. They were so very taken with European fascism. Raymond learned from his father and I am afraid Michel has learned from Raymond rather than his mother, a sweet girl. There is little compromise to be had from the people of the mountains. I rather think it is the terrain that creates absolutism. It forgives so little, the mountain.'

The entrée arrived. Beef, carved at the side table and

served with creamy potato and a pouring of dark red wine into the cut glasses.

Maalouf was solicitous, his eyes following Chalabi's increasingly grandiose gestures like a bodyguard. It dawned on Lynch she was quite drunk as he speared a rosy slice of beef. 'This is the best beef I have eaten in many years.'

Madame Chalabi inclined her head graciously. 'I am glad. The compliment is particularly appreciated from an Englishman.'

Lynch smiled, his Irish Catholic heart black. 'It is heartfelt, Madame.'

Nathalie leaned forward, her cheek dimpling as she smiled. 'All too many men are governed by their stomachs. But what governs Michel Freij, Madame?'

Vivienne Chalabi placed her wine glass carefully upon the linen. 'The most dangerous people are those who can convince themselves that a convenient thing is true. Why? Because they can use that skill to rationalise their selfishness. It is the key to good acting, I think. Michel is being presented for election as a moderate candidate, as a man who is against sectarianism. Selim helps him in this, his Shia business partner held up as a reason we should trust this new coalition, this new Lebanon. Their success, we are being told, could belong to us all. It is a *lie*.'

The old lady glared at Lynch unsteadily, raising her glass, the rim smeared with pale lipstick. Her eyes were moist. Lynch wanted to gather her frailty up in his arms for her bravery, compassion and wit, while also rejecting her fakery, the pomp and formality of Cedars, its staff and its carefully arranged place settings. It was living in a photo shoot, he thought as he regarded her. She was shaking, her fist clenched on the table cloth. Maalouf spoke for her, his hoarse voice breaking across the table.

'Yes, this is a lie. Michel is a fundamentalist, a racist. Like his father, like his grandfather. Michel is a dangerous absolutist and always has been.'

Lynch raised his glass. 'A toast. To be saved from absolutists.'

Madame Chalabi raised her glass to him and so, after a short pause, did Maalouf.

As they left Cedars, Maalouf took Lynch to one side. 'Forgive Vivienne, Lynch. She is old and has seen, has lost too much.' He waited for Lynch's nod. 'You have a significant operation building against Michel Freij, Mister Lynch. For myself, I am no supporter of this young man. But I would caution you to take great care. He is not to be trifled with.'

'I rather think I've already found that out. He's bad, like his father.'

'Good luck. Anything to do with that man is bad business and I would frankly not wish to see Nathalie involved in it, but this vocation of espionage obviously runs in the family. She's an extraordinary girl, the daughter of a very extraordinary woman. Take care of her, Lynch. If I thought for a second her father would consent to speak to me, I would offer you my assistance. I feel we have much to contribute to your investigation. You may like to mention the offer to him.'

If Maalouf had meant his words to be infuriatingly oblique, Lynch reflected he could have hardly done a better job.

The old man pushed him away genially, stemming his questions with a handshake as they joined Nathalie, who was propping up the quite drunk Madame Chalabi. Nathalie handed the old lady into Maalouf's care.

Lynch escaped with her across the courtyard and, at the street door, they turned and waved their farewells like an old married couple.

Chapter Fourteen

The bright morning sunshine bathed the square, people chatting as they hurried by. Nathalie and Lynch sat together, basking. She ate her croissant delicately, picking off slivers of toasted almond and placing them on her tongue. Lynch read the newspaper. He groped absently for his coffee across the café table.

'So you start every day like this?'

'Pretty much. I happen to consider this one of the many perks of living in Beirut.'

Nathalie tore the crisp pastry, releasing the warm almond fragrance. She bit, licking brown flakes from her lips. Lynch watched her above the paper, took in her dark, bobbed hair and slender fingers. Her eyebrows were strong, her dark-edged green eyes alive and inquisitive.

She wiped the corner of her mouth. 'I have been talking to some of our contacts here. Michel Freij is to address a rally later this week. His agenda is centrist, his One Lebanon party that will apparently bring the peoples of Lebanon together, as Madame Chalabi said. They are running on a ticket of constitutional reform and non-sectarian values. The rally will be very large and take place in the *Place des Martyrs*. It is expected over two hundred thousand will attend.'

Lynch harrumphed. '*Your* contacts?'

She smiled sweetly at him. 'Yes, our contacts. You surely recognise the French government has an extraordinary relationship with Lebanon. We founded the country, after all. My father lived and worked here throughout the civil war. My mother was Lebanese. I probably know more people in Beirut than you do,

Monsieur Lynch. For instance, our dinner last night was with my contact, was it not?'

Lynch snapped the newspaper shut. 'And here was me thinking we were Europeans.'

'And so we are. But some of us are, after all, a little more European than others. Shall we ask for the cheque?'

Lynch caught the eye of the man at the till, his voice genial. '*Antoine? L'addition, s'il te plait.*' He leaned towards Nathalie. 'You know, my dear, this isn't *your* city. It isn't even what you'd call *my* city after over thirty years living here. It never has been anything but *their* city. The sooner you grow up and realise it, the better off we'd all be. It does not matter one shit how many contacts your daddy scooped up during the civil war. This is Beirut and this is now. They don't need colonising or patronising anymore.'

Lynch pushed his chair back and walked out, giving the bobbing, grinning Antoine a familiar punch on the shoulder as he wove through the little forest of tables. Nathalie followed Lynch down the sunny street as he flagged down a passing *servees*, a battered yellow Mercedes. She slammed the door as the driver pulled away, the car's engine coughing. 'Where are we going?'

Lynch sat back and gazed out of the window as the driver urged the old car into the jostling stream of morning traffic with a hand flapping to cajole his passage.

She was silk and she was jasmine, ivory and frankincense, her skin a pale golden slide for the smooth satin riding up her legs as she mounted the stairs. Her hips moving under the wrap were a provocation, her long hair cascaded down her mobile back.

Reaching the top ahead of them, she strutted across the dance floor and sat on a high stool at the bar. Lynch ducked behind the counter and started to fix coffee at the gleaming red La Marzocco espresso machine. This was obviously some sort of well-worn ritual – Nathalie noted Lynch's deft movements. The white filter of Marcelle Aboud's cigarette was reddened by her lipstick, her dark, kohl-lined eyes coolly gauging Nathalie as the younger woman waited, her hand resting on the back of a bar stool.

'Come, sit,' Marcelle purred, gesturing at the stool. Her very movements were sensual, her voice husky, rolling and dirty. Nathalie caught the flash of a full breast trying to escape the cascades of smooth bronze material as Marcelle turned her magnificent face to Lynch.

'So you're buying or selling, Lynch?'

He brought the espresso cup over to her. 'Her? You can have her for free.'

Nathalie twisted off her stool. 'Sorry, not putting up with this.'

'Sit down,' Marcelle's languorous voice wasn't raised, but her tone stopped Nathalie in her tracks. 'Make her a coffee, Lynch, Play nicely.'

Lynch busied himself with the machine as Marcelle examined Nathalie, who met the dark brown eyes after they finished travelling lazily up her body like a slow touch. The clink of the espresso cup on the bar broke the moment.

Marcelle turned to Lynch. 'So what do you want, you and your *assistant*?'

Lynch waited behind the bar with his hands laid on the marble top. Nathalie was surprised at how he eased into the role of barman and fancied perhaps he had worked here many, many years ago as a young man.

Lynch was diffident. 'Michel Freij. He's a customer, no?'

Marcelle's eyes narrowed. She lifted the espresso cup

to her full lips, watching Lynch warily. Nathalie, fascinated, was a *voyeuse* as Marcelle made her decision, a little sag of her fine, proud shoulders. 'Michel? Sure. For years. Since Raymond brought him to be broken in.'

'One of yours?'

Marcelle raised her head. In the name of God, thought Nathalie, she's like a horse. Proud, Arab and untamed.

'My fucking business.'

'How regular?'

'Every month or so. Usually on a Saturday night.'

'What's he like?'

Marcelle pulled a cigarette from her packet. 'What do you mean?'

'What does he like to do?'

'Just straight. Nothing funny. He can get little rough on the younger girls. We've had to pay a few extra. One girl needed some little piece dental work.'

Lynch grinned wolfishly. 'You mean he knocked her teeth out.'

Nathalie watched the tension in the older woman, the way she treated Lynch like a hunter, was scared of him and yet seemed somehow to own him.

Marcelle pursed her lips. 'Maybe.'

'He come alone or with company?'

'Sometimes with company. His friends. Hanging on.'

'Hangers on?'

'*Adi*, like this. So what you want, Lynch?'

Lynch reached into his jacket pocket, passing an envelope across the counter. 'I want him in our little room. I want her to sweet talk him and ask him about a place called Deir Na'ee. I want to know where it is.'

Marcelle slid off the stool, the sinuous rotation of her hips pulling the soft material up her leg as she leaned over to scoop up the envelope. Nathalie caught a glimpse of the dark mound at the top. The woman's rich scent mingled with strong coffee. She started at Marcelle's touch on her cheek, a warm fingertip, purring. 'Bring her next time, Lynch, will you? I like her.'

Nathalie couldn't help the blush washing across her cheeks.

Chapter Fifteen

Lynch paused at the edge of the square. The soldiers hunched for warmth by their little green huts in the early Beirut spring morning air, the growing tide of pedestrians jinking past the red and white painted barriers and concrete blocks marking the secure areas of Beirut's Solidere district. The Beirutis called it Sodeco. The cobbled streets echoed to an increasing number of feet, shuffling, striding and skipping as the crowds grew. The tide flowed into the open spaces of Martyrs' Square, traffic blocked by the streams of people.

Lynch and Nathalie joined the growing throng, their breath puffing in little clouds. The sound of Koullouna lil-watan, the Lebanese anthem, started to play tinnily across the square, the embarrassed bastard child of the Marseillaise and an Edith Piaf lament.

The scent of charcoal and hot sweetcorn from the vendors who had moved their carts from their pitches on the corniche mingled with tobacco smoke on the cold breeze, a faint hint of the sea behind them. The usual miasma of car exhaust was absent, the barriers diverting the traffic from its habitual course, creating little jams, confusions and jostling altercations on the roads around the big square.

Banners hung all over the huge open area, the clusters of logos intensifying towards the large stage set up in the centre. Speaker stacks were mounted on each side of the stage, its red, white and green decorations proclaiming

'One Lebanon'. Traffic barriers festooned with banners declaimed 'One Lebanon, One People'. Polo-shirted staff handed out decorated plastic flags at each entry point.

Lynch scowled at a huge panel carrying Michel Freij's portrait as they passed it.

'Unhappy, Lynch?'

'Uncomfortable. There's a difference.'

Nathalie dug her hands deeper into her jacket pockets. 'Sure.'

The echo of the parping, staccato music from the brass band on the stage splashed back from the frontages of the buildings lining the open area, Ottoman stone and ironwork mixed with smoked glass and restored finery, each a unique testament to its era. Lynch brooded, surveying the chattering crowd of excited youngsters, their breath misty in the morning air, their faces reddened by the cold. Behind them all, Mount Sannine glowed against the Mediterranean sky.

Nathalie hooked Lynch's arm as the crowd grew denser and started to gravitate toward its focus, the big stage in the centre of the square. Militiamen in camouflage fatigues dotted with glittering insignia, all carried the stylised green One Lebanon badge on their arms and breasts, an upraised sword. The euphoric throng washed against the stage. The smiling militiamen formed a benign wall, stopping people from crushing against the steel supporting formwork, the banners tied to it flapping lazily. Her hand was cold and, unthinkingly, he cupped his warmer palm over it. He scanned the solid wall of young, shaven-headed men standing arm in arm, smiling and chatting with the crowd.

The music stopped, halfway up its rousing crescendo. The shuffling and murmuring died with it. Lynch surveyed the expectant faces, registering the hope and curiosity reflected there. He focused on a girl, pretty and lush-haired, her brown eyes flickering from the stage to meet his as she sensed his interest. The crowd shifted and compressed. Thousands of voices built into a gathering roar, a wave of hands punching the air. He lost the girl as the crowd surged forward.

'Michel! Michel! Michel!'

It settled into a rhythmic pattern, two syllables: *Mee shell*, each repetition punctuated by a handclap. Lynch hated crowds like this. He darted a glance at the ecstatic faces and felt the first quivering of fear, the resonance of childhood turning the massed chants into the tinny cacophony of dustbin lids, the raised faces losing their dusky, Mediterranean tone and gaining the pasty, desperate pallor of Belfast.

He was back on the Falls Road and his body prickled, sweat running down inside his shirt. Jerked into to the present, he caught the concern on Nathalie's face.

'You okay, Lynch?'

'Never better,' he lied. He was back there in a flash, surrounded by the shouting throng and throwing stones, feeling the weight in his hand, as a bottle flew over his head to hit the khaki Land Rover, petrol splashing across the white face of the Brit who'd been stupid enough to jump out of the big car. The liquid ignited with a great whoomp. The deep roar and crackle of the flames was pierced by the soldier's high pitched screams as he ran, flailing at himself, in ever-diminishing circles.

The stone fell from Gerry Lynch's limp fingers as the thing that had been a soldier dropped to its knees in front of him, its blackened face bursting with the heat. It finally fell forward. Transfixed by the sight, Gerry was pulled away by his friends.

Nathalie was shouting at him over the crowd noise. He

let go of her hand and she took it back, gripping it under her armpit.

'*Merde*, Lynch, you nearly crushed me to death. What's wrong with you?'

Scattered clapping broke out, welling into an ovation as Michel Freij took to the microphone, smiling and waving acknowledgement at the crowd, his eyes taking them all in and locking, for a sickening instant, with Lynch's.

Freij's hands descended, palm down, calming the crowd. 'Thank you, thank you all.' He smiled, pausing to grip the sides of the lectern. 'It is my intention to speak to you today in Arabic, but I wanted to say a few words in English first. Please, I beg your indulgence.'

Freij scanned the crowd. His voice rang out across the square. 'We are here today because we share a vision. A vision of one Lebanon. A strong Lebanon. A country we can all be proud of. A united country, a country whose people can finally, after all these years of conflict, be free of fear and suffering. A country rid of the evil of sectarianism, proud of its nationhood and unity, of its one identity and its one people. If you are Orthodox, Copt, Maronite, Shia, Sunni, Druze, you are all one people. South and North, Bekaa and Chouf, you are all one people. From the camps or the cities, the mountains or the farms, you are all one people. If you were born in this country, you are Lebanon's child and Lebanon shall love you, be proud of you and nurture you. We are all, all of us, one people. One Lebanon.'

Freij waited as a tide of applause broke across the square, acknowledging it with a magisterial wave. The sound died, a few whistles then silence. In his dark blue suit, Freij held the lectern, his head bowed. Lynch could almost feel the indrawn breaths of the crowd, the sense of anticipation. Freij raised his head, throwing his hand towards Mount Sannine's white peak.

'Lebanon's tragedy is that we have been weak. We have too long been subject to the forces around us, we have too long been others' battleground. We have been forced to depend on others for protection as foreign armies clash on our soil. No longer. Lebanon will rebuild herself as a nation, a nation of unity and prosperity, of fairness and equality because we will be capable of repelling all outside interests, of defending our shores against all force. Our new Lebanon will be a nation of strength, capable of deterring others from interfering in our rights and sovereignty. Never again will war be waged on us in the name of another nation's security or interests. Lebanon shall have peace because she demands peace. And she shall be strong enough to *make* demands.'

The crowd erupted, roaring approbation. The air filled with flags, scarves and waving hands. The sound of clapping echoed off the buildings. Lynch managed to turn in the press, his arm around Nathalie keeping them together as they shoved their way through the tightly packed crowd, returning the smiles and grins of the people they passed. Freij was speaking again, in Arabic, his voice rising and falling, his tone urgent and declamatory. The message was the same.

Another wave of cheers rippled through the square as Freij embarked on a series of rhetorical questions, his voice low, raising in enquiry and each time answering, after a perfectly timed pause, in the negative: '*La.*' The crowd rustled in reaction to his voice, breaking into cacophonous applause and cheering.

Lynch and Nathalie finally pushed through to the top edge of the square, standing by the imposing bulk of the Al Amine Mosque to gaze down over the huge sea of people to the blue Mediterranean beyond.

Nathalie pointed to their right. 'Lynch, look.'

A noisy crowd was pushing its way down Gouraud Street and starting to burst into the square, blowing air horns and chanting. They carried black banners daubed with flowing white Arabic script. Towards the back of the insurgent crowd, Lynch could make out placards with a turbaned, white-bearded mullah on them. Others carried green flags. They were joined by a second flow striding down Damascus Street, the leaders' faces wrapped in black scarves.

Scanning the scene, Lynch did a little double take. A face he recalled drew his eyes back to the shadow of a shopfront by the entrance to Gouraud. Their eyes met, the other man's gaze dropped. A trench coat and green tartan scarf. The man turned away and walked uphill through the sparser crowd along the square's edge. Frank Coleman, by the grace of God, thought Lynch as he lost the big man's figure. Lynch lost no love on the CIA's station chief in Beirut, an old hand who'd been stooging around the Middle East since the civil war. Lynch shrugged off his curiosity. Coleman had a nose for trouble and there was certainly trouble breaking out today. He searched the streets behind them, assuring himself of a safe exit and started to pull Nathalie away. The crowd rippled as the new wave of marchers pushed into it like a wave breaking against a sandcastle. The wail of sirens echoed from the streets uphill of them.

Two black Lincolns pushed across the crowded square, blocking Gouraud Two more backed across nearby Damascus Street, stemming the flow of new entrants into the square. The packed knots of demonstrators jostling for position tried to retreat, confronted by a flow of One Lebanon militia wearing combat fatigues and brandishing laths. Their arms started to rise and fall, the leaders of the incursion cut off by the Lincolns and falling to the hammering sticks. Between the two black cars on Gouraud, Lynch glimpsed many more uniformed men beating the demonstrators up towards Gemayzeh and away from the crowded square, many running from the relentless beating of the militia, their banners dropping.

The screams of the beaten demonstrators were drowned by Freij's echoing voice as he started the run to the finish, calling out to the crowd as they cheered, raising his voice above their cheers to tease more noisy support from them. They gave it, crying out and punching the air, their voices combined in chanting his name. He finished with a flourish and the square rang to the sound of thousands of voices calling out, the roar drowning the sound Lynch had been waiting for: automatic gunfire.

Lynch pulled Nathalie away from the square. 'Come on, time to get out of here. They're shooting.'

'Who are they? They're not Lebanese Army, for sure.'

Lynch strode ahead, passing through the people walking towards the square, latecomers curious as to the fuss. 'Freij's militia. Those demonstrators looked Hezbollah but there were Sunni factions in there, too. Funny bedfellows. Jesus, but those militia guys were brutal altogether.'

A surge in the crowd parted them. Lynch caught a glimpse of features he recognised, a man in militia uniform. He scanned the blur of faces for Nathalie, struggling to place the man even as he craned to get a glimpse of her black hair and pale skin. He spotted her across the sea of people being ushered by a group of uniformed men. She turned her head anxiously but her arm was gripped and her head jerked back. She was engulfed by the crowd. Lynch was jostled hard. He elbowed his way after Nathalie. A hand gripped his right arm. He turned. That face again. He placed it, the thugs who had ransacked Stokes' apartment, the car that had followed him from the airport. Forage Cap's friend. The one he hadn't shot. Looking at the reddened face of the man shouting, he reflected what a pleasure it would have been.

The man's lips were spittle-flecked. 'You must come with us.'

He felt another hand clamp on his left arm. He let both arms stay loose. A hand scrabbled in his jacket for his holster. Lynch moved fast, head-butting the man to his right, feeling cartilage breaking as his head bore down onto the top of the man's nose. The grip on his arm loosened and Lynch drove his fist into the man to his left. Lynch wheeled to send him flying over his outstretched leg, following through with a powerful lip-splitting blow. Lynch span to forge ahead into the crowd, waving his drawn gun. He cried out Nathalie's name. He caught glimpses of her ahead, but was constantly frustrated by the press of people. The clashes on the side streets triggered unpredictable eddies of people fleeing the conflict at the exits to the square. Lynch fancied he could smell the growing fear, tension on people's faces, wide eyes and flared nostrils as the sound of screams mingled with the crack of gunfire. The crowd was thickest around the group of black Lincolns. For a second it parted and Lynch glimpsed Nathalie struggling in the grip of two militiamen. He redoubled his effort to push through the crowd, earning himself several blows on his shoulders and back from aggrieved people he shoved out of his way.

Lynch turned to see the man whose nose he'd broken following him through the crowd, shoving people aside with his big, bloody hands and leaving a swath of outraged expressions and stained clothing in his wake. Lynch held the gun out, a double-handed grip. The man saw the gesture and stopped, fear replacing anger on a face half-covered by the hand holding his nose. Lynch gestured him back with the gun, the crowd parting miraculously as they saw the weapon, to leave an empty corridor between Lynch and the blood-spattered militiaman. For the second time in days, the man held his hands out in supplication. Lynch lowered the gun to point at the man's leg, the movement earning a look of terror. Lynch turned and pushed toward the Lincolns.

One of them moved, squeezing its way through the crowd and sounding its horn. Lynch lashed out at the people in his way as he struggled through the press of bodies trying to avoid the big car. Moving fast along its black slab sides, he shot out the front tyre and pushed to the back of the car to take out the rear and driver's side tyres. Lynch wrenched open the driver's door and shoved the Walther into the man's shocked face. 'Stop the car. Now.'

The blown-apart tyres flapped on the tarmac. The driver braked hard, slamming Lynch against the open door. He recovered too slowly, the driver's foot lashed out and caught him hard in the stomach. Lynch doubled up, instinctively he reached out to catch the foot. He pulled hard and twisted to yank the man from his seat. Lynch hit him a crushing blow on the cheek with the butt of his pistol, dropping the the man. He jumped into the driver's seat and shoved his gun into the face of the nervous young militiaman in the back of the car next to Nathalie. Lynch barked, 'Get the fuck out now or I'll shoot your fucking face off.'

After a second's hesitation, the militiaman opened the door. He turned to speak and Lynch fired, the report deafening in the car's confined space. Nathalie screamed. The militiaman dropped out, his hands over his head, a neat hole drilled in the roof.

Lynch slammed the SUV into gear and leant on the horn, the crowd angry and fearful as he drove into them, the broken tyres slapping, the heavy car harder to control. The flop of tyre was replaced by the screech of metal as the big car forged through the fleeing press on its rims. The crowd thinned beyond the edge of the square and Lynch put his foot down, struggling with the steering wheel. Reaching Debbas Square, Lynch gave up and pulled the Lincoln up, its battered rims smoking. He helped Nathalie get down and they jogged uphill, Lynch checking behind them for signs of pursuit.

Out of breath and feeling battered, he holstered his gun.

Chapter Sixteen

Lynch and Nathalie returned to the apartment after the rally and cleaned up, both coming down from the tension high, laughing too much and still a little breathless. Nathalie left with a French Embassy driver to join her digital surveillance team. Lynch went down to Manara to meet an informant who knew a lot less about Michel Freij and Falcon Dynamics than he had made out when they talked on the phone. After returning, Lynch settled down to spend the afternoon going through Paul Stokes' laptop. He worked systematically, jotting down directory names as he pored through them looking for anything that Stokes might have kept there.

Flicking through Stokes' memoir again, unable to stay away like a man whose eyes are drawn to a car crash, Lynch hadn't noticed the light failing and now it was evening. He closed the document, stretched and hobbled over to switch the light on, hours of crouching over a keyboard taking their toll.

Nathalie pushed the apartment door open with her back, heaving the four bulging jute bags of shopping to kick the door shut behind her. She staggered down the corridor to the kitchen. Lynch reached her as she hoisted her loot onto the kitchen worktop.

He laughed. 'What on earth are you up to?'

She blew on her reddened fingers. 'I'm cooking dinner tonight. I decided. I had one of the security guys go shopping for me.' She smiled impishly. 'Isn't that what security guys are for?'

Lynch was wide-eyed. 'Cooking? At a time like this?'

Nathalie smiled defensively. 'Yes, cooking. I am French

and it is time you ate decent food. To thank you for saving my life.'

Why not, indeed. Lynch tried to contain the little surge of anger her presumption had caused in him. He desperately missed Leila, his dark, clever dissident girl. Nathalie Durand was entertaining, intelligent company, graceful and, yes, beautiful. But Leila was wild, angry and bursting with the challenge and certainty of rebellious youth. And she was *his*, given to him and part of his inner life, a secret within a life already lived in secret. Nathalie was only a colleague operating within cover.

Leila hadn't returned a single call since she had walked out. Lynch checked with the concierge and yes, she had moved in to the flat in Hamra. Yes, she had indeed taken male company, the old crone told Lynch, laughing dirtily and pocketing the fifty thousand lire tip.

Lynch banished the thought and threw his hands up. 'Sure, why not?'

Nathalie smiled bravely. 'Why not? You are too enthusiastic, Lynch.'

'Sorry, I didn't mean to bring you down. It's just that I had a life here before—'

'Before what? Before I came? Before *she* walked out?'

Lynch steadied himself against the wooden worktop. 'How did you—'

'She left herself behind, Gerry. She's all over this place. Whatever has happened between you, I cannot help. But I am here to do a job. If I need to stay in a hotel, tell me and I will find some way. If not, I will try to have a life as well I can as I do this job. But staying here was supposed to be cover, no? You remember this thing, this *cover*?'

Lynch fought the urge to correct her. *It's Gerald.* He held his hands out, palms down against her passion, 'Okay, okay. Look, I'm sorry. We—'

The doorbell sounded, its staccato repetitions stilling him. He took in Nathalie's silent response to his glance and padded up the corridor to the echoes of its clamour.

He spoke through the door. 'Hello?'

Marcelle's urgent voice was throaty. 'Lynch, open the fucking door.'

Lynch tore off the security chain, the door handle yanked from his hand. He fell back as the door smashed against the wall. Marcelle stumbled through, half-carrying the blood-smeared deadweight of a girl in her arms. He lunged forward to take the burden, carried the girl into the living room and laid her on the couch. She was badly bruised, her lip split and a cut above her right eye. Her cheek was swollen and scraped. Her tumbling blonde hair was matted and stiff with so much blood she smelled of iron. Feeling her head, Lynch winced as he encountered the massive swelling at the side, carefully parting the sticky hairs to find the moist lips of the ragged gash where her skin had split like a tomato. One of her arms hung limply and her breathing was ragged. Lynch pulled her smeared blouse open to show the massive mauve contusions on the pale skin stretched over at least one broken rib. Her breast was milky and full with a dark, tight nipple, obscenely beautiful amongst the bloodied cloth and bruised skin.

'What the fuck?'

Marcelle stooped, breathless, flinging a small memory key at Lynch. 'Here. This is what you wanted. This is all your fault, Lynch. Get her a doctor.'

'Jesus, Marcie, Couldn't you find one?'

Marcelle braced herself against the door and snarled at him. 'Get her a fucking doctor, Lynch. You know how. One who don't talk about whores who billionaires beat to death. Do it.'

She collapsed against the frame, her cheek pressed to the painted wood. Nathalie caught her as she slid, supporting her to guide her into a round wicker seat. Marcelle's harsh breathing slowed as Nathalie sat beside her, stroking her hair.

Lynch talked on the mobile. 'This is Nikola. I need the *doktor* now, *bil bait.*' He listened, nodding. *'Na'am. Daroori. Ta'al, bsiraa. yalla.'*

Lynch used a damp flannel to clean the girl up as best he could. They waited silently together for the doorbell to ring, the long silences broken by the girl's ragged coughs and Marcelle's low-voiced reassurances and endearments. It seemed an age, but could only have been fifteen minutes when the bell rang. Lynch opened the door to a small, white-haired man in his late sixties wearing a tweed suit and thin, gold-framed glasses.

'The patient's through here.'

Lynch grasped the memory key Marcelle had thrown at him in his pocket, the little chip containing the video of whatever had happened to this girl in the room at Marcelle's cathouse Lynch used to 'burn' the occasional politician or business leader. The little camera in the wall was virtually obsolete, but then Channing wasn't interested in Beirut these days; he was frying bigger fish in the Gulf and playing European politics. Lynch's thumb slipped on the memory key and he realised he was sweating.

They moved the girl to the spare bedroom where the doctor worked for over an hour. Lynch admired the fussy little man's work. He finished treating the girl and rose, puffing himself up to his full height. His combed-over wisps of white hair barely reached Lynch's chest.

'This is very serious. You understand it is a matter for the police.'

Lynch gazed down at him. 'Yes, it likely is, but that is not our arrangement.'

The doctor pulled a rumpled handkerchief from his breast pocket and wiped his glasses. 'The girl has been seriously assaulted. This was not an accident or any,' he graced Lynch with a bitter little smile, 'operational expediency.'

Lynch tried to curb his impatience. 'No. No, it wasn't. But your help was necessary.'

The doctor's lined face cleared. 'Ah, yes. My help is necessary. Then I can sleep well tonight knowing I was, as you say, *necessary*.'

Lynch took the old man's arm as they went up the corridor, squeezing his withered bicep through the thick tweed jacket. 'We all do everything we can, *Doktor*. Everything we can. Even *in necessitas*.'

The old man turned at the doorway, his lined face smoothed in repose. 'Do they all suffer for a *reason*, then, these poor faceless people you bring me to see, Mister Nikola?'

Lynch smiled sympathetically down at the frail man facing him. 'You are being emotional, *Doktor*. I ask for your help rarely and only when there is no reasonable alternative.'

'And you sit in judgement of what is reasonable, I see. The girl belongs in hospital. She is very seriously injured. She is lucky to be alive. She will need further attention.'

'Thank you, *Doktor*. We will transfer your fee as usual.' Lynch pulled the door open and waited for the old man to move but he shook his head.

'No, no. Not this time, thank you, Mr Nikola of the Russian Embassy. No fee.' He put on his hat, a shabby tweed trilby with a tatty Alpine feather in its green band. 'Please do not call me again. I will not do this more.'

He strode out of the door. Resolution straightened the old man's back. Lynch closed the door. Marcelle sat in the living room staring into a tumbler of whisky, her dark hair tumbling down her shoulder as if she had arranged it. Which she probably had, Lynch thought. He poured himself a glass and went to the balcony. He clipped, then lit, a Cohiba and drew the smoke down as he gazed across the streetlights and surrounding buildings to the distant lights of the boats at sea. He really needed to stop smoking these things. The spring air was cool.

The balcony door slid open and the musk of Marcelle's perfume carried on a waft of warmth from the apartment. She put her hand on his hip, her voice low. 'Thank you. I was scared for her.'

'She'll be okay. What the hell happened?'

'You'll see on the video. He came by after lunchtime. He called ahead. He does that sometimes, in the mid-afternoon. There was a rally this morning, you know? He was on a real high, you could tell. He had been drinking. After they made love, Mirielle asked him about this place like you wanted. Michel went crazy, Lynch. Really crazy. Okay, he likes a little roughhouse, but this was insane. My boys are ex-army, yes? They are tough. There are three of them before they stop him. His security they arrive then, with guns. It was bad. Like those days, you know? The war. Like that again. They nearly tore the place apart. I was scared of the police so I had Hassan bring us here.'

He curled his arm around her shoulder. 'I didn't realise this would happen, Marcie. I'm sorry.' He felt her tears on his hand as he rubbed her cheek. A car horn sounded twice on the street below, a pickup. She broke free to drink from her glass and nestled her head against his shoulder again.

Marcelle's voice was concerned. 'Will she really be

okay?'

'I think so. The doctor wasn't happy. She'll need to rest, might need to see someone else later. Is there somewhere you can take her?'

Marcelle nodded against Lynch's hand. 'Yes, but not tonight. Please not tonight.'

'No, no. Not tonight.'

Marcelle's wrap parted and Lynch flicked his cigar butt over the railing to spin down into the darkness. His hand slid inside to cup the warm weight of her breast. The balcony door slide open. He turned with Marcelle to see Nathalie framed in the soft light from the living room, her mouth open in shock.

'How many women do you need, Lynch?'

Marcelle moved first, pulling her wrap closed. 'Nathalie, please.'

Lynch let Marcelle follow Nathalie through the door. He admired Marcelle's red-painted toenails and lithe, gypsy feet. He stood on the balcony and took a reflective drink from his glass, letting the sound of raised voices from inside the apartment mingle with the night-time sounds of the *Ain Mreisse* area, the traffic noises mixed with the clink of glasses from the balcony of an apartment below. Laughter from a party across the street carried on the cool breeze. He went inside in time to hear the slam of Nathalie's bedroom door. Marcelle stood perplexed in the living room.

'Well?'

'She wouldn't talk to me. She's a crazy one.'

The girl Mirielle was sleeping, her breathing relaxed. Lynch turned off the light and closed the bedroom door softly. Marcelle followed him down to the kitchen. He pulled an ice tray from the freezer, cracked a series of lumps into his glass, and filled it from the stand of bottles in the living room. She held hers out and he obliged. He took her hand and they held onto each other as they strolled into the master bedroom.

Lynch woke. The moonlight shone through the window across the bed; he'd forgotten to draw the curtain. He lay, his mind racing with inchoate thoughts, watching the rise and fall of Marcelle's breathing as the moonlight cast shadows down her elegant back. She was half covered by the duvet, her leg bent so the smoothness of her perfect skin glowed blue, a slope that led down into the mysterious warmth in the shadows.

He crept out of bed and into the living room. He opened his laptop and inserted the memory key from his jeans pocket.

The camera in Marcelle's 'special room' had been there for three years, replacing the microphone that had served for the ten years prior. London had grudgingly sent a technician to replace the mike, but the camera was already an obsolete model, only recording an hour of low resolution footage onto a memory key. Wireless connection was deemed insecure and Lynch's constant requests for an upgrade had eventually earned a lecture from Channing on budget cuts. Little wonder, he thought. Nobody gave a shit for anything he caught in Marcelle's little honey trap anyway, although Lynch took care not to tell her. A little over a year ago, Marcelle had delivered some juicy footage of a high-ranking member of the armed forces and a couple of underage girls. Lynch's proposal to burn the man had been turned down by Channing, who had pointed out that 98 percent of Lebanon's pitiful armoury was supplied and maintained by the Yanks and anything the Lebanese armed forces had to say in bed or out was likely to have been dictated by the Americans. So all you had to do, Channing was acid, was Google what you wanted to know.

The video file opened. Michel Freij watched the girl strip. Freij tapped the arm of his chair, grinding his cigarette out in the glass ashtray. When she was ready, he was peremptory, gesturing at her to kneel on the bed. He undid his belt and advanced on her. Facing the camera, she closed her eyes. Her face was pretty, milky skin and heavy lashes. Freij's voice was indistinct and Lynch cursed the old equipment. He watched, mesmerised as Freij thrust, the girl's eyes snapping open and a cry forced from her lips.

Later, she cradled Michel Freij's head and stroked his hair. The sound was still indistinct, but her mouth formed the words, 'Deir Na'ee'. Freij scrambled to his feet, shouting as the girl cowered. He lashed at her with his fists then his heavy-buckled belt, looping it around his knuckles and punching down at her pitiful, hunched body. He screamed at her, a strange mixture of French and Arabic, 'Who told you about that? Who told you to ask me about it, whore?'

He rained down blows on her, pulling her head back by her hair to repeat his questions before lashing out at her again. Blurred figures rushed the room, the amount of movement overwhelming the ageing camera, the recording breaking up. The video file ended in static. Lynch sat at the blank laptop screen, his face illuminated by its dull light, until Marcelle softly called his name. She stood in the doorway, wearing his shirt.

'Come back to bed. Leave it.'

Closing the bedroom door behind him, Lynch thought about Paul Stokes. Every time he sent someone in to find out something about Freij and Hussein, they got hurt.

Maybe it's time to go yourself, Gerald, and stop getting others to do your dirty work.

The thought slipped away as Marcelle reached out for him.

Chapter Seventeen

The insistent treble of his mobile woke Lynch. He scrabbled for the handset, his face screwed up against the daylight streaming through the window. A Beirut mobile, an unknown number.

He croaked. 'Lynch.'

'Mr Lynch. I trust you are well. It has been too long since we last talked.'

Lynch sat up, stilling Marcelle as she turned, the duvet rustling. He had last heard the voice on a video file: Michel Freij. 'Too long for you, maybe.'

The velvet laughter was synthetic. 'I thought perhaps we could meet. The Le Gray? At eleven for coffee? I am sure you would find the assignation in your interest.'

'Sure. I'll see ye there.'

He cut the line and turned to Marcelle. 'Freij.'

'What did he want?'

'To meet. This is going to be interesting. Are you okay to take the girl home while I'm gone? Hassan will come over, no?'

Hassan, Marcelle's driver, was devoted to her, loyal in a way only an older generation would understand loyalty: absolute, unthinking, and pure as the fire of faith. Hassan had been there when Lynch had come to Lebanon as a kid to work as a barman at Marcelle's shady little club in Hamra, *Le Chat Botté* – The Puss in Boots. Hassan had always been there.

Marcelle's eyes flickered uncertainly, scanning Lynch's face for signals. 'Yes, of course. I think we'll be okay. I'll call him.'

'Good. Do that.' He was half out of bed, his body hair

dark against his pale skin. He turned, the cotton duvet billowing as he threw himself across the bed, his swift kiss drawing a surprised gasp from her. 'Thanks, Marcie.'

Her eyes were bright. It wasn't until Lynch was sitting in a *servees* in the stream of traffic on Clemenceau he realised Marcelle was scared.

The back door of the big limousine opened, blocking the pavement in front of Lynch as he rounded the corner towards the two pristine ornamental bay trees in stainless steel containers marking the entrance to the Gray Hotel.

'Mr Gerald Lynch?' A blonde in a tight-fitting black dress rose elegantly from the leather seat and invited him into the car.

He stopped walking. 'Yes.'

'Would you like to come with me? Mr Michel Freij sent me for you.'

He gestured towards the sleek, brushed facade of the hotel. 'I thought we were meeting here?'

She smiled, efficient yet sympathetic. 'A change of plan. Please?'

Lynch got into the car. She closed the door, joining him from the street side, her skirt parting to show her long legs as she sat, her perfume heady and floral.

The Maybach's smooth acceleration pushed him back into the leather. 'So where are we meeting, then?'

'At the Freij Foundation's private museum. Michel had an urgent meeting with the trustees regarding an important acquisition. He hopes you understand.'

Lynch gazed over the city's towers, some new and clad in smoked glass, others older, concrete and bearing the pockmarks of history. 'Oh, sure. I understand totally.'

She missed the irony and smiled at him. The sunlight

escaping between the city's shadowed tower blocks flickered across Lynch's face as she chattered in Arabic on her mobile. He was surprised at how short the drive was. The car slowed at a security checkpoint and then turned to halt in an enclosed cobbled courtyard. He surveyed the garden, Beirut laid out below like a carpet of matchboxes. The formal walkways and shrubs were dotted with white marble Byzantine busts and pillars, each carrying a little brass plaque. Lynch wandered through them as the woman finished her call. She caught up with him as he admired a thirteenth-century piece, a woman in flowing gowns.

He gestured at the statue. 'This is beautiful.'

She snapped off a smile. 'Mr Freij shares his father's impeccable taste in fine *objets*. Shall we?'

Lynch followed her up the stone staircase into the large villa dominating the gardens. She left him in the reception area filled with cases displaying opaque pieces of fine green Roman glass.

Michel Freij's voice echoed down the marble staircase. 'Mr Lynch. Thank you for joining me.'

Lynch waited as Freij's footsteps clacked down the ornate stairs, taking in the man's crisp linen shirt, glistening cuffs and English wool suit. Freij's hands were manicured and his oiled hair was swept back. Lynch was dressed in a crumpled cotton shirt and jeans. *Mind you, wanker, you have to pay for what I get for free.*

Freij shucked off his jacket and swung it over his shoulder. 'I am so sorry to have diverted our meeting, but business calls on occasion, does it not?'

'Oh, yes,' said Lynch, 'it surely does.'

Freij relaxed, gesturing at the high-vaulted room 'Come, Mr Lynch. I shall show you some of my collection and we shall perhaps talk a little.'

Lynch wandered alongside Freij as he led the way into the colonnaded central hall of the building. Peach, white and black marble cladding decorated every surface. They turned left into a long, shaded room with a sumptuous Ottoman roof and a long central cabinet packed with artfully arranged pieces of age-frosted glass. Each wall space carried cabinets of artefacts. Four alcoves held white marble statuary – Roman noblemen in perfect condition, their aquiline noses and sightless, decent eyes gazing into the middle distance. Each piece in the impeccably curated collection was lit by its own cluster of tiny halogen lamps.

'This is the Roman room. This collection was amassed by my father. I have only added a few *objets* such as this,' he gestured to a collection of tiny amphorae, 'set of early Roman ladies' scents. Amazingly, research chemists at one of my companies was able to take samples from these bottles and use spectrometers to recreate the scents. They are fascinatingly complex. We hope to market it in the near future.' Freij's voice echoed in the cool silence.

Lynch nodded. 'Impressive.' He dropped behind, glancing over the greenish, matte shapes of the ancient glass. 'These must be worth an amazing amount of money.'

Freij surveyed the garden, his hands clenched behind his back, his smiling face in sharp relief in the sunlight. 'Yes, they—'

He wheeled at the crash of Lynch's fist slamming down on the glass case. The sound reverberated through the building. One of the amphorae fell over, rolling across the dark velvet.

Lynch beamed at Freij. 'Just wanted to check it was secure. You can't be too careful, can you?'

Freij's fury gave way to confusion as Lynch turned to face the bulky figure framed in the doorway. 'And you can put the gun away, monkey man. Mickey and I were only having a little chat.'

At a nod from Freij, the suited gunman relaxed and placed his pistol back in its shoulder holster.

Lynch was genial. 'Shall we sit down and talk, Mr Freij? I think I've seen enough history for now. I'm not safe around valuables, I have a nasty habit of breaking beautiful things.'

Freij opened his bunched fists, his mouth a grim line. He nodded slowly, scanning the jumbled objects in the case. 'Very well.' He led the way from the room, the gunman standing aside for him. Lynch followed, snapping a grin at the sour-faced guard as he passed.

Leading the way up the ornate stone staircase to the first floor, Freij's handsome face was illuminated by the afternoon sunlight streaming through the large vaulted windows. His movements were stiff, Lynch guessed from suppressing his anger. It gave Lynch enormous, childish pleasure.

Freij halted by a double doorway framed by brass-studded carved woodwork. 'I regret ever trying to buy that yacht, Mr Lynch. I am now in litigation with Luxe for the return of my funds. Please, after you.'

Lynch entered the meeting room, blinking at the transition from Ottoman marble to minimalist chic. He sat on the black leather sofa.

'Coffees please, Annette,' Freij addressed the tall, pencil-skirted girl who had appeared through a connecting door. He draped his jacket over the back of a chair.

Lynch leaned back, an arm stretched along the sofa and gazed around the room. 'I'm getting a bit upset by your militia, Mr Freij, if I were to tell you the truth. They appear to favour the heavy-handed approach and I can't say I appreciate it. Attempting to abduct one of my associates was...' Lynch cast his gaze to the ceiling. He threw a broad smile at Freij, his blue eyes twinkling, 'rude.'

Freij's composure flickered. 'I am not aware of any attempt to abduct anybody, Mr Lynch. I understand there was some unpleasantness at the One Lebanon rally. Were you involved in this?'

'Where is Peter Meier?'

Freij's smile was Siberian. 'Who, more to the point, is Peter Meier?'

'Come on, Mickey, stop fucking around. Meier's the hood you bought two nuclear warheads from.'

Freij sat back into the armchair by the coffee table, his face an incredulous portrait. 'Have you taken leave of your senses, man? This is all too much. I am a man of standing in Lebanon, a public figure and I am respected. I will not have this, this idiocy bandied about. This is the wildest, most ridiculous accusation.'

Lynch remained silent, examining Freij's body language. The man was so precise in everything he did. Now he leaned forward, his elbow on the coffee table and his finger raised at Lynch, who wanted to lean forward and snap it. 'Can you prove this, Mr Lynch? Do you really think you have a case to make?'

The silence roared between them. Freij leaned back in his chair. 'No, no you don't, do you?' He crossed his arms. 'I told you in London, I have no interest in smuggling arms – I intend to stand as the president of Lebanon and my very expensive campaign has started. I do not want this affair hanging over my head.' Freij reached into the jacket and withdrew an envelope, which he pushed across to Lynch. 'Here. Take this and go. I almost regret putting the effort into it now.'

Lynch pulled out a folded sheet of vellum of the same

type he had found by Paul Stokes' corpse. He opened it to find a set of coordinates written in the careful, black script he recognised from reading Paul's name on a note in a stinking farmhouse down a dusty track near Tripoli.

'What the—'

'It is the location of a farm in the Bekaa owned by a man called Jamal. He was a hashish farmer forced out of business following the last government's crackdown on the drugs trade. Apparently he does odd jobs for money. Dirty jobs others don't like to do. He is the man who killed Paul Stokes.'

Lynch gestured with the folded paper. 'This you carrying on the tradition? Raymond leave you that little Indian teak desk of his, did he?'

Freij rose, distaste on his proud face. 'I promised you this information. I have delivered. As I said, I almost regret it.'

Lynch smiled as he got to his feet, his hands held palms up. 'What, an' no coffee?'

Freij smiled coldly. 'I find I, too, have lost my interest in history for now.'

Lynch escaped into the cool, sunny garden, admiring a fine Byzantine statue of a woman carrying a baby. Electric motors whirred: the cameras tracking his progress out to the street. There was no limo to take him back to the Le Grey. He strode uphill to a T-junction. He glanced behind, but the streets were quiet. He called Tony Chalhoub.

'Hey, Lynch, 'sup?'

'Okay, Tony, I've got a name and location for Stokes' killer. It's in the Bekaa.'

'How did you get it?'

'Freij gave it to me just now. On one of those pieces of

paper he's so fond of. It's pretty mad, I know. I can only imagine he wants to burn his boy for some reason and I'm perfectly happy helping him do it. You can have your moment of fame, Tony. Freij thinks this'll buy me off and he's got another thing coming.'

'Fine. I'll pick you up in, say, an hour?'

'Done. I'll bring Palmer so we're, um, *diplomatic* about it.'

The quiet snoring from the back of the car grew louder. Lynch turned to view Palmer slumped across the beige leather back seat of Tony Chalhoub's Audi Q7. He noticed Chalhoub using the driver's mirror for the same purpose. Palmer's trademark linen suit was rumpled on his corpulent frame, his hand dangling off the edge of the seat.

Chalhoub's brow was wrinkled. 'Jesus, Lynch, why'd you have to bring him?'

'For the same feckin' reason as you want to meet up with your boys from Baalbek. I need consular cover if this all goes to fuck. Just like you'll need the local lads to clear up.'

Chalhoub grunted as he steered around the last roundabout out of Zahlé , leaving the agricultural town behind as they drove up the Bekaa Valley. Wood smoke rose in little pillars across the misty plain. The air was fresh after the late morning shower, the clouds parting to reveal the cobalt sky.

Lynch stared at the farms and villas, a cluster of Bedouin tents steaming in the cool spring sunlight. He wanted to smoke. He turned to Chalhoub.

'So who's yer man, this Dubois bloke? He was here in the civil war, wasn't he? French intelligence. You must have known him.'

Chalhoub's hand was light on the wheel. 'It's beautiful, isn't it, the Bekaa? It's God's Own place, this. Fertile, magical.'

'Sure and you're a poet, Tony.' Lynch tapped the leather dash. 'Dubois.'

Chalhoub frowned. 'He was the French head of station here during the war, a double act with his wife. She was some lady. She used to stop talk in rooms when she walked in. I mean, I'm talking halting conversations in Beirut, right? She was a Christian, from Jounieh. He was good, one of those operators who is everywhere and nowhere. They kicked him out in the end. He was very thick with Raymond Freij.'

'He was close to *Freij*?'

Chalhoub nodded, his eyes scanning the lush planted fields as he drove. 'Very much so. The Americans had Dubois thrown out. The French were backing Raymond a little too enthusiastically and his goons started shooting up the US Marines in his sector with Sarpac rockets. The Yanks had a real problem with their boys getting killed with French munitions for some reason, but they couldn't pin anything on Dubois. Then some guy at the UN comes along with a story about a brutal interrogation in Saida, a couple of Palestinian kids were killed by Maronite militiamen and Dubois was present. The Yanks went for him. They got their man.'

Lynch watched the scenery ahead of them. Arid, rocky terrain rose to their left framed by the hazy white-capped mountains. Palmer shifted and grunted in the back. 'You know a woman called Chalabi? Rather grand old dame, lives in Hamra, big old place called Cedars.'

'Sure. Everyone knows her. Vivienne Chalabi. Big money. Her husband used to be close to Gemayel. He was a big shot in the Lebanese Forces. Got himself killed near the end of the civil war. What about her?'

'I was at her place having dinner with Ghassan Maalouf.'

Chalhoub whistled. 'Maalouf, wow. He's a spider with a big old web. You're moving in high circles these days, Gerald. These guys are all big players in the old Christian power base. That's more of Dubois' clique.'

'Were *they* close? Maalouf and Dubois?'

'Dubois' wife was from one of the big Maronite families in Jounieh, so they would have socialised for sure. Why?'

Lynch shook his head. 'Ah, sure, it's nothing. Curious, I guess. Maalouf asked me to talk to Dubois about cooperation, so I called the guy and he was pretty cold about the whole idea. Strange, no? I mean, you'd want Maalouf and his boys onside, wouldn't you?' He tapped the map on his knee. 'You're taking a left here just at the end of the village. Are these your coppers?'

Chalhoub hit the horn as they passed the black police car and it swung out behind them to follow. The sound of the horn woke Palmer, who rubbed his face and moaned, propping himself up.

Lynch's voice reflected his contempt. 'With us now, are you?'

'Sorry.' Palmer's mouth pursed. 'Dropped off.'

His drool glistened on the seat.

Chalhoub turned off the main road towards the mountains, leaving the russet soil of the valley behind as they jinked through the village and then up the dusty road curving toward the foothills.

Lynch held up his hand. 'It's off to the left, there. Looks like farm buildings.'

Chalhoub pulled off the main track and stopped the car. 'One second. I'm going to tell my friends to hold back here for now. I don't want anyone getting scared.'

As Chalhoub walked back to the police car, Palmer shifted in the back seat, his clothes rasping in the silence. The car rocked with his weight.

'What do you think you'll find here, Lynch?'

Lynch glanced back in the vanity mirror, regretting his decision to bring the Embassy man. *Jesus, but he's got a silly fucking face on him. He's scared witless.* 'I don't know, Palmer. Maybe another dead body. You gonna throw up again, son?'

Palmer was querulous. 'That's not funny. You must have some idea of what's here, surely?'

Lynch shook his head, speaking up at the grey hills. 'He's Michel Freij's man, this Jamal. Freij has given him to us to avoid taking the rap for Paul Stokes' murder. Freij doesn't need the hassle right now. He's running for the top job. So boy Jamal will have been paid off handsomely to take it on the chin on Freij's behalf. Christ, with good behaviour and some of that Freij *wasta,* he'll be out in three to five. Michel's betting I'll take the credit for the nick and shut up like a good boy. He thinks I'm just a plod, see? Like the Lebanese plods he bribes.'

Palmer frowned. 'Whatever. But you *know* it wasn't Jamal. You know Michel Freij ordered Stokes' murder.'

Lynch turned in his seat, his steady regard making Palmer look away. 'Yes, I do. But right now we're going to play by Michel's playbook.'

Palmer was sweating, his hands kneading his crotch. Chalhoub returned to the SUV. 'What's up?'

'Nothing,' Lynch growled. 'Let's get this over with.'

They drove up to the scattered outbuildings. The land was rocky, the spring grass forming a fine green down over the unkempt fields. The door hung off its hinges on the large, rusty barn. An old American motorhome was parked by the barn, a battered white caravan stood behind it. The carcases of several battered cars lay abandoned to one side near a single, tired tree.

'What a mess,' said Lynch, 'Some farmer.'

Lynch left the car door open. He scanned the buildings. Chalhoub joined him. They paced towards the caravan together. The car door slammed behind them and Palmer cried, 'Wait for me.'

Lynch turned back to the caravan. He caught the glint from above the low wall behind it and shouted to Chalhoub. Lynch dived left and reached for his shoulder holster. He felt the bullet twist the air by his ear as he went down, his shoulder smashing into the dry ground. The echo cracked back from the hills.

Palmer's heavy body crashed into the ground behind. The air filled with a series of short, high-pitched screams and the noise of Palmer kicking and threshing in the dust. Lynch crabbed left, knowing left-handed Chalhoub would move right. He jabbed his gun out, scanning the rough wall-top for any movement. Lynch risked a glance behind – Palmer's back was arched, his hands held to his face. Blood pulsed through the man's fat fingers and dribbled down his arm.

Lynch scrambled for the cover of a pile of damaged tractor tyres as Palmer's shrieks cut off, leaving a terrible silence. From his low vantage point, Lynch glimpsed the blotched linen, the white hands flat on the ground and Palmer's bloody face turned to the right, away from him. Acutely conscious of minutiae, he watched the first fat fly settle on the corpse's pudgy white finger.

Chalhoub called a warning. A figure behind the wall was silhouetted for a second against the mountains.

Chalhoub's shot rang out. The figure collapsed. Lynch sprinted for the wall. Chalhoub was first. The Lebanese police car's siren wailed. Lynch stared over the wall at the body spread before him, the revolver still clasped in the man's hand and the back of his head blown away, dusty gore splashed behind him. Lying on the ground some ten feet beyond was a camouflage-patterned forage cap.

Lynch holstered his gun. 'Well, that's him done, then. Nice shot.'

Chalhoub bent down, patting the man's pockets. 'Thanks. Nothing on him.'

Lynch returned to Palmer's bulky corpse. The bullet had hit him in the eye and taken much of his right temple with it. No stranger to violent death, Lynch still had to clench his mouth and fight the impulse rising in his throat.

'Sorry, Palmer. You weren't cut out for this, son. Should have stayed home.'

Chalhoub joined Lynch, the two Lebanese policemen behind him. 'This is going to be a little messy, I think.'

Lynch shook his head. 'No, we needn't be involved. Your two boys here can take the credit. Terrorist, kidnapped British Embassy official, cannabis farmer driven to extremes. Terrorist kills embassy man, brave police shoot terrorist. This *was* a cannabis farm, wasn't it?'

'Likely. The fields haven't been tended for years. We kept ploughing them up until they stopped.'

'Only one small detail you'll have to brush over, Tony. Jamal there's got a gunshot wound in the right leg. A nine mill parabellum.'

Chalhoub glanced at Lynch. 'You've met before, then.'

'Twice before and he didn't mean me any good either time. He's Freij's man all right, but not a freelance. He's militia. He was expecting us. Now I'm not sure if Freij was trying to use him to waste me or use me to waste him.'

Chalhoub held up his palm, his fingers fanned in the universal Arab gesture that means everything from *what's going on?* right through to *what the hell's your problem?* He turned to the policemen and spat a string of Arabic at them. They brightened and, with a *'shukran sidi'*, thank you, they raced back to their car and started their urgent report over the radio.

Chalhoub followed Lynch over to the caravan. The door was open. 'I reckon we've got about fifteen minutes before half of the Bekaa police force arrives here,' Chalhoub warned.

'We can leave now, Tony. I have everything I need.'

Lynch turned in the gloomy interior and offered the piece of paper he'd picked up from the grubby, lino-topped table. Chalhoub took it, unfolding the thick parchment to reveal the bold, flowing calligraphy: *Gerald Lynch*. There was a photograph of Lynch clipped to the note.

'You recognise it, yes?'

Chalhoub stared. Lynch's voice was bitter. 'One of Freij's little notes. That photograph was taken in London.' Lynch bent to sit at the table, which bore the remnants of a meal, a crumpled bag of sugar, a glass with a tea bag in it and a full ashtray. Next to the ashtray was a half-empty jar of pickles, which Lynch picked up. He turned it and watched the cucumbers dance in the cloudy, green-tinged brine. 'At Paul Stokes' funeral. I met Freij there. The bastard must have had a photographer with him.'

'So he likes you.'

'He's in fucking love with me, isn't he? The kiss of death is what he wants to give me, right enough.' Lynch banged the jar down on the table, making both the ashtray and Chalhoub jump. 'I'm going to have him, Tony, I swear to God.'

'Let's go, Gerald. This place stinks.'

'Everywhere stinks. Everywhere Freij goes smells of death. He's fucking evil.'

Chalhoub put his hand on Lynch's shoulder. Lynch knocked it away, his dive for the door rocking the caravan.

Chapter Eighteen

For over 180 years, the Ottoman Grand Serail has commanded Beirut from its lofty position atop the city, a huge quadrangle of pale stone capped with a red-tiled roof. Lynch didn't spare the great building a glance as he hurried along its sun-splashed frontage, passing the towering gates and ignoring the bored glances of the soldiers guarding the prime ministerial headquarters. Nathalie Durand fell back and called to him. Lynch turned and cast his eyes to heaven. She leant against the wall, massaging her reddened ankle where her shoe had rubbed it in the walk uphill from where the *servees* driver had dropped them in Sodeco.

'Sorry,' she gasped. 'I did not expect —'

'Wear flat shoes in future. You're operational, not on a shopping trip. Come on.' Lynch forged ahead, her limping clatter following him up the street.

Entering the British Embassy building, Lynch ignored the security guards and their scanner and strode to the lift, stabbing the call button. Nathalie regained her breath as Lynch glared around him, tapping his foot.

They waited together for the ambassador to see them, the only sound in the room the faint echo of voices from the visa section echoing through the oak door and the electronic tick of the clock on the wall. Minutes of aching silence later, the great doors opened and St John Winterton marched out.

He waved them into the office as he left. 'Go on, go on in. What the hell are you waiting for?'

Brian Channing and Yves Dubois sat at the head of the long mahogany table, both working at laptops. Dubois looked up, beamed and rose to kiss Nathalie on both cheeks.

'Take a seat, guys.' Channing gestured along the table.

Lynch sat, Nathalie three seats away from him.

Channing waited until the doors were closed. 'He really doesn't like you, does he?'

Lynch was momentarily mystified. 'Oh, Winterton? Sure, he's a teddy bear under that gruff exterior. Laugh a minute when you squirt a couple of scotches into him.'

Dubois closed the lid of his laptop. 'To bring you up to date, we have located the *Arabian Princess*. We have a satellite fix on her and we have a British patrol boat following her in long pursuit using radar. The analysts think she will try to refuel in Malta or possibly Tripoli.'

Channing grunted. 'My money would have said Tripoli, but we have additional intelligence that points to Malta. Thank God, because we're damn close to the Maltese and the very idea of the bloody Libs getting hold of two hundred kilotons of mayhem makes me want to shit, to be honest, post-Gaddafi or not.'

Something on Channing's screen caught his eye and his focus shifted to his laptop. He pecked at the keyboard.

Dubois raised an eyebrow. 'C Company, the Maltese special forces, are planning to take the boat when it docks. Their unit has been strengthened by a unit from the British Special Boat Squadron. They're flying in now. This boat will not leave Valetta if it docks there.'

Nathalie crossed her arms. Lynch caught the movement in time to see her blouse part to expose the curve of her breast as she spoke. 'Then it is end game, no?'

Dubois made for the window, surveying the city below, his hands in his pockets. 'That rather depends on you and Monsieur Lynch. We still don't have Peter Meier and we still have no tangible evidence against Michel Freij and Selim Hussein.' He turned, his face half-shadowed. 'Unless you have something for me.'

Nathalie bit her lip. 'Nothing new. We have flown the team in and they are established at the Résidence des Pins, but Falcon's security is highly sophisticated.'

Channing's head lifted. 'Residence de what?'

'The French Embassy.' Lynch answered him. 'And no, we've still got nothing on Freij beyond a dead man who was sent to kill me.'

Dubois steepled his fingers. 'What do you think the president of Lebanon and the head of a successful defence systems manufacturer would want with two nuclear warheads, Monsieur Lynch?'

'He's not president yet. Parliament has to vote him in.'

'Oh, I rather think he has put it in the bag, Monsieur Lynch. The Americans are being very nice to him. He is very close to them. He will be interviewed by CNN, I understand. His rally this week was widely televised. Parliament knows he carries a populist card. He will almost certainly gain the parliamentary vote. He has been paying all the right people very generously indeed. His posters are all over the city. The campaign has been extraordinarily slick and very expensive. Mark my words, Michel Freij is the next president of Lebanon.'

Lynch frowned. 'Close to the Americans? His father was a major thug, Michel is no better. Why would he be close to the Yanks?'

'American and Israeli interests are closely aligned, as you well know.' Dubois allowed himself a taut smile. 'And so are Israel and the Christian militia. Falcon works extensively with American companies, Monsieur Lynch. They're the biggest overseas contractor to the US defence industry outside Israel. It's a virtuous circle of interests.'

'Do you know if Freij has links to the CIA?'

Channing stirred. 'Why would you ask that?'

'Frank Coleman was hanging around at his rally the other day. He didn't like being seen in public.'

Dubois leaned over and made a quick note. 'We'll look for it, but I would not be surprised at some degree of contact given Freij's involvement in military procurement and defence.'

Lynch rubbed his chin. He'd forgotten to shave. 'Is this nuclear thing part of the presidential grab? You think he's going to pull a Geagea if he doesn't get the vote?'

Nathalie shot him an irritated glance. 'Pull a what?'

'A Geagea,' Lynch grinned. 'Sure, haven't ye ever met a Geagea?'

Nathalie pushed her chair back, smoothing her skirt. 'I'm sorry, I don't have time for this. I have work to do.'

Dubois looked from Lynch to Nathalie. 'It is good to see you are getting on. Sit down, Nathalie. What did you mean, Monsieur Lynch?'

'Sure you know yourself. You were here, weren't you? Samir Geagea and Michel Aoun held the Lebanese Parliament to ransom by surrounding it with militia in the late eighties. Geagea the kingmaker. Isn't that Freij's game? You know, back me or I push the button?'

'I cannot find that conceivable. We are a long way from 1988. Lebanon has left that time behind it. Nobody would be mad enough to take the country back there, let alone use a nuclear device on their own country. No, Monsieur Lynch, there has to be another reason Freij wants to acquire two nuclear warheads. I need you two to work together and find what it is. We don't know when we stop this attempt he is making he won't make another one.'

'If the Yanks are so fond of him, get Coleman to rein him in.'

Dubois wheeled to face Lynch. 'May I remind you we

are not talking to "the Yanks" right now. We are very hopeful to avoid telling them the European Union has lost two nuclear warheads. We might have traced the boat, but we haven't secured it yet.'

Channing surfaced from his laptop again, beaming at Lynch and Nathalie. The screen cast a blue sheen over his face. 'Need you to go to Malta, Gerald. Your friend Mister Freij owns a nice executive jet and it flew there this morning, apparently. Funny thing to be doing in the middle of a race for the presidency, isn't it? Tootling off to Malta. At least Libya's totally out of the picture now, so that's one less worry. The *Arabian Princess* is making for Malta for sure.' Channing closed his laptop and stood, the computer under his arm. 'Right, must dash. Lovely to chat with you all. Come on, Gerald, let's get you sorted with flights and things. You'll like Malta. Nice weather. Food's pants unless you know where to eat.'

Lynch opened the door and turned to Nathalie. 'Coming?'

'No. I want to talk to my father.'

Lynch shrugged and followed Channing, the door slamming behind him.

Dubois breathed deeply. Channing irritated him at times. He feared the Englishman's political capability, wondered at times if Channing was goading him with his affectations. Lost in thought, he jumped when Nathalie hit the table and cried out. She spoke in French, the words tumbling from her.

'In the name of God, he's impossible, Papa. He spends all his time chasing women, drinking and fighting. It's too much. He is infuriating. He has no... subtlety.'

Dubois laughed. 'He is a man of action, Nathalie. You

need a man of action to protect you, to follow up with the physical work that is undoubtedly going to be necessary. You need to work with him, to incentivise and guide him. You have the background in pure intelligence, in gathering data. Use him to help you in this, to provide the human intelligence. You will find you need this in Beirut. You are leading this effort, your team is here now and I understand they are working well. Manage Lynch. This is your big chance. Use him, Nathalie.'

'But he is,' Nathalie's fists were clenched, 'impossible. He takes the *servees* taxis and yet he can drive. He even has an embassy car but refuses to use it. He breaks every rule of cover constantly. He drinks like a fish. And his temper...'

Dubois breasted the table, taking her in his arms and hugging her, his hand stroking her back. 'Come, *Nino*. I have too much to do for now. Make me proud, eh?'

She nodded into his shoulder and Dubois tried not to think of her mother, but Beirut brought back too many memories and he had to let her go and turn away so she wouldn't see his tears as she left.

Dubois looked over the city that had been his home for five years and where he had met the proud, glorious Lebanese girl with green eyes. Gazing over the rooftops, something cold crept over him, making him shudder. He felt the spectre of the vicious civil war that destroyed this beautiful city and taken away his humanity. It had all happened decades ago, was buried in the distant past now.

Surely it couldn't happen again? He realised he had voiced the thought aloud. He stood at the window and let the past wash over him.

Lynch was sitting outside on the balcony smoking a cigar when Nathalie entered the apartment. She went into the kitchen, fished out the ice cube tray from the freezer, and filled a tumbler with ice, taking it through to the living room where she picked up two glasses and a bottle of Tyrconnell from the tray. She slipped through to the balcony, placed the glasses down on the plastic table and poured two drinks. She pushed one towards him and kept the plain tumbler with the blue glass teardrop in its base for herself. She quite liked it.

'Ice?'

Lynch stared at the drinks and up at Nathalie. 'Not that glass.' He got to his feet and held his hand out to her barely in time to stop her flinging the drink in his face. 'I'm sorry, I don't mean to be funny, but not that glass. Here, I'll get you another one.'

She sat, mystified, while he took the glass away and brought her a crystal tumbler. 'Ice?'

She shook her head. 'What was this about?'

'Can I tell you another day?' Lynch implored.

She nodded. She opened her mouth to speak but he caught her eye, his face solemn, holding his glass up between them pinched between his thumb and forefinger, his other fingers held up to silence her. 'Look, I want to say I'm sorry. I haven't been very considerate to you and I think you deserve better. We have a job to do together and I haven't made it easy, I know. I'll try and watch my mouth in future.'

He seemed sincere enough, Nathalie reflected as she looked into his eyes. And yet she wanted to scream with frustration. She drew breath and touched her glass to his. He smiled, the waning sun catching his blue eyes, the sudden urchin's grin making her smile in return. She drank to hide her confusion.

Oh, Maman, mais il est dangereux.

'Peace?'

'Peace.'

Lynch sat back, puffing on his cigar. She liked the smell. It reminded her of being a child and sneaking downstairs when her parents had held dinner parties. A car horn sounded below them in the jostling traffic, the sun warming her back.

'When do you fly to Malta?'

'First thing in the morning. No private jets for me and there aren't any direct flights. Seven bloody hours.'

'Lynch, can I ask you a question?'

His shoulders stiffened. He tapped the cigar against the balcony railing and nodded. 'Sure.'

'Who was Paul Stokes, exactly?'

He turned away from her to look to sea, the orange glow of the sun on his skin. He took a deep breath and faced her. 'Paul was a young man I met in Jordan. He was working for a government ministry there, producing a magazine for them. I sort of hooked up with him because my masters had an interest in the ministry's work.' Lynch drew on his cigar. Nathalie waited. Lynch's gaze was drawn back to the sea. 'He was in love with a Jordanian girl, Aisha Dajani. Her brother was involved in a hare-brained scheme to drain the Israeli water supply in order to bolster Jordan's. The Izzies wanted him stopped and the alternative to his scheme was a nice, profitable British consortium. So we stopped him.' Lynch closed his eyes briefly. 'There was some...' he caught Nathalie's eye and smiled humourlessly. 'Confusion. The Jordanians were too heavy-handed and Aisha was killed. I took Paul under my wing and brought him here. He was working for *Beirut Today* as a journalist. He did the occasional bit of research for me on the side.'

She sipped her drink, the ice clinking. 'And you were friends with him.'

'I suppose I felt responsible for him. After all, she died because of me, even if that wasn't something I intended to happen. When we picked up the first clues Michel and his partner Selim were fiddling around with clandestine money transfers, I sent Paul to interview Freij and rattle his cage. They killed him. *Michel* killed him. Worse, it was casual, like, done as a warning to me, you know? They took a man's life just to pass on a message. It was swatting a fly, no more than that.'

Lynch was so far away he had forgotten her. She sat and let him speak, the sunlight glowing red and the shadows deepening the lines on his face. Lynch closed his eyes for a long time. He reached to the bottle and refilled their glasses.

'I mean, I thought we were talking about a money-laundering racket, not an out of control Lebanese Christian militia smuggling nuclear warheads. I'd never have used an irregular on something that dangerous if I'd known.' He fell silent again and she turned to scan the skyline of *Ain Mreisse*, almost missing his whisper. 'Christ have mercy on me.'

Nathalie was surprised. 'You are religious?'

'It's more a figure of speech.'

The sound of raised voices carried from the street below. Nathalie leaned over the balcony's cast iron railing. Two men were arguing. One of them was selling radishes and herbs from a cart, a cigarette dangling from his mouth as he waved the other man away, the other calling on those around him to witness some iniquity or another.

'They always argue here. It must be the water.' She turned to Lynch. 'You cannot blame yourself for Paul's death.'

He took his time to answer her. 'They both died, that young couple, because of me. I owe it to Paul to at least avenge his murder, so an' I do.'

'What about the warheads?'

'It's strange, you know. I've never got out of the habit of being grateful for being able to stand on this balcony without worrying about being shot. In the war, you'd not have lasted two seconds out here.'

Lynch turned his back on the shimmering blue expanse to face her.

'Your father was right. There's nothing to stop Michel trying again. We'll be very lucky to pin any involvement with those warheads on him, particularly if he gets the presidency. But the question is what he wanted to do with the damn things and to answer that, we need to get inside Falcon Dynamics.'

'We haven't been able to penetrate their networks. My team here has been working on it for days. And they're good, the best.'

'So why don't we get all old-fashioned and go for humint? Find someone who'll let us in?'

Nathalie nodded. 'Agreed. My thoughts entirely. We have been looking for known defence contacts with links to Falcon. We have also been trying to find local contacts, employees and so on. It's not easy. Strangely, Falcon Dynamics is highly advanced digitally, but Lebanon is still a very analogue country in so many ways. It makes things harder than you would imagine.'

'Grand. If you focus on that, I'll go and play around in Malta. Is that okay with you?'

Nathalie held her glass to clink against and then drained her whisky. 'Not bad, this stuff. We need to get some Ricard, though. I miss Ricard. I am going to get dressed, I have promised to have dinner with a friend.'

*

Nathalie put her head around the door. 'I'm going. Don't wait up for me. Good luck in Malta.'

Lynch whistled. 'You brush up well, so. I hope he's worth it.'

She grinned. 'You'll never know.'

He stared at the diamonds around her neck. 'Are those real?'

'Again, you'll never know.' She laughed and turned away, her heels clacking down the corridor. The front door closed. After a short time staring at the sea, Lynch took his mobile and called Leila. This time she picked up.

'Lynch.'

'I didn't know where you were,' he said. 'I was worried.'

'What does it matter? Are you enjoying your games?'

He looked up at the whiteness of Sannine's peak towering beyond the city in the waning light. 'They're not games. It's what I do. You've always known that. It'll be over soon. Will you come back?'

She sighed. 'I don't know, Lynch. My head's in another place right now. I have some living to do.'

'I have to go away for a while. Can I see you when it's over?'

'Where are you going?'

'I can't tell you.'

Her voice trembled. 'Then I can't trust you. You understand that? I'm a secret from your secret life. That's just not me.' She sniffed, the sound faint through her hand cupped over the receiver, he guessed. They shared the silence for what seemed like an eternity, the line was hissy.

'Okay. If you come back, Lynch. Call me first, yes?'

'Thanks. Thanks, I will.'

Lynch should have felt elation, but he was filled with a terrible sadness. Sitting back with his whisky, he drifted, the sound of the city street below him lulling him as the shadows gathered. Someone was cooking in the apartment below and had the window open. He could hear pans. He was a child again, dustbin lids clattering on the Falls Road. He was upstairs, fighting for his life as Cathal tried to take his money from him, the two quid from his paper round. He was in the kitchen, shouting at their foster mother, her kind, lined face shocked at his words. He was standing in the bathroom over Cathal's still form, the older boy's lips blue and a needle lying on the tiled floor.

Gerry Lynch was sent back to the Sisters of Charity after that. The family hadn't been able to cope with the trouble. Nobody had told them the older boy was an addict. Nobody had known, to tell the truth. Nobody except Gerry. And somehow they blamed him for knowing. For not telling them. For Cathal's death.

He woke with a start, the air cool. His cigar had gone out. He checked his watch and swore softly. His mobile was ringing and he hurried inside to answer it, Marcelle's smoky voice his reward. 'Can you come over, Lynch?'

He pocketed the phone and headed for the door. He paused for a second, uncertain whether to take the Walther. On the balance of it, he decided, no.

Lynch leaned against the bar, drinking an Almaza, tearing up a beer mat and trying not to want to smoke. It was early and the club was almost empty, a few huddled couples whispering in the dark corners and a party of loud suits drinking champagne at the other end of the long walnut counter.

Marcelle joined him. She was angry, her tone urgent. 'What the fuck happened there, Lynch? Freij has paid me ten thousand bucks to say sorry and hopes that the girl wasn't hurt in the "unfortunate accident".'

Lynch tossed the soggy shreds onto the bar. 'So it's a win-win, Marcie. Your girl gets patched up, you get to earn bank and Michel stays clean. Why buck that?'

Decorated for the evening shift, Marcelle was resplendent in a clinging black velvet dress accentuating her curves, cut perfectly under her taut breasts. Gold hung from her ears and neck, her bangle glittered with diamonds and kohl framed her eyes.

'Come on. Have a drink and celebrate your luck.'

She gauged him, her lips tight. He smiled at her and patted the red leather stool. She sat and snapped her fingers at the barman. 'Martini. Dirty.'

Lynch's gaze ran up her legs to her face and met her frown.

'Forget it, Lynch. You got a freebie. Count your blessings. But forget it.'

He smiled, shaking his head. 'I don't remember a thing.'

She leaned forward, drawling, her touch light on his thigh. 'Babe, I have known a shitload of men. I so know you.'

Lynch lowered his gaze, smiling. 'Marcie, take his money and keep the girl quiet. Did he mention anything else to you?'

'Nothing. That girl almost died. He's an animal.'

'Sure, but he's playing nicely, so just go along with it. You have my number. Please take care.'

The barman placed her Martini on the bar, waiting on her reaction as she lifted the frosted cocktail glass, the queen olive speared on its cocktail stick rolled into her full lip as she sipped. 'Good. Thank you.' She tipped her chin, dismissing him.

She turned to Lynch, her deep eyes half-lidded. Her contempt was languid. 'Lynch, you have a short memory. I used to take care of you, remember? You were a kid when you came to Beirut. You were scared of loud noises. You pissed yourself in the air raids. Don't presume to mother me.'

The lights dimmed and music started to pump. The first floor-show of the evening was starting.

Lynch stepped down from the bar stool, smiling. His hand caressed her thigh with a light, passing touch that slid inside her leg fleetingly. He leaned into her to speak over the music. 'You're getting older, Marcie. You can't afford all that pride.'

He left her without a backwards glance, ignoring the two listless girls on the stage as they stroked each other's breasts theatrically in time to the pumping music.

Ghassan Maalouf sipped his Caipirinha delicately. Nathalie tried not to feel out of place. She knew her dress was elegant and complemented her slim figure and full bust, was perhaps even a little too daring. She had checked her makeup and it was the best she could do, the red lipstick contrasting with her fine skin and black bobbed hair, a touch of colour on her cheeks and her green eyes framed with mascara. She wore diamonds, borrowed from the ambassador's wife, an elegant lady in her fifties who had declared herself Nathalie's surrogate mother. She clutched an Hermès evening bag that had likewise been pressed on her by her new companion. Yet she felt like an intruder, a dowdy little sparrow in the opulence of the Casino du Liban and its outré occupants. They swept by in a tide of silk and tumbling hair and pumped-up breasts, chattering parties of fleshy-lipped brilliant white smiles on the arms of dark-suited, swarthy men with blue-shadowed chins and male pattern baldness.

Nathalie had watched as Maalouf won and then lost five hundred dollars at roulette. He walked her through the gaming room to the bar afterwards, acknowledging the attention of the many people who greeted him or stopped him to offer their wishes. Always deferentially, Nathalie noted.

Maalouf's rumbling voice brought her back to earth, to her seat at the table in the elegant salon. 'You are not drinking.'

Nathalie smiled and lifted her glass to her lips, the cold, sweet aniseed flowing over her tongue. 'It is very kind of you to invite me to join you here. I had not visited this place before.'

'But you lived in Lebanon.'

'As a child. This is not a place for children, Monsieur.'

Maalouf chuckled, his merry eyes looking her up and down. 'Absolutely not. You certainly are no child now, though. You are every piece as beautiful as your mother was.'

'You are a flatterer.'

He shook his head, his expression becoming serious. 'No, the truth. It is important to be aware of the difference between flattery and truth as it is to be aware of the difference between love and hate. Both are too close, so some subtlety is required. But truth is important.' He studied her face.

She held his gaze. 'Then let us practice, Monsieur. What do you seek, precisely?'

His white-whiskered face broke into a smile. 'Ah, so the interrogation begins. Are you, I wonder, as effective as your mother was? Are we to anticipate the same mixture of intellect and persistence?'

'You said you knew her. Did you know her well?'

'Yes, since before she met your father. She was a famous beauty, but you know this. She was well known here.' He gestured at the opulent bar, taking in the whole hillside complex of concert halls, gaming rooms, bars and restaurants overlooking the bay north of Jounieh. 'In better times.'

Nathalie's face clouded. 'Her family was from Jounieh. Before ...'

'I am sorry. We should perhaps change the subject.' Maalouf brushed the lapel of his tuxedo. 'It was insensitive of me to talk like this of the past.'

Seeing the little red thread in his buttonhole took Nathalie back to Vivienne Chalabi's house and their first meeting and reminded her of Lynch. She wondered what he was doing and rather thought he would still be drinking whisky.

Maalouf shifted in his chair and sighed. 'I shall cut, as they say, to the chase. I run the organisation ultimately responsible for Lebanon's antiterrorist operations.'

Having checked him on the European Joint Intelligence Centre database, Nathalie knew this. She also knew he had graduated from a long career in the *mukhabbarat*, the secret police, had a history of affiliation to the Syrians and enjoyed close ties to Syrian intelligence. Maalouf was a highly respected and influential member of the Christian community, an assiduous networker and one of the few figures to enjoy the confidence of key leaders in every one of Lebanon's many, many political camps. An assassination attempt against him in the early nineties by a group of Shi'ite hotheads had led to the would-be assassins being handed over personally to Maalouf by

Hezbollah. An unfortunate and fatal accident had sadly prevented the young hotheads from being brought to justice. Maalouf was thought to be a strong candidate for head of Lebanese intelligence when the current incumbent retired. It was thought the date of the retirement would be set by Maalouf himself.

Maalouf smiled at Nathalie, pushing his drink on the tabletop with his forefinger, a shy gesture for such a powerful man. 'We have been watching you and Mr Lynch with some interest. It is clear you are involved in a major operation targeted against Michel Freij. Are you not?'

Nathalie felt her pulse rising. *Careful girl.* She sipped her drink and met his eyes over the brim of the glass. 'We are.'

'You have been adding significant resources to the French Embassy staff. Given your own role within EJIC, this would lead me to believe you are involved in an electronic surveillance or interception operation against a Lebanese target.'

She smiled, relaxing. 'We are all led to belief, are we not? How much nicer to have belief brought to us. So much more convenient.'

Maalouf banged his glass on the table. She managed not to jump. Maalouf lifted a finger to her. 'Don't be facetious. You and your British friend are playing around in my backyard and we would have stepped in many days ago if we did not happen to share a common goal.'

'And what is that, Monsieur?'

Maalouf snorted. 'Freij, of course. Michel Freij. We know what he's doing. And we want him stopped. We can help you.'

Chapter Nineteen

Gonsalves stood at the wheel, the dark sea stretched ahead of him, the big boat's pale wake kissed by the full moon. He checked the route; they were set to make Malta the next morning. He scooped three chunks from the ice bucket and sloshed the last of the Macallan into the crystal tumbler at his side. He took the big boat to fifteen knots, enjoying the iodine night air.

They had passed through the strait of Gibraltar the night before. Gonsalves was relieved as he regarded the lights of the rock twinkling on the horizon behind them. He had been keyed up about the nosy Brits and their fast little Scimitar-class patrol boats, but the passage through the straits had been uneventful. They had hugged the Moroccan shore through the night before Gonsalves had handed the wheel to filthy little Martinez and turned in.

Gonsalves was running the boat with a skeleton crew of four: the plodding Lebanese Boutros; little Panamides the silent killer from Bogota, a surly Frenchman called Blanc who cooked like an angel and swore like a trooper and Pedro Martinez, a wheezing, dirty old bastard with black fingernails who knew boats like other men knew their wives.

Martinez had taken them back into the busy Mediterranean shipping lanes as Gonsalves had slept, charting a fast, steady course for Malta. Gonsalves had relieved him as dusk fell and now, after the long day's rest, he was back at the wheel and exulting in the power of the great engines working under his feet. The surge reminded him of the blood in his own veins, the feeling of liberation and victory coursed through him.

Gonsalves called down to Boutros on the intercom.

'Come up and take the wheel.'

He increased the thrust and the big twin engines responded, sending a powerful shudder through the boat to lift the prow, the wash rhythmic and the salt of the open sea in his nostrils. He sipped his whisky and steered the big yacht. Twenty knots and more in reserve. He grinned. Damn, but she was a fine ship.

Gonsalves was laughing when Boutros arrived, his puzzlement at his skipper's mood clear on his big face. Gonsalves moved aside. 'Here. Take over. Keep us at this speed. Charts are over there.'

'Skip.'

'Give me the key to the girl's room.'

'Skip?'

'The key to her room. Give it to me.'

Boutros held the wheel, grinning sycophantically. 'But Skip...'

'Just do it.'

Boutros handed over the key. Sipping from his glass, Gonsalves held the key in his other hand, stroking the little metal sliver between his thumb and forefinger as he picked his way down the stairway. He took his time, his hand sliding on the steel railing of the spiral staircase and the icy, pale liquid warming his mouth as he took the last turn onto the lower deck. He stopped by the guest cabin door and inserted the key in the lock, pushing it in smoothly. His heart hammered, his mouth dry with anticipation. He locked the door behind him.

She was awake, disoriented. 'Who are you?'

He smiled at her, placing his tumbler on the bedside table. 'I am the captain of this ship.' His German didn't even sound rusty. He exulted in his control as he sat on the bed beside her. 'Do you feel better?'

Her voice was thick. 'Better? Better than what? I have been kidnapped. I demand to be released.'

'And so you shall be,' Gonsalves reassured her. 'There has been a terrible mistake. Would you like some water?'

She studied his face for a moment and he was careful to stay impassive and calm. 'Yes, yes please.'

He fetched a glass of water from the sink in the bathroom and she took it from him in the palms of her two hands, her extended fingers shaking as she gulped. The Fentanyl did that, thought Gonsalves. Dry mouth or retches.

He reached out and touched her cheek. 'You're hot. Want more water?'

She recoiled from his touch. 'Where are we?'

'At sea. It's okay now. You're safe. We've sorted out the mix-up and we'll get you to land soon enough.'

'What mix-up?'

'Your father has done some bad things. The authorities thought you were involved. Were you?'

'In the guns thing? No. No, I wasn't.' She glanced wide-eyed around her. 'Where am I? What boat is this please?'

He was calming, his voice gentle as he took her empty glass. 'I think you should get some rest now. We're going to stop off at Gibraltar so you can leave the boat. You should never have been here in the first place.'

Elli lay back against the damp pillow, smiling. 'Thank God I'm finally safe.' He watched her face, serenity giving way to a troubled expression. 'But—'

Gonsalves was fast, his hand on her mouth and nose, blocking her from breathing or screaming with one movement. Her face reddened as she struggled beneath him. He slapped her across the cheek, hard, with the other hand. He pulled the bedclothes away from her, tearing at her pyjamas. Still groggy from the Fentanyl, she tried to fight him off but she was too weak and Gonsalves was expert. He pinioned her arms and punched her in the stomach, her reflex action giving him the leverage to jam his forearm between her legs and then push his fingers into her.

Freed of his grip on her face, Elli Hoffmann screamed, a hoarse cry of abject despair. He slapped her again, harder. The blow seemed to take the fight out of her in an instant. She relaxed, moaning and stretching out, her hands slipping under the pillow. Gonsalves, taking her movements as a sign of submission grinned. He tore at his belt and knelt between her parted legs in triumph. He bent to enter her.

Surprised by her violent movement, he caught the glitter of the fork in her hands as she lunged for his face. He flung up his arm too late. The sharp tines dug deep into his cheek.

Later, a lifetime later, Elli felt as if her reason was once again going to flee her, leaving her in the darkness, screaming for release. Slowly, her body aching, she uncurled from her foetal position.

He had fallen back, roaring, the fork sticking out of his bloodied face. And then he had simply pulled it out and dropped it to clang on the floor as he lunged at her, hitting her so hard she had thought she would die. He started to kick her, the heavy blows to her stomach doubling her up.

By the time she had fallen off the bed to the floor, he had decided she was too tainted for rape. The Lebanese man had come and reasoned with him, but Elli didn't remember the words, just a vague sense of meaning from the tones of their voices. She had lain there retching blood until the blessed release of her assailant's leaving. Then the darkness came with its chattering little things screeching at her. They always came in the darkness.

Elli pushed herself off the bed and hobbled to the bathroom. She poured water into the sink, scrubbing hard to remove the dirt of his touch on her skin. She cried, the hoarse sobs breaking out of her bruised mouth as she scoured herself with the flannel. She rubbed until her skin burned away the shame, until it reddened to mask the contusions, blood coming to the surface with the force of her chafing. The bathroom door burst open and she looked up to see Boutros framed in the steam. He leapt to restrain her.

'Fucking hell. What are you doing? Are you crazy?'

She struggled against him but he was too strong. He wrapped a towel around her.

'It's okay, it's okay. He's over in the sick bay now, getting the wound seen to.' He took her shoulder in his big hand. His touch was cool. 'It's okay. It's over now. Stop hurting yourself. It won't happen again.'

She regarded him, her eyes pleading, desperate to believe in him. 'How you know this?'

'I won't let it.' he said, smiling. 'I'm no angel, but rape wasn't in the deal.'

She wrung her hands, focused on the bulkhead. 'What *was* in the deal, please?'

Shaking his head, he rose. The gentle giant looked down at her. 'I'll get you some ointment. I'll see you're all right from now on. But stop hurting yourself. Please?'

Elli's weary visage dropped. 'Yes, okay.'

Boutros took a deep breath, knocked and entered Gonsalves' cabin. Gonsalves was standing at the mirror in his bathroom, examining his wounded cheek. Boutros stared at the plaster and the swelling around it.

'Christ, Skip.'

Gonsalves glared at him in the mirror. 'Never mind. I have a job needs doing. It's worth ten thousand US to you.'

Boutros gulped. He had a feeling he knew what was coming next. 'Sure. What do you want done?'

'The girl,' Gonsalves' lips tightened. 'I want her got rid of...'

Boutros was very glad indeed he'd played this scenario out already in his mind. He sat down slowly, using the table for support. He had known Gonsalves for years, had done many small jobs for the man and knew him to be both ruthless and violent. He had also seen Gonsalves crossed by a woman before; had helped patch her up afterwards. 'That's going too far, Skip. Shit.'

Gonsalves turned from the mirror, his face a mask of cold rage. 'That's why I'm paying you ten thousand to do it. What did you think would be worth ten thou? Clean the decking? Nip down to the store and get some smokes?'

Boutros glanced down at his hands. *Yallah, gently now, Magdy, not too keen, now.* 'I don't know, Skip. I never did that before.'

'Time to grow up then, Boutros. It couldn't be easier, man. Give her a jab and put her over the side. Weigh her down. Job done. But I want her off my fucking boat. I swear to God the only reason I'm not doing it myself is I don't want to cover the fucking place in her blood.'

'But Martinez, the other crew...'

'Will be asleep. I'll take the watch.'

Moving his hand left a wet mark on the veneer table top. Boutros hesitated, an iron tang in his mouth. 'Twenty.'

Gonsalves shifted his weight. Boutros managed to stop himself cowering. He raised his eyes to meet Gonsalves' glare, his voice strengthening as the immediate danger passed. He licked his lip. 'Twenty thousand dollars.'

Gonsalves moved to the door and pulled it open. 'Fifteen. Now get the fuck out of my sight before I change my mind. Midnight, I want her gone. Nice and clean.'

Boutros turned in the doorway, but Gonsalves was already closing the door, forcing him to step backwards. His nose almost touching the door, Boutros nodded to himself.

Earlier that evening, Magdy Boutros had made a decision. Now he knew it was the right one and he felt calm and certain, despite the sweat and his trembling hands. He was going to save Elli Hoffmann's life.

Taking one of her tablets chased the darkness away. Elli was grateful they had left her handbag. Her sense of time seemed to have deserted her, day and night flowing into each other. She watched Boutros working. She shivered as he plunged the syringe into the last of the four vials of Fentanyl, sucking the drug up to spray it into the sink.

He turned off the tap and placed the kidney dish by her bedside. 'Don't be afraid. It's going to be okay.'

She smiled at him. 'I am not afraid. I am cold.'

He placed some twists of cotton wool soaked in alcohol in the dish next to the syringe and vials. 'I'm sorry. I'll try and get you new clothes later. You ready?'

She nodded. 'Yes. Thank you.'

He pulled at the heavy bundle of sacking wrapped in her clothes, dragging it to the door.

He opened the door a crack and peered out. 'Now.'

He dragged the bundle behind him down the corridor, Elli followed, clutching the greatcoat he had brought. She crept along in her bare feet. He pushed a cabin door open to his right, pausing to hold three fingers up to her as he heaved the bundle down the corridor towards the aft deck and the swimming platform. She recalled his urgent words to her. *I'll open the door to my cabin on the way down. There'll be no funny business. You're to lock it and only open to three taps. Hear me? Three taps.*

She ducked into the cabin and shut the door quickly. She turned the lock, pausing to listen at the door to the heavy sliding sounds of Boutros dragging her sacking-filled doppelganger down the corridor. The aft bulkhead banged. She strained to hear more.

Elli was in a stranger's cabin on a ship wearing little more than a greatcoat, a crazy notion which made her grin briefly. She scanned the room, similar to hers, a functional space with a single bed and a locker, a small desk squeezed between the bed and the wall. A metal-lined hatchway set into the carpeted floor glittered in the halogen lighting. She supposed the doorway opposite the bed led to a bathroom, the same as her cabin. She pulled the coat tight and sat on the bed to wait.

The silence was oppressive. Footsteps sounded in the corridor outside, breaking into her reverie. She tensed at the knock on the door. Two taps. She tried not to breathe. It was wrong. He had said three taps. Two taps again, a confident double rap. *Efficient. A confident knock. Can you knock a door confidently?* She shook her head, banishing the silly thoughts. Thank God for her pills. The key snicked in the lock and she bit her lip to stop herself crying out. Dread seized her and she tried desperately not to move back from the danger in case she made a sound. A violent ague shook her. She was sweating. Her hands trembled. She held her breath. Her throat ached from locking the screams in. The darkness crept back, satanic laughter in her ears as the door was pushed open.

*

Boutros staggered on the moonlit aft deck, hands on hips, panting. The foaming wake stretched into the dark expanse. The bundle bobbed once before it disappeared into the foam, the anchor he had tied to it taking it deep down to the seabed below.

Not a religious man, Boutros nevertheless crossed himself. He smiled at the gesture given he had consigned some sacking and women's clothing to the deeps. He turned away, striking out along the aft deck to the rear door, stepping over the bulkhead into the corridor serving the crew quarters. He froze. Gonsalves stood at his cabin door with a key in the lock. His heart hammering, he pushed the door shut behind him and forced himself to walk as normally as he could up the corridor.

'Skip?'

'Done?'

Boutros swept his hand back through his hair. 'Yes. Done.'

'Good. Good job, Magdy. Clear out her cabin, then. Get rid of all the Fentanyl.'

'Yes, Skip. Leave it with me. Something you wanted?'

Gonsalves looked down at his hand and pulled his master key from the door. He shook his head. 'No, no. Nothing. Just thought you were in there and hadn't heard me knocking.'

Gonsalves smiled, nodded and strode up the corridor. Boutros turned to his cabin. The door swung open in the swell to reveal Elli on his bed. She was holding the duvet to her as protection, her legs pedalling on the mattress, trying to push herself into the wall. Her face reddened and crumpled. He moved quickly, signalling her to silence and whipping the cabin door shut behind him. Squatting by the bed, his finger held to his lips, Boutros waited for her to calm.

Her voice quivered. She wiped at her eyes. 'It was him, wasn't it? He knocked wrong. I felt him in my head. He's evil.'

'It's okay, it's okay. You're safe now. Just keep very, very quiet. I need to get you some clothes from the laundry. We dock at Valetta in two hours. We need to get you off this tub while it's still dark. Can you swim?'

She was wide-eyed. 'Yes, yes I can. Did you keep the pills from my bag like I ask?'

'Sure. Here. What are they for?'

'It doesn't matter. Do you have some water? I'm thirsty.'

He fetched her a glass of water and she drank. He paused by the door. 'Remember, no noise. And three taps, right?'

She nodded. 'Right.'

Boutros crept down the corridor to the guest cabin, where he gathered up the syringes and ampoules, and scanned the room for any other trace of Elli's stay there. He added a bloodied flannel to his collection and took the staircase up to the pantry on the main deck, where he placed the kidney dish and unused syringes in the medical store. He wrapped the rest in a plastic bag, weighted it down with a tin of beans and pushed it out of the porthole, the cool night air filled with the splashing of the big boat's progress through the calm sea. He took the companionway down to the crew quarters and stepped into the laundry room, thankful one of the washing machines was still on, its noise masking his movements. Boutros rooted through the clothes in the drier, hoping to find some of little Panamides' clothes. The dark, silent man from Bogota hadn't been teased about his tiny stature by the other crewmembers, perhaps on account of the knife he was always sharpening.

Boutros pulled out a t-shirt and a pair of pants. Rolling them up tight and tucking them under his arm he stole out of the laundry, passing the silent crew's mess.

Boutros stole past the other crew rooms and gave three gentle taps on his cabin door before pushing it open. He stepped into the room.

She stood behind the door, the heavy-based table lamp clutched in her hand. Boutros' puzzlement gave way to a grin and he prised it from her trembling fingers. 'Relax. It's going to be okay. Everyone's asleep apart from Gonsalves up on the bridge. Here, I brought some clothes. You'll just have to wear socks until we can get you to a shop or something.'

Boutros waited by her as she slept, looking down at her fragile form curled up on the bed. There was something about her made you want to protect her, he mused, noting the dark shadows around her eyes. He thought back to the journey from the hotel in Hamburg to the boat, holding her down and giving her the first dose of the Fentanyl which Gonsalves believed Boutros had used to kill her. Now Boutros' own life was in danger, too. He reached down and shook her gently, his hand poised over her face in case she screamed. She woke slowly. She opened her mouth, peeling her dry lips apart. 'Water. Why I am so thirsty?'

'It's a side effect of the anaesthetic. Sorry.'

She sat up as he filled the glass, took it from him with a smile and drank. Her voice was croaky. 'Why you decide to help me, Magdy?'

Why, indeed? Because I'm sweet on you? Because I'm

perhaps not as big a bastard as I thought I was? Just because

'I don't know. There's no time for talking about it right now, though. We're coming into Valetta. We've only got a few minutes before we dock at Marsamxett. You'll need to strip down to your underwear.' He handed her a plastic bag. 'We'll put your clothes in this and tape it up. Hopefully they'll stay dry.'

'Where do I go? To the police?'

Alarmed, Boutros almost cried out. 'No, God no. Gonsalves would kill me. I'm not joking, I mean it. Please no. We'll find somewhere you can go until the *Princess* has moved on. I'll come ashore and join you as soon as I can.'

'It all seems crazy.'

'Do you have a better idea?' Boutros' voice was soft, but she flinched.

She shook her head, her lip trembling and her hands clasped. 'No.'

'Let's move, then.'

'Actually, yes.' She was smiling as if touched by angels and Boutros felt his heart could break. 'Yes, I have the better idea. My father has a friend in Valetta. We can call him.'

'Elli, listen to me. I know this is difficult, but you are here because of your father. You can't go near him.'

'No, no you have not understood. Joseph Scerri is an old man, he is nothing to do with all of this. He will help me, I know. We can call him.'

Her voice had risen in her excitement and Boutros held her shoulder, his finger to his lips. 'Hush, for God's sake. Okay, we'll call him, but keep your voice down.'

She nodded and he dropped his hand. 'Do you know his number?'

She opened the laptop on the little desk. 'No, but we can look for him. What is your password, please?'

'It doesn't matter. The Inmarsat's down. We can't get Internet.'

She frowned. 'Okay, doesn't matter. Give me the password anyway.'

He reached across her and keyed it in. She waited, then tapped on the keyboard, her pretty face screwed up in concentration. 'Here. Can I borrow the mobile?'

Boutros marvelled at the change in her. 'Here. What are you doing?'

She flourished it at him. 'A signal, see? Vodaphone. I can get online.'

Boutros gave up trying to understand and watched her frowning concentration as she stabbed at the keyboard and thumbed away at the mobile's screen. Eventually she sat back with a triumphant look on her face. 'There. Now I can call him.'

'Yes, but you have to be quiet.'

'So I talk under the bedclothes like a little girl, then.' She flashed a grin at him, and took the handset, keying in the number from the laptop's screen. She dived under the duvet. After a few seconds, her muffled voice apologised for waking whoever it was she was talking to.

Boutros ran the shower to cover any sound she made. He stared out of the porthole in his bathroom at the lights of Valetta twinkling in the grey morning half-light as they slid past. She emerged triumphantly. 'You see? I knew he would help. My father has a reservation at the Excelsior Hotel. Mister Scerri is making another in my name. We can go there and hide.'

'Please, hush. We need to move now, we are about to dock. There is no time.'

She handed the mobile to him. 'Good. What do we do?'

'You need to take your clothes off now. So you can swim.'

She stopped smiling and stared at him, a long silent weighing up that pressed in on Boutros, who felt the colour rising to his cheeks. She reached down and pulled the t-shirt over her head, her full breasts held by her bra, the shadows of her dark nipples showing through the sheer material, pushing against it. The cold had hardened them. Boutros turned away in confusion. The plastic bag rustled. He helped her to press the air out and tape it up with masking tape, then taped it firmly to her warm upper leg.

He handed her the dark greatcoat. 'Here, put this on until you get into the water, it's better in the dark. Ready?'

She scanned his face uncertainly. 'Yes. Ready.'

They made it to the aft deck and its swimming platform as the big boat bumped against the wharf. When the lines were thrown, they made their move. Crouching low, Elli slipped into the water. Her pale skin flashed as she wriggled free of the greatcoat's dark embrace, twisting as she dived. He was surprised at how strong a swimmer she was, the long dive took her at least twenty-five metres from the yacht and Boutros could barely make out when she broke the surface to head around the rear of a smaller boat moored several empty berths over.

Boutros watched for a second more before he turned and hurried along the right hand gangway. He climbed to the bridge deck, waving at Blanc and Panamides standing on the wharf. Gonsalves was smoking and gazing at the lights of Valetta as dawn broke over Malta.

'Magdy. You did well last night.'

'Thanks, Skip. It was my... you know, the first...'

'You said. I appreciate that.' He blew smoke and smiled, clapping Boutros on the shoulder. 'Good man,

Magdy.'

'Is it okay to go ashore later, Skip? I sort of need to. You know. Let off steam.'

Gonsalves' face clouded. He regarded the tip of his cigarette. 'Sure, why not? We're sailing before lunchtime though, so you can't go too crazy out there. Not that there's much to do in Valetta, you understand? You can pick up a mobile SIM for me while you're there.'

Boutros nodded fervently. 'Aye, Skip. It's good to breathe in the land air sometimes. To get a taste of it, you know?'

'You're a romantic, Magdy. It'll get you in trouble one day, that big heart of yours. Be back by eleven, you hear? You don't tell anyone a word about this boat. Not a word.'

'Sure, Skip. Thanks.' Boutros grinned. He slid down the stairwell and spent an hour pacing in his berth, marking time so he didn't appear too eager to get ashore.

Boutros took a long shower, splashed on aftershave, slicked back his hair, and took care to dress well. Finally, he strode down the gangplank past surly little Panamides leaning on the railing and smoking. Boutros' heart felt like a kettle drum, the blood rushed in his ears, every second an eternity expecting to hear a shout behind him. The early morning sunlight was on his back.

He struck out down the wharf and rounded the corner towards the main road leading off Manoel Island. He had arranged to meet Elli at the Excelsior, and he looked forward to being with her in safety.

It wasn't until he reached the main road he patted his pocket for his mobile phone. He hesitated for a second, but there was no way he was going back on that boat now. Boutros cursed and walked on, glancing back every now and then, just in case.

Chapter Twenty

Lynch hadn't been in Malta two minutes before catching up with his old friend – Paul Tomasi was waiting at the top of the jetway as the plane disgorged its weary passengers. In his early forties, tanned and fit, Tomasi was flanked by police officers. Lynch recognised him instantly, the swarthy features and impish grin that marked a man who didn't necessarily take a career in law enforcement as an invitation to lose his humanity or lust for life. One of the policemen took Lynch's wheelie-bag as Tomasi stepped forward and threw his arms around him.

'Gerald Lynch, you old rascal. Welcome to Malta.'

Lynch grinned. 'Paul Tomasi, by God. It's been a long time.'

They backed up to survey each other. Tomasi laughed. 'Come on, we'll whisk you through immigration like magicians.'

They chatted as the police officers managed the formalities. Lynch punched his old friend's arm. 'So how the fuck did you get involved in this one, Paul?'

'A job like this would naturally come to me these days. I got promoted to Director of Enforcement last year. They reckoned I'd messed up enough over at SIAT and pushed me uphill, some idea I'd do less damage behind a desk.'

The easy, self-deprecating lie wasn't lost on Lynch, who had known Tomasi as the head of Malta's small but efficient Special Investigation Action Team. Lynch cast his memory back into his turbulent history as an SIS operative in the Levant and to the operation against the Iranian-backed gang smuggling Lebanese-refined heroin into Europe through Malta. 'It's been, what, five years?'

Tomasi was lost in thought for a second. He nodded, 'Sure. Five years. And you know what? Those bastards we worked so hard together to put behind bars got free before we ever got the chance to meet each other again. They released Renzo last August, you know? The fucker's back in Malta now walking free on the street and there's not a thing we can do about it. Tell me, how does that work, eh, Gerald?'

Lynch's face darkened. 'I didn't know, Paul. It's crap. He was down for a fifteen-year stretch. I attended court for that one.'

'Yeah, right. Good behaviour. Like someone fucked up enough to ship heroin will ever understand good behaviour. We should have kept him in Malta to do his stretch. I'd have made sure he didn't get out before his time.'

'Sorry. You know how the deal panned out.'

'Yeah, yeah. I know. Is this going to go the same way, then?'

'This is way bigger. Way, way bigger.' Lynch grinned. 'And it's travelling the other way, too. This one's going from Europe to the Middle East.'

Tomasi held Lynch's eyes for a second then nodded. 'We're two minutes away from my headquarters. You can brief us when we get there.'

As they left the airport building, a large black Lincoln pulled up. They got into the back, the front seat taken up by a burly army man with a shaven head and high cheekbones.

Tomasi did the honours. 'Gerald, this is Captain Gabriel Lentini. He heads up the unit of C Company we're working with on this one. You might not know C Company, but they're the Maltese version of your Special Boat Squadron. We've got some SBS boys here helping us out with this too. They're reporting to Captain Lentini.'

Lentini leaned back, his thick neck creasing as he turned to offer his hand. Lynch took it. 'Good to meet you, Captain.'

'Call me Gabe,' Lentini replied in a soft, high-pitched voice.

Tomasi's voice was tight with excitement. 'There are four teams watching the yacht and we have patrol boats on standby on the seaward side of Grand Harbour. We've delayed their refuelling with a cock and bull story about shortages on the island because of a fuel-workers' strike. Gabe and his boys are going in tonight.'

Lynch had nodded in acknowledgement. 'I'm impressed, Paul. What about Freij?'

'We don't know where he is. His jet's parked up at the airport but we got the heads up from Brian Channing too late to track him. And we have no record at all of any Peter Meier coming to Malta. Certainly not by air.'

The ancient city of Valetta sped past, winding streets of deep yellow stone buildings capped by terracotta-tiled roofs. Lynch longed for a shot of energy drink or another strong coffee. The car smelled of leather, the pale seats soft and comfortable, the powerful engine a soporific bass hum.

The jerk of the car drawing to a halt wakened him. He glanced around to discover Paul Tomasi looking sympathetically at him from the open door. 'Come on, Gerald, let's get on with this. You can sleep after tonight.'

Lynch rubbed his eyes. 'Where are we?'

'Police headquarters, Floriana.'

'Sorry, Paul. Too much flyin' around I guess.'

*

Lynch rang the doorbell, replaying Channing's words in his mind. 'Joseph Scerri. Expert on Enigma, Ultra and all that wartime stuff. Lives alone out in the country, place called Sh'ayra. He's an old man, Lynch. Go gently, you hear me? None of your rough house stuff.'

He waited on Scerri's doorstep, shivering. The early afternoon light was pale and weak, presaging more rain. His patience was rewarded with the sound of shuffling footsteps and fumbling chains. The door opened and Scerri peered at him from the dark interior. Lynch smiled reassuringly.

'Peter Jones. We spoke on the phone.'

Scerri's white hair was combed over a balding head spotted with age freckles. His eyes were red-rimmed with heavy bags. He wore a loose-fitting jumper, a remnant of a younger man's clothing. His deep voice was stronger than he looked.

'Yes, yes, I know. You had better come in.'

Lynch brushed past the old man into a corridor lined with books and tottering stacks of papers, the swirled brown and beige carpet matched by dark cream textured wallpaper. The over-warm house smelled musty and airless.

'Living room's first on the left,' said Scerri as he closed the door. 'Coffee?'

'No thanks, just had breakfast,' Lynch replied. He had, too. A tray of lukewarm omelette on the plane from Beirut treated with a powerful flavour-removing process and a mean cup of cold coffee served just in time for him to have finished eating the food. Lynch wasn't a happy flier.

Scerri gestured to the room. 'Sit, sit, do.'

Lynch avoided the worn armchair, obviously Scerri's favourite. He found a space on the sofa between the piles of books. He picked up one of the weighty volumes and read the dust jacket. 'Enigma Symposium. X and Y Sections.'

Scerri let himself down into his chair. 'Yes. It's rather been my life's work, you know. That's one of Hugh Skillen's books you have there. A great researcher into Enigma. He worked on de-Nazifying German radio with Airey Neave, actually. A wonderful man. Marvellous linguist. A Scot.'

Lynch shifted on the soft cushions, stemming the slide of a pile of books with a grab. 'Well, as I said on the phone, I am writing a feature for the magazine on Enigma and the community around it, particularly Bletchley and the museum. Mr Hoffmann was very kind to give me a great deal of his time and he did suggest that you were *the* authority.'

Scerri harrumphed. 'Enigma killed my parents, Mr Jones. The breaking of the Enigma code meant the Allies were able to read German naval and army signals. The intelligence this gave them was obviously of inestimable value. So much so that when the British found the Germans were planning a major air assault on Malta through an intercepted Enigma message, Churchill decided to sacrifice our island rather than let the Germans know the Allies had broken the code. They bombed us mercilessly day and night as we cowered in the caves, unprepared and ill-supplied to withstand their terrible rage. I was barely more than a child. I left my parents in order to forage for scraps. They were gone when I returned. There was nothing remaining of them. Nothing.'

Lynch was silent as Scerri took off his half-frame glasses and polished them on his tie, his watery eyes lidded. He replaced them on his prominent nose and glared at Lynch. 'I grew up wanting to know what it was my parents died for. I was in the army here, made it something of a specialisation, you see. And when I retired, particularly after Fran died, it gave me a focus. Something to *do*.'

Lynch nodded. 'So this shared interest is how you met Gerhardt Hoffmann.'

'A shared *passion*. We met at an Enigma Symposium in the UK many years ago. As you'll know, his father was in the Abwehr. He is a respected authority. We are to meet this week. He is coming to Valetta.' Scerri blinked owlishly. 'I am surprised he did not tell you, in fact, if you had already interviewed him.'

'He didn't mention it.'

Scerri's face showed his growing confusion. 'But he is meeting his daughter here, joining her on his yacht. He would surely have mentioned it if you were talking to him about Enigma and coming to Malta.' Scerri scanned Lynch's face. He raised an accusing forefinger. It trembled. 'You're not a journalist at all, are you? What *are* you, Mr Jones?'

Lynch's voice was gentle. 'No, no I'm not.' He hunched forwards, his hands opening. 'I am sorry, but Gerhardt Hoffmann is dead.'

Scerri slumped back, winded. 'Good God.'

The shock and confusion on Scerri's face turned to indignation. He straightened. 'So what the hell are you doing here then?'

'I'm working with European intelligence. I'm investigating Hoffmann's death. We believe he was murdered by a man called Meier. Peter Meier.'

'His brother-in-law? Why would Meier kill Hoffmann? I am sorry, Mr Jones, but you have introduced me to a new world and I rather think I prefer my old one,' Scerri gestured at the book-strewn room.

Lynch sat forward. 'Do you know Meier?'

'I have met him. He tried to sell me an Enigma once, but I refused it. I believed it to have been stolen. I did not much care for the man, to tell you the truth.'

'Where did you meet him?'

'Here. He was in Valetta earlier this year, in fact. A flashy type, stayed at the Excelsior. Hoffmann always stayed at the British Hotel, although for some reason this time he asked me to book the Excelsior. I joked with him about coming into a fortune and he said that indeed he had.' Scerri paused, musing. 'Was it over money, then, he was killed?'

'Do you know why Meier was in Malta, Mr Scerri?'

Scerri rounded on him with the unpredictable asperity of age. 'No, I didn't. He was on his way to Albania.'

'Albania?'

'Yes. Vlorey. Vlora? Something like that. He was going on a cruise, he said. Seemed to find it highly amusing. Didn't seem the type to tell you the truth. Fran and I used to enjoy cruises, you know. We toured every summer.'

Lynch rose to leave. 'Thank you, Mr Scerri. I believe I have disturbed you enough. I am sorry to have brought you bad news.' He turned at the doorstep. 'This is my number, Mr Scerri. If you think of anything which might be of assistance to our investigation, I'd appreciate a call.'

Scerri took the card in his age-spotted hand. 'His yacht. The *Arabian Princess*. It docked here this morning.'

Lynch froze in amazement. 'How did you know that?'

Scerri blinked, a look of mild puzzlement on his face as if the knowledge had come as a surprise to him as well. 'Why, his daughter of course. Elli. She called me. Very early, in fact. Woke me and I'm an early riser as a rule. She wanted to know where her father was staying. I made a reservation at the Excelsior for her as well. I did think it was odd she hadn't called her dad. I supposed it was on account of the argument. They had fallen out, he told me. He was hoping they could reconcile here in Valetta. But now we know she couldn't have called him at any price, could she? Poor, lost child.'

'You *know* her?'

Scerri whickered crustily, one hand on the door. 'Of course I know her. I dandled her on my knee. They found it difficult recently, I understand. Getting on, I mean. But children are like that, aren't they?'

'Do you have children?' Lynch regretted the automatic question as Scerri withdrew into himself with a pained look.

'Yes,' he said, with an air of finality. 'We did. Goodbye, Mr Jones.'

Lynch nodded. 'Thank you, Mr Scerri. Thank you very much.'

His boots skittered on the tiled steps down to the nondescript car Tomasi had lent him. The customs guy, Duggan, had said Elli Hoffmann was kidnapped by Meier, that he thought she may be on the boat. The boat was here in Malta, Freij was here and now Elli Hoffmann was here. Everything converges on Valetta, Lynch thought as he sped through the country roads. Meier must be here, too. If he had kidnapped Elli, he must be with her now. The thought of catching Michel Freij tied to a kidnapping, a murderer and a boat full of nuclear warheads brought Lynch great and savage joy.

Lynch called Paul Tomasi. 'Paul? Gerald. Okay, Scerri's been in contact with the Hoffmann girl. She's at the Excelsior.'

Tomasi's voice was incredulous. 'She's supposed to be on the damn yacht. What's she doing at the Excelsior? This all gets more insane by the minute. We have one of the crew in custody. He just walked off the yacht this morning, shortly after she docked. The watchers tracked him for a while then picked him up when he was well clear. He didn't seem to know where the hell he was going. Or at least, he wasn't saying.'

Lynch shifted the mobile against his ear as he negotiated a turn in the winding coast road. 'What does he know?'

'Whatever it is, he's not telling. He's crying for a lawyer and much as I'd like to, I can't torture the bastard.'

'I'll be there as soon as I can. Can you put the Excelsior under observation?'

'We'll have the place locked down within thirty minutes. We're holding the crew member here at Floriana. You want to come here or meet at the hotel?'

Lynch thought fast. 'I'll come to you. There's something odd about an international weapons smuggler wandering off his ship for tea in Valetta. I'll call you when I get lost. Give it about three minutes.'

Tomasi laughed easily. 'Sure enough.'

There was a small gap between the piles of books and papers on the table next to Joseph Scerri's armchair and it was here he carefully placed his cup of tea, giving himself up to the chair's embrace with a sigh. Living in a fine, scholarly solitude, he resented journalists who weren't journalists. Sighing, he picked his gold-rimmed glasses up from the tatty cloth and settled them on his nose, peering at the text in his hand until it came into focus. He settled back, licking his finger to turn the dry paper, the muted clock marking insistent seconds. The sunbeam falling across the top of the chair warmed him and the paper fell as he dozed. The sound of the kitchen door closing woke him and he sat up, blinking and peering to bring the room into focus. The blur in front of him resolved into a man.

Scerri frowned. 'Oh. It's you.'

Peter Meier smiled. 'Good morning, Herr Scerri. I trust you are well.'

Scerri nodded. 'As can be expected. What brings you here?'

Meier stepped forwards. 'Oh, just tidying up a few loose ends. You took a telephone call this morning.'

Puzzled, Scerri was querulous. 'Yes, from Elli Hoffmann. She is here in Valetta.'

'Staying where, precisely?'

'The Excelsior, room 255. I told the journalist that.'

Meier stilled, poised with his hand in his jacket. 'What journalist?'

'Jones was his name. Peter Jones. He was looking for Elli. 'What happened to Hoffmann, Meier?'

Meier's face was grim as he withdrew his hand. 'Never you mind.'

The bullet punched through the back of the armchair, blowing out a cloud of kapok and cloth tatters. Scerri's hand spasmed, his cold tea splashing upwards, papers tumbling to the floor. The impact pushed him back deep into the chair and his body bounced slackly.

Meier turned away. The kitchen door opened and closed again, a slight coolness in the air.

A band of steel tightened around Scerri's chest and stopped his breath. He tasted blood, but felt no pain as the dark sleep crept up on him. He fought against it, scrabbling for his pen, his hand shaking as the strength ebbed from his fingers.

Breathing in the iron tang of his own blood, Joseph Scerri cried out to his beloved Fran in exultation. He let the sleep overwhelm him and take him to her.

*

Tomasi strode up waving a sheaf of papers as Lynch was getting out of the car outside police headquarters in Floriana. 'We've got Scerri's call records. One incoming call from a roaming mobile this morning. He's placed a number of calls to Albania in the past ten days as well. We're trying to get a trace on the numbers from the Albanians. You ready to have a chat with sailor boy? Name's Magdy Boutros. Sounds Lebanese, right? He's being smart and we can't get a thing out of him. He keeps insisting on a lawyer. We thought you might be able to help. The one thing we know is that he walked off the *Arabian Princess* and seemed to be very glad to leave the boat behind him.'

'Sure. What about the girl?'

'In her room. Checked in early this morning and hasn't moved since according to the staff. We've got a surveillance team on the hotel. I've instructed them to observe and report, no intervention. They're plugged into the hotel's CCTV system.'

Tomasi led the way from the spring sunshine and into the shade of the police station. 'I've asked Gabe Lentini to come over from the barracks and join us. He's very keen to find out more about the layout of the boat and Boutros should be able to help. Ah, here he is. I was just explaining to Gerald your interest in our friend from the boat.'

Lentini fell in with them. 'Sure. Logically the ordnance is stored in the pool area, but we can't be sure. It complicates the action. And I don't like assumptions.'

Lynch stopped dead in the corridor. 'Ordnance?'

'Yes, the guns these guys are smuggling,' Lentini piped.

It never failed to anger him, this insistence on putting

brave men's lives at risk for dumb lies. Lynch's career was crammed with incidents where the men on the ground were misled as to the true aims and goals of operations, the real risk of the actions they were asked to undertake. *Secrecy be fucked*, he thought.

'Gabe, the *Arabian Princess* is believed by my masters to be carrying two stolen one hundred kiloton Soviet nuclear warheads. If they were triggered, Malta would be a new Atlantis. You need to be taking radiation precautions.'

Lentini turned to Paul Tomasi, who had placed a hand against the wall for support, his face a picture of amazement. Tomasi held up his hand to ward off Lentini's questions. 'Gerald, are you fucking us around here?'

Lynch frowned. 'No, Paul. I'm not. That's the payload they're tracking this boat for, not a few guns. Your best bet would be to pass a Geiger counter over that poor fucker in your cells, not a lie detector.'

Lentini's high voice was furious. 'This is unacceptable. We were going in with no knowledge of this.'

Lynch forestalled him. 'Look, just kit your guys up properly now you know. I didn't tell you, right? There's a lot riding on how you do this tonight. I don't know why they haven't told you guys the whole truth, but I do know they were very keen indeed to keep this from going public. Like I said, just make sure your guys are well equipped. And don't tell anyone I told you.'

Lentini stared at Lynch for a few long seconds, then nodded slowly. 'Sure. Thanks.'

They reached the door of the interview room, a police constable standing by. Tomasi signalled for him to open the door and let Lynch enter first. The small room was bare, two cheap plastic chairs either side of a wooden table. The strip lights hummed, casting a pallid light over the gloss-painted walls and grey floor.

Boutros was sitting hunched on one of the plastic chairs. He wore a t-shirt, a leather jacket slung over the back of his chair. His back straightened up as they entered, a look of forlorn hope on his swarthy, drawn face.

Lynch pulled up the plastic chair facing Boutros. Tomasi and Lentini took up positions behind him. Boutros' eyes darted between the three of them. His knuckles were white, the muscles on his forearm knotted.

Lynch smiled, his voice factual and a little bored. 'You are Magdy Boutros, a member of the crew of the *Arabian Princess*. Am I correct?'

'I want a lawyer.'

Lynch's tone didn't change. He leaned back. 'You are being held in Maltese police headquarters in Floriana. The gentlemen behind me represent the Maltese police and special forces. I am an officer in British intelligence and I will beat the living shit out of you if you do not cooperate fully and immediately because I do not have the luxury of time. Do you understand me?'

Boutros scanned Lynch's face, his eyes again darting to Tomasi and Lentini, both silent against the wall. He swallowed. 'Yes.'

'You are, I understand, a Lebanese national. Is that correct?'

'Yes.'

'How old are you, Magdy?'

'Thirty-two.'

Lynch scrutinised Boutros' face as he responded, noting the direction of the man's eyes as he answered.

'When did you leave Beirut?'

'I moved to Munich four years ago.'

'Really? Why?'

'A girl, a German girl. We were going to settle down.'

'The *Arabian Princess* is a fifty-metre Luxe Marine

superyacht that sailed from Hamburg just over two weeks ago. Is that correct?'

'Yes. Yes, it is.'

'Do you like sailing?'

The question disconcerted Boutros. He thought for a second. 'Yes.'

Lynch had it now. Eyes left for recall, right for invention. The behavioural pattern in all of us that betrays our lies in the hands of trained interrogators.

'Where did you join the yacht, Magdy? In Hamburg, the Czech Republic, or Bremerhaven?'

Either Boutros was a brilliant actor or he was genuinely puzzled. 'Czech Republic?'

'Never mind. Do you know what cargo the *Arabian Princess* is carrying?'

Boutros shook his head, 'No cargo. Just ...'

'Just what, Magdy?'

Boutros took a deep breath. 'Just a girl.'

'Just a girl. Elli Hoffmann.'

Boutros shifted in his chair, his eyes wary. 'Yes. Elli Hoffmann.'

Lynch leaned forward, his voice still measured. 'Has Michel Freij visited the boat?'

Boutros shook his head. 'Don't know any Michel Freij.'

'Tall man, Lebanese. Oiled-back hair, goatee beard.'

'No. I left anyway, soon as I could.'

'Why did you leave the boat, Magdy?'

Boutros was sweating. 'To help Elli. They hired me to sedate her and make sure she was looked after. Gonsalves tried to rape her and it was too much. I helped her escape. He wanted her killed.'

'Gonsalves?'

'The captain of the *Princess*. Joel Gonsalves. He's a Portugese.'

'Do you know where Elli Hoffmann is now, Magdy?'

Boutros stared at Lynch, sweat beading his forehead. His mouth tightened in resolve. Lynch whipped his hand across the table, the stinging flat-palmed blow to Boutros' cheek unseated him. Lentini moved fast, picking Boutros up and pinning him against the wall. A fast, economical punch to the stomach forced a cry from Boutros' throat. Lentini picked him up and pushed him back onto the plastic seat Lynch had righted. Boutros sobbed.

'I told you.' Lynch shot a cuff. 'We haven't got time to mess around, Magdy. Where's Elli Hoffman?'

Boutros' eyes were on his clasped hands. 'At the Excelsior, waiting for me. She had a contact here, a guy that knew her father.'

'Joseph Scerri.'

Boutros nodded.

'Where is Peter Meier? Is he with Elli?'

'Elli's alone. I don't know any Peter Meier.'

'Have you looked in the pool area of the boat, Magdy?'

'No.' Boutros glanced at Lentini and Tomasi before his eyes returned to Lynch. 'What's in there?'

'Is there any other area of the ship that is blocked off or being used as a storage space?'

Boutros wiped perspiration from his forehead, his hand shaking. 'No. There are cabins that aren't being used, we're on a skeleton crew, but we haven't been told we can't go anywhere.'

Lentini's voice shrilled. 'How many crew?'

Boutros turned to face the big man. 'Four. There's myself, a cook called Blanc and two sailors, both speak Spanish and little else. Panamides and Martinez.'

Lentini crossed his arms. 'Have you been taking any precautions against radiation? Monitoring?'

Boutros' face was ashen. '*Radiation*? What the fuck's

going on here?'

Nobody answered him. Lynch turned in his chair. 'Paul, I think the best thing we can do right now is pick up the Hoffmann girl. I think we should bring Magdy along if he's what she's expecting. And then I think Gabe and his boys need to do their thing as fast as possible.'

Tomasi opened the door. 'Agreed. Come on, I'll get you a firearm organised.'

Chapter Twenty-One

The black Lincoln pulled up under the portico of Valetta's Grand Excelsior Hotel. Lentini snapped instructions into his walkie-talkie. The driver opened the door, helping Magdy Boutros step down. He was handcuffed. Lynch waited as Paul Tomasi rounded the big car to reach them. Tomasi waved the hotel staff back. The Lincoln pulled away and they waited under the portico for Lentini to finish giving instructions to his team.

Lynch started at the splash of red light across Boutros' forehead. He turned to shove the man. Boutros stiffened oddly, rooted to the spot with a look of comical surprise on his face, a neat hole in his forehead. The beige wall behind him turned misty red. The busy traffic outside the hotel compound masked the sound. Time stood still for a moment. Silence reigned. Stasis.

Boutros collapsed. Lynch cried out and reached for his gun. Lentini was already crouched with his pistol held in both hands, scanning the one building that had a clear line of sight to them. The tower was on the opposite side of the road. Tomasi was slower to react, his hand on his mouth, staring.

Lynch called to Lentini. 'Gabe. The girl.'

The big man nodded once and Lynch was off, sprinting along the hotel's frontage towards the tower, gun in hand. He passed a puzzled pedestrian. Alarm registered on the man's face as he saw the gun. Lynch's feet hammered tarmac. He ran into the road, his jacket flapping. Car horns sounded. Tyres screeched. He raced for the apartment building, rounding the corner to its rear to come up against an area of scrubland. Nothing moved. The fire escape door was closed.

Lynch stood panting, the Walther hanging useless in his hand.

Sirens sounded as Lynch returned to the hotel. Someone had already put a blanket over Boutros' body, but it hadn't stretched to covering the dark splash on the steps or the carmine stain on the wall. He strode past into the plush hotel lobby, two soldiers in brown and green camouflage stood to one side holding machine guns, white on black 'Malta' labels on their chests, an incongruity in the opulent setting. Tomasi peeled away from the girl at the reception desk and took Lynch's shoulder.

'Come on, it's upstairs.'

Lynch caught his tone. 'She's dead.'

'Yes.' Tomasi pressed the lift button.

They didn't speak as they waited in the lift. Lentini's men greeted them as they walked out, more camouflage and crew cuts in the corridor. They nodded at Tomasi. 'That way, sir.'

The door was very broken indeed. Beyond it, Lentini stood with another soldier who avoided looking at the bed.

Lynch turned to it.

She had been pretty, he had to admit. She had short cut, bleached-blonde hair, an elfin attractiveness. In death, her pale skin had become alabaster. She had given up the struggle to live, the peaceful look on her face a counterpoint to the livid marks around her neck. She had been strangled.

Lynch pulled out a hankie and picked up a packet from the bedside table. 'Risperdal?'

Tomasi shrugged. Lynch opened the packet and shook

out the folded wad of thin paper. He read the fact sheet intently. Lentini murmured instructions to his trooper, who left the room without ever looking at the bed. A squeamish soldier, thought Lynch. Interesting.

'It's used to treat schizophrenia.' Lynch laughed. 'Oh, sweet mother of Jesus, she was a schizophrenic.'

Tomasi frowned, gesturing at the corpse. 'Please, Gerald. Come on.'

Lynch rounded on him. 'Paul, do you not see this? We are about to mount an armed raid on a billionaire presidential hopeful's superyacht, with patrol boats and the air force in support. I have been chasing around Europe like some mad fucker for a week and we've got a major intelligence operation ongoing in Beirut. There's a pan-European manhunt on for Meier. And it's all based on the testimony of a mad German prostitute.'

Tomasi held his hands up. 'Yet you tell me the arms dump was real. And this poor girl, Gerald, is clearly very dead and clearly very strangled. First Boutros, then her. Someone's clearing up.'

Lentini's eyebrows were raised, his walkie-talkie held near his ear as he waited for Lynch's verdict. Lynch's mouth tightened.

'Fuck it, we go ahead. We raid the boat.'

Lentini's bark into the walkie-talkie was helium-high, but it was a bark all the same.

Lynch sat in the car scanning the *Arabian Princess* through field glasses, the big boat's lights twinkling and joining the dancing reflections across Valetta's Lazaretto Creek in the dusk. Two Zodiacs were to approach from the seaward side of the big yacht, while the main boarding force would move in from land. He peered through the growing shadows.

'Coffee?'

Paul Tomasi offered the tiny plastic cup and Lynch's nose wrinkled at the pungent drink. He took it and raised it to Tomasi. 'Thanks.'

'I think we have a little time yet, Gerald. They will be very careful to plan everything and make sure they are perfectly set up. We don't get this sort of thing very often, so I know Gabe and his boys are keen not to fuck it up. The captain, Gonsalves, has been kicking up merry hell all afternoon about not being able to refuel, threatening lawsuits and all sorts. Strange, you'd have thought he'd want to keep his head down.'

Lynch nodded, sipping at the thick coffee. 'We go in straight after Lentini's boys, right?'

'They'll let us know when they're comfortable for us to join them. You know, this is a little more complicated than most enforcement operations.'

Lynch cupped the little plastic cup of hot drink in his hands, although the Mediterranean night was warm. 'Sure, I understand.' He gazed across the wharf and the water rippling in the distant moonlight. Lynch scanned the dock again through the glasses. Something shadowy seemed to move beside a rocky outcrop built into a wall, but he couldn't be sure.

Lynch adjusted the focus of the binoculars. 'Did you get the warrant for Freij's arrest?'

The silence made Lynch turn. Tomasi's face showed he had been dreading the question. 'No, Gerald. I'm sorry. There are no charges against Freij.'

Lynch's voice was as tight as his hands gripping the binoculars. 'What about fucking murder?'

Tomasi tried to keep his voice steady. 'No evidence, Gerald. My prosecutor wouldn't touch it with yours. I got told to leave well alone. Hands off. Official.'

Lynch jumped at the flash to his right. Shadowy figures swarmed across the concrete wharf like bounding rats. Muffled concussions reached them and he hit the window button to better hear the action. Tomasi strained for a view from the driver's seat.

The warm breeze bore the distant echo of shouts and the thump of smoke grenades. Shadows flitted across the boat's three stacked decks. Lynch fancied he saw one stick figure swallow-dive from the bow of the big boat. There was a brief, crackling burst of live fire.

Lynch jumped at Tomasi's shout. 'There. The signal.'

Lynch's head was slammed back against the headrest as Tomasi hit the accelerator, taking them down to the dock level. They pulled to a sharp halt. Blue lights flickered on the road above them and sirens sounded across the sleepy docks of Manoel Island.

Lynch sprinted up the gangplank. Lentini was waiting for him at the top, his white teeth gleaming in his blacked-out face. He was wearing a dark biohazard suit, a stark contrast to the bright white suits Lynch and Tomasi wore. Their hands slammed together.

'It's fine,' said Lentini. 'A walk in the park. She's ours.'

Lynch rasped urgently. 'The cargo? The pool space?'

Lentini's radio spat a series of urgent voices. 'We didn't open it yet. But there's no radiation reading at all from the counters. You want to go there first?'

'Sure,' Lynch said.

Lentini led the way to the pool on the afterdeck. Four of his men rolled back the heavy panelling covering it. Two freestanding floodlights had been set up and, together with the boat's own lighting, the whole area was bathed in light. The brass fittings glittered, the wooden decking faded into the shadows.

They peered as one into the area that should have been a swimming pool and the extra space created below it by the unpaid workers at Luxe Marine. Lentini gave a low whistle.

'Oh, fuck,' Lynch whispered.

The modified pool space was very deep indeed, a yawning chasm stretching at least four metres down, its depths shadowed despite the lighting Lentini's men had erected.

It was empty.

Chapter Twenty-Two

Lynch gazed around the butterscotch marble floors and red-carpeted staircases of the Hotel Grand Excelsior's lobby. 'It feels like I'm in the damn Gulf,' he complained to Paul Tomasi, who sipped his morning espresso.

He broke off as Gabe Lentini's bulk wove towards them through the clusters of tables and chairs scattered in the lobby lounge. Lynch pushed himself out of the dark wooden chair to stand and slap palms.

'Gabe. Great job last night.'

Lentini threw his rucksack down and sat. 'Thanks. But we didn't get what we were looking for, did we?'

'No.' Lynch shook his head. 'We have to keep that very, very quiet. London's in a massive panic about it. At least we know the boat's going nowhere.'

Tomasi cleared his throat and reached for his water glass. 'Well, not right now, Gerald. We can only hold the crew for forty-eight hours.'

Lynch gaped. 'They're a bunch of damned pirates, for God's sake.'

'Gerald, they've done nothing wrong. Without the cargo you were expecting, they're clean.'

'What about kidnapping Elli Hoffmann? What about Boutros saying the captain tried to rape her?'

Tomasi fingered his collar. 'There's a problem. The Hoffmann girl's medical history means she wouldn't have stood as a reliable witness. It's unfortunate, but there we are. She was travelling on Hoffmann's yacht on her way to meet her father, according to Gonzales, the captain. He says Boutros was hired as a nurse to look after her properly and he was a troublesome and disaffected employee who left the boat in Valetta in a huff. They were to meet Hoffmann here at Valetta and he claims not to know Hoffmann was dead. The boat is registered in Freij's name, there's a valid contract of transfer, the papers are all in order. The public prosecutor has advised that he doesn't believe we have a case to bring charges. To be frank, he told me to drop it like a stone. We've nothing to link any of them to Elli Hoffmann's murder. In fact, they have an impeccable alibi – we had them under close surveillance all day. We have to let Gonsalves and his crew go, Gerald. There are no legal grounds to hold the *Arabian Princess*.'

Lynch tried to keep his face impassive while he struggled to digest the information and map it to the events playing out around him. Now doubt was making him feel sick. If those warheads weren't on the yacht, where were they? Lynch found himself back in the damp of a cold war bunker talking to Branko Liberec, the huge doors that had guarded the missiles, the tyre tracks and churned up forest floor around the loading entrance, damp leaf mould and urgent voices. Men and women in white coveralls moving in taped-off zones.

Lynch gazed across to the hotel's reception area with sightless eyes, lost in thought. A figure standing there brought him back to reality. A tall figure, suited with a tiny gold tie stud. Wealthy. A goatee beard and brushed back hair. Michel Freij was laughing with the reception clerk. A portly man in his fifties next to Freij followed him from the reception desk to sit in the front area of the lobby. Lynch tried to rein in his racing mind, his heart thumping with the surge of adrenalin, the need to act coursing through his veins.

Mickey Fucking Freij. The cheeky bastard.

Lynch marched across the lobby, suppressing the urge to slide the Walther out of its holster under his left shoulder. The balding man talking to Freij was making a point, karate chopping one hand with the other. Lynch confronted them. Freij looked up with a quizzical smile that faded as he placed Lynch.

'Who the fuck do you think you are?' Lynch spat. 'You think you can just fly in here, arrange a couple of convenient murders and nip off home?'

Freij glanced across at the balding man, who was staring open-mouthed up at Lynch. 'I am sorry, John. This is Mr Gerald Lynch. He represents British *Intelligence*. He is becoming rather a nuisance.'

Tomasi and Lentini caught up with Lynch and paused behind him. He pointed at Freij, his Northern Irish accent thickened by his anger, his raised voice turning heads in the lobby. 'There is a dead girl upstairs in this hotel and a man murdered outside and do not tell me you didn't know it.'

Freij smiled up at the three men standing in front of him. 'I am so sorry, gentlemen, but this has absolutely nothing to do with me.' He rose and smoothed his jacket. 'Mr Lynch, I rather think that is enough. John is my legal counsel here in Malta, where we have today made a substantial investment in the Smart Village technology park. I have been in meetings with government representatives and developers for the past two days and can account fully for my movements. Your wild accusations are not only baseless but actionable. If you do not leave, I will instruct John to indeed act.'

Tomasi put a hand on Lynch's shoulder. 'Come on, Gerald. We can't do anything here.'

Lynch stepped forward and for the first time he saw Freij's brown eyes flicker. He stabbed his finger into the impassive face as he ground out the words. 'You're cool, Michel. But I am going to fucking nail you. So help me God

I am going to nail you.'

He turned on his heel and strode across the lobby. Tomasi and Lentini stared at Freij, who sat down again. Ignoring them, he turned to his lawyer. The pair exchanged a glance, shrugged and followed Lynch.

It was an uncharacteristically gloomy spring morning, the air bearing a mist of fine droplets, the precursor of rain. Lynch clicked the remote and crossed the road as the car beeped twice. The stippled sea was behind as he mounted the steps to the house, the green sward blowing in the freshening breeze.

He knocked on the front door and waited, surveying the sea and the patchy, wan sunlight dotting its surface. Lynch had a dreadful premonition. Someone had, indeed, been 'cleaning up' and he had been drawn back to the little house by the coast in Sh'ayra precisely because Scerri hadn't answered Lynch's repeated calls.

Lynch knocked again, cupping his hand over his eye to see into the dark interior. He picked his way through the garden rubbish along the side of the house, the air shimmering above the rusty heating flue. He pressed down on the kitchen door handle and felt it give, pulling it towards him and letting the warmth escape from inside.

He pulled a handkerchief from his pocket and placed it over his nose and mouth.

Striding through the kitchen and across the dining room, he pushed the living room door open to see the body of Joseph Scerri slumped in his chair, the carpet stained black with dried blood. Stuffing was spread in an arc on the floor behind the armchair. He felt oddly dispassionate at the sight of Scerri's violent end. The old man had lost control of his bowels at the moment of death.

Most of them do.

Belatedly, the reaction hit him and the room seemed to spin, bile forcing its way up his throat, an acrid tide he managed to stem as he turned and fled for the fresh air.

It had started to rain, the light drizzle carried on the cold breeze and Lynch held his face up to catch the water, rubbing himself in a washing ritual which didn't take away the dirt of Scerri's violent death or the memory of the cloying stench in the over-warm house. He called Tomasi.

'Gerald.'

'Scerri's dead.'

'Natural?'

'If shooting's natural.'

'You touch anything?'

'Nope. Looks like Scerri told Freij where to find the Hoffmann girl.'

'If it *was* Freij, Gerald.'

'Nobody else had a reason to want her dead, Paul.'

'What about the German? Meier?'

Lynch stood rooted to the spot, the cold drizzle making him shiver. Meier, the man they'd lost somewhere in Europe. The man who had killed Hoffman and his wife, Meier's own sister. There had been no *billets doux* left by the corpses in Malta, if that was truly Freij's pugmark. Meier, the deadly shadow.

'Gerald? Gerald? Look, I'll send our boys up. You'd better make yourself scarce if you want to avoid spending the rest of the year filling out paperwork.'

Lynch wiped the rain from his face again and used his coat sleeve to wipe the door handle. He walked along the side of the house and down the steps to the road and his car, staring at the grey horizon and the dark clouds gathering overhead.

Glad to leave the stench of death behind him, he drove quickly. Lynch had a flight home to catch and, at the end of it, an invitation to meet Leila in a sunny little apartment in Hamra.

.

Chapter Twenty-Three

Relieved to be back in Beirut, Lynch left the airport terminal and breathed the cool evening air, remembering his last arrival at the airport with Nathalie in tow. He was startled to see Tony Chalhoub walking towards him. Chalhoub's car was parked illegally on the kerbside directly outside arrivals. As head of police intelligence, Chalhoub rarely faced the consequences of his sloppy parking habits and, in fact, there was a policeman standing guard beside the car. Chalhoub was grim-faced as he approached and Lynch's stomach tightened with the premonition of bad news. Chalhoub took Lynch's hand in a two-handed press.

'Gerald, I'm sorry. Leila's dead.'

Lynch opened his mouth to speak, but his lips felt glued together. He shook his head, tears filling his eyes. Chalhoub's hand was around his shoulder propelling him towards the car, the policeman standing aside and saluting. Lynch wasn't there. Leila on top, smiling down at him. Leila laughing as they raced down the bumpy piste at Feraya, she skiing like a professional and he, military trained, rusty and less fluid in his movements. Her middle finger raised at him in triumph as he caught up with her at the bottom of the slope.

God, but she was gorgeous.

Lynch was silent as Chalhoub pulled away from the terminal, ghosts filling his head with perfume and softness and tears coursing down his cheeks.

The body on the gurney looked tiny, covered in green and

washed by the morgue's greyish light. The attendant was about to pull the cover back, but Chalhoub stayed her with a peremptory palm. His baggy, sad eyes asked Lynch if he was sure and Lynch nodded. Yes, he was. He wanted to see her.

The cloth was folded back. Lynch felt he was outside himself looking down on them both, he fearful and she in repose. The assistant, her gaze downcast, left the room. Chalhoub stayed.

Leila's face was calm. She looked as if she were asleep. Lynch stepped forward, touched her icy cheek, held a strand of her hair. He spoke for the first time since leaving the airport. 'How, Tony?'

Chalhoub winced. 'Heroin. A big dose. I know, she wasn't a user. No track marks. Did you ever know her take drugs at all?'

Lynch shook his head. 'No. Never. She wasn't against them per se. Just didn't do anything for her. Liked whisky. Smart girl.' His lips trembled. He shut his mouth, his lips tight.

Chalhoub cleared his throat. 'There was... there was a note.'

Lynch nodded. Of course there was. *Oh Christ, please not let this be because of me, because of us.* He wondered where she'd got the heroin. Why heroin? Why suicide, come to that? Lynch's mind was reeling. Leila was about *life.* 'What did she say?'

There was something desperate in Chalhoub's eyes. 'No, not suicide. One of *those* notes. She was tied. Cable ties, from the marks.'

Lynch stared at Chalhoub. *Those* notes. The vellum, the thick paper with its flowing calligraphy. He whispered, '*No.*'

Chalhoub held him close. Lynch clutched at his friend,

resting his chin on his shoulder. Chalhoub patted his back. 'I'm sorry, Gerald. I'm sorry.'

Unseen by Tony Chalhoub, Lynch's eyes were dry and his face was set hard.

Lynch rounded the corner of the cobbled street, his eye distracted for a second by the sun reflecting off the little pair of blue enamelled plaques on the pale stone wall. Every street in Beirut had them, one in French and one in Arabic, displaying the area and road number in white lettering. Nathalie was waiting for him at the café. Lynch was profoundly grateful she hadn't been there when he had returned to the apartment the night before. He had picked up a bottle and a glass, filled a bowl with ice and shut himself in his bedroom. He ignored her knocking on his door in the morning, but he had felt strong enough to talk to her by noon and had taken her call.

Nathalie glanced up from her seat under the striped red and white awning. 'I am sorry, Gerald. They told me.'

His head hurt and he had a raging thirst. There was a large bottle of Perrier on the table and Lynch sloshed the cool liquid into a glass and drained it. He glanced up from the glass at Nathalie, his face creased with a winning grin. 'Well, an' that apart, it's a lovely day to meet a beautiful woman for lunch in this fantastic old city. So why be caught in the doldrums, eh? Why waste all this *life* we have?'

Her shocked face told him anger had made him loud, couples turning to see what the fuss was about. For a second his head dropped and then he caught her gaze, his voice quiet. 'She was killed with an overdose of heroin. Freij's killers left her a little note. I will have my day yet.'

Nathalie was patently at a loss for words and Lynch

reached out to touch her hand. 'It's okay, Nathalie. It's something I'll have to deal with one day when there's time. Right now, I just want Freij. Her mouth softened, ready to form a platitude. 'No. I *really* want Freij.'

Lynch struggled to rein in his fury. He needed an ally right now, even a shoulder to soak up the tears when they came back. He didn't know when they would, but for now anger had dried them up. He tried to lighten for her, paused to control himself. Lynch knew his voice was too bright. 'Did you get anywhere with Scerri's phone records?'

She shook her head, her eyes wary. 'No, not yet. My team is looking for any connection with Falcon Dynamics and this company Scerri had called in Albania, an oil company called PIL. He had placed several calls there over the past ten days.'

There had been a scar on Leila's arse where she had fallen on glass as a child. In the war. It was a tiny sideways cicatrice like a smiley. He used to find it in the dark, like a blind person finding '5' on a mobile or F and J on a keyboard.

Lynch forced his thoughts back to the present. 'So what else have we got to go on?'

Nathalie leaned forward slightly. 'The night before you left, I met with Ghassan Maalouf. And he wants Freij as well. He wants him very badly.'

Lynch's eyebrows raised, an appreciative look at her. 'But your father doesn't want Maalouf. He's made that clear before. Why's Maalouf so interested in Freij, anyway?'

'We met in Jounieh, at the Casino du Liban. For dinner. He is an interesting man, you know? He knows we are going hard after Freij. And he, they, want us to succeed.'

'They?'

'The powerful Christians. They don't trust him. Falcon has close ties to a number of American companies and right-wing think tanks. It is true Freij has been courting both America and Israel. But at the same time, his business partner Selim Hussein is Shia and he has been visiting Damascus and Tehran. The people aligned to Maalouf have a large dossier on Freij. There is much that is unexplained. Beyond this, a number of the more powerful Christian families are concerned at how much popular attention Freij has managed to attract. There are many vested interests. Many jealousies.'

'So what's on the table?'

'Maalouf has given me a contact, a man we can use to gain access to Falcon Dynamics' networks. Lebanese intelligence don't have the advanced digital resources we do, but they do have extensive human intelligence. He has offered their cooperation in return for an equal share of our product. And Freij's head.'

'What do you think?'

'The alternative is that he'd arrest us, which he has the authority to do. They're aware we're involved in an operation against Freij. They could make it look bad for us. He made this quite clear. He knows our operations and networks in Lebanon are all compromised.'

Lynch was sharp. '*Our*? Is that a European '*Our*' or a French '*Our*', I wonder?'

Nathalie tutted. 'It doesn't matter.'

The waiter arrived with a breadbasket, fussing around the table and laying out cutlery.

'*Steak et frites*,' said Lynch. 'And an AlMaza. Cold.'

Nathalie pointed to the menu. '*Le poulet, s'il vous plait.*'

The waiter's features softened perceptibly. '*Mais vous etes bien sûr Francaise, Madame.*'

'*Oui.*' She smiled. '*Bien sûr.*'

'*Bienvenu! C'est mon plaisir de vous servir.*' He retreated, beaming.

Lynch glowered at the waiter's back. 'Christ on a bike, what did you people do here to make them so bloody grateful to see you?'

'Us? The French? Honestly, Lynch? We took sides. We were clear. Something you English never managed to do. At least the Lebanese Christians love the French. In the *Monde Arabe*, everyone's agreed on what they think of the English.'

'That's not true and I'm not bloody English.'

Nathalie broke a bread roll and delicately changed the subject. 'The French Embassy people are unhappy about my team. We have set up a mobile surveillance unit in the grounds of the Résidence des Pins. They are bureaucrats, these people. They are very old-fashioned. Papa says things were better in his day.' She grinned at Lynch. 'It always is like this, *non*? It is always better in the old days, as they say.'

Lynch finished his beer and signalled for another. 'I wouldn't know. I haven't quite had my day yet.'

Nathalie popped a piece of bread into her mouth and sat back, one eyebrow raised at Lynch. 'We could benefit from the help of the Lebanese now. Falcon Dynamics is highly secure and we have not been able to gain access to any systems at all. It also has an Internet footprint that is very vague, with little information that bears the scrutiny. Many third party sources and reports, blogs and so on can be traced back to Falcon Dynamics itself or become the dead ends – they have created their own *legend.* You call it this, *non*?' Lynch nodded and she continued. 'So, there is this *legend* on the Web. When we look at known contacts, there exists almost nothing. Every senior associate we have investigated has been pure as the snow. We have only one contact who is viable, and likely still has security access to Falcon and that is the man Maalouf told me about. We are, after all this effort, reduced to one man.'

'So who is he?'

The waiter arrived, Nathalie acknowledging his bowing and scraping, Lynch's plate delivered without ceremony. Ravenous, he started to eat, the steak tender and the fries breaking with little puffs of steam.

Nathalie picked up her fork. 'He is a lecturer in Middle East history at the American University of Beirut. His given name is Anthony Najimi, but he is known as Spike. He is something of a character, apparently. A big rebel figure. A folk hero to many of the students.'

Lynch's heart quickened as he recalled the note Paul Stokes had left: 'Spike' and 'Deir Na'ee'. Here was that connection with Stokes' legacy and the words that had triggered Michel Freij's brutal assault on Marcelle's prostitute after she had whispered them across a pillow. Delivered randomly out of thin air.

Nathalie pulled a tablet from her handbag. 'This is him.'

Lynch took the device. He signalled the waiter for another beer and propped his elbow on the table, his food cooling as he swiped his way through the document. Lynch's eyes widened as he read. 'Jesus. He's a fucking drug dealer.'

Scanning the last page, Lynch's body tensed. He tried to stay calm, slowing his breathing before he was sure enough of himself to slide the tablet back to Nathalie. The food he had eaten tried to come back up. Lynch struggled to stop himself from puking. He avoided her direct gaze and scanned the empty tables under the awnings on the sunny cobbled street, his breath rasping. He swept his hands back over his hair. 'Jesus wept.'

He couldn't stop thoughts of Leila flooding his mind. Leila, mentioned in the Lebanese intelligence file on the tablet he was holding. Last seen by Lebanese intelligence in the company of a drug dealer, activist and rebel called Anthony Najimi whom everyone knew as Spike. What had she said as they'd stood together on the Beirut corniche? *I'll not wait for you, Lynch. Not while you play with your Bond girl.* She hadn't been kidding.

'What is it, Lynch?'

He signalled for the cheque. 'Nothing.' He tossed the file back to her. 'Come on, we're supposed to see your father at two. We're late.'

Standing, Lynch tossed a bundle of lire notes onto the table. Mystified, Nathalie joined him as he strode up the street towards the British Embassy.

Dubois watched Channing stalk up and down the ambassador's meeting room, pausing at the picture window that looked over the sunny stone buildings and terracotta-tiled roofs of Sodeco, and onto the azure Mediterranean beyond. He turned his back on the idyll and jabbed his finger at Dubois.

'It's finished, Yves. We close the whole operation now. This is in danger of turning into the biggest fuck-up in intelligence history.'

Dubois was the older man but technically junior to Channing, the British deputy director for security and public affairs. He laid his hand on the French-polished wood, his melodious voice thickened by the effort to contain his rage. 'We have every reason to believe Freij and Hussein are attempting to acquire viable nuclear warheads.'

'No, you do not. What you have is a couple of Lebbo

parvenus who tried to buy a luxury yacht for cash from a dodgy Kraut bankrupt whose daughter, our only witness, happened to be psychotic and is now, in any case dead. That's what you have. In short, sweet fuck all. I should never have agreed to the operation in the first place.' Channing grabbed a blue-capped bottle of spring water from one of the place settings at the table, wrenched the cap off and swigged from it. He gestured at the newspaper on the long table. 'Worse, one of those parvenus is the future president of Lebanon and he's given half a page of the Daily Star to explain why the Brits are the root of all fucking evil. Our host, His Excellency, is currently busy petitioning the Foreign Office for my balls on a plate.'

Dubois' lips were drawn tight. He glared up at Channing's bulk, framed by the window. 'Could you perhaps stop swearing at me, Brian?'

Channing threw the plastic bottle to the floor. 'No, I fucking can't. I've got the Maltese government baying for my blood, the Special Boat Squadron bitching me out and the PM asking my boss why I've lost my fucking wits. Your big fat hunch led to a dead end, Dubois. That boat's as clean as a whistle, Freij and Hussein are even more squeaky fucking clean and whoever Meier is, he's nowhere to be found. It's over, full stop. I'm pulling the plug. Sod European cooperation.'

Channing sat at the head of the table and ran his fingers through his greying hair. He closed his eyes and threw his head back, linking his hands behind his neck. Dubois studied the man. Middle-aged, Channing wore jeans and a striped shirt, the casual clothes offset by a pair of expensive-looking silver cufflinks. A consummate politician himself, Dubois had to acknowledge Channing's ability to play the game brilliantly. More brilliantly than he, Dubois admitted to himself with a twinge of envy. He almost fancied Channing had dozed off, the man was so still.

'You're wrong,' Dubois blurted.

Channing's eyes snapped open. 'Prove it.'

'I don't need to. If those warheads aren't on the *Arabian Princess*, where are they? We need to find them and we know there is a direct link with Hoffmann, Meier and the arms cache they came from. We also know there is a direct link between them and Falcon and Freij. We have a payment from one party to the other. In case you had forgotten, Brian, Hoffmann and his wife were murdered. So was Paul Stokes. Then there is Elli Hoffmann, Joseph Scerri and the man from the ship, Boutros. This is a lot of dead people around the purchase of a luxury yacht, is it not?'

'I don't care. Murders are for the plods. We have to find those warheads all right, but they're not in Beirut, are they?'

Dubois paced the table. 'Not yet, no. But this is where they are coming. I know it.'

'Another hunch. Enough hunches. It's over.'

'French intelligence has supported the Freij family for many years. I cannot tell you by what degree, but our support has been significant. The French government has been very involved in Lebanese politics since the foundation of this country, as you very well know. Something is happening here. I do not know what yet, but something. It is not good. Michel Freij is not what he seems to be. He has become a client of the Americans but they do not understand him as we do. We need a little time. Just a little time.'

Channing sat forward. 'No. No more time. It's over, Yves. Listen to yourself, man. You're waffling. Whatever interest the French government has in him, Freij is not a

European problem and I won't let you make him into one.' He waved down the meeting table to the folded newspaper. 'And he's certainly not a British problem except now we've obviously got to go on the biggest arse-licking exercise since the invention of diplomacy.'

Dubois lunged across the room and placed his hands over Channing's. 'We must stop him, we must.'

Channing snatched his hands away, his face screwed up in disgust. 'Stop him? Get a grip on yourself, Dubois. There are no warheads on the ship and Operation Beirut is closed with immediate effect.'

Dubois snapped. 'You can't close it. You don't have the authority. This is an EJIC operation and therefore under my purview.'

Channing's voice was mellifluous, *creamy* thought Dubois, realising his naiveté as Channing pronounced sentence.

'I bloody can because I have been given precisely that authority by your mealy-mouthed political masters in Brussels. This is my show now and I can stop it or start it as I see fit.'

Dubois opened his mouth to protest but Channing cut him off. 'Check before you say something you'll regret. I want us to work together. You'd best accept the new reality.'

Both men's heads turned at the tap on the door. Lynch entered, holding the door for Nathalie, whose hand flew to her mouth at her father's abject demeanour. Lynch returned Channing's glare with a raised eyebrow.

'Sorry, did we pick a bad moment?'

Dubois' voice was husky, 'No, no. Come in.'

Standing in front of the fireplace with his hands behind his back, Channing's tone was matter of fact. 'Operation Beirut is over. Michel Freij and Selim Hussein are no longer of interest to us. Official.'

Lynch tested the coffee pot and poured a cup for himself. He tipped the pot at Nathalie but she shook her head.

'What about the murder of Paul Stokes? Or Elli Hoffmann? Or Leila Medawar?' Lynch's face was taut, his knuckles white on the cup's handle.

Channing craned forward. 'Leila who?'

'The activist girl.' Dubois answered, watching Lynch and fearing violence.

'Up to the police. Not an issue for us.'

Lynch put the cup down, spilling the coffee. 'Not an *issue*? How's that, then?'

'No. I said let the Lebboes handle it. I've had enough wild crusades to last me the rest of the year and I won't have us playing cops and robbers in a foreign jurisdiction. Particularly not this one right now.'

Lynch nodded. 'Fair enough. Your call.'

Puzzled by Lynch's meek acquiescence, Dubois caught the glance between the Irishman and Nathalie. Lynch, he realised, was about to take the law into his own hands.

Channing shoved his chair back. 'What a fucking mess. Right. You.' He waved at Lynch. 'Get on with whatever you were doing before all this. You.' Nathalie raised her head. 'Get back to France, soonest. It's over. Goodbye.'

'You can't—'

'Yes, he can,' Dubois interjected. 'Brian is heading up the operation and the decisions are his now.'

Dubois felt a lump in his throat at Nathalie's horrified look. She knew well what a setback to his career this was. He glared down at the table to avoid her pity, his distorted, pale features reflected on the polished mahogany.

Lynch took Nathalie's arm, his touch startling her as he

drew her away. Dubois looked up as the door closed. Standing at the window, Channing was a silhouette.

'Yves, you and I are in a unique position, my old son. Together, we have managed to lose two nuclear warheads capable of wiping out a reasonably large city. They aren't on the damn boat, and they sure as hell aren't here in Beirut. So my best suggestion would be that we nip off back to Brussels and start to find out quite where the hell they, and Mr bloody Meier, have got to.'

'I told you. They're on the way here.' Dubois fought to keep the desperation from his voice.

Channing strode from the window, bending down to hiss in Dubois' ear. 'No, they're bloody not. Not without proof.' He straightened. 'We're focusing on the wrong place and we're wasting valuable time here.'

Dubois waited for Channing to bustle from the meeting room before slumping back in his chair. He felt dull. He had been so sure the boat was carrying the warheads. Much as he disliked the idea, Channing had reason: the funds transfer from Beirut to Hoffmann had been the pointer. Without the certainty of the warheads' destination, Dubois faced widening the scope of the investigation massively. They had no choice but to go public with the loss of a pair of hundred kiloton Soviet Oka-class nuclear warheads.

Lost in thought, Dubois let his mobile ring out. It rang again and he surfaced and reached for the slim black case and the green key.

'Monsieur. Dubois? Branko Liberec, in Prague. I hope I don't disturb you.' Liberec's voice was tense.

Dubois rubbed his eyes. 'No, not at all. How are things with you, Branko?'

'The missing warheads, sir. They are not on the *Arabian Princess*.'

Dubois sat back, marvelling at God's sense of timing. 'Really, Branko? Where are they, then?'

Lynch and Nathalie wandered down into the cobbled streets of Sodeco, passing the army guard and the red and white painted barriers. The café tables on the street were empty under their striped awnings, the weather too cold for anyone to sit outside, despite the sun that fell across the rich beige frontages of the restored buildings.

Nathalie's mobile rang and she pulled it from her pocket. She bit her lip as she listened to the voice on the line. The signal, as usual in Beirut, was bad.

'*Oui. Maintenant. 'Voir.*'

The sunlight lit the side of her face as she stopped walking and turned to Lynch, her expression worried. 'It is my father. He wants to meet again. Something's changed.'

Lynch screwed up his face in disgust. 'Jesus. Are we going to spend all day walking up and down this fucking hill?' He turned on his heel and led the way back up to the British Embassy.

They entered the meeting room. Dubois was a man transformed, his eyes alive with excitement. Channing sat at the head of the table, feigning sleep, his hands clasped on his lap.

Playing with an empty coffee cup, Dubois was losing his English in his excitement. 'They are in containers. The Czechs have traced them. They have crossed the Slovakia-Hungary border before four days. The Croatian, Romanian and Serbian road borders with Hungary are all closed. All of the Balkan border posts are on high alert. We have them. They are entrapped.'

Lynch whistled. 'They had balls, all right. How did

they expect to get away with that?'

Dubois beamed. 'Oh, come, it is not so difficult, is it? Meier, he knows every corrupt officer and easy customs post in Europe with his history of trafficking. They will have been using different sets of documents.' Dubois paused for reflection for a second. 'Most customs men do not really look for nuclear warheads, is it not? It is not the... *everyday* problem.'

Lynch drew a map of the Balkans in his mind. 'So what was the plan? Through Romania and down through Turkey?'

'We cannot know for sure, but this would seem likely. The operation has expanded to cover a wide area, but we are keeping the nature of the cargo confidential. It is still top secret.'

'Because you don't want the Yanks to know?'

'Because we want nobody to know. Imagine the media and the public reaction, without even to think of the political backlash. That is my waking nightmare at this moment. It is why Brian and I have to return to Brussels and manage the operation. We must leave you both here to try to find what Freij intends for these warheads. I surely know he is behind this. If we fail and those weapons get to Beirut, I want us at least to be ready for them when they come.'

Channing's lazy drawl froze the conversation, his eyes still closed. 'They won't. Half of Europe's armed forces are mobilised to stop them now.'

Lynch poured another coffee, even though the stuff was vile. 'Fair enough.'

Nathalie reached across the meeting table and touched her father's hand. 'We have been approached by the head of the Lebanese security directorate. He is an associate of Madame Chalabi's. He is offering their cooperation.'

Dubois' face darkened. 'What is his name?'

'Ghassan Maalouf.'

Dubois shook his head. 'Not in a million years. I already told Lynch that.'

Nathalie glanced at Lynch, who met her eyes. She nodded, her lips tightening. 'He said you'd react like this. He said to tell you he was genuine, that this matter is of great importance to Lebanon. That I should give you this.'

Nathalie handed a plain silver memory key over to Dubois, who regarded it with mild revulsion and dropped it into his pocket. 'Where did you meet him?'

Nathalie gestured to Lynch. 'First we met with Madame Chalabi at Cedars. I had dinner with him a few days ago at the Casino du Liban.'

'Alone? With *him*?'

Lynch paused, studying Nathalie's bewildered reaction to her father's cold fury. 'But, yes.'

Dubois got to his feet, glaring down at Nathalie, his hand held up to her. 'Never again let yourself be alone in the company of this man. Do you hear me? Never.' Striding to the door, Dubois turned. 'I will not hear of it.'

As the door slammed behind Dubois, Channing opened his eyes and glanced around the table. He closed them again, a smile playing on his lips. 'Odd fellow, that. Very odd.'

Chapter Twenty-Four

Lynch and Nathalie stepped downhill together, away from Hamra's garish shopfronts and flickering light displays, towards the vast American University of Beirut campus. The full moon cast a milky glow over the quiet streets, the deep-set doorways and side alleys plunged into shadow. Lynch hopped into the street to avoid a telegraph pole rooted in the uneven pavement. Nathalie brushed against his arm.

They made way for a passing group of revellers, the bright chatter of the men and laughter of the women fading into the dark behind them. They rounded a corner and headed for the orange light and bustle of *Baromètre*, the student bar by the American University, known simply as AUB.

Lynch leaned on the counter, surveying the smoky bar, the rough tables piled high with glasses, the ashtrays overflowing. The benches and chairs were dense with animated young people, some sitting on each other's laps to squeeze into the haphazard arrangement of tables and chairs. He signalled to the shiny-haired young barman with a twenty-dollar bill. 'A beer and a white wine.'

Nathalie stood with her back to the bar. Her dark hair reflected the orange light, her pale cheeks flushed from the walk in the cool night air. She turned and caught Lynch looking at her, flashed him a smile.

The barman banged the drinks down. 'Twelve.'

Lynch handed the note to the barman who took it with studied indifference. He passed the warm glass of white wine to Nathalie, who winced when she tasted it.

The barman tossed the change on the countertop.

Lynch left it there. 'Know a guy called Spike?'

The barman's eye flickered to at a table near the door where an older man was holding forth to a small but attentive audience of female students. He recovered, indifferent again. 'No, never heard of him.'

'Thanks for your help,' said Lynch, taking his change and walking away from the bar to the table by the door. He slammed his bottle on the table, flashing a grin at the group. 'Hi. Sorry to interrupt. Anthony Najimi?'

Najimi's beard gave him a dashing air and, Lynch noted, masked a weak chin. He wore a black and white Palestinian *keffiyeh* around his neck, his dark green linen shirt and beige photographer's waistcoat hinting at a revolutionary, a man of action. He brushed a wavy strand of hair aside as he turned to Lynch.

'Do I know you?'

'Peter Dominic, The Guardian. I'm working on a piece on AUB and several people told me you'd be a good guy to talk to. I wondered if we could have a quiet word or two alone.'

'No thanks, dude.' Najimi turned back to his audience with a superior grin. 'I only talk to Arabic newspapers.'

There was a dutiful ripple of laughter around the table, which settled down to wait for Lynch's next move. He made it.

'Oh, that's such a shame. I thought you might be interested in talking about a friend of mine called Paul Stokes. I don't really care which fucking language you do it in. Do you remember Paul Stokes, Spike?'

Najimi rose and turned to face Lynch, who gripped his beer bottle by the neck. Lynch's voice was silky, his eyes boring into Najimi's. 'Or Deir Na'ee? Ring any bells with you? Or Leila Medawar?'

Najimi's furious expression froze, replaced by animal

panic. His glance flicked across the room. He snarled, 'Fuck you, man.'

Flinging his drink in Lynch's face, Najimi leapt for the door, sending a girl flying. Her glass tumbled to smash on the floor. Screaming broke out. Najimi threw a punch at Nathalie as she moved to cut him off. His shoulder caught the doorway a glancing blow. He sprinted through the tables scattered outside the bar.

Lynch gave chase, a more powerful runner. He rounded the street corner downhill from the bar, grabbed a handful of Najimi's shirt and pushed him into the side of a garage exit, using the ramp to pull the man round and slam him into the concrete wall. Najimi held his hand up to shield his face as Lynch hammered a series of twisting blows into the man's face, chest and stomach.

Nathalie caught up with them. She pulled Lynch away from the huddled figure on the dusty floor. Blood streaked from the man's nostrils across his face in a dark parabola. 'Christ, Lynch, leave him. What has taken over you?'

Lynch wiped his mouth with the back of his hand, regaining his breath. 'Nothing. We've got to get this pile of shit off the street. Hang on.' He fished his mobile from his jacket pocket and dialled. 'Marcie, I've got a problem. I need a room and a loan of Hassan. Sure. Thanks. Barométre. No, right now.' He turned to Nathalie. 'Done. He'll be here in five minutes, there's no traffic this late. If you go back up to the bar, he'll be in a black Touareg. Bring him down here and I'll take care of this fuckwit.'

'Okay, but stop hitting him, yes?'

'Sure, fine. Just go.'

He listened to her fading footfalls for a few seconds. Turning to Najimi, he swung his boot into the man's ribs, feeling the bone crack.

'So I lied,' Lynch spat. 'That was for Leila.'

*

Lynch helped Marcelle's driver Hassan carry Anthony Najimi into the small room and let him down onto the bed. The movement forced a groan from the man's broken mouth and renewed the flow of blood from his tissue-packed nose.

Marcelle drew on her cigarette nervously. 'Was this all because he slept with your Leila?'

Nathalie wheeled to face Lynch. 'Leila? The girl in the apartment?'

'He's too fond of secrets, *habibti*, is our Lynch.' Marcelle chuckled nastily. 'He was screwing a student chick from AUB. She walked out on him and even then he was fool enough to pay for a flat for her.'

'Shut up, Marcie.'

Marcelle gestured at Nathalie with her cigarette. 'She walked out when you walked in, dear.'

Nathalie shook her head. 'How do you—'

'Because I make it my business to know things. That piece of shit is a heroin dealer and he sells to a few of the girls. They sell it on to their clients. Sometimes they don't have enough left. Then he takes payment in kind.'

Lynch steadied himself against a chair, part of the room's sparse, cheap furnishing, his hand gripping the plastic back. He had to clear his throat to speak. 'He didn't just sleep with Leila. He killed her for Freij. She was found injected with an overdose of heroin. There were signs she was tied, had struggled. One of Freij's notes was beside her. Leila never touched junk. Ever. He was the last person she was seen alive with.'

Marcelle's calculating gaze weighed Lynch up. She nodded, her dark eyes dropping. 'I'm sorry, Lynch. I didn't know.'

Lynch glanced at Nathalie, who was staring at Najimi moaning on the bed. Her voice was a whisper. 'If I hadn't come, she would never have moved away.'

'It doesn't matter.' Lynch ran a hand over his tired face, his voice lowering. 'It doesn't matter. But the only reason this piece of shit is alive is that he's key to finding out what Freij is up to.' Lynch glared up at them both. 'The only reason.'

An Indonesian girl in a housecoat bustled into the room carrying an enamel bowl and a wad of cotton wool. She started to dab at Najimi's broken face.

'She's good. Used to be a nurse. Come on, I need a drink.' Marcelle led the way from the room, glancing back to her driver. 'Look after him, Hassan. He's not to go anywhere.'

Hassan nodded and closed the door behind them.

They followed Marcelle down the corridor and up a short flight of steps to her plush, modern office, the furnishings contemporary and minimalist, abstract art on the walls and coffee-table books scattered. The right-hand wall had an angled floor to ceiling window overlooking the club. Nathalie watched a skinny, pale girl on the stage pretending to masturbate with a teddy bear.

Marcelle glided over to the drinks cabinet and poured whisky into two tumblers, handing one to Lynch, who helped himself to ice. She went over to the window, draping her hand on Nathalie's shoulder and massaging it gently. 'Would you like a drink?'

'No, no thanks,' Nathalie said, her face reflecting the purple glow of the stage lights, the audience of Japanese businessmen, solitary figures and noisy groups of balding suits oblivious of her regard behind the one-way glass. Marcelle drawled, gesturing at the stage with her tumbler. 'You like?'

'No. No, I don't actually.' She turned away.

Lynch poured another drink. 'I'll need your help, Marcie. We'll have to keep him here for a while. Okay?'

Marcelle rounded on Lynch. 'Lynch, you've already had one of my girls near-killed.' She searched his face. Whatever she read there, her mouth pursed in resolution. 'You're paying, Lynch. Five hundred a day.'

'Done.'

'Dollars.'

'I wasn't talking lire, Marcie. It's fine. Just don't let him go anywhere.' Lynch topped his glass up. 'Najimi was a dealer. Was he a user?'

Marcelle sat down on the white leather sofa. 'How do I know? Go ask him.'

'Thanks, I will.'

Lynch went back down the corridor and nodded at Hassan, who let him into the room. The maid had taken off Najimi's shirt and had bandaged his ribs, the livid bruises already forming a patchwork across his torso. His eyes opened, one swollen and bloodshot, nestled in a livid, blackening bruise. Hassan had bound his feet with cable ties.

Lynch reached over to his arm and wrenched it, making Najimi cry out. The track marks were there. It was a mess, the vein collapsed. The other arm was little better. He grabbed Najimi's chin.

'Leila Medawar. Why?'

'I know nothing, man. I swear.'

'Okay. You want to tell me about Deir Na'ee now or you want to wait until tomorrow when your skin's crawling?'

Najimi's voice was a croak. 'No. I know nothing.'

'*Kazab*. Okay, you made your choice.'

Lynch turned to Hassan. 'Tie his hands. Gag him, too.

He'll start making a noise soon enough. Tell the Indonesian chick, "nil by mouth." Got that?'

Hassan nodded. Lynch returned to Marcelle's office to find the two women sitting together, Marcelle's hand on Nathalie's thigh.

'*Kiss immak*, don't you ever knock?'

He pretended not to notice Nathalie's blush. 'We're going. We'll be back in the morning.'

Marcelle smiled down at Nathalie. 'I look forward to it.'

It had been a long day. Nathalie had disappeared into the bowels of the French Embassy where her team of hackers was trying to squirrel its way into Falcon's security system. Apparently doing so undetected was the hard bit. Lynch had feigned interest. He himself had visited a number of people with dubious histories, including a dangerous foray into the heart of Chatila, the infamous Palestinian refugee camp. It had all come to nothing and Lynch could barely wait to get back to Marcelle's club. When he did, he bounded up the stairs to find the dutiful Hassan on guard.

Lynch nodded to Hassan, who opened the door. Anthony Najimi, gagged and lying on the bed, was mumbling. His skin had a sweaty sheen. There were livid red marks on his wrists where the cable ties had bitten into him. He strained against himself, his unfocused gaze roamed the room.

Lynch grinned. 'Good evening. How's she hangin'?'

Najimi jerked at the sound of a voice, then collapsed back on the bed, breathing heavily, his eyes screwed shut. Lynch sat on the side of the bed and removed the gag. He cupped the man's head and offered him water, watching him gulp.

Najimi gasped, water running down his chin. His breath stank. 'Stop it. You know you can. Stop it. Give me some stuff, man.'

'Here's the deal.' Lynch's voice was a gentle whisper and Najimi had to crane his head painfully in order to hear. Lynch pulled a plastic bag from his pocket. It contained a disposable syringe and a small bag of white powder. He held it out. Najimi tried to reach for it, but Lynch pushed his shoulder, making him wince with pain at the grip on his tender skin.

'Talk. You talk first.'

Najimi's bruised mouth worked as he held his tied hands out to Lynch, drool streaking his cheek. 'Jesus, man, have some fucking mercy. Look at what you've done to me.'

Lynch's smile was cold. 'Mercy? You show Leila Medawar any mercy? You sell drugs to kids, *Anthony*. Don't you presume to lecture me about mercy.' Lynch got to his feet, looking down on the mess on the bed. 'And for the record, son, I had my mercy glands removed a long time ago. So, Leila Medawar. Why?'

'I know nothing, man.'

Lynch slapped him. Najimi cried out. 'Freij. Michel Freij made me do it. I was seeing her. She'd just split up with some guy. Freij gave me a choice, it was me or her. I chose her. No brainer, right?'

'Sure,' Lynch confided. 'No brainer.'

Najimi's breathing was ragged. His eyes tracked Lynch moving the syringe to the other side of the room. Lynch returned to the bed but the tied man's eyes stayed on the little bag of gear in the corner.

'Now,' Lynch said, sitting with his bended knee on the bed touching Najimi's leg. 'Deir Na'ee. What can you tell me about Deir Na'ee?'

Najimi moaned and licked his lips, jerking his head painfully. 'I don't know anywhere called Deir Na'ee.'

Lynch's hard-handed slap bounced Najimi's head off the mattress. His sodden hair flew up, suspended like a halo for an instant. He drew his legs and arms foetally into his stomach. Snot ran from his nose and onto the cotton sheet in a constant stream he didn't bother to sniff up.

'We've got all evening, you know,' Lynch said. 'It's only you that can't get what you need. I'm good, see?' He called to Hassan and the door opened, the driver's brown, lined face impassive, a flash from the door handle as the red stone on his crude signet ring caught the light.

'*Seer*?'

'Get me a scotch on the rocks. A double.'

'*Seer.*'

Lynch sat back, his tone conversational. 'How did you first meet them, Anthony? Michel and Selim? You're great pals, aren't you?'

Najimi glared sideways at him, his eyes fixed on the bag in the corner of the room, his words tumbling out between shuddering breaths. 'AUB. At the university. They were hiring.'

'Did they hire you?'

Najimi shook his head, sniffing and swallowing with an effort.

Lynch waited as the man on the bed gulped and gagged, heaving for breath. The bed was cast iron, the white-enamelled frame topped with dented brass ornamentation. It was Marcelle's cheapest room, ill-favoured and above the kitchen to the back of the club. A faint stench of boiled vegetables and frying had soaked into the mean fittings.

Najimi tossed his head back to flick the lank, damp hair

from his eyes. 'I heard you talk to the French chick. You're British intelligence.' He licked his lips. 'We're on the same side you know, man. My people are gonna be pretty pissed when they find out how you've treated me.'

Lynch snorted. 'Your people? Who might they be when they're at home?'

'That's how I met Freij and Hussein. I was Michel's bag man, see? Look, let me have some stuff. I'll tell them I was hurt in an accident. They don't need to know. You'll be okay. I can fix it.' His smile of triumph was cut short by a grimace as his lip split again. 'Ah, shit.' He sniffed again. 'Come on, dude, we can sort this out—'

'Shut up,' Lynch said, shaking his head in disbelief. 'What intelligence outfit would be stupid enough to trust a piece of shit like you?'

Najimi was eager now, his battered face lit up with hope. 'See? I knew you'd be okay with it in the end. It's gonna be cool, it's okay. I work for the CIA, dude. The Americans. I'm their man, see? Their man in the university, that's me. Come on, man, the stuff. It's cool, we're on the same side. We're good, no?'

'Where's Deir Na'ee?'

The sweat was beading on Najimi's high forehead, running down his cheek. He pawed at Lynch, nodding and smiling. 'In Dannieh, in the mountains. It's their big hideout, man. Their research place. All top secret, see? It's where they do the heavy shit. Nobody gets near that place that Michel doesn't know it. Big security, see?'

Lynch spoke to himself. 'How's nobody heard of the place?'

Najimi's laugh was a broken, high-pitched cackle. 'It's the biggest secret in Lebanon, man. In the world. There's more security around Kalaa than anywhere, man.'

'Kalaa?'

Najimi nodded. 'Yeah. The mountain. Where it is. Deir Na'ee. Kalaa. It used to be a nunnery. The whole place belongs to the Freij militia. One Lebanon.' He stretched an entreating hand. 'Come on, man, give me the stuff.'

'Soon enough.' Lynch pulled a micro recorder from his pocket and switched it on. 'But first take me through this one bit at a time. I'm feeling stupid.'

The man they called Hassan had come into the room and cut his hands free. His wrists were sore but he didn't notice, curled up in a ball on the bed and shivering, sniffing away as much of the constant tide of snot as he could, his hands shaking so hard he could barely focus on them when he did summon the energy to lift his head. His skin crawled, sago with cockroaches scuttling on its pliant surface, slipping off his bones in great strips of sloughing lifeless matter.

Najimi cried out, the soft rasp of the linen on his ear. He had pissed himself, the warm pungency from his damp groin filled his nostrils. He forced his caked eyes open, focused on the sordid little room. The bag was there, where Lynch had tossed it in the corner. He regarded it for some time, starting to cry with the need but too weak to make the effort to get to it. Eventually he focused, summoned his will and forced himself upright on shaking arms, groaning with the pain in his side. He pushed the plastic water bottle from the bedside table onto the floor. He slid to the floor as gently as he could, his legs still pinioned by nylon ties. He cried out from the pain in his bruised thighs and broken ribs.

He fell, crashing to the ground. He lay weeping with the pain and the need, the latter driving him to drag himself along the floor with his elbows, wriggling as much as he could despite the screaming of his bound ribs. Each breath too short to fill his aching lungs, he could hear his own ragged gasps and the rustle of his clothes on the faded rug.

He cried with relief when he reached the little bag. With a last effort, he propped himself up to sit against the wall, his head lolling as he struggled to fight off the wave of tiredness enveloping him.

He woke with a start, the blessed relief of sleep replaced by the shrieking of his jangling nerves. For a second he gazed around the room unseeing, trying to gain his sense of place. The pain and the sharpness of his need brought him back to the little bag.

Licking his dry lips, he opened it. It was a neat and complete works, a spoon, cotton wool and a vial of alcohol, a tiny clip-seal bag of fine, off-white powder and a lighter. It even had a little metal stirrer. His hands shook so much he had to stop several times. He burned a small pile of powder on the spoon, adding a splash of the bottled water and stirred it up to mix the powder in. He pulled the plastic covering off the syringe and pushed it into a tiny wad of cotton wool in the middle of the liquid so there were no lumps in it as he drew up the plunger. He tied his arm with his belt, swabbed the bulging vein with alcohol and then slid the needle in, a moment that always caused a slight rise in his trousers, a penetration that he always wanted to see under a microscope so he could better appreciate its shiny metal perfection against the warm embrace of his skin and blood. He pressed the plunger slowly, withdrawing the needle and pressing the swab to the tiny welling of blood, the belt falling to the floor.

He prepared to receive it, his eyes rolling back as his heart pumped and the first waves of the rush tumbled over each other like the tide coming in. The waves started to crash like a tsunami and his eyes snapped open with ecstasy and burgeoning fear. It was too much, too fast. The waves started to crash down on his head, a tide become a torrent.

Anthony Najimi gasped for air but there wasn't enough in all the world.

Chapter Twenty-Five

Nathalie hadn't noticed the lengthening shadows fading to dusk outside. She screwed her eyes shut as Lynch switched on the lights. His eyes looked bruised in his pale face, but he smiled for her. 'Hey, bookworm. You been sitting there since I left you?'

She nodded. He sloughed off his jacket and flung it on the back of a dining chair. She gestured at her screen. 'We have traced this PIL. It is a company in Albania. Petrolifera Italo Libanese is owned by Sakhr Investments, an offshore investment vehicle ultimately owned by Selim Hussein and Michel Freij, together with other Lebanese partners. Sakhr is Arabic for Falcon, but I think you know this.'

Lynch sat beside her. 'Sure I do, but where's the connection with Meier or the warheads?'

'PIL has a facility, an oil terminal near Vlorë in southern Albania. Scerri's phone records show a number of calls over the past month to numbers in Vlorë, including the International Hotel, PIL's offices and two private numbers. The hotel holds a booking in Hoffmann's name made by Scerri. We are working with RENEA in Albania, their counterterrorist army unit. They tell us both of the private residences are now under surveillance.'

Lynch spoke haltingly. 'You think the idea is to load these warheads onto the boat at this oil terminal?'

Nathalie smiled at Lynch with what she hoped was the pitying smile a teacher would bestow upon her slowest pupil. 'Michel Freij flew out of Beirut this morning to Tirana in his private jet. Once over Albanian airspace, his pilot put in a request to divert to Vlorë.'

'And the boat? Where's the boat?'

'We don't know.' Nathalie looked embarrassed. 'We cancelled the original satellite tracking request to the Americans and it's apparently taking effort to convince them we are serious this time around.'

'Is it now?' Lynch rubbed his face in his hands. 'Why does that not surprise me?'

Lynch insisted they go to eat before he would share his day with her and they strolled together down the street from Lynch's apartment in *Ain Mreisse* towards the sea. He made laughing small talk all the way. He puzzled her, the way he was obviously under stress – the amount he was drinking testament to that alone – and yet he insisted on being flippant and irresponsible. At the same time, she sensed a burden had been lifted from him.

They sat at a table for two by the window in an Italian restaurant overlooking the rocks at Raouché. The great stone humps seemed to float on the moonlit sea. The lanterns hanging from the weathered wood rafters cast a warm orange glow over the red-checked tablecloths and candles in Chianti bottles. The wine Lynch ordered arrived, two large claret glasses poured with exaggerated panache by the white-aproned waiter.

They touched glasses, Nathalie inhaling deeply, then appreciating a sip of the expensive Vino Nobile. Lynch gulped.

Nathalie surveyed the restaurant, empty in the early evening. 'So what about you? What happened with Najimi? Enough holding out on me.'

'Najimi? Ah, sure, just a heap of shit an' piss. He's nothing. He reckons Falcon's got a massive underground facility in the northern mountains where it develops high-tech missile systems with American investment. It's totally sealed off by the One Lebanon militia. Sure, nothing interestin' about the man at all.'

He grinned and she scanned his face, his blue eyes twinkling in his pale features. She gave up trying to make sense of his words, laughing. 'Shit, Lynch, you are teasing me.'

'Nope. He sang like a canary. We have everything we need. I even found out where bloody Deir Na'ee is.'

'So what else did he sing?'

Lynch slid the silver-cased voice recorder across the checked tablecloth. 'Here, put this in yer handbag and ye can listen to it later. He said all that and more. Freij is a hood, an honest-to-goodness employee of Uncle Sam's defence industry, a joint venture partner with all sorts of big business interests. Selim's the engineering brains, Freij is the frontman. They've got huge research and development, something like four hundred software engineers alone, hardware development in drones and tactical missile systems. It's all sanctioned and signed off by the State Department, albeit hush-hush. Falcon isn't allowed to sell to the home market without permission but they can sell outside their backyard. The whole shebang is up there in the mountains surrounded by Christian villages where nobody who doesn't belong ever goes, hidden behind a disused fruit cannery and named for a nunnery that has been a ruin for more than a hundred years. Deir Na'ee, the lonely homeplace.' Lynch sought her eyes. 'And you know the best bit, Nathalie? The very best bit?'

She shook her head.

Lynch drained his glass and waved it at the waiter. 'That was the last place Paul Stokes went before he was killed. He overflew Deir Na'ee with a rogue chopper pilot called Marwan Nimr, a real gun-for-hire type. Nimr used to deal drugs, but got busted. He was pals with Najimi. And Najimi was one of the bastards who kidnapped Paul Stokes. Would ye ever believe it?'

Nathalie sipped at her wine, the candlelight glinting from the glass marked with her fingerprints. She regarded Lynch, trying to make sense of his strange, brittle humour.

'You must hate him very much, this Najimi.'

'No, no I don't,' said Lynch. 'Not anymore.'

Nathalie wondered quite what that meant but a glance at his face in the candlelight decided her against asking any more questions.

It was late. Lynch sat outside his favourite late night café in Marmara, smoking apple *shisha* and drinking *arak*. Quite drunk by now, he was genial; well known to the locals who cheerily greeted the *Ingleez* among them. He sat back and smoked the sweetened tobacco, a little *pasha* or perhaps a caterpillar. The thought drew a manic giggle from him. The pile of charcoal brightened on top of the little ceramic cup every time he inhaled. He held the snaking pipe with its furry grip aside and blew the smoke up into the air.

Nathalie was back at the apartment. They had returned from their early dinner, Nathalie refusing Lynch's offer of a drink with a shy smile and a half-lidded glance, waving the little silver voice recorder at him. 'No, I'll listen to this first. Work first, play later.'

Lynch had wondered what *play later* meant, watching her swinging arse push against the black cotton dress as she sashayed to her room in her high heels. She had emerged from her room an hour later, ashen-faced, hurling the recorder at him as he sat smoking a cigar and drinking his whisky on the balcony.

'You bastard.'

He caught it neatly as it skittered off the white plastic table in front of him, laughing. 'Steady, girl, you could have damaged it. That's British government property, I'll have you know.'

'How could you have—'

'Shut up.' Lynch raised his hand to her, his pointing forefinger moist from the condensation on the glass he held. 'I got the results. Your job is to use them.'

'Don't tell me my job.'

'Fine. So don't tell me mine.'

The light caught the tears running down her cheeks as she glared at him. 'You did not have to do it like that, not brutal like that. Not cruel like that.'

Lynch was pure fire, ardent anger. 'He killed her, Nathalie. He made his way into her fucking bed and then he injected her with a lethal dose of heroin because Michel Freij wanted him to. Paid him to.' Lynch stumbled to his feet. 'That part of his confession isn't on the recording. Neither is his account of lifting Paul Stokes and imprisoning him before leaving him to the mercy of Freij's drugged-up thugs.'

She couldn't hold his burning stare. She dropped her gaze. Lynch strode past her through the sliding door into the apartment and picked up his jacket from the sofa in the living room. He turned to her. 'Don't you dare judge me, Nathalie.'

She was silent, her back to him.

'Fine,' he had said, as gently as he could. 'I'm going out.'

And go out he had. To get drunk alone. He was getting maudlin and thinking about staggering home when Tony Chalhoub pulled up a plastic chair. The sound brought Lynch from his reverie. He glanced up at Chalhoub then picked up his *shisha* pipe and took a toke. Chalhoub gestured at the waiter for a glass and poured himself an *arak* out of Lynch's bottle.

'Know anything about the dead druggie at Marcie's?'

Lynch's pipe bubbled as he took a long drag, his baleful red-eyed gaze on Chalhoub. 'Nope.'

'Thought you might.'

'Know anything about a flyboy called Marwan Nimr?'

'Christ.' Chalhoub drank from his *arak*. 'There's a blast from the past. Nimr, he's locked up in Roumieh Prison, unless he got time off for good behaviour. In which case he must have behaved like an angel because he was doing something like a twenty-stretch.'

'What for?'

'Jesus, Lynch, I've got a dead man on my hands and the hysterical madam of Beirut's poshest brothel calling through her Swarovski-covered iPhone contact list and you're asking *me* questions?'

'Anthony Najimi, AKA 'Spike'. On the staff roster at AUB.'

Chalhoub noted down the name. 'So what happened to him?'

'What did Nimr go down for?'

Chalhoub sighed and slapped his notebook down on the table, looking to heaven for succour. 'He got caught, Lynch. It's why most hoods go to prison. Those that survive meeting members of Her Majesty's Britannic Government, of course.'

'I had nothing to do with him. He was in a hit-and-run accident.' Lynch took a pull of his *argileh*. 'Out of interest, how did he die?'

'Heroin. Odd, that. The same way Leila died.'

Lynch had the little plastic disposable mouthpiece of the *argileh* pipe between his lips, but he didn't draw on it.

His gaze on Chalhoub was impassive. 'Leila who?'

Chalhoub held Lynch's eye, then gazed around the café. 'Uncut laboratory grade. He took what would have been a normal dose of street stuff. How'd he get hyper-pure gear like that, do you think?'

'I wouldn't know, Tony. Sure, I'm just a jumped-up researcher in the commercial section, you know that. What did Nimr go down for?'

'He used to fly for the big warlords, the drug runs. He's good, the best. He made good money, bought some land and went into business for himself. The big boys didn't particularly like that but he kept them sweet and they turned a blind eye. After the war, they had the sense to crystallise the profits, as it were, and leave the trade. Nimr kept flying.'

'Until?'

'Where did Najimi score lab grade smack, Gerald?'

'Must have been a mix-up with his dealer, ain't that the case?'

Lynch regarded Chalhoub with distaste. He just wanted to be left alone and he was starting to resent the incursion into his wallowing. He sucked on the pipe and waited.

Chalhoub sighed. 'Okay. Marwan Nimr was traded in by one of the warlords. We'd got a little too close to some stuff that the big guy wanted to avoid having to answer to, so he gave us a few little gifts and the news that if we didn't take the gifts, he'd start another war. One of the gifts was Nimr. We hesitated, then my boss got hit in the shoulder by a sniper on his way to the office. We took the gifts. Nimr went to prison.'

Lynch drained his glass, resting the *shisha* mouthpiece across the arm of his chair so that he could lean over and slosh *arak* into his and Chalhoub's glasses. 'Which warlord?'

'You already know, Lynch.' Chalhoub sighed. 'Raymond Freij.' He splashed water into the glasses, the *arak* clouded.

Lynch grunted and drank. He'd had enough and more and he knew it. He focused on speaking as clearly as he could, but Chalhoub's expression told him that he was drunk enough to alarm even his old friend. 'Anthony Najimi was a known associate of both Michel Freij and Selim Hussein. He knew them both as students and was an early employee of Falcon Dynamics. He was on their payroll for years, a highly talented programmer with a particular specialisation in security applications and encryption. Najimi crashed out with a nervous breakdown three years ago. He got the job at AUB thanks to an effusive reference and the personal intervention of Michel Freij with AUB's board. Najimi was financially wealthy, held Falcon shares and had liquidated about four million dollars' worth in the past year.'

'So why kill him?'

Lynch blinked slowly, surfacing to grin roguishly at Chalhoub, tipping the *argileh* mouthpiece at the policeman. 'Naughty, Tony. Very naughty.' He drank from his *arak*, putting the glass down too roughly, the sound of it smacking on the tabletop stopping conversations around them. People glanced across to see what was happening.

Lynch sat back. 'A good question, though. Why would someone want to kill Anthony Najimi, broken genius, brilliant lecturer and mature student activist? Why would someone think that it would be appropriate to kill a man who would never want for money again in his life and yet who chose to be a drug dealer, to peddle smack and dope as gaily as he peddled influence among the young people he preyed upon?'

Chalhoub nodded. 'And he killed Leila Medawar.'

Lynch kept his face impassive as his heart leapt. He wanted the cleansing fire of anger to come, but everything was just turning woolly. He sighed and gazed into his glass, deciding he was being metaphorical.

Chalhoub persisted. Lynch wanted him to go away and leave him to rot in his plastic chair under the neon light. He felt his sleeve tugged as the urgent whisper came to him. 'So who killed Najimi?'

Lynch smiled. *Who indeed?* 'Harry did, Tony. Harry killed Anthony Najimi.'

With exaggerated care, Lynch rested the *argileh* mouthpiece on the little silver pan of the decorated pipe. He drained his *arak* and got to his feet, swaying to maintain his balance. He threw some notes down on the table.

'Gotta go, Tony. Good luck with the druggie files.'

Lynch wove between the tables and then turned to pick his way back to Chalhoub. Lynch leaned against a chair to ask, 'By the way. Where would I find Nimr?'

Chalhoub hesitated, then shrugged. 'He used to drink at the Red Lady in Monot.' He leaned forwards. 'Take care, Gerald. You know if I can help—'

'Yeah, I know. Thanks, Tony.'

Lynch left, consumed by the darkness.

Chapter Twenty-Six

It was cold and Lynch waited, huddled by the airstrip. Vlorë wasn't the most important of Albania's military bases, but it was seriveable enough. It formed part of a network of facilities deemed critical in the cold war and still being decommissioned. The old stockpiles were slowly being identified and destroyed, some disappearing into shadowy hands that would pass them on to Iraq, Afghanistan or Africa. Hands like Peter Meier's. Lynch scanned the tatty runway.

Brian Channing had confounded Lynch's plans to track down Marwan Nimr, the bent helicopter pilot. Lynch had left Tony Chalhoub and struck out for his apartment, arriving exhausted and very drunk at midnight. Channing's call delivered the news Lynch was booked on the 4.30am flight to Albania. As usual, there were no direct flights. He'd have to route through Istanbul. Lynch just made the flight, was almost refused boarding and had to be shaken awake in Istanbul. He slept again on the light plane that took him down the Adriatic coast to Vlorë.

He was to meet up with Gabriel Lentini, the Maltese special forces officer who had planned the raid on the *Arabian Princess* in Malta and so knew the big yacht's layout. Lentini's brief was to liaise with the Albanian special forces, offering his expertise on the interior of the ship. Tirana had been grateful for the help, according to Dubois, who had been in constant contact with his counterpart there since Nathalie had unravelled the PIL connection. Albania had immediately extended its fullest cooperation in the European-led operation against arms smugglers. Whilst eager to help, the Albanians had been mildly puzzled as to why anyone would want to smuggle arms into a country still in the process of destroying and decommissioning one of the greatest concentrations of weapons and military assets remaining in the post-cold war era. Dubois, his imperative as ever to keep international embarrassment and public panic to a minimum, hadn't been too clear on precisely what cargo they were seeking. Lynch had again been warned to go to all and any lengths to maintain that lack of clarity. It had led to a number of awkward conversations when he had arrived in Vlorë.

Lynch had instantly disliked his assigned liaison officer when he arrived at the airbase. Lieutenant Colonel Adam Meshkalla came into sight, scuttling across the crumbling concrete apron, leaving the low building next to the hangars behind him. Lynch returned his attention to the sky above the northern end of the airfield, an approaching aircraft's lights resolving into a shiny little CASA C-212. One of the newer additions to the tiny Maltese Air Force, the light-blue liveried plane wavered in the coarse shear wind as it swooped down to meet the weed-whiskered concrete runway.

Meshkella reached Lynch. There was almost comical

Oriental effusiveness about the man. Like a Turkish pimp, Lynch thought as he allowed his hand to be enclosed and pumped in a double handed display of Meshkella's eternal good intentions. Meshkalla's clipped military moustache, his oiled, dark hair and the ridiculous little baton he carried under his arm along with his peaked hat all made Lynch want to round on the toy soldier and demand a real officer to talk to.

The turboprop passed them by. It slowed, its engines' noisy buzz rose for the turn then lowered as the plane went around parallel to them. It drew to a halt, the engines cut. A few seconds later, Lynch watched Lentini's uniformed bulk descend, the wind gusting so the big man had to hold down his cap as he approached them.

At Lynch's side, Meshkalla gushed, his voice filled with delight and camaraderie. 'Very good. We have help from Malta. Now we may proceed together to solving this greatest mystery.'

Lynch breathed deeply and strode to greet Lentini. 'Gabe. Great to see you.'

Lentini grinned, his hard hand gripping Lynch's, his castrato's voice raised against the strong breeze. 'Good to see you, too, Gerald. Paul Tomasi sends his regards and says you're to get the bastards.'

Meshkalla joined them and clapped them both on the back. 'Welcome to Vlorë, gentlemen.'

Lynch bit his tongue and forced a smile. 'Thank you, Adam. This is Captain Lentini. Gabe, this is our liaison here in Vlorë. Lieutenant Colonel Adam Meshkalla is in charge of the operation against Meier's illegal shipment.'

Lentini and Meshkalla shook hands, Meshkalla patting Lentini's arm and bobbing his head as he displayed his profuse gratitude at being able to host such a luminary. He led them to the low administration block. Lentini's hand darted to catch the door as it swung in the wind. It slammed behind them as they reached the warmth of the administration block. They clattered into a waiting area with chipped metal seating bolted to the floor in sections, an embarkation point for the military. Rubbish was scattered on the floor of the empty terminus. The air was stale and oily.

'There will be a storm,' grinned Meshkalla. 'We must all take care tonight, I think. Please, take a seat here, gentlemen and we will arrange the necessary transport. We believe our quarry has passed the border with Macedonia a little before the dawn. We are in wait for them. We are crouched like the tiger.'

As Meshkalla strutted off, Lynch leaned over to Lentini. 'Gabe, he's either an incompetent fuckwit or a dangerous waste of space. I can't make up my mind.'

Lentini laughed. 'Let's see. These guys still have a formidable military machine. I flew in over Sazan Island. It used to be a huge Soviet military base and it still seems like an active military zone. I'd heard about it before, never expected to see it, somehow.' He leaned forwards in response to Lynch's raised eyebrow. 'What I mean is, I doubt Meshkalla could have got to where he is by being incompetent.'

*

There was no sunset as such, just a deepening of the gloomy cloud cover to a sulky slate and then charcoal. Lynch paced along the windows overlooking the airfield, retracing his steps like a cage-happy animal. He caught his reflection in a glass panel. The neon lighting made his face ghostly.

Lentini inspected his firearms, laying them down on the bench. He had stripped the two pistols he carried, scrutinising each piece and reassembling the guns with loving care.

He peered up from his labour. 'Take it easy, Lynch. You'll wear a path in the flooring.'

Lynch rounded on Lentini, exasperated. 'Gabe, we've been sitting in this dump for over two hours now. I'm sick of waiting.'

Lentini chuckled. 'Relax. You've obviously never been in the army. We do more waiting than anything else. The Albanians shut the border as soon as we talked to them. It's their operation and we have to respect that. Meshkalla's in charge now.'

'So how long do we give them?' Lynch gazed out of the window at the deepening gloom outside, raindrops starting to dot the glass. The *Princess* must be here by now. They could even be loading up and we don't know what the hell's happening.'

Lentini sighed. 'I understand your frustration, but there's really nothing we can do. We can't search the Vlorë coastline by ourselves, can we? These guys have got the resources and Meshkalla's the man in charge. They'll have patrols at sea, and overflights, too. There are only two places with jetties that could load a boat as big as the *Princess* and Meshkalla's bound to have them both covered.'

'What about the houses Scerri made calls to?'

'Both under surveillance. The Albanians have had people there since we called this morning. Really, we can do nothing more than wait.'

Lentini's mobile rang and the big man's shoulders stiffened as he listened, turning and nodding at Lynch. Lentini hung up and bent to lift the heavy holdall he had brought with him. 'We're go. Customs have picked the consignment up, they've let it go through as agreed. The tail is good. There's a team ready to move on the Petrolifera facility and the port's been shut down. The navy is moving to blockade the straits between Sazan and Vlorë. The cargo's moving. Meshkalla's sent a driver. We can follow him. So you can stop champing at the bit. We're good.'

They strode to the door. This time the soldiers on the other side nodded and escorted them. They bustled through the empty, grey building, gathering more men as they made their way, finally bursting through the glass front doors as a large group of uniformed men with Lynch and Lentini at its centre. There were two big Land Cruisers waiting for them, new matte camouflage paintwork and regimental insignia above their back bumpers, whiplash antenna waving in the air. Two staff cars were queued up behind them, engines running. Officers barked commands and they were surrounded by commotion. Behind it there was a low beating sound. Lynch craned his head to try to hear better over the noisy military around them. He strained to catch the noise, tapping Lentini's arm.

'Did you hear that?'

The big man shook his head. 'Hear what?'

'Choppers.'

'How many times? Relax. There should be choppers up there. And spotter planes. And patrol boats on the sea. These guys are going all out to help us here and we haven't even been truthful with them. At least you told us what we were up against back in Malta.'

'Yeah, well. I got double warned off letting anyone here know about our two little problems.'

Lentini was sour. 'Not my call, anyway, is it? Come on.'

They passed the airbase to their right, another two military cars joining them as they raced through the city's suburbs, the front car flashing blue lights to push the sparse traffic out of the way.

A signpost to their left proclaimed 'La Petrolifera Italo Libanese'. Lynch glanced at the army driver. 'Here?'

The driver pointed ahead of them. 'No. Not here. This way.'

The driver switched on the headlights as the darkness thickened, the trees shadowed. The woodland cleared ahead of them, blue and red lights flashing against the tall trees at the periphery of the clearing. Floodlights had been set up. The roadblock was lifted as they slowed to approach. They drove into the floodlit area. A military transporter stood at the centre of the circle of lamps in the clearing.

'Those are NATO insignia,' said Lentini.

'It figures,' said Lynch. 'Explains how they sailed through all those border posts, doesn't it? Christ, but Meier's got balls, all right.'

They pulled up, the wheels crunching on gravel. Lynch joined Lentini at the front of the car, the driver by their side. The evening had cooled, and Lynch turned away from the buffeting cold of the strong breeze. The military transporter carried a single container, which was being opened as they approached it. Lieutenant Colonel Adam Meshkalla walked up to them, his face a picture of joy and pride. He gestured at the clearing, military trucks and cars joined by police cars, a collection of at least twenty vehicles, tape fluttering at the periphery and floodlights set up to pick out the transporter.

'You see? We have your contraband under control perfectly!'

Lynch scanned the huge display of activity. He let his incredulity show. He focused back on Meshkalla's beaming face, glowing with perspiration under the floodlights. 'The fuck you do,' he said, striding towards the container.

The big doors were open as soldiers unloaded it using

a lifting platform, pulling crates out and stacking them. A light drizzle had started to fall. The canvas covering the lorries glistened under the floodlight.

'Look here,' said Meshkalla, pointing with his little silver-ferruled swagger stick. 'These are 122mm missiles designed for the Soviet RM70 launcher. Here there are Trnovnik missiles. According to our experts, they are equipped with cluster bomb warheads.' He jabbed the stick at another stack of crates. '9M22 Grad warheads. HE fragmentation. These are very dangerous weapons, you understand?'

'Very,' said Lynch. 'But they're not what we're looking for.'

Meshkalla peered at him from under his peaked cap, his brown eyes lively and his face suffused with excitement. 'Not what you are looking for? How is this? We were given alert for illegal shipment of arms coming from Czech Republic and here they are. They are shipped using NATO lorry and with NATO paperwork that authorise this shipment. Even they have two motorcycle riders for this lorry. Everything was in order. This is why it reach this far. But we are better than these bad men.' He grinned. 'We catch them, no?'

Lynch scanned the floodlit clearing. 'Where is the driver?'

Lentini took a call on his mobile, walking away from them and cupping a hand over his ear as he talked urgently.

Meshkalla's face was a picture of deep regret, his hands

thrown out in sympathetic despair. 'He get away. Still my men they are hunting him in the forest. You understand it is difficult in this darkness. We do not yet have the equipment the Americans promised to us, the night vision and the helicopters.'

Lentini piped, 'And the outriders?'

'Ah, yes,' Meshkalla gestured up the road with his swagger stick. 'Tragical they are too fast.'

'Excuse me one second,' Lynch nodded to Meshkalla and joined Lentini a few paces away. Lentini signalled to Lynch to wait. After a few seconds listening and a terse '*Grazzi*,' he cut the line, his face grim.

Lynch hissed, 'Gabe, this guy's fucking us around.'

Lentini nodded. 'That was my liaison officer. He checked with the Macedonians. They let three trucks through in total. We're missing two trucks.'

'So we check out the Petrolifera facility? It's the most likely of the two places they could offload the warheads.'

Engines started up behind them as they broke into a run, Meshkalla shouting protest. Lynch clambered into the driver's seat of the Land Cruiser, momentum slamming the door as he rammed the big car into drive and floored the accelerator, wrenching the steering wheel to turn the vehicle back the way they had come. Scattering gravel behind them, they swerved onto the road back to the Petrolifera facility.

The light drizzle had turned into steady rain, forming big

puddles. Lynch, peering into the darkness, spotted the turning too late and jerked the wheel, sending them sliding across the tarmac. He over-corrected and they swerved in the other direction before he managed to tame the bucking wheel. They sped through woodland, emerging into an area of industrial units interspersed with scrubby open spaces. The patchy sodium lighting cast a rusty glow over the unkempt buildings. Barbed wire fencing surrounded many of them. Others were protected by high walls. The rising wind sent a cardboard box tumbling across the wet tarmac.

Lentini leaned forwards. 'Lynch, do you know where you're going?'

'I took a look at the satellite images of Petrolifera's facility back at the hotel. They've got an area of deep water wharfage. If they were going to embark the warheads onto a boat as big as the *Princess*, it would make sense to do it from here.'

They broke into a large open area with brighter perimeter lighting, the dark mass of the sea stretched in front of them. The moonlight glittered on the waves, picking out the vague silhouettes of two loading cranes on the wharf.

Lynch slammed on the brakes and the big car slewed to a halt. He sat with his arms crossed on the wheel, squinting at the stark shapes of the cranes, the detritus strewn on the ground and the weeds pushing up through the cracks in the concrete. The fat raindrops beat a steady tattoo on the roof of the car.

Lynch got out of the car and peered into the shadows.

Lentini joined him. 'Nothing.'

'Hang on,' said Lynch. 'Listen.'

Lentini tipped his head to one side, straining to hear against the drumming of the rain. His face relaxed as he recognised the sound. 'Choppers. Heavy ones.'

'Over there.' Lynch pointed to the lights rising from beyond the industrial units. 'They're taking off from the airbase.'

Lentini reached into the car, pulling open his dark holdall and grabbing a pair of binoculars. He adjusted them and whistled, handing them to Lynch. 'Here. Night vision.'

Lynch picked out the shapes of the two big helicopters, each harnessed to a container, lumbering seaward from the direction of the airbase. 'Where the fuck are they going?'

Lentini shouted above the noise of the rain and the increasing din of the rotors. 'They're almost going to pass overhead of us. They must be headed for that base on Sazan island.'

Lynch boiled with impotent rage. 'What the hell can we do to stop them?'

'Nothing. I've only got handguns. We'd need SAMs to bring those bastards down.'

'The navy?'

Lentini's frustration mirrored Lynch's. 'Meshkalla was in charge of liaison. I don't have any other contact here.'

Lynch got back into the Land Cruiser. Lentini opened

the back door as approach lights from behind them picked out the Land Cruiser in their glare. The reflection in the rearview mirror blinded Lynch, an army lorry and two staff cars, a bullhorn barking at them, Meshkalla's voice rendered oddly mechanical. 'Stop now. Do not move.'

Lynch swore, turning to Lentini who still stood outside the car. 'What do we do?'

'Nothing. Don't move.'

Troops disembarked from the lorry, taking up kneeling positions. Meshkalla leaned behind the open door of the staff car, cracking out orders on his bullhorn. 'Move away from the vehicle now and nobody will get hurt.'

'Fuck me,' Lentini spat. 'This clown thinks he's in a movie.'

Jesus, but it's like listening to Mickey Mouse swearing. The incongruous thought hit Lynch, bringing a cold grin with it. The rain was falling in sheets, the noise of its spattering modulated by the gusts of wind masking the dying sound of rotors in the sky.

Lentini stretched for his holdall. 'Gerald, listen to me. Meshkalla's bent. You have to get word out and have those containers followed. When I say go, hit the accelerator and get out of here. You hear me?'

Lynch shook his head. 'I can't leave you behind.'

'We don't have time to argue. This is what I do, it's not what you do. Go and get hold of your people. I'll catch up with you.'

'You can't take out eight soldiers armed with machine guns.'

Lynch caught the glint of two big semi-automatic pistols as Lentini snapped off the safeties, a wolfish grin on the big man's face. 'You got a million pounds to bet me?'

Lynch was silent. Lentini's grin widened. 'Thought not.'

Lentini spun away, the deafening guns bucked in his big hands. Muzzle flashes strobed across the Land Cruiser's interior.

Lentini screamed 'Go! Go! Go!'

He launched himself away from the car. The rear window hazed as the soldiers returned fire. The noise of its implosion and the cacophony of gunfire forced Lynch's foot to the throttle and the car jerked forward, the huge engine roaring. Bullets hit the front wheel arch, a series of tinny plunks. Muzzle flashes lit up the night air. Lentini rolled on the ground and soldiers threw up their arms, diving aside for cover. The big car jinked along the wharf, a bullet smashed the side window. Lynch lifted his hand against the flying shards of glass. The wheel flew from his grip as the front tyre blew out. The rubber slapped the wheel arch and sloughed off. The Land Cruiser spun on the slick concrete with sickening momentum.

The door vibrated against his leg with bullet impacts. The warehouse wall loomed, and Lynch threw up a hand to cushion himself against the shock, the airbag smeared with red in front of his face as the crash sucked the air from his lungs and slammed his limp body back against the seat.

Chapter Twenty-Seven

The whiteness of sunlight on clean linen hurt his eyes as he tried to open them, the lids glued together and his mouth parched. His head throbbed. He tried to move, but the effort was too much for his bruised body.

Lynch tried to speak, but could only croak, the consequent cough driving a bolt of pain into his chest and side. He relaxed, letting his breathing and heart slow again. He sniffed, antiseptic and a hint of something else, possibly scent.

He took another, slower, breath. It came back to him.

The trolley crashed to the floor. Lynch lashed out, his own pain forgotten as he struggled to raise himself, flailing against the tubes and his own weakness. An alarm sounded; raised voices and footsteps echoed down the corridor. By the time the first nurse arrived, his shouts had died to whispers. He plunged back into unconsciousness.

Later, he woke again, a better awakening with the memory of a conversation with Leila falling away from him despite his efforts to recall every little detail of the dream. She had been standing by the railings overlooking Raouché's rocks, posing for a photograph with the famous landmark behind her, shielding her eyes from the sun and laughing at Lynch trying to take a picture and simultaneously fend off the various hawkers and urchins gathering around the *khawaja*, the gentleman. She took his arm and they wandered down the corniche towards Manara, Leila teasing Lynch as she held on to him.

'So you spy on me too, Lynch? Are you keeping a watch on the activists?'

'I don't know anything about you. I don't want to

know.'

'*Kazab*. Liar. Of course you want to know. It's in your blood. You're a spy.'

'Deputy Commercial Attaché. Only information I have an interest in is commercial opportunities for the boys and girls of the DTI.'

'DTI?'

'Department of Trade and Industry.'

It was a conversation from the early days and recalling it brought a smile. At that point, Leila faded, become a dove and flew up into the blue Mediterranean sky above the green sea, circling the Manara lighthouse and swooping in the warm currents of the sunny afternoon.

Lynch opened his eyes. He focused slowly, resolving Dubois' face staring down at him. 'Good afternoon. How are you feeling?'

Lynch licked his dry lips, taking Dubois' proffered plastic cup of water. He flopped back on the pillow. He let his breathing slow. 'Lentini?'

'In ICU. He has been shot six times. He's a remarkable man. They think he will pull through now, but he has been in theatre all night.'

'He got Meshkalla.' It was a statement.

'Yes, he did. Meshkalla was Meier's man, had been selling arms from Albanian caches and stockpiles to Meier for years. They flew the warheads using two army choppers to the Sazan Island base. The Albanians have arrested a number of officers and men who have links with Meshkalla. They are very embarrassed. The warheads are in two containers, both painted with NATO markings, according to the men we caught at Sazan. We've got a whole team wrapping up the Albanian end of this.'

Lynch reached for the water cup and Dubois helped him to sip from it. Lynch moved his head, his voice still slurred. 'And me?'

'Injuries, you mean?' Dubois used his fingers to enumerate Lynch's wounds. 'You have a gash to your forehead, a bullet graze. You have two nasty contusions from mild bullet impacts, one in your thigh and one in your stomach, both bullets had passed through the door panel at an angle and had lost most of their force. You have numerous glass cuts and extensive bruising. You have some grazing from the airbag cover and some bruising on your shoulder and chest. You have been remarkably lucky. You are almost untouched.'

'And now?'

Dubois paused, scrutinising Lynch's expression. He seemed to reach a resolution. 'Nathalie's team has finally compromised Falcon Dynamics' security and we have teams now working to assess and catalogue the product. The facility you identified in the mountains north of Beirut is, we believe, the destination of the two Soviet warheads. We do not know what they intend to do with them, but we believe there is a mobile missile system developed there that would be compatible with the warheads. We suspect the target may be Israel.'

Lynch wasn't sure if it was the drugs or the battering he'd taken that made everything seem as if it was cosseted in cotton wool. He struggled to think clearly. 'You didn't get them, then? The warheads?'

Dubois shook his head. 'We were too late. We must focus on Beirut now. We'll fly in the morning.'

'Will we get there before the *Princess* does?'

'We have alerted the Greeks, the Turks and the Syrians as well as the Lebanese. All believe this is a drugs enforcement operation, all have stepped up patrols. We are being, sadly, a little economical with the truth, but we think this wisest given the nature of the boat's cargo. There is a major regional patrol operation being run by helicopters from RAF Akrotiri quartering the Lebanese coast in conjunction with the Lebanese air force. I think the *Princess* will not get there.'

'And if it does?'

Dubois stared out of the window. 'We will have to tell the Americans.'

'So why not tell them now?'

'No,' said Dubois. 'Our instructions from our masters are quite clear on this. The nature of that cargo remains top secret. As far as the world is concerned, we are on a drugs enforcement mission. Besides, we're starting to wonder quite how the Americans are involved in this.'

Lynch fought the tiredness overwhelming him. '*Involved*?'

Dubois was silent and Lynch fell back on his pillow, a jolt of pain in his side. He could hear his own breathing, the bang of a distant door and voices. There was a rush of blood in his ears, his own heart carrying life around his exhausted body. Lynch thought Leila again. A dove in Manara.

Darkness.

Chapter Twenty-Eight

Yves Dubois called Nathalie to check on progress as they sped from Rafic Hariri International Airport to the British Embassy, where Channing had arranged a temporary office for him. Dubois had the feeling that Channing just wanted him where he could see him. He would have been a thousand times more comfortable at the Résidence des Pins.

An efficient, middle-aged woman met him as the car pulled up and showed him to his office, *my jail*, Dubois thought bitterly. He threw his bag onto a chair and stalked the small, airless room. He pulled his mobile from his pocket and slipped it onto the desk. He glanced at it and away at his bag. Wracked by indecision, he thought about the contents of the documents Nathalie had been given by Ghassan Maalouf. He had read them on the flight by private jet from Tirana to Beirut.

He reached for the mobile and thumbed the screen.

'Maalouf.'

Dubois steadied himself, his mouth dry. 'You understand talking to you gives me no pleasure.'

Maalouf's voice was cautious. 'I appreciate this. There is nothing, I know, I can say to you. But I am sorry. And I am truly sorry to hear of your loss. Of her death.'

'Where did these documents come from?'

'That is not germane. They are genuine. We are offering our cooperation, a partnership. We can help with more information of this nature. You have access to the resources and tools I believe we need if we are to bring this matter to a conclusion. Our friend is dangerous to us all and must be stopped.'

'And if we choose not to cooperate?'

'You are on Lebanese soil, Yves. I would be perfectly within my rights to protect our sovereignty. I told this to Nathalie.'

Dubois sighed. 'We meet, then.'

He had dreaded the prospect of this meeting ever since he had read Maalouf's information and realised he needed the man's help. He had thought of any reason he could not to make the call in the first place.

Now the die was cast and he felt relieved. And, if the truth be told, he was glad to be given an excuse to escape Channing and his Embassy.

Dubois trod up the stone front steps of the old house. It loomed, shadowed and disused-looking, the plasterwork cracked and the stonework green with lichen and streaked rust marks from the rotting ironwork. He pushed open the flaking door. There was a mean bulb hanging from the ceiling at the end of the long corridor, its yellow glow shadowing the peeling walls, the littered floorboards. Dubois picked his way down the corridor, the doors to the left and right shut against him, but that at the end ajar, a crack of light showing through.

He pushed open the door. Ghassan Maalouf sat by the cold fireplace facing him, two men in greatcoats flanking him. They held guns. Maalouf examined him, then dismissed the men, who left either side of Dubois.

Theatrical Lebanese bastard.

'Please, sit. My French is rusty, forgive me.' Maalouf spoke in impeccable French. 'It has been a long time.'

Maalouf gestured to the chair facing him. Between them was a thin-legged coffee table which held a small crystal ice bucket flanked by two glasses and a bottle of

Johnny Walker Black Label.

'Not long enough. I'm not here because of us. I'm here because of the operation against Freij. I will never forgive you, you must know that.'

'I understand. Sit anyhow, you can't stand.'

Dubois scanned the shabby room distastefully. 'Your standards are slipping.'

Maalouf smiled. 'As I become old, I find I have developed a fine eye for decrepitude.' He poured himself a drink, waving the bottle at Dubois, who shook his head, standing with his hands behind his back.

'The documents you gave to Nathalie assert Michel Freij is in the pay of the American government and his controller is an Israeli working in a joint Mossad and CIA operation.'

'That is correct. You see why we cannot possibly accept his accession to the presidency of Lebanon. A man with a successful defence company and links to America would be a great asset to Lebanon, particularly if it brought us more American aid, funding and investment. But to have a man who is a puppet of the Israelis? Even elements of the Christian community would find it hard to swallow that. But the rest of them...'

Dubois rounded angrily on Maalouf. 'This is a remarkable assertion and one I cannot support. We have very good reason to believe while Freij does indeed have remarkably close links to a number of American defence companies, he is most certainly operating against American and Israeli interests in this region.'

Maalouf inclined his head. He sipped his drink and regarded Dubois cautiously. 'Your good reason being based upon quite what evidence, Monsieur?'

Dubois ignored him. 'Do you have corroboration for your assertion regarding Freij and Israeli interests? Who is this Israeli controller?'

'His name is Amit Peled. What is the reason for your very strong interest in Michel Freij, if I may ask? He is hardly a... *European* problem, is he not?'

'Nothing much.'

Maalouf chuckled. 'Of course, only a minor investigation, this. An Anglo-French joint operation under the aegis of EJIC, involving elements of British forces in Cyprus, specialist communications equipment being flown in by military freighter and installed in the Résidence des Pins, along with something like fifteen French digital intelligence operatives. The rise in the level of data traffic between here, Brussels and London has been phenomenal.' Maalouf sipped his whisky, talking to himself. 'Quite phenomenal...'

Dubois remained silent. Maalouf continued. 'Let alone the traffic to Valetta and, Vlora, isn't it? Albania. Remarkable.' He paused, unrewarded with a response. 'Tell me, Yves, tell me about the *Arabian Princess*.'

Despite years of training and experience, Dubois blinked. 'How did you...'

Maalouf leaned forward. 'Michel Freij is not intending to target Israel with these warheads he has acquired, Yves. His target is Iran. Your analysts have over-emphasised the role Selim Hussein has played in this. Hussein is Shia, yes and he is also Freij's partner and close ally. But,' Maalouf raised a finger, 'no, listen to me, Yves. Freij is the Israeli's monster and he is dancing to their tune. As his father was before him, as you well know. Remember Raymond Freij? Sabra? Chatila?'

Dubois was silent, his gaze on his clasped hands.

Maalouf rose, brushing down the front of his trousers. 'Anyway, I have to go. I can't sit around in tumbledown houses all night.' He offered his hand to Dubois, who did not take it. Maalouf shrugged. 'Do your stuff on Peled, then get in touch with me. You have the number. I know we should be working together on this. I know you'll come round. We can't heal the past, but we can surely be aspirants to a better future. For *her*, Yves, if no-one else.'

Smiling, Maalouf walked past Dubois who stared into the empty fireplace, his knuckles white with the effort of keeping his fists at his sides rather than smashing them into Maalouf's smug face.

Lynch woke in pain to the sound of knocking on his bedroom door. He called out, nothing coherent but a cry to let the knocker know he was awake and wanted them to go away.

'Lynch. It's me. Get up, we need to go to the embassy.'

Nathalie.

He propped himself up on the bed, his bruised body protesting. He had flown in with Dubois that morning. He felt as if he hadn't slept in years. He reached for the plastic bottle of water he kept by the bed and drank.

Lynch called out hoarsely. 'What embassy?'

'French. We have total access to Falcon's security system. We need you.'

He slid from the bed, propping himself up against the wall.

'Okay, okay,' he croaked. 'Give me five.'

When Lynch emerged, red-eyed with his hair still damp, she handed him a pint glass of orange juice and soda. He reached into the kitchen cupboard for the blue packet of Panadol and took four. He gulped the drink and wiped his mouth with the back of his hand.

'Coffee?'

'There is not time. Come, we need to go to the

embassy.'

He threw the rest of the juice into the sink and followed her from the apartment into the ancient lift, leaning against the wood panelling as they creaked their way down to the ground floor.

Nathalie brought a *servees* to a halt with a wave, opening the door for Lynch who clambered in, noticing the crucifix dangling from the battered old Mercedes' cracked rearview mirror.

How does she always manage to get fucking Christians?

Lynch sank into the worn upholstery as they jerked through the busy streets, the stench of exhaust fumes overpowering and the erratic driving reawakening every wound. He noticed the driver's hand, blue veins standing out with age spots, blue fingertips too. *No wonder, the guy must be half dead with carbon monoxide poisoning.*

Lynch paid off the driver outside the French Embassy compound and followed Nathalie through security and into the impeccably groomed formal gardens of the imposing Résidence des Pins, through the dappled shadows cast by the big trees behind the colonnaded classical building. A guard stopped them. Nathalie showed her ID. Waved on, they rounded a corner to a large mobile home with a whip antenna and a brace of satellite dishes on its roof. Nathalie smiled at the guard by the side door.

Lynch followed her up the steps and inside, his eyes adjusting to the gloomy interior as Nathalie closed the door behind them. An impressive display of technology greeted him, banks of screens and racks, displays and keyboards. Two men sat on swivel chairs at the far end of the cramped space, wearing earphones and peering at screens, their ghostly faces illuminated by the displays. A third figure, podgier but younger than the other two, was stretched out on the floor, a dreamy, delighted expression on his fleshy face as he tapped on a Mac keyboard.

Nathalie kicked the kid's booted foot and his head jerked around in surprise. He focused, peering up at them.

'Oh, hi.' He scrambled to his feet, flicking a switch on a rack and pulling off the headphones. Breathless from the exertion, he gasped. 'Sorry. Rammstein.'

Nathalie turned to Lynch. 'This is Jean. He's heading up our local surveillance and interception resources. Jean, this is Lynch. He is an English spy with bad manners.'

Lynch's hand met a damp grip. Brown eyes took him in and a sensual little mouth smiled. 'Jean Meset. Nice to meet you.'

Lynch replied in French. 'A pleasure to make your acquaintance.'

Nathalie gestured to the wall of blinking electronics. 'So where are we?'

Meset ran a hand through his sparse light-brown hair, grinning as his eyes flickered between Nathalie and Lynch. 'We have penetrated the security system of Falcon Dynamics and we are analysing the product. For now we are being careful so we are not detected, but I can give you access to the CCTV system at the Deir Na'ee facility. We believe we have layouts of the facility, too. We have not identified any R&D systems on the networks we have compromised, but this is to be expected. The very sensitive data would not be directly online and would be protected with more sophisticated layers of security.' He sniggered. 'I must say, the systems we have encountered have been of a surprising sophistication.'

Lynch rubbed his eyes. 'Okay, let's take a look.'

'Here.' Meset turned to his right. 'I will scroll through

screens and you can tell me when to stop or ask where we are, okay?'

'Fine,' Lynch said.

Meset brought up a camera view, a classroom of some sort. Next a corridor, then another set of theatre-style seating. The screen flickered again, an empty storage space, an entranceway then a larger warehouse.'

'Stop. Can you zoom?'

'A little. It's risky, in case they're using this camera themselves.'

'There,' Lynch pointed at the screen. 'Zoom there.'

Two grey shapes became larger, more distinct. Meset licked his lips, fiddling with the keyboard and mouse. The screen wiped down as the pixellation hardened, blurred and then the screen redrew once, twice.

Lynch peered at the image in front of them, unmistakeably a mobile missile launcher. Behind it was the soft focus outline of another. The cradles were empty. He whistled softly. 'It looks as if they are waiting for something, no?'

Meset hit a key. 'Printing it.'

'Okay. More, then.'

They scrolled through more corridors, a series of workspaces divided into cubicles and empty warehouse areas. Lynch stopped the procession of grainy images in an open storage area. 'There, no, back. Yes, there. Enhance it.'

The shadowy cylinders flickered as the screen redrew once, twice. Finned tails, long bodies held in cradles. At their heads where there should have been a nose cone, they presented a flat surface.

'Okay, print that for me too,' Lynch said.

*

Nathalie Durand pressed her finger to the panel and presented her eye to the scanner. The door clicked and they left the opulent reception rooms of the Résidence des Pins and entered a plain white corridor, their shoes clacking on the shiny floor. They entered a side room, a large open-plan office filled with terminals, piles of equipment and banks of electronics. Cabling snaked between the racks and LEDs flashing on the black and silver panels.

Jean Meset called out in English, his voice stilling the group of people working at the terminals, mostly men but a handful of women, all young.

'Guys, meet Gerald Lynch from England. And of course you know our own lovely Nathalie.'

There was a ragged cheer from the group. Nathalie smiled and waved her hands to silence them. 'Okay, guys. What have we got on Falcon? Maurice?'

A youth wearing a torn black denim jacket and sporting a chin strip ran his hand through his untidy hair. 'We are proceeding carefully. We are in and nobody knows this so we try to keep it. We have the building security systems, as Jean will have told you.' He raised an eyebrow at Meset. 'You have been in the mobile, yes?' Meset nodded and Maurice continued, wiping his hand on his jacket. 'We have start to look at email traffic and we have mirrored the mail server, so this let us analyze the email archives offline. The financial system, it is on a different server and we are not in there yet, but soon this will happen. Their security, it is good, but some of the deeper network is not well done. We also think there are other systems at this site. It is probable there is a supercomputer for the modelling and other research work.'

Nathalie nodded. 'Janice?'

A girl rose, grinning nervously. A London accent, skinny and nervous. Curly hair, pale skin. 'Um, thanks. We've started tracing the subsidiaries Maurice's team is identifying and deep diving into the public records on each one before we assign a team to profile their security systems. Bryony's team is managing the subs. So far we're finding a lot more interests and holdings than any public source would acknowledge. It's a very big company indeed. And very privately held.'

Nathalie smiled, 'Tha—'

'And diverse,' said Janice, wringing her hands.

'I'm sorry?'

'Diverse. It's a diverse company.'

'Thank you, Janice. Gerald?'

Lynch started at the unexpected question. He tried to think of something useful to ask. Dubois' words to him, it seemed like a lifetime ago, came to his aid – a comment about Falcon working for the American defence industry.

He scanned the room. 'Has anyone come across any obvious links to US companies? Particularly in the defence sector?'

Several people threw their hands up, but it was Maurice who spoke for them. 'Yes, a lot. There are many, many references.'

Lynch glanced at Nathalie. 'Can we get someone to start profiling and analyzing the scope of that relationship? It seems odd to me that someone who actually makes missile systems would want to steal them.'

Nathalie nodded. 'Carmen? Can you make this your focus?'

'Sure thing. Will I report results to you or Gerald?'

'To both of us, please.' Nathalie paused for a second to scan the room. 'Let's keep the information moving, people. Carry on.'

Lynch found himself smiling at Nathalie's obvious command of her team as they left the room. He had to admit he was impressed at the way the gang of misfits looked up to her – and at the fact they seemed to know what they were doing.

Walking in front of him, her swinging hips a provocation, she spoke back at him. 'What are you grinning about, Lynch?'

'Ah, sure and ye know yerself,' he replied, watching the outline of her legs moving in her tight skirt.

His side still hurt, though.

Chapter Twenty-Nine

Lynch and Nathalie sat together on the sofa watching CNN's Middle East Report. Michel Freij was looking sharp, an open-necked white shirt and black suit, composed and relaxed. The woman interviewing him announced a report on the man who had come from nowhere to set Lebanese politics alight, the head of the One Lebanon Party. The programme cut away to the package, a voiceover announcing that Freij and his unlikely partner had founded the Lebanese computer and electronics company Falcon Dynamics when they were at university, recruiting the brightest talent from around the Middle East and even bringing young people back from Dubai to join in the success of the growing defence and communications company. Freij and Hussein crossed the sectarian divide, successful business partners from the Christian and Shia Muslim communities who worked together to build operations in the Middle East, West Africa, Central Europe and now mainland Europe. Diversification had taken Falcon into telecoms, dotcoms and even tourism and transportation. Falcon's significant contributions to charitable work, social development programs and educational programs were a major element of its work and had won it award after award.

'I feel sick,' said Lynch. Nathalie shushed him. The programme cut back to the studio, the CNN anchor gesturing with her pen.

'So, Michel Freij, you and Selim Hussein have built a multibillion-dollar business together. Why this move into politics now?'

Freij inclined his head. 'Well, first let me say thank you for having me here on Middle East Report, Tina. It is truly an honour and privilege for me.' He paused to smile. 'To answer your question, it is something that Selim and I have often discussed, that our nation is partisan, too polarized and built around sectarian lines and self-interest. I am already wealthy. I have no need of corruption or what we Arabs call *wasta*. I consider myself a testament to the success of a non-sectarian approach to building something significant in the shape of our business and I think Lebanon has the same opportunity to build and grow if it can put sectarianism behind it. So I think I can make a difference.'

'There were disturbances at your recent Beirut rally. What do you have to say to those who oppose your point of view so strongly that they use violence?'

Freij nodded. 'Yes, thank you. I do not believe this is the solution. We all know where violence has taken the Lebanese people in the past. I am proposing a new Lebanon, a Lebanon that can rebuild herself. A Lebanon of unity and prosperity, of fairness and equality because we will be capable of repelling all outside interests, of defending our shores against all force. Our new Lebanon will be a nation of strength, capable of deterring others from interfering in our rights and sovereignty.'

'You have often referred to a Lebanon that can defend

herself against outsiders. How will you achieve this?'

Freij sat back in the chrome and leather studio chair, throwing his arms out expansively. 'The key is strength as a nation. We are not a football for others to kick around. The key to a strong Lebanon is a strong deterrent to others. We must have a strong police, a strong civil defence so we have the rule of law in our country. At the same time, hand in hand with this, we must have a deterrent against others who choose to make incursions into our airspace and onto our land. Once we have that deterrent in place, and our enemies accept we can and will use this deterrent, we can focus on rebuilding our nation together as one people. We can focus on our future. We need to secure our outside so we can focus our efforts on ourselves, on our nation. One nation.'

'Shit,' said Lynch.

Tina adjusted her clipboard, leaning forward for the killer question. 'You have said that Lebanon must work with America and the United Nations. How can you reconcile that with a policy of military aggressiveness in the region?'

Freij's features relaxed into a picture of reasonableness. He leaned forwards, his hand outstretched, palm up and fingers curled. 'I do not talk of aggression, but of deterrence. What purpose would aggression serve? It is aggression that has done this to Lebanon, brought her low. Now we will bring her high, but not through aggression, but by asserting our right to sit at the table with other nations, to take our rightful place as a leader in the region and the world.'

'If you are successful in your bid for the presidency, does any ambition remain for you, Mr Freij?'

'My ambition is for Lebanon. Winning the popular vote and gaining the presidency through a parliamentary vote is only the start for my ambition, because it will mark the start, *insh'Allah*, of a new era for our country. One of hope, togetherness and prosperity for all people born in Lebanon. One people.'

Tina laid her clipboard flat on her knees, slapping the pen down on top of it with a satisfied air.

'Michel Freij, head of the One Lebanon Party, thank you.'

Lynch snatched the remote and snapped the television off. 'Fuck, are you seriously telling me anyone buys that schtick?'

Nathalie rose, rubbing her back. 'Of course. They love him. He is a hero in the Palestinian camps because he offers them nationality, passports in place of travel documents. They are treated as second-class citizens and now he is offering Lebanon to them on a plate. The Christians love him because he is such a strong figure. His father was a hero in the civil war and Michel has carried on with brilliance. Some even credit him with an informal leadership of the big Maronite families. The Shia love him because of Selim. He has built schools, workshops and factories employing thousands of Druze. He's almost a hero in areas of the Chouf. He is a very powerful man. And he does truly appeal to them all.'

She walked into the kitchen. Lynch threw down the remote and pushed himself out of the sofa, walking towards the drinks cabinet. He poured a whisky.

'Really, Lynch, it is only four o'clock.'

He turned, the tumbler in his hand and his finger pointing at her. 'Did I ever tell you what to do with your life?' She halted, the apple she had taken held halfway up to her mouth. He dropped his gaze to the glass and breathed deeply. 'Ah, look. I'm sorry. I didn't mean to snap, I—'

'No, you're right. It's none of my business if you want to be drunk all the time. It must be a secret British intelligence strategy, this drinking. You are *very* good at it. Here, let me try.'

Grabbing a bottle, Nathalie poured a stiff measure of whisky into a tumbler. 'Not the blue teardrop one, right?' She knocked it back. '*Bon.* So now am I more *intelligent,* Lynch?' She glared at him, the glass held almost sideways in her hand.

He stepped towards her. 'Look—'

She raised her face, her eyes flashing defiance. Her pouting lips full and her black hair shining as it tumbled against her cheek, her warning gesture too late as he moved into her and put his hand on her lower back, pulled her to him and kissed her, tasting the whisky from her open mouth. Her hand was behind his neck, the tumbler spinning in the air as their bodies coalesced and she met his tongue with hers.

The glass smashed, unheeded.

*

They lay together in the darkness, the sheets on the floor and their bodies cool. Lynch broke the long silence.

'I'm going up there.'

'Deir Na'ee?'

'Yes.'

'When did you decide this?'

'Just now. Lying here, thinking.'

'So you don't think about making love?'

'Yes. No. Well. You drift, no?'

She laughed, her breath on his ear. 'Yes, you drift.' She ran her fingers across the hairs on his chest. 'Why?'

'Why do I want to go up there?'

She moved onto her elbow, reaching to pull his chin to face her. 'Obviously, you irritant.'

'I want to get a GPS marker for that shed, the one where they're storing the transporters, but I want to try and see what the hell it is they've got going on up there. I want to have a look around. You know, take a walk.'

'Lynch, that is insanely dangerous.'

'We don't know what's up there, do we? I think it's time we did.'

She felt his nipple stiffen under her fingertip. 'Can we plan this properly?'

'Sure,' he said, sliding his hand down her back. 'No rush, like.'

Chapter Thirty

Peter Meier gazed over the wooden railing, the sea breeze whipping his hair. He sipped from the mug of coffee, putting it down to light one of Gonsalves' cigarettes. He pointed to a thin blue line on the horizon.

'Where's that?'

Gonsalves flicked the base of the soft pack and shook a cigarette free for himself. 'Zakynthos, boss. Greece.' He lit it, his signet rings clinking against the glittering gold lighter. 'We've made good time.'

They had left the storm far behind, the early morning sky clear and warming from grey dawn to the cobalt blue of a Mediterranean spring day. Meier smiled, drawing on his cigarette and reflecting on the sense of freedom and space the open sea brings to a man who has faced an impossible and deadly challenge and won. Hoffmann's blundering stupidity had come close to wrecking everything Meier had built so carefully, his mad bitch of a daughter running around and telling her wild stories. Meier was amazed she hadn't gone to the newspapers, but grateful she had chosen to go to ground in Malta. He had enjoyed killing her, which perturbed him a little. Meier had no issues with death as an operational necessity, but he didn't approve of killing for pleasure.

A cloud descended on Meier's sunny outlook. He shook his head and stubbed out the cigarette in the ashtray Gonsalves kept on the bridge. Michel Freij hated smoking and this was, technically at least, now his boat. Meier clapped Gonsalves on the shoulder, letting his hand stay there and weigh down on the man. 'You did well to find that mobile in Malta, Joel. It let us tie up those loose ends nicely.' Meier didn't let his voice miss a beat or change in pitch. 'Why didn't you kill her when I told you to?' Kneading Gonsalves' shoulder, he felt the man's muscles stiffen. Gonsalves' forehead was damp. 'I thought I had, boss. Boutros was supposed to take care of it.'

'You want to be careful, making mistakes like that, Joel. You could get hurt. Worse than the nasty bruise you have on your face.' Gonsalves swallowed, the puncture wounds from Elli's fork still livid scars on his cheek. Later, Meier thought. There was time to take it out on Gonsalves later. For now, he had a more pressing problem on his hands. 'How is Mister Freij enjoying the stateroom?'

Gonsalves' voice was shaky. He wiped his wrist across his mouth. 'No complaints, boss. Guess he'll be having breakfast now, one of the crew woke him up almost an hour ago.' Gonsalves flicked a switch on the small black panel beneath the screen to his side, a view of the dining saloon showing a slim figure standing by the sideboard. 'Yup. Breakfast.'

Meier peered at the screen. 'Arrogant pig. Right, I'm going down. How long until we get to the island?'

'We should be there this time tomorrow. I'm trying to stick to the busiest shipping lanes, change our course a little bit in case we're being tracked but still behave like a regular old gin palace.'

'Talking of which, where are Meshkalla's girls?'

Gonsalves grinned. 'On the sun deck already, boss. They're real babes.'

'Hands off, Gonsalves. They're for the pleasure of my client.'

Gonsalves' face was a picture of innocence. 'You know you can trust me, boss. Besides, I'm not sure that's where your client's tastes lie, if you—'

'Shut up, Gonsalves. Drive the Goddamned boat.'

Gonsalves' gaze dropped. 'Boss.'

Meier turned and left the wheelhouse, taking the spiral staircase down to the dining saloon, his face genial as he spied Michel Freij sitting at the great twelve-seater maple and walnut table, a collection of plates spread in front of him. A uniformed crew member poured coffee, one of four Albanian waiting staff they had taken on in Vlorë. Meier saw no reason why he shouldn't make his customer comfortable while they handed over the boat and its cargo.

'Michel, Michel. How good to see you.' Meier pulled up a chair, flinging his arm out to encompass the saloon. 'Is she not beautiful in the daylight?'

Freij dabbed at his lips. He chewed at some length as Meier waited. He swallowed, bestowing a thin smile on Meier that didn't reach his watchful eyes. 'When do we reach Anhydrous?'

Meier signalled for coffee. 'Tomorrow morning. All that remains is to sit back and enjoy this beautiful craft and the company on board.'

Freij scanned the dishes in front of him, taking a piece of flat bread, scooping up a piece of herbed cheese and pinching an olive to make a little parcel. He stared at Meier. 'We are carrying two tactical nuclear warheads, Meier. We hold the future of a nation on this ship. This isn't a pleasure cruise.' He popped the parcel in his mouth, wiping his hands on the napkin. Chewing, Freij regarded Meier.

'But of course.' Meier smiled as he reflected on his newfound pleasure, the contemplation of an act of murder. He rolled it around in his mind as one would a fine brandy in the mouth.

Meier stood in the wheelhouse next to Gonsalves and

watched the island's dusty light brown soil and green clumps of scrubby vegetation slide past. Dressed in white trousers and a polo shirt, feeling every part the mariner, he wore a pair of binoculars around his neck. Gonsalves turned the wheel as they rounded the headland, taking them closer in. Michel Freij's sure, light-footed step came up the stairs to the wheelhouse.

'There we go boss,' said Gonsalves, pointing as a large white building came into view.

Meier brought the binoculars to his eyes and scanned it. 'Good God.'

'Ah, so you like our little holiday home?' Freij smirked.

Meier let the binoculars fall. 'This belongs to you?'

'Welcome to The Near East Institute for Oceanographic Research.' Freij bowed slightly. 'It was built as a hotel but we took the site over and extended it. As you can see, we have made a number of additions to the original building.'

Trees surrounded the hotel building, a green lawn stretched down to the white, sandy beach. To its side was a large concrete structure that looked like an aircraft hangar, its sea-doors open.

Meier beamed to hide his intense dislike for Freij. The man's proprietary air irked him intensely. His cheeks hurt as he nodded. Freij swept his arm to encompass the buildings jutting out from the barren hump in front of them. 'This is the island of Anhydrous. It is, as you will deduce from the name, waterless. We lease it from the government of Thira, who are most accommodating in many ways. The lack of water was the eventual downfall of the hotel project. The developers lacked vision and purpose. We funded a proper hydrographic survey and brought up the water that had been there all along. We have a Jordanian team that specialises in such technologies.'

Meier bowed slightly. 'You are most astute.'

'Yes,' Freij seemed surprised. 'I suppose we are. Gonsalves, you can enter the hangar, dock to the right if you please.'

Meier, burning with resentment, stood by as Gonsalves acted on the instruction. It was technically Freij's boat, but the man's casual assumption that Gonsalves was now *his* man was infuriating. Meier glared towards the island and the hangar as it loomed up towards them. He shivered as they slid into the big space, lighting hung from the gantries above, boiler-suited men standing on the dockside, staring. The huge sea-doors started to close behind them, the rattle of the heavy chains echoing in the yawning depths of the big chamber.

The closing impact boomed in the great space, a signal for the men on the dock to start moving. The crew cast ropes to them, snaking white lines picked out by the floodlights. The yacht slowed to a standstill, its wash sloshing inside the hangar. The gangway lowered and a team of men in white biohazard suits raced up it, deploying across the covered pool area and directing the crane swinging around over the boat.

On the upper sun deck, Meier watched the heavy panels covering the pool roll back. Michel Freij was impassive at his side. More lamps snapped on high above them, lighting up the two green, tapered cones nestled in their sophisticated aluminium and black foam cradles.

'They don't look so evil, do they, Meier?' Freij chuckled, a new sound to Meier. 'Yet each one can destroy a city.'

'I know their capabilities, Mr Freij.'

'Do you? Do you really? How fascinating.' The low

chuckle sounded again. 'The standard Russian missile was capable of propelling these almost five hundred kilometres. It was unbelievably,' Freij cast about for the right word, smiling when he found it, 'crude. Solid fuel, barely better than a Scud, really. We have developed hybrid propellant systems that will send this warhead four times the distance and yet are still capable of a mobile launch with fast deployment. We have, of course, developed the most sophisticated electronic countermeasures to protect our delivery system.'

Meier made an effort to keep his voice steady, his mind racing to try to assess the potential of Freij's assertions. 'You are to be commended. But why would you need such long reach? I had thought your target to be the Zionist state.'

Freij patted Meier's shoulder heavily forcing Meier to steady himself against the handrail. 'Why? Because we can reach London from anywhere in Lebanon if we wish to, Herr Meier. Imagine. London, this great city. And of course we can reach out to touch any other great city in mainland Europe. Or indeed into Asia. Any city we choose, and with pinpoint accuracy. Is that not... *splendid*?'

Meier watched the first warhead rise in its cradle as if in a dream, gripping the varnished wood to steady himself. The whir of the crane and the muffled sound of men calling instructions echoed in the great, covered space came to him as if through cotton wool.

Freij turned away from the handrail. 'Come, Herr Meier. Our work here is done. We can leave this good ship to the careful ministrations of my men now. We can celebrate our success.'

The cone encased in its cradle swung onto the dockside where it was grabbed by a team of men in white coveralls and guided onto a trolley. The straps dropped and the crane moved back over the boat. Meier hastened after Freij down the spiral staircase to the bridge deck. He called out as he descended. 'Where are you taking them now?'

'To Beirut, Herr Meier.'

'Yes, yes, but how?'

They reached the main deck and Meier caught up with Freij. 'How are you going to get them to Beirut?'

Freij glanced down at Meier's hand on his arm and Meier let it drop. The dark, glittering eyes flickered and Meier felt like prey. 'To Beirut, Herr Meier? Why, I am going to fly them there like little angels.' He grinned. 'I shall give them wings.'

They descended the gangway to the dockside, the workmen making way for Freij and two supervisors attending him anxiously. Meier paused and watched the second warhead being hoisted from the yacht, its cradle glittering in the overhead lights. Meier tore his gaze away from the warhead and turned to follow Freij away from the wharf into the corridor beyond, his heels sounding on the concrete floor.

They waited by the brushed steel lift doors, stepping in when they opened to a soft digital tone. They turned and waited as the door closed. Meier gazed at the orange display counting the floors until they stopped on the third. He was surprised to find himself in a corporate-style office, partition windows sandblasted with striped patterns lining a light blue carpeted corridor that carried them along to a small reception area. A wooden door opened and a smiling, efficient-looking woman in her thirties emerged to meet them, speaking English then impeccable German with a soft, Alsatian accent.

'Mister Freij, welcome back, sir. Herr Meier. *Bitte, kommen Sie herein.*'

Chapter Thirty-One

Freij's office was impressive indeed and Meier, despite his growing dislike for Freij and his damned arrogance, had to admit the man had taste. He breathed in the smell of leather from the beige hide sofa and chairs around a glass coffee table perched on a stone head of Buddha, *killims* strewn on the floor and a hidebound desk to one side. The desk was flanked by shelves containing books, little figurines and pieces of ancient glass. The wall to the right hosted a bank of plasma screens showing the *Arabian Princess* at her mooring, the second missile now sitting on the dockside.

Michel Freij draped his jacket over the back of a chair. The woman directed Meier to a sofa by a coffee table. She left and Freij turned from the dark wood sideboard, two champagne flutes in his hand.

'Herr Meier, I think you will find everything you expected is in the attaché case before you.'

Meier leaned forward to pull the gold latches of the red calfskin case with his thumbs. He pulled open the lid of the case, which contained a single cream parchment envelope with his name written on it in careful calligraphy worked in dark brown ink. Tucked into the document pockets attached to the lid were more envelopes and a passport.

Freij placed a flute in front of Meier and one by his own seat. He went back to the sideboard. 'All as we agreed, Herr Meier. A price of one hundred and twenty million dollars. Eighty million has already been transferred to Herr Hoffman's company account, as you are aware. A Lebanese passport in the name of Hans Allawi, whose mother is German and whose father is Lebanese. Herr Allawi holds an account with Bank Audi containing ten million dollars. He is also the sole owner of Allawi Holdings of Bermuda and this company owns a mixed portfolio of stocks and bonds with a current market value of thirty million dollars held in Beirut, Bogotá and six other markets. The case also contains a first-class ticket from Beirut to Colombo booked two weeks ago in that name. You may keep the case with our compliments. We thank you for your efforts.'

Meier nodded, trying not to react. 'It has been a pleasure to do business with you and your esteemed partner, I am sure.' He opened the envelope and unfolded the expensive-looking parchment. The fine calligraphy read 'Peter Meier'. Meier waved it at Freij. 'What is this?'

'An old family tradition, Herr Meier. It is a gift tag. Here.' A gentle pop sounded. Freij returned carrying a green bottle. 'Lamiable, Herr Meier. A fine, single grower extra brut champagne. It is a particular indulgence of mine.' He poured the fine, pale liquid into the glasses. The dancing bubbles glittered.

'*Bi sahtak*. Your health.'

'*Auf Dich*,' Meier responded, raising his glass to toast Freij. He sat back, watching the screens where the second warhead was being lifted into a white container marked with blue lettering. He gestured with his glass at the screen. 'UNWRA?'

Freij turned to the screens. 'Oh, the containers? Yes, we are now an aid shipment.' He beamed at Meier. 'A small container vessel will take them to Thira and then we shall take them to Beirut. You also, Herr Meier. Ellen has booked you a ticket from Santorini to Beirut under your new name. Sadly, your flight must connect in Athens and then Larnaca.' Freij pulled a tragic face. 'Direct flights are so often a problem for us in Lebanon.'

Meier nodded graciously. He sipped his champagne, noticing how fine the flute was, holding the dry, complicated drink in his mouth and revelling in the fact that a lifetime's work had culminated in this – a new identity, a new life of reward and luxury. The stress of the past few weeks was making itself felt now as he relaxed, a feeling of lassitude creeping over him.

He placed the glass down on the coffee table, and Freij reached over to top it up.

'It is a particularly fine champagne, no, Herr Meier?'

Meier nodded. 'I have always preferred Sekt, of course, being German. But I have to confess, when the French get it right...'

Freij sat back in his chair. 'Lamiable is a small house, a grand cru, of course, from near Tours. Sixty percent Pinot Noir, forty percent Chardonnay. We can enjoy champagne because of the Levant, you know this, Herr Meier? The Chardonnay grape was taken back to France by the Crusaders. My ancestors, in fact.'

Meier shook his head, tiredness slowing his movements. He settled back into the big chair, letting Freij's enthusiastic torrent of words wash over him. The man was positively garrulous now he had his blasted warheads safe. Meier would be pleased to turn his back on Michel Freij, for sure. Having said that, however irritatingly superior the man was, he had made Peter Meier a rich man. He gave up a private toast to that. He reached for his glass, but his hand wouldn't respond.

'You must be tired, Herr Meier. So much achieved, so much energy. This has been a flawless operation on your part, carried out with considerable... what is the word I need here, Herr Meier? I am so very clumsy sometimes with these words. My English is not so good. *Brio*? Is this the word?'

The stitching on the sofa was a pale terracotta colour, the new leather soft and welcoming. Meier tried to move his head, to nod assent. He was gripped with panic, incapable of movement. His breathing was reduced to gasps.

Freij's voice was chatty. 'It is a powerful form of potentiated chlorzoxazone developed by our pharmaceuticals company. Sadly, it did not result in a clinical compound we felt could find a market, but it is a very powerful muscle relaxant indeed. It dissolves quite nicely in alcohol, which further potentiates the drug. It must feel strange, Herr Meier,' Freij leaned forwards to peer into Meier's eyes, 'To find oneself relaxing to death.' There was garlic on Freij's breath. Houmos for breakfast, thought Meier.

Meier's breath rasped as Freij sat back, beaming at him. 'I forgot to mention that the flight we had booked for you to Beirut was a cargo shipment. I am so sorry that my memory is such a traitor to me.'

Meier made one last supreme effort, sweat beading his upper lip as he forced his mouth to move, Freij craning forwards to catch the word as he formed it.

'Fucker.'

'Herr Meier, I am shocked,' Freij mocked, standing. 'Shocked, I tell you. I think perhaps you had better take a chill pill.' He looked down with a dry chuckle. 'Oh, sorry. You did already.'

Meier's breathing froze, his lungs betraying him an instant before his heart stopped beating. Peter Meier expired with a long sigh, hate burning in his furious eyes and his face frozen in calm repose.

The darkness claimed him.

*

Gonsalves swept an appreciative hand over the fine hide of the attaché case, the gold catches glittering in the lights from the *Arabian Princess'* bar area.

Michel Freij gestured at the case. 'Go ahead, open it.'

Gonsalves snapped the catches and pulled the lid up to reveal neat packages of twenty dollar bills. He nodded, swallowed and looked up at Freij, who was gauging his reaction. 'There is one hundred thousand dollars in the case. You may consider this yours to keep.'

Freij leaned towards Gonsalves, offering an envelope. Gonsalves took it.

'This is the necessary information to access your account with the Bank Audi of Lebanon containing three million dollars, double the fee that you agreed with Herr Hoffmann and Herr Meier, I believe.'

Gonsalves swallowed. 'I —'

Freij waved him silent. 'We may well do business again, Mister Gonsalves. You now know that we are generous and fair-minded employers and so I consider this to be in the way of an investment. The bonus in front of you is to ensure that you get this hulk to Tripoli quickly and in good order. I want to be able to enjoy my yacht without Meier's stink all over it.'

Gonsalves nodded. 'Not a problem. Where is —'

'Gone.' Freij got to his feet. 'He never did join the boat. His whereabouts is a total mystery. You can leave that with us. He did not fulfil his obligation and we are only generous,' Freij scrutinised his fingernail, 'with those who deliver.'

Gonsalves' quick eyes flickered from Freij's goatee-bearded face to the burgundy case on the black marble-topped table. He licked his lips. 'I understand.'

'Tripoli, then. Thank you, Captain.'

Freij wheeled around and left without a further word, his shoes clattering on the steps down from the bridge.

Gonsalves had an erection. He sat back and luxuriated in the sight of a hundred grand in notes, just like in the movies, running his thumbnail absently, if pleasurably, up and down the tumescence pushing against the length of his zip.

The two Albanian girls Meier had brought along in case Freij had wanted to be entertained were still on board. A Mediterranean cruise on a fifty metre yacht with a hundred big ones in cash and two hookers all to himself. Gonsalves grinned. Life was about to become very good indeed.

They were in the open sea again, free of the hangar on Anhydrous. Joel Gonsalves scanned the blue horizon in front of him and took the cigarette smoke deep into his lungs. He was shot of Freij and Meier and their toxic cargo. He'd finished the job and gotten paid. Now he was clean and free. It doesn't get better than this, he reflected. He sipped his whisky and laughed out loud for joy and exhilaration.

One of the girls, the brunette, was lying topless on the sun deck above and Gonsalves had the feeling she might need some suntan lotion. He picked up his lighter and softpack, cut the boat to autopilot and climbed up the circular stairwell. Sure enough, she was on her back, her skin glistening with tanning oil, naked and shaved. Shading her eyes from the sun to look at the new arrival, she smiled, turning so her legs opened. His eyes flickered across her breasts, firm and dotted with beads of sweat. She smelled of coconut oil.

'Gonsalves. You have cigarette for me?'

He swaggered over to kneel beside her sun lounger, its blue foam covering darkened with the moisture from her lithe body. Her toenails were painted crimson and she wore an enamelled gold Snoopy ankle chain. She opened her full lips for him to insert the cigarette, holding his wrist as he lit it, her fine gold bangle sliding down her arm. He laid his hand on her belly. She exhaled, moving to push it downwards. Gonsalves let his fingers glide down her slippery skin. He took his time, revelling in the smell of her, licking his lips as her legs parted wider. His finger poised at the top of her, trembling a little. She moaned. A bead of sweat rolled down her inner thigh.

The explosion tore them apart. The fireball engulfed the big yacht, ripping through all five decks and sending great hunks of wreckage wheeling high into the Wedgwood sky. The sea around the *Arabian Princess*, compressed by the hammering force of the concussion, threw up a great wave that reflected the mass of flame in glittering golden splashes. The black smoke rose, smearing the sky above the red flames that roiled at the centre of the great conflagration, detritus splashing into the water, falling into scattered fires of polystyrene and fuel stretched across a huge area of water.

Michel Freij was nothing if not fastidious when it came to tidying up loose ends.

Chapter Thirty-Two

Lynch sat at the dark wood bar and ordered an Almaza, paying in dollars. He took back the change. 'I'm looking for Marwan Nimr. Know him?'

The barman turned away. Lynch sighed and sipped his beer. He sensed movement beside him, turning to face the stocky, round-shouldered figure in the faded green army shirt pulling up a barstool.

'And say you found Marwan,' the man growled. 'What then?'

Lynch grinned, his blue eyes wrinkling with delight. 'Sure, I'd buy the man a drink. Any friend of Spike's is a friend of mine.'

'I never heard of no Spike.'

'Come on, Marwan, we're both big boys. Spike AKA Anthony Najimi. Small time hood, smack dealer and the sex pest of AUB. Sure you know him.'

Nimr was bald, his head creased above the ear from wearing sunglasses. His dark goatee beard framed full lips. His prominent nose arced to indolent hazel eyes beneath his heavy eyebrows.

'Jack and Coke, double. Easy on the Coke. Heavy on the ice.'

The barman was already making the drink. Lynch studied the glass as it was banged down on the bar. He glanced at Nimr. 'I understand you offer transportation services. Did you offer them to Paul Stokes? Journalist fellow. Remember him?'

'I charter helicopters, yes.' Nimr toasted Lynch with the frosted glass. 'Cheers. Don't remember the name.'

Lynch sighed. 'You're not very good with names, are

you Marwan?'

Nimr shrugged and Lynch shifted to face the big man. 'You took Stokes up into the mountains, high up North. Did you land up there?'

Nimr sat silently, his eyes half-lidded. Lynch fought the urge to smack the man's face. 'No, no we didn't. Just an overflight.'

Lynch drank. 'Will you take me up there?'

Nimr's smile died. 'Who sent you here?'

'Tony Chalhoub mentioned you drank here.'

Nimr nodded. 'Yeah, I know him. Cop. You a cop?'

'Nope.' Lynch lowered his voice mock-conspiratorially. 'You still a robber?'

Nimr finished his drink. 'Again, Mike. His tab.' He turned to Lynch. 'Up where?'

'Place called Deir Na'ee. Kalaa Mountain, near Dannieh. Where you took Stokes.'

Nimr drained his glass. 'I know where it is. Why you wanna go there?'

'I'm a nosy tourist.'

Nimr laughed, a throaty chuckle. 'Bullshit, dude. You ain't got no Nikon.'

'I left it at home.'

'What's your beef with Michel Freij?'

Lynch leaned forwards, lowering his voice. 'I want the motherfucker behind bars. What's yours?'

'So you *are* a cop.'

'No, I'm not. I'm James Bond, me. I'm what students of oxymorons laughingly call British intelligence.'

'No, thanks, man. I don't need all this cop stuff. I'm private enterprise.'

'So I understand. Which is why you ended up in Roumieh Prison. I'm offering you a nice stable government job, Marwan. You know, guaranteed hours and a good, clean salary check. Even a little, how do I express this, gratitude if you should ever find yourself needing a friend.'

Nimr cast up his eyes at the bottles stacked on shelves behind the bar, took a drink from his glass and shook his head. 'No, thanks, man. Nice of you to think of me.'

Lynch turned to Nimr. 'You were supposed to learn from jail, Marwan. They're meant to be correctional institutions. You're still running shit from the Bekaa.'

He glimpsed the big man's fist bunched in his trouser leg, stretching the material.

'No way. I'm clean, man.'

'Bullshit. Look, I'm offering you a sweet, all expenses paid chance to help me fuck up the Freij family. I think you owe them something, no?'

Nimr considered Lynch's words. He nodded. 'Sure I do. But I don't do public sector, man. No way.'

Lynch fished in his pocket, emerging with a black pellet that he held under Nimr's nose. Take a sniff of that,' he said appreciatively. 'Really first-class stuff.'

Nimr's eyes were fixed on Lynch, his face pale. Beads of perspiration dotted his head. He inhaled hesitantly, his nose crinkling.

Lynch was still smiling. 'Hash laced with opium. Very nice, top quality. From the Bekaa. You know they farm that stuff up there still? Land belongs to a flyboy who doesn't get that the civil war is over. You might have heard of him, Nimr. Marwan Nimr. Flies fruit by day, gear by night. Fat bald guy.' Lynch pulled on his cigar, ignoring Nimr's raised hand. 'Chalhoub will take you down the second I call him, Marwan. For running dope but also for the murder of Paul Stokes.'

Nimr's knuckles were white. 'I had nothing to do with the kid, I just took him on a ride. Najimi had business with him, not me. Najimi worked for Freij.'

'Worked? Past tense? My, but word gets around quickly.'

The sweat was running off Nimr's bald head. He turned to face Lynch. 'Was it you killed him? Najimi?'

'Not me, Marwan. Harry.' Lynch handed the pellet of marijuana to Nimr, who nodded and slipped it into his pocket.

'Okay. But you pay.'

Lynch lifted his second beer. 'I just said that. Jesus, Marwan, can we not be a touch more subtle about the money stuff.' He screwed up his face in disgust. 'I hate talking about fucking money.'

'Ten thousand.'

'Lire?'

'Fuck you man. US.'

'Five. You have a vested interest in helping me, believe me.'

'Ten.'

'So how long did you spend in Roumieh? Time go quickly, did it? Or did you settle in nicely with all the pretty young things they sent in there to keep you company?'

Nimr growled. 'Don't fuck with me like that, man.'

'Five thousand, Marwan.' Lynch tapped on the bar with a beer mat. He threw it down and faced Nimr. 'I'll buy the fuel. Last.'

Nimr nodded. 'Okay. I'll live with that. You better have a strong stomach, though, James Bond.'

Lynch considered this for a second. 'Uh, no. My name's Lynch. Gerald Lynch.'

'I preferred Bond.'

'You'll get used to it.'

*

Soaring above Beirut in Nimr's helicopter, they left the city behind. The great mountain, Sannine, loomed to their right as they banked away from the sea and flew over the foothills. The aircraft, an ex-army Alouette II, was registered as a crop sprayer. It wasn't carrying any tanks or spray rig.

Nimr was in his element, his hands deft on the controls and joy in his voice on the radio link between them as he pointed out landmarks to Lynch, the wooded slopes below dotted with farmhouses. They flew across a green valley, the white-capped mountains rising to their right. Nimr gestured to the land ahead of them, his voice carrying over the intercom above the insistent whine of the engines. 'That's Feraya, where Beirut likes to go ski. Nice place. We're about half an hour from Deir Na'ee but I have to make a quick stop first.'

Lynch turned, but the helmet, glasses and microphone made Nimr's expression impossible to gauge. 'Why?'

'I have to get some stuff prepared. No big deal, take about fifteen minutes.'

Lynch turned back to see the dramatic folds of the mountainside below them, dotted with greenery with occasional patches of white as the spring sun started to reclaim the ground from the winter. 'This used to be deep snow through this time of year right up to June. Snow's been pretty erratic last few years, comes late, comes early. It's fucking up the skiing industry.'

They passed a freestanding crucifix perched on a rocky outcrop, which Nimr pointed out. 'See that? You're in Christian country big time now, *Kartaba*.'

They climbed, banking to fly north above the valley, rising to its left. Nimr leaned across Lynch pointing to the left and dipping the helicopter so they looked down to the rocks that breasted the top of the valley, a smattering of snow dusted across the rockscape. 'See there? That's Jaj. I got a sister-in-law lives there.'

'Too much detail, Marwan. Let's get the fuck on with it, eh?'

'Only being friendly, dude. Don't wanna waste the scenery now.'

Lynch laughed, shaking his head. 'Fuck, no. Sure am't I a tourist only?'

They passed a village to their right, terracotta roofs and an area of cultivated fields rose, then dipped down, descending fast towards a small wooded valley, the hillsides closing in on them as it deepened. A blue warehouse building loomed ahead, blacktop laid to its front. They dropped to the tarmac and landed gently, a last bump before Nimr killed the rotors, slowing their insistent whipping.

Nimr unclipped his seatbelt and removed his helmet. The shades stayed on. 'Cigarette break.'

Lynch stepped down from the chopper, his breath misty in the cold mountain air, tucking his hands under his armpits for warmth. Nimr turned to him. 'See that bowser over there? That's fuel. Pull the pipe over this way and fill her up. You engage the red handle.' He strode towards the warehouse, unlocking the side door and wrenching it open with a screech.

Lynch wandered over to the small, rusty lorry and unhooked the dirty pipe from its side, dragging it over to the Alouette. He found the fuel tank and was trying to snap the red handle of the feeder pipe to the notched tank-mouth when Nimr returned with a pallet truck.

'Here, let me.' Nimr took the metal fitment and twisted it with a single practised movement, the two pieces snicking together smoothly. He handed Lynch a pair of keys on a plastic fob. 'Start her up and hit the green button on the dash.'

The engine of the bowser kicked into action after a few coughs. Lynch found the green button and listened to the pump kicking in. He dropped down from the cab and went back to the Alouette. 'How do I know when it's full?'

Nimr was stretched underneath the body of the aircraft, wrenching a complex assembly to the fuselage. 'When it's full.'

'What's that?'

Nimr grunted as he tightened the wrench, sliding out on the trolley under his back. He blinked as the wintry sunlight caught his brown eyes. 'Mind your own business.'

There was a snapping sound and the pump cut off. Nimr grinned. 'Full. Disconnect it and I'll put this junk away.'

Lynch eyed the fuel pipe distastefully. 'That didn't seem worth it.'

'This baby's got a 350 klick range. You never know when you might need that last thirty or so. Best fly full when you can, *kapisch*? Unclip it, man, we need to get going.'

Lynch did as he was told. Within a few minutes they were sitting back in harness and Nimr hit the starter. The Alouette's engine coughed and roared into life.

They rose above the blue warehouse, the sheer face of the valley in front of them dropping away as if they were going up in a lift, the Alouette steadied by Nimr's sure rudder-work, his legs flexing. They breasted the valley, skimming over the snow-whitened, rocky landscape to another valley beyond, the road below clinging to the steep, far side of the valley, snaking between the dark trees in the wintry landscape. They rose farther, leaving the valley and then banked right to follow a steep ravine.

'This is Bcharre. People up here are real headbangers. Khalil Gibran came from here. Over there are the famous Cedars of God. You heard of them, right?'

Lynch laughed. 'Marwan, I first came to Lebanon in my twenties. I remember The War. I told you already, you can keep the patter.'

'Fuck me for being helpful.'

'Fuck you anyway. How far now?'

'Just around the corner, few minutes. I'll take us up over the top, yeah?'

'Sounds good. Can we approach it from the sea as well?'

'Sure, no problem. Two passes is about it, though. Those Freij boys can get itchy, know what I mean?'

Banking left above the red rooves of the little mountain town of Bcharre, they floated in blue sky above white folds of barren mountain, the land below shining with the glare of the light reflecting from the snow. Lynch grinned with the sheer liberating delight of skimming untrammelled above the peaks, his heart racing with the thrill even as the anticipation of danger ahead made his gut tighten. He reached for the camera bag and dug out the high speed camera. He cleaned the 28-300mm zoom on his sleeve.

Nimr's voice was edgy. 'Okay, we're about forty-five seconds from the edge.'

He tilted the Alouette to give Lynch clear shots as they flew over the edge of the high, snowy escarpment. Deir Na'ee was nestled below, the snowy rocks falling away from them in a vertiginous curving tumble. Lynch spotted a grouping of outbuildings, snapping away as they passed by. Nimr brought the Alouette round for another run. They had agreed on an approach that would allow the complex to be accurately waymarked and the manoeuvre took them up over the cliff edge again, the whump of the rotors echoing back at them as they rose up the rock face.

'What's that over there?' Lynch pointed to the left as they climbed over the edge of the escarpment, a long double strip of black etched on the mountainside lost as they breasted the ragged top. Nimr took the Alouette around and left, sliding back over the escarpment with consummate skill and giving Lynch a clear series of shots of the runway below them, a double line of tarmac airstrip and a cluster of buildings to the southern end, a road dropping directly down from the airstrip to the Deir Na'ee site. An Ilyushin 76 sat to the side of the apron, the big Russian freighter dwarfing the executive jet next to it.

'Shit. A whole private airport.'

'Coming around now to give you that approach from the sea.'

'Nice and slow now.'

'We can't go too slow. I told you, man, these guys are headbangers up here. This is tribal country, they're armed to the teeth and they'll shoot at shit.'

Lynch was snapping on auto, the high-resolution camera struggling to keep saving the bursts despite its unusually advanced specification, each shot a triple-play of 28mm, halfway and then a 300mm zoom of the relevant feature. A high-pitched alarm sounded.

'Fuck!' Nimr wrenched the cyclic and rammed the Alouette right. Lynch was flung against his harness, the camera flying from his hands, the precious shots and expensive body saved by the strap double-wrapped around his wrist. Nimr shouted, 'Radar. We got radar lock, man.'

Nimr gunned the engine, taking them fast towards the escarpment. He slapped his hand on a mushroom switch to the right of his dash. Lynch caught the flashes pulsing behind them. Nimr was releasing flares as they sped towards the rock wall.

Lynch looked down. Flashes lit the ground. 'SAMs.'

'Seen 'em. Trust me, man.'

'Fuck all else I can—' Lynch could see individual stones on the rock wall in front of them, stark in the bursts of light from the flares behind them. Nimr clutched the cyclic to his gut to bring the Alouette vertical to the cliff, blowing a cloud of snow from the rocks. The helicopter's turboshaft engine screamed. They scraped up the rock face and careened over the escarpment edge in an explosion of powdery snow. The missiles struck below, the concussion wave flipping the Alouette over. A hail of rock flew from the roiling core of the explosions. Nimr fought to bring the bucking chopper back under control. They rolled, the throttle cut as Lynch pushed back as deeply as he could into his seat, his legs scrabbling. He clutched the camera and gulped sweet life from the cold air. He was snivelling and fought for control, gasping for breath and reasserting himself. The violent rearing calmed as Nimr righted the Alouette. He switched off the flares. The fingerless glove on his right hand was shredded, blood streaming down the ball of his thumb.

'Shit man, fuckin' cyclic bit me again.'

Lynch unwrapped the strap tied on his wrist, the flesh rubbed raw. The harness had dug into his shoulders, which screamed pain. 'That was close.'

Nimr shrugged. 'Told you they were headbangers, man.' He leaned forward and banged his fist against the display. 'Crap.'

'What?'

Nimr's voice on the intercom was matter of fact. 'We got trouble. Fuel tank's hit.'

Chapter Thirty-Three

Nimr was jabbering in Arabic on his radio, negotiating by the sound of it. Lynch craned to peer at the fuel gauge. It was showing empty. Nimr's voice rose an octave and he started to gesture with his left hand. The sea was spread far beyond, the land below swathed in green vegetation. They were still climbing.

'Okay, we're going to land at Hamat. It's a disused military base. I got some guys coming out to meet us.'

Lynch's response was lost in the sound of the engine coughing and then dying in a slow, whining wheeze. He froze, consumed by a sudden rush of absolute fear, a cold sweat breaking out all over his body. The rotors whooshed in the silence.

Nimr pulled on the lever to the side of his seat, using the pitch of the blades and guiding the cyclic between his legs back and forth. They started the descent towards the runway shimmering into sight ahead of them. Nimr guided the Alouette with skilful touches of the controls. Lynch, once again recovering from staring death in the face, stuttered.

'What the the the—'

Nimr glanced at him, grinning, his hands working the controls of the Alouette. 'Autorotation, man. Only a fuckin' idiot crashes a chopper. This beauty's gonna land like a fuckin' sycamore leaf on a baby's belly. You gotta control her careful, but the rotors slow us down with updraft if you pitch 'em right. We're going to glide down, see?'

Lynch watched the ground approach them, gripping his seat as the last few seconds rushed past and the earth rose to meet them, the nose of the Alouette tilting up and then the sliding impact as Nimr fought to keep the aircraft stable. They careened to a standstill, the rotors whirring silently. Lynch thumbed the catch and pulled apart the harness, tumbling left to dismount. Nimr held him back. 'Wait a second, man,' Nimr cackled. 'I mean, like, shame to beat SAMs and an autorotation landin' then get fucked up by the blades when you hit ground, no?'

Lynch nodded, dumbly, only grateful he hadn't soiled himself. He fought the strong urge to puke. The long concrete runway was blistered with craters, gouged and uneven. Weeds pushed through the surface. The rotors slowed and he jumped down from the Alouette, shocked at how weak his legs felt. He fumbled for his mobile, dialling Nathalie.

Nathalie took the call sitting at the dining table in Lynch's apartment, her screen displaying the scrolling repository of information streaming in from the hack of Falcon Dynamics' server farms. She had been trying to make sense of the meta-tagged datasets and follow leads through the quagmire of information. Her teams in Beirut and Brussels were struggling to download, process and tag the huge volumes of unstructured data flowing in.

She had been working for hours trying to build a picture of the events she and Lynch had seen unfolding over past weeks. The task was complicated by the richness of data – video, images, eyewitness reports, intelligence updates and white papers, snippets of news that had been catalogued and tagged into the files all jostled for attention alongside the raw data from the Falcon systems. Nathalie was silent, tight-lipped and fatigued as she tried to make sense of the information streaming into the feeds.

She held the mobile under her cheek with her shoulder as she worked on the screen. 'Durand.'

'It's me, Gerald.'

'How'd it go?'

'Ah sure, you know yourself. We got shot down.'

She took the mobile in her hand, standing. 'You are kidding, right? Are you okay?'

'Right as rain. I've got the photos but it'll be a while before I can get to you, I'm at Hamat Airbase. Listen, There's an airstrip up there at Deir Na'ee, newly built from the look of it. There are two planes there currently, an IL76 and an executive jet. The Ilyushin is marked OD-256. I couldn't see a marking on the small plane. Not sure what make it is. I'm going to try to send you a photo from the camera, but it'll take time to upload. The Lebanese mobile networks are pretty fucked up.'

'Okay, we'll try to look it up. I'm searching —'

'Sorry, gotta go. We've company and they don't look like family. Let Dubois know we're here, yes?'

The line cut. Nathalie closed her eyes and held the mobile to her forehead for a second. She shook her head to clear it. An Ilyushin 76. She Googled it. A big plane, a freighter and underpowered at that. Built to circumvent strategic arms limitation treaties, the IL76 could be converted into bombers at the drop of a hat, it would seem. She searched OD-256. A Lebanese aircraft ID, the plane registered in Tripoli, Lebanon. She smiled. To Falcon Tourism and Logistics.

Nathalie miskeyed the name in her haste and corrected herself with a whispered curse. The links came back, the list growing as the database scanned the product from Falcon's servers. Set up two years ago, Falcon Tourism and Logistics was a freight forwarding company that also operated charter flights. Oddly, it linked to the Near East

Institute for Oceanographic Research, an organisation that operated a marine research facility in Santorini. Her lips moved as she scanned the data, her eyes flickering over the links, her fingers flying on the keyboard. Based on an island near Thira in Santorini. A lease from the Governorate of Thira. She whistled. The lease had cost Falcon five million dollars. She put in a request for OD-256's flight log, tapping the tabletop as she waited, the data confirming that OD-256 had been cleared for take-off from Santorini International Airport that morning, cleared to fly to Beirut, carrying two containers of United Nations aid supplies.

Nathalie shuddered, her skin clammy. She whispered, just to make it sound real, 'They're here already.'

She lunged for her phone.

'Dubois.'

'It's me. The warheads have already landed. They are up at Deir Na'ee. Lynch has identified a plane that flew from Santorini today, we have found Falcon owns a facility near there. They must have taken them from the boat and transferred them. What shall we do?'

'Wait. Slowly. How is it Lynch is at Deir Na'ee?'

'He took a helicopter.'

Dubois almost shouted. 'Is he mad?'

'He found the missiles, *Papa*.'

'Tell him to come back immediately. Thank you, Nathalie.'

'What should we do?'

'Find the guidance systems in that damn network.'

Nathalie dropped the handset. She ran her hand through her hair and walked to the balcony to look out over *Ain Mreisse*. They had failed. There were nuclear warheads in Lebanon. She tried not to think of what might happen next.

A message flashed on her screen from Jean Meset.

'Found rogue system. IBM Blue Giant. Attempting access now.'

Nathalie tapped at her screen and sent back, 'Odd. Not listed anywhere.'

The world's biggest supercomputers are listed, the opportunity to boast about how big yours is being one everyone finds too good to pass up. Nathalie opened a window, a status bar flashed and Jean Meset appeared onscreen.

He spoke French. 'Hey, Nathalie. It's the core research and development mainframe. It's big, very big and the latest configuration. This should rank top twenty at least. Maybe top ten.'

'Jean, we need to find out if that system contains the missile command and control infrastructure.'

'It's certainly the machine you'd use for that. We're trying to get in now, but it's very secure.' Meset paused, distracted by events off-camera. 'One second, if you please.'

Nathalie reached for her coffee while Meset clacked on his keyboard. The drink had gone cold and she pulled a face.

'Here.' Meset looked pleased with himself. 'See what you make of this.'

Nathalie opened the folder he sent, clicking on the first file. 'Right. What's this?'

'It's an exact match for the two images we captured from the CCTV system. It's an intermediate-range missile system. The design is American.'

'What's its range?' Nathalie asked.

Meset nodded. 'The original design was a ballistic missile system that sat between tactical and medium-range use. We think this one has been extended. The analysts in Paris are onto it, but a preliminary guess would be somewhere around three thousand kilometres.'

'Why would they want a missile with such range to target Israel?'

Meset was interrupted again, holding his hand up to his unseen colleague. 'Sorry. About the range, I don't know. This missile system has a sophisticated guidance system that doesn't rely on GPS. The Americans can't switch it off, that is to say. I'm sorry, I have to go. Is there anything else, Nathalie?'

'No thanks, Jean. Let me know when you get into the big machine.'

His shy smile in response was rather sweet, thought Nathalie. But her heart was thumping in her chest for other reasons.

The jeep bumped towards them on the broken concrete runway. Lynch turned away from it, switched his mobile to silent and slipped it into his boot. He gave up a silent thanks to God for his insistence on using his mobile rather than the bulky 'highly secure' MI6 issue handset. He reached for the camera and slid out the memory card.

'Whatever you do, don't piss them off,' urged Nimr, climbing down from the cockpit. 'They're headbangers, I'm tellin' ya.'

The jeep shrieked to a halt, side on to the Alouette. Four men, all wearing camouflage fatigues and caps, jumped out. Lynch and Nimr waited in front of the helicopter.

The first of the men jabbed at them with the AK47 slung over his shoulder. 'Hands up.' They raised their hands. Lynch read the nametag on his chest as he strode towards them: *Danni*.

'Turn around. Spread. Now. Hands on the chopper.'

Lynch staggered as one of the men patted him down roughly. The search was thorough, but stopped at the top of his boots. *Amateur.*

'Okay.' They turned. 'What the fuck are you doing here? Who are you?'

Banging came from the helicopter behind them, the fourth guy searching it. Lynch beamed winningly. 'Depends who you are.'

The man unholstered his pistol, clicking off the safety. He pointed the Desert Eagle towards Lynch and fired. The bullet hit the Perspex of the Alouette's windshield, sending shards of plastic into the side of Lynch's face as he flinched. Nimr shouted out, moved forwards and then halted at the distinctive click-clack of AK47s being cocked. Red-faced, the pistol still held out in front of him, the man screamed, 'I asked you who the fuck are you.'

Lynch answered, his hand coming away from his cheek streaked with blood. 'I'm a tourist. I chartered this guy to take me up into the mountains. Someone shot at us.'

The gunman twisted the pistol to point at Nimr, who stammered, 'True, man, true.'

'Liars. On your knees.'

They sank to their knees and their hands were pulled down behind and tied, the distinctive little 'zip' of cable ties coming an instant before the pain as they were overtightened.

The crackle of a radio. 'Danni. I got the guys with the chopper here.'

A response from the radio, 'Okay. Bring them in.'

Lynch kept his eyes on the ground. A boot crunched on the broken concrete. His chin was pulled up, gripped in the gunman's big hand. Blinking with the violence of the movement and the bright sun, Lynch stared into the swarthy, sneering face. The Desert Eagle was placed against the top of his nose.

'A tourist packing countermeasure flares? You think we're fucking idiots?'

Lynch shook his head minutely, his eyes focused on the face above him. He wished he could stop blinking, the cold metal of the gun triggering the reaction. A click sounded, Lynch screwed his eyes shut. His head was pushed back contemptuously.

'*Oom wla*,' the man commanded Lynch and Nimr in Arabic. They staggered to their feet and were jabbed towards the jeep by the butts of AK47s.

They drove up the valley, climbing the face of Kalaa mountain, the road wet and the ground white with snow. Lynch tried to lessen the pain of the cable tie but moving his wrists worsened it, the rocking motion of the jeep making him cry out in pain. The gunman barked at him to shut up.

Deir Na'ee looked more ramshackle from the ground. They drew up to a barbed-wire fence where a surly-faced militia man raised the barrier. A second barrier a hundred metres later was protected by tank traps and a machine gun emplacement. Waved through again, they drove through the big compound, warehouses to the left and right. There was a building set into the side of the steep escarpment to the left, jutting from the rock wall and fronted by huge picture windows.

They arrived at a large hangar backed into the mountain, the big double doors opened for them by invisible hands. The area inside was cavernous, a roadway running down the centre of the steel-framed building, leading to a far doorway in the back of the hangar. The jeep's engine roared, the noise bouncing back off the steel panels. They approached the doorway and stopped, the engine idling as they waited.

A red light flashed above the studded heavy steel door and its two leaves opened outwards to the intermittent loud beeping of an alarm.

They drove into the mountain, a long tunnel. They passed side tunnels, pulling up at a loading bay several hundred metres in. They were pulled from the jeep and marched through into a warehouse-like area. Lynch had seen rooms like this on the compromised CCTV system. That meant Nathalie's team could see him now. He searched for the camera, earning himself a ringing punch on the ear from Danni and a barked 'Eyes down'.

They marched into another corridor. Lynch was driven into a side room with a brutal blow to his side from a rifle butt. His knees gave way and he slid to the floor, gasping. The door slammed behind him.

Lynch took time to regain his breath, his eyes closed and his face upturned. He drew a deep breath and opened his eyes to take in his surroundings. The room was small, a shabby camp bed against the wall. There was no window. Lynch got up from the floor, bent in a painful, low crouch and reached with his tied hands into his boot for the mobile. He overbalanced and fell on his side. He tried again by balancing against the wall. The mobile fell to the ground by his foot and he managed to slide it toward him.

Held dn il gone militia hold hamat. ok.

Lynch pressed send. The door flew open. Two gunmen burst into the room, screaming abuse. He leapt to his feet, unable to stop the mighty blow to his face. A flurry of damaging punches to his stomach doubled him up. He tried to retaliate, but his legs gave way again and he fell backwards against the wall.

Danni towered over him, the mobile held in his big hand, screaming '*Kiss ikhtak! Kiss ikhtak ya kalb!*'

On the floor, Lynch fought for breath, his pinioned arms painful behind his back, knees drawn up, and his head lowered. The door slammed again. Lynch thought of the grubby farmhouse near Batroun where he had found Paul Stokes' body. The stench of death and the buzzing of flies came back to him.

Chapter Thirty-Four

Yves Dubois arrived at the fourteenth floor of the opulent Phoenicia Intercontinental Hotel and headed straight for room 1430. He tapped on the door, noting the service trolley outside the room two doors down, the uniformed staff member meticulously folding a piece of linen. A guest walked up the corridor towards Dubois, again in no particular hurry. Dubois noted both men and, given who he was about to meet, assumed both were CIA operatives.

The door was answered by a grey-haired man in shirtsleeves. 'Yves. Good to see you again.'

Dubois smiled thinly. 'Frank. Good to see you too. It must be, oh, years since we had the chance to talk.'

'Come in, come in. Don't be a stranger now.'

Frank Coleman was CIA station chief, Beirut, and a man whose past was intimately intertwined with Dubois' own. Coleman's call had come out of the blue, a surprise so total it had left Dubois in a state of shock. He and Channing had argued bitterly about the decision to accept Coleman's request for a crash meeting. It was only when Dubois agreed to absolve Channing of any knowledge of his decision to agree to meet the CIA man that he had been able to talk Channing down from his towering rage. The news that Maalouf had precise knowledge of the cargo the *Arabian Princess* carried hadn't helped Channing's temper.

Dubois strode past Coleman's outstretched hand into the room.

'Buddy, this is Yves Dubois, an old friend and a good friend to America.' Coleman grinned, his teeth dazzling. The gesture never quite reached the washed-out blue gaze even as Coleman gave the impression of being in a rush to spread *bonhomie* on the world. Dubois held his hand out to the man who had risen from the sofa, leaning over the coffee table with a smile. He was stocky, pale but dark haired, his brown eyes nervous and his greeting given with a fleeting, uncertain smile.

'Hi. Buddy Steele. Steel with an e on the end.'

'Can we get you a coffee, Yves?'

Dubois sat. 'No, thank you.'

Coleman took the opposite armchair, Steele between them on the sofa. Coleman's smile made his crow's feet wrinkle up. *Sun damage*, thought Dubois, who sat with his hands clasped together, his forefingers against his lips.

Coleman picked up his mobile and tapped it against his palm. 'I am so glad you could join us today, Yves, and we truly appreciate your fitting us in at such short notice. Especially as you are travelling so far from home. Mind you, this place must seem like home to you after all those years.'

Dubois inclined his head in acknowledgement, watching Coleman's face transform into a picture of earnest friendliness.

'You're normally in Brussels these days, aren't you? What brings you back to Beirut? You on a nostalgia trip?' Coleman laughed, alone. Steele smiled dutifully, sitting back and draping his arm on the back of the sofa.

'No, Frank. Only duty, as usual. I am afraid I am not very interesting these days. I merely push paper.'

'Sure, sure. I understand. Well, listen I got a little local problem here that I thought maybe you could give me a hand with. See, we got an operation going here that's real tough, so we're working with our good friends next door on it. It's kind of sensitive, so much so that it's run strictly on need to know, all the way up the chain. So I don't really have the clearance to, you know, go into so much detail as

I'd like.'

Coleman's easy smile transported Dubois back to the Lebanese Civil War, to his past in another world, one of fear and intrigue amongst the wreckage of Beirut, the great city torn apart by sectarian factions, militia and Israeli bombardment before the Palestinians left, a ragged mob deserting the broken ruins.

Coleman had smoked back then, a lazy-looking fat kid with pale cheeks and brown hair who wore wide-collared shirts. Dubois had denied the charges made against him, but couldn't deny that he was present during the interrogation of the farmer by Christian militia. Dubois remembered Coleman back then, stabbing his two fingers, the cigarette held between them as he peered through the smoke. The snarled rebuke, 'You could have stopped them, Dubois. You killed that old man as sure as if you used your own fucking hands.'

Looking across the coffee table at the smiling American, Dubois knew that Coleman was back in the early eighties as well, striding around the little dark interview room as Dubois sneered back at him, still pumped on the adrenaline and arrogance of war.

Coleman's eyes shifted to Steele, who nodded. He turned to Dubois. 'Our operation is very important to our Israeli allies. It will stop a man who has gone too far, a former client of the United States who has become a terrorist. It is an entrapment operation of some complexity that has been ongoing for a great deal of time.'

Dubois listened raptly. There was something strange about the way Buddy Steele spoke English and he couldn't place it. He opened his hands flat and hammed up his accent. 'A terrorist in Beirut? *Dis donc!*'

He was rewarded with a momentary tightening of Coleman's silver brows. 'We're asking you to suspend your operation against Michel Freij and Falcon, Yves. We are perfectly well aware that the search for the Arabian Princess is not about drug enforcement. We will take care of Michel Freij and his partner. But we need clear space to operate in.'

Dubois rose and Coleman, with an alarmed glance, did the same. Walking to the closed curtains, Dubois pulled them open, gazing from the picture window to the sapphire Mediterranean. He half expected a bullet through the glass. The street below was busy, traffic roaring past the Rafic Hariri monument. *The blast that killed Hariri blew every window out of this hotel.*

He wondered why they had used Coleman. Anybody else would have done, but they sent Coleman. He watched a small speedboat at sea, its white wake spreading behind it in the dappled turquoise. He closed the curtain and turned to face the room.

'Absolutely not. This is a EJIC operation which concerns assets stolen from an European Union member country by European nationals and you have no jurisdiction over it. I will not countenance any interference in our operation.'

Coleman's face flickered with a brief wave of naked hate. He composed himself and forced a sympathetic smile, a reasonable man who appreciated the issues that caused Dubois to be so hot-headed.

Behind him, Buddy Steele clapped slowly. 'Bravo, Monsieur. I would have done no less than you. But you must understand we are at the end of a long and expensive operation that could result in tens of thousands of deaths if this terrorist is allowed to get away with this. They are intending to target nuclear missiles.' He paused to raise his finger. '*Nuclear* missiles at Israel. We can take no chances. If you insist on interfering, we will inform all EU member states that EJIC has lost two nuclear warheads. You will be paralysed from operating in the uproar and we will have the space we need to finish our work. We would obviously prefer to come to a,' Steele smirked, 'quieter arrangement.'

Intuition came to Dubois. He swung to face Coleman. 'Do you have authority for this?'

The American rubbed his chin. 'We are deniable, but believe me we have sanction.'

'Then fuck you.' Dubois strode towards the door. Coleman moved to block him but Steele stepped in and restrained the American. Dubois slammed the door, rewarded by the sight of the nondescript hotel guest, still lounging in the corridor, taking a dive sideways and fumbling towards his left armpit.

Dubois stood outside the Phoenicia Intercontinental and glared across the Hariri monument to the ruins of the St. Georges Yacht Club and the blue sea beyond. He ignored the staff asking if he wanted perhaps a taxi, lost somewhere in an interview room in the 1980s, drenched in the smell of cigarette smoke and sweat. He fished the pack from his bag and undid the elastic band around it he used to make himself think twice about smoking. He lit up with deep pleasure.

The black Mercedes slid by in front of him, its back door opening as it halted to reveal a beige leather interior.

'Come, Yves. It's time we talked.' Ghassan Maalouf beckoned him in. Dubois hesitated, his mind rebelling at the idea of getting closer to the older man. 'We must act. Forget who I am to you. Forget the past.' Maalouf's face implored him, a weak, conciliatory smile so uncertain it had to be genuine. 'Give me a few minutes. I have no right to ask you for anything, I know, but I ask you this.'

Dubois flicked his cigarette into the gutter and got into the car.

Maalouf spoke French. 'Thank you.'

'Save your breath.'

'You met with Coleman and a guy called Steele.'

'What do you want?'

'We track them. They track us. We track them tracking us. We all play games. It is our way of all staying employed. Coleman asked to speak with you because we rattled his chain. He is scared.' Maalouf gazed out of the window as they left the Phoenicia and joined the road. 'It is always better when we play parlour games like this than when we make wars. Better to have men behaving like children on the playground than like savages.' He sighed. 'Forgive me, Yves, I am an old man and have much to regret.'

'Spare me.'

'Buddy Steele is Israeli. He is operating under the protection of the US Embassy. His real name is Amit Peled and he is a Mossad operative of senior rank. It is a clever name, this, a new Israeli name for an old Diaspora name. Peled is Hebrew for steel, replacing the Germanic name Stahlman. Amit means friend. So we have a friend, a buddy, of steel. Why are you not laughing, Yves? It is a subtle joke, no?'

Dubois recalled Steele's odd accent and awarded Maalouf a brownie point. An Israeli, then.

'They tried to stop you, Yves. We know this because they had no other option. Their operation is illegal. We have been watching them for a long time. You have the data from Falcon. I know you do. Together we can find out everything, apart we are blind. I know you hate me and I don't pretend to be anything other than the monster you think I am. But we need to work together. There is no time.'

Consumed by a dangerous lassitude, Dubois faced Maalouf and looked him in the eye. 'Why do you even take an interest? Let the Israelis stop them.'

Maalouf's gaze flitted between Dubois' eyes, his lined face registering his surprise. He cried out in frustration. 'I told you, Israel is not the target of these missiles. Steele is Michel Freij's control. Israel is Freij's *backer*, not his target. Freij will fire these missiles at Iran in a deniable strike to eradicate the Iranian nuclear programme. And the missiles will come from Lebanon. We will have another war after this. A real one. The Gulf will be in flames, the oil wells will go up. And Israel will have everything it wants. So will the right-wing Americans behind them.'

Dubois and Maalouf stood listening to the waves together. They leaned on the cold metal railing that snaked along the wide-paved corniche. Maalouf was first to break the long silence. 'I live with it even now, you know. I see her still in my dreams and wake up crying because I am sorry for what I did.'

'I don't want to talk about it. I agreed to talk business, not about this. I will not let you unburden yourself to me. Shut up. Talk business.'

'We become brutal at times like that. Brutal times. Do you remember they used to fly along this very stretch of corniche, dropping their flares before they came inland and dropped hell on us all?'

Dubois shifted uncomfortably, but didn't move away. 'Business. Now. The future. Not the past.' He drew on his cigarette and glared at Maalouf, who was also smoking. 'I will not go back there with you. You are on your own.'

'Even you, who are so self-righteous. Even you were sent home because you let your precious standards slip.' Maalouf turned to him. 'She wasn't your wife then, Yves. You didn't even know her.'

Dubois' lips were drawn. 'Enough or I walk. Warheads or not. Enough. No more of the past.'

Maalouf turned to look across the rocky foreshore to the iridescent sea. Dubois followed his gaze, the waves breaking against the abandoned concrete of some long-forgotten restaurant or gun emplacement. He couldn't remember which.

'Their target is Iran. Two strikes against the remaining Iranian nuclear research facilities, two nuclear explosions near Qom and Tehran. All evidence will be wiped out in the explosions, which they will claim were caused by Iranian negligence. If by chance any evidence remains, it is Russian nuclear technology and a missile made from stolen designs. The missiles flew from Lebanon, not Israel.'

Maalouf puffed on his Gitane. He waved the cigarette at Dubois. 'Michel has prepared his militia. They will strike against Hezbollah and other Shia targets, hard. They are well equipped. When Freij talks of a strong Lebanon, this is what he means. When he talks about ceasing outside interference, this is what he means.'

'What about Selim Hussein? His partner? The guy is Shia, no?'

'Hussein is technical genius, but he is stupid with people. He believes Freij is the best of men. He loves Freij. Not like a brother, more than this.'

Dubois ground out his cigarette butt with his heel. 'And if Iran retaliates?'

Maalouf sighed. 'They have anticipated this, of course. It will be against Lebanon. And the Middle East will erupt into flames in any case, you know this.' He turned to Dubois, his palms up. 'Now, Yves, will you work with us?'

Maalouf flicked his cigarette butt over the railings and lit another one, crouching over his lighter to shield the guttering flame from the sea breeze. Dubois waited until he straightened up. 'The missiles arrived here this morning by air. They are at Falcon's main R&D centre, a mainly underground facility called Deir Na'ee in the Northern mountains.'

Maalouf was grave. 'We know this place.'

Dubois faced Maalouf, his hand and forefinger raised. 'You do not speak to her, you understand? Not one word. Especially not about—'

'I understand. If I would say something, I would have said it to her by now. She has her life and she can live it without concerning herself about me. And so can you, Yves, if you will only allow it.'

Maalouf offered his hand and Dubois, surprising even himself, took it.

Chapter Thirty-Five

Brian Channing sat back in his armchair, his hands behind his head and his eyes closed as Dubois paced his office. Channing didn't move a muscle, his fleshy face in repose. Dubois wondered quite what it was about Channing that scared him. Perhaps it was this very languor, a state that Channing seemed to retreat into when at his most dangerous. The man was certainly smooth, always dressed in fine blue pinstripes, with tie-pins, collar studs, cufflinks and other accoutrements. Every bit the English gentleman, cool and poisonous behind the politician's smile. Yet Channing was very good at his job, a genial host and unmatched in his ability to feel his way around the corridors of power, a call here, a *bon mot* there. He was, in short, everywhere.

Channing's voice was a drawl, his eyes still closed. 'Frank Coleman's an old warhorse, but his remit has been eroded by the current round of power-grabbing in Washington and station chiefs have nothing like the authority they used to have. They're being marginalised by the more vertical approach to counterterrorist operations that Washington's taking. It seems odd, though, that they'd shake sticks at you here at the operational level. It would make more sense to escalate the back off request up to Daddy in Washington so your mealy-mouthed buggers over at Berlaymont pull their noses out of the trough long enough to call us off the kill.'

A knock on the office door snapped Channing's eyes open. 'Come.'

A plain girl in her early twenties entered, handing a file to Channing with a deferential murmur. His salacious gaze followed her leaving. He grunted. 'Now, Yves, let us take a look at what we've got sitting under Frank Coleman's little rock, shall we?' He ambled over to the desk, spreading the file out and picking through its contents. He tapped at the keyboard of his notebook PC.

Dubois found it difficult at times to keep up with Channing's idiomatic drawl, one of the many aspects to the man that got under his skin more than he'd care to acknowledge in public. Channing liked to test his patience and Dubois, as ever, waited so that he wouldn't give the man the pleasure of a reaction.

Channing tutted. 'So our buddy Buddy is a fully paid up Mossad hood. Kidon boy. Speaks Arabic, long history of involvement in southern Lebanon, AKA Amit Peled, Harry Stahlman and Rutger Stahl. He's been all over, has Buddy. Munich, Dubai, Gaza and Saida. A lot in Saida. Funny you hadn't come across him before, Yves. Used to be your stamping ground, didn't it? Saida?'

'I have never met him before, no,' Dubois shook his head, consigning the hazy remembrance of a young Frank Coleman shouting at him back into the past.

'Peled's been spotted snuggling up to a number of right-wing US groups, suspected of involvement in a couple of operations that have caused great embarrassment to the current government, starting with that Hamas murder screw-up in Dubai.' Channing became garrulous. 'There's talk of an ultraright-wing cabal in Israeli intelligence and political circles and our boy fits the profile perfectly. Old Sharon thought the sun shone out of Buddy's little brown arse.'

'The Americans have run with the Israelis before here. This is hardly news. They have told us to get off their patch.'

'Oh, I don't think we're going to do that,' Channing

drawled, reaching for his mobile. 'One second, Yves.' He dialled, waited. 'Karl, hi, it's Brian over in London. Well, not actually. In Beirut at the moment. How's Celia? Great, great. Look, Karl, I wonder if you could do me a quick favour. We were having a look around over here and wondered if you chaps had any ops running in Lebanon right now, particularly anything going on with our friends from David's Land? Sure, no problem at all. Thanks, Karl.'

He dropped the line with a look of smug satisfaction. 'Now that, Yves, is why you need to cultivate contacts.'

Dubois smiled wanly and sat back as Channing continued to pick through the file with his tender, thief's fingers.

Brian Channing let the mobile ring five times before answering it, the nearest Dubois had ever come to snapping and shouting at the man to react for the love of God.

'Channing.' He listened for a time. 'Can I take that as Gospel, Karl? I mean, there's no chance that anyone particularly *clandestine* might be operating here? Under Frank Coleman's direct purview, for instance? Okay, thank you very much. No, no, nothing at all.' Channing held the phone between shoulder and cheek as he scanned the papers in front of him. 'No, Karl, absolutely not. You know if we do, you'll be the first to know. Be great to catch up next time you guys are in London.'

Channing beamed, a gesture purely for the benefit of the man on the other end of the phone. Dubois couldn't help feeling that he had, somehow, to admire the way the man worked even as he knew Channing's gain would always somehow end up being his colleagues' loss.

Dubois was surprised at the look of fear that passed

across Channing's face as he laid the mobile down on the desk like a playing card. Fear was something he had never seen in the man before. Channing was about cunning and determination, not fear. Dubois was silent as Channing sat, his eyes closed.

'They're freelancing, Yves. The CIA has no operations running in this area currently. Absolutely none. Coleman is retiring next week and is off effective duty.' Channing rose from the table and reached again for the mobile. 'The innocent questions I have just asked are about to start creating fucking chaos in Washington. I suggest you talk to your masters as I am about to talk to mine. If Maalouf is right, the whole Middle East is about to go up in flames.'

Dubois nodded and headed for the door. As he pulled it shut behind him, Channing's silky tones sounded. 'Minister, it's Brian Channing in Beirut.'

Chapter Thirty-Six

The meeting room deep in the heart of the Résidence des Pins was functional, blue carpet tiles and scuffed white walls, the plastic-covered table surrounded by a motley collection of swivel chairs. The whiteboard on the wall was scuffed and grubby in the corners from long use. There was a kettle and a tray with coffee packets, tea bags, sugar and a tin of condensed milk.

Channing stood by the projection of the ground plan of the Deir Na'ee facility, his face stark in the projector's light as he glanced around the room. Ghassan Maalouf and Yves Dubois sat to his right, to his left Jean Meset, the programmer from Nathalie's team. The young man's face was bathed in the harsh light from the screen.

'Okay, this is the situation right now. The team here has access to the CCTV systems in the Deir Na'ee complex and to the core security systems. We are in effective control of Falcon Dynamics' networks and can shut them down if we so decide. The question I believe is timing. The Lebanese Army is moving in. Ghassan?'

Maalouf got to his feet. 'The army is deploying units from Bahjat Ghanem, the air force is readying Fourteenth Squadron, which has modified Bell Huey helicopters. It will be an hour before the army units are within range of the complex at Deir Na'ee. We fear it will be too little, too late, but sadly Lebanon is hampered militarily by lack of supply and technology. We know that Freij's militia is numerous, well-armed and entrenched in Kalaa, the area around the Deir Na'ee facility.'

Channing turned to Jean Meset. 'Jean, where's the missile guidance system? Can we hack these missiles?'

Meset rose with an odd bowing motion, his hands clasped together and fidgeting. 'We have missile analysts from Dassault and BAE working on the data we have gathered on these units and we know that the guidance system is highly sophisticated, but we haven't been able to find the control network. We think it might be totally independent of the systems that we have gained access to. This would be sensible, actually. We think it might be linked to the supercomputer we have found. We have not gained access yet.' He turned to Maalouf. 'Erm, you can tell your army guys that when they're ready we can open the automatic doors, but not any manual ones. Obviously. I mean—' He shuffled a little and glanced at Channing. 'We can't take the networks down without losing control of the access systems, so we have to leave them up for now. I would suggest we open all doors then shut down the networks when the army is arrived.'

Channing nodded. 'Thanks, Jean. Yves?'

Yves Dubois stood. 'As the European Union, we have no significant military assets close by. There is a British airbase in Cyprus, but it is set up for search and rescue helicopter missions, not for major combined attacks. The British have the Armilla patrol in the Gulf, which does have a combat aircraft capability and has been put on high alert. We could call on support from the Turkish air force, but there simply isn't time. We believe these missiles could be readied to fire imminently.'

'Guys,' Jean Meset's voice was tight with excitement. 'There are two prisoners being brought into the building. Here.'

He twisted his tablet screen and they watched Gerald Lynch, blindfolded and bound, marched past the CCTV camera. The bulky bald man walking next to him stumbled, urged on by the gunman from behind.

The shock hit Dubois, an icy blow. He turned to Channing, who was staring at the screen. 'What do we do?'

Channing was silent for a moment. He glanced away from the screen, shaking his head. 'We must proceed as we can. The army goes in, the networks go down. We try to find the missile guidance systems. I'm going to make a couple of calls to America to see if they have any assets close by.'

Chapter Thirty-Seven

Marcelle Aboud was sitting on the sofa in Michel Freij's sumptuous office when Lynch was marched in, Danni the gunman's hand on his shoulder. The heavy door slammed shut behind them. She was wearing a long red dress, diamonds glittered above her full bust. Her smile at his entrance turned to a frown and Lynch realised he must look one hell of a mess.

He stared around the big room. The walls were stone, a free-standing fireplace divided the workspace from the sofas and a bar, the flames dancing merrily. To the right was a massive picture window looking out to the wintry mountains beyond, the huge pane of floor-to-ceiling thick glass at least thirty feet wide to give a breathtaking, vertiginous view of the snowy slopes of Dannieh.

'Mr Lynch.' Michel Freij sat at the big glass desk. He issued a command to the gunman in Arabic and Lynch found himself shoved across the rug-strewn wooden floor and into a black and chrome chair. The movement made the cable tie on his wrists cut even deeper and he fought to suppress the cry of pain in his throat.

Freij nodded a dismissal. 'Thank you, Danni.'

Freij was wearing a white shirt, open at the collar, and jeans. His dark hair was slicked back and his handsome face turned to Lynch with a pleasant, relaxed smile.

Lynch's mobile was on the black mirrored surface of Freij's desk. The only other object on the obsidian surface was a slim black notebook computer parked to one side. Freij followed his eyes.

'Yes, Mr Lynch. Your mobile. I should have Danni punished for that oversight, should I not?' He smiled regretfully. 'He is normally so very... effective.'

Lynch croaked through his dry lips. 'He's just another thug, Michel. Like you, but without the suit.'

Freij tapped the desktop with his fingertip, which instantly became a display. He swept a finger across an area of coloured symbols.

'There,' Freij mused, scrolling the screen with a fingernail. 'Yes, the polls are once again excellent. *Au contraire*, then, Mr Lynch, this 'thug' is well on track to becoming the next president of Lebanon. Marcelle, do you think you could be so kind to give Mr Lynch a glass of water? He seems to have been in the wars.'

Marcelle sashayed over to the bar and brought a heavy tumbler of water to Lynch. She cradled his neck as he drank, leaning into him and whispering, 'There,' when he had finished.

She took the glass away and Lynch glared at Freij, his voice stronger. 'What's she doing here?'

Freij feigned surprise. 'Marcelle? Oh, I invited her to join me for this moment. I find this type of event so very *stimulating*. Marcelle is very good at her job, Mr Lynch. You should save up and perhaps give her a try one day. Although I understand it could be difficult on a British civil service salary.' Freij tapped the desktop again. 'It is over, Mr Lynch. As you so correctly pointed out when you sent this text to your friend Ms Durand, the Ilyushin is indeed gone from our airfield here. It flew to the Baazaran Air Base with two mobile missile launchers, each armed with a highly sophisticated medium range missile. These have both deployed on schedule. You have been looking for two Russian Oka class nuclear warheads, have you not? Let me fulfil your quest for you. They are both at Baazaran. You have heard of Baazaran?'

Lynch glared at Freij, his breathing quickening with his

anger.

'It is a disused airbase in the mountains, in the area we call the Chouf. The Druze made great use of it during the civil war and I am making use of it now. Any Iranian retaliation will be, of course, directed at the place the missiles originated.' Freij chuckled. 'Not a good time to be Druze, I think.'

Lynch struggled against the sharp-edged cable ties. 'You'll never get away with this.'

'My God, could you come up with nothing better than that?' Freij kicked his chair back and rounded the desk. 'Is that it? Your last great line?' He gripped Lynch's chin, forcing his face up to meet Freij's furious eyes. 'You're not going to escape, Lynch. You're not going to blow up my mountain retreat and walk away with the girl. You're too late and, if I may be frank, not very good.'

Freij let Lynch's head drop and strode to stand in front of the picture window, a dark silhouette against the blue sky. 'In a little under five minutes, those missiles will launch and in under ten minutes will be suborbital over Syria. This, *habibi*, is game over.'

Lynch's mobile buzzed on Freij's desk. Freij turned from the glass. 'What could we have here, Mr Lynch?'

Lynch was silent as Freij read the message. He dropped the mobile and strode to the door, barking a command in Arabic as he left. Danni entered the room, shutting the big door behind him very carefully.

'Marcie,' Lynch craned his head back to try to see her. 'Fancy reading what that text said?'

Marcelle rose from the sofa where she had been reading a magazine and walked up to the desk, pushing away the gun that Danni brandished.

'Don't you dare lay a finger on me, boy,' she drawled.

She picked up the phone. 'Army coming. Hold on.'

Lynch nodded, his urchin's grin lighting up his battered face. 'Yes, I can see how that would piss him off.'

The beat of helicopters penetrated the thick glass of the picture window, the impact of concussions coming soon after. Craning his neck, he could see the first Huey rising up the valley towards Deir Na'ee. An instant later, white missile trails streamed from its pods.

Overwhelming relief made him boyish, the impish grin coming easily.

'You made a will, Danni boy?'

Danni leapt for him, the punch smashing into Lynch's cheek and rocking the whole chair. '*Kiss immak!*'

Lynch braced for another punch.

'Stop,' Marcelle cried out. 'You have no authority to harm him. Get out.'

'Michel asked me to—'

'Get out.'

He reminded Lynch of a whipped cur, unsure of Marcelle's authority but cowed by her fury. With a snarl at Lynch he left the room. *Good doggy*, thought Lynch. His vision was blurred by the punch and he tried to clear his head. SAM fire was returned at the helicopters, an awful moment of impact as the lead chopper blew apart in a ball of flame. The wreckage plummeted down, pulling a plume of smoke behind it. The crack of gunfire sounded, the distinctive clacking of AK47s joined by heavier answering fire.

Lynch meant his voice to sound airy, not nervous and croaky. 'Marcie, do you fancy, you know, untying me?'

Marcelle gazed coolly across at him, her deep eyes weighing him up.

Another Huey went down to SAM fire from the

ground, explosions throwing up clouds of dark charcoal smoke farther down the valley. A series of white streaks rammed down the valley from above them, the salvo of Katyushka rockets throwing up enormous gouts of red soil.

Dubois punched the air in frustration. 'Come on, Jean, we must be able to do something.'

Meset was sweating, his plump hands flying across the keyboard. 'We're all on it, Dubois, give me a break.'

The room was packed with people using screens, clamorous with raised voices, telephones and clattering keyboards.

Ghassan Maalouf replaced the handset he had been talking into. 'Radar went down two hours ago in Beirut International. It affected both civil and military traffic. Our analysts believe it was some kind of electronic countermeasure. It came from the blue and only lasted twenty minutes.'

'What could that possibly —'

'It's happening again now. We are also hearing reports of two very large missiles seen launching from the area near the Baazaran Air Base in the Chouf mountains. I think this is where Mr Lynch's Ilyushin 76 went. It makes sense.'

Dubois flicked through the banks of camera views on the Deir Na'ee CCTV system, his eyes on the display as he talked. 'Why launch the missiles from the Chouf? Why not directly from Deir Na'ee?'

Maalouf was impassive. 'Because this dirty bastard wants any Iranian retaliation to hit the Druze.'

Brian Channing re-entered the operations room at the

Résidence des Pins, having left to take a call on his mobile. He was grim-faced as he approached Dubois and Maalouf. The room was quiet, everyone watching the scene unfolding on the CCTV screens as the Lebanese army battled the One Lebanon militia in the mountains of northern Lebanon.

Channing's voice rang out in the silence. 'Right. We've been told to clear our forces from Deir Na'ee. My PM and your PM,' he gestured at Dubois, 'have agreed with the Americans. Ghassan, your CiC has confirmed receipt of the instruction and his compliance. He has ordered a retreat. We are to leave this to them. The Americans will take any further action.'

Dubois' fists balled. 'What the hell does that mean?'

'It means we're pulling out. We're leaving it to the Americans. They have launched a major cruise missile strike vectored from the Eastern Mediterranean and the Western Gulf.'

Meset leapt up. 'We've got it! We're in! We have control of the missiles.'

Channing wheeled, incredulous. 'Where are they?'

'Here, just here. Over Syria.'

'Can you disarm them?'

'Yes. We've initiated that sequence.'

'Ditch them, then, man. Ditch the fucking things. Here, in the Aral Sea. There's nothing much worse you can do to that poor, benighted bloody pond.'

Marcelle regained her seat on the big sofa moments before Freij re-entered the room. She composed herself, shooting him a too-bright smile. Ignoring her, Freij strode to the big picture window and gazed over the valley below.

The helicopters were pulling back, gaining altitude and

banking to turn towards the sea. The sound of heavy gunfire, muffled by the thick glass, ceased and, gradually, the little puffs of smoke on the mountainside abated.

Freij turned with a cold smile at Lynch. 'As you can see, Mr Lynch, we are very well defended.'

The door burst open. Danni's face was flushed with excitement. 'They have withdrawn. It is over. We won, we won.'

Freij smiled and held out a hand to him, palm down to slap Danni's upturned hand, dismissing him with a gentle shove on his shoulder.

'*Shukran*, ya Danni. Take Marcelle up to the eyrie for me.'

He turned to Lynch. 'So you see, Mr Lynch, we are well protected.'

'Oh, I wouldn't say that,' said Lynch, staring fiercely out of the window. 'In fact, I'd say quite the opposite. Goodbye, Michel.'

Freij turned to the picture windows. Lynch lunged from his chair. He raced for the door, which Danni was keeping open for Marcelle with his back. The gunman reacted too slowly. Lynch's rabbit punch, delivered with all his momentum, smashed down on the man's cheek, driving his head back against the metal door with a crunch of bone. Danni slumped as Lynch powered through the doorway. He caught Marcelle around the waist. His weight crushed her against the rough wall of the corridor. He recovered his balance. He pushed away from the wall and dragged her. Confused, she hesitated and he screamed at her, 'Move! Move! Move!'

Marcelle's dress caught in her legs, she stumbled and Lynch overtook her, caught her hand and dragged her behind him down the corridor.

Michel Freij barely had time to raise his hands in a futile denial as the phalanx of brutal, finned cruise missiles loomed into the glass like sharks in a tank, shattering the thick pane with a massive impact that sent a wave of brilliant shards bowing inwards.

The freezing air sucked into the room blossomed into orange fire, the cloud of flying glass became flechettes shredding anything in their path before they melted and vaporised. Michel Freij's face was lit for a microsecond in a fierce orange glow like a million sunsets. His lips were forced back by the force of the first concussions, a macabre, manic grin that melted as his flesh was flensed by the tiny shards, his bones carbonised by the hellish heat of the first wave of explosions, his ashes thrown into the air and atomised by the second and third waves of missiles as they slammed into the boiling mountainside.

The heavy door smashed open and was obliterated, a roiling fireball raced down the corridor, sucking the oxygen from the air to feed its devouring flames.

A second door, farther down, caught the violence of the first explosion and held, the vacuum extinguishing the flame for an instant before it sucked in the powerful concussion of the second wave. The door blew apart and the shards of metal glittered as they were driven forwards by the massive force of the second wave of detonations. The corridor was stripped back to bare rock by the metal and flame until the whole punch of fire met the mangled wreckage blocking the ruined lift shaft. Everything in the two hundred foot length of passage was destroyed.

The cold air rushed in from Dannieh to fill the vacuum left by the fireballs. Cracking, ticking and dripping, the various materials that formed the remains of Deir Na'ae cooled in their various ways.

In a tiny side room off the main passage, its door blackened but intact, a woman sobbed.

Chapter Thirty-Eight

Brian Channing stood at the head of the boardroom table in the British Embassy. Around it were gathered Nathalie Durand, Jean Meset, Yves Dubois, Ghassan Maalouf and Tony Chalhoub. The gold tassels on the velvet curtains glowed in the Mediterranean sunlight streaming in through the faux Georgian windows.

'It falls upon me to draw a line under yesterday's events and to clarify them for your benefit. After we leave this room, we will likely never speak of this again. However, I believe we all need to walk away having shared the intelligence we worked together to collect, and to understand that we did a fucking good job.'

Channing took them in, rewarded with wan smiles. 'First, the American angle. As we now know, there was never an...' Channing's fingers made quotes in the air, 'official American operation. A right-wing group well placed in the corridors of power in Washington worked with Israeli intelligence to devise an attack on Iranian nuclear programme sites that would be deniable by Israel and the United States. It was Michel Freij's aim to use the attack to ensure that any reprisals would take place against the Druze and Shia areas of southern Lebanon.' Channing paused and scanned the weary group. 'The Greek Navy is currently conducting a mop-up operation at the so-called Near East Institute for Oceanographic Research.' He lowered his hands and continued. 'The

Iranians are making a huge song and dance about two missiles fired in their direction, of course. And the Kazaks are not so happy about two new additions to their environmental disaster zone. The Yanks are crawling all over the Aral Sea trying to get to those missiles before the Russians do. Our friends in the home of the free and land of the brave are inventing some cock and bull story that you'll be reading in tomorrow's press. You can enjoy a sneaky laugh at whatever it is they come up with.'

There was indeed, despite the drawn faces of those at the table, a quiet murmur of anticipatory amusement. Channing waited for it to die down.

'Michel Freij is also dead, as is anyone who was within several hundred yards of Deir Na'ee. The Americans loosed over a hundred cruise missiles in total. Much of the facility has been totally destroyed and the fires are still burning there.'

Channing scowled at the room. 'And we mourn our colleague, Gerald Lynch, who died bravely fighting for truth, for fairness and for justice.' He glanced at Nathalie, sitting back from the table. She avoided his gaze. Tears streamed down her cheeks. Her hands worked together in her lap, her knuckles white.

Channing's mobile peeped insistently. The people in the room started looking at the damn thing and he grabbed at it. They watched him take the call. He shook his head, steadied himself against the table. Stammering, he ended the call and dropped the mobile.

'Fuck me,' Channing told them. 'It's Lynch.'

Dubois cracked first. 'What about him?'

Nathalie looked up, wiping her eyes. Channing spoke to her rather than Dubois. 'It would seem the bastard's still alive.'

Fin

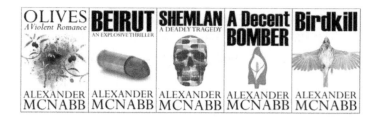

Also by Alexander McNabb

Olives – A Violent Romance

Shemlan – A Deadly Tragedy

A Decent Bomber

Birdkill

You can sign up to Alexander's newsletter, find
out more about new releases, giveaways and
other updates at **www.alexandermcnabb.com**

Thanks

To 'beta readers' Bob Studholme, Micheline Hazou, Kamal BinMugahid, George Kabbaz and Alice Johnson. Thanks, too, to Sara Refai and Taline Jones for early reads and constant friendship. To the Grey Havens Gang, as always, for support, laughs and shoulders. Roba Al Assi once again inspired a scene in one of my books. This time she gave me Barometre which gave me Spike. But for Roba, Leila Medawar would still be alive.

To Eman Hussein I owe a great deal, not least for sharing her Beirut with me as we walked and walked in between death-defying *servees* rides. Maha Mahdy tottered across the city with me in her Louboutins and gave Nathalie another reason to bug Lynch. Carrington Malin has been a staunch ally in this whole book thing.

Derek Kirkup gave me the *Arabian Princess* and a great deal of help and guidance on matters nautical, while Andy Drew helped with whizzbangs. Jessy Shoucair created the 'bulletstick' for the cover.

Thanks, too, to Robb Grindstaff, my editor, who curbed many of my more outrageous tendencies.

Finally, most importantly, thanks to my long-suffering wife Sarah, for putting up with a husband who has his head in the clouds 99 percent of the time.

Reading club notes, FAQ, newsletter and more at:
www.alexandermcnabb.com

Complaints and demands for refunds can always be
directed at @alexandermcnabb

Do please feel free to leave your review of *Beirut –
An Explosive Thriller* **over at Amazon!**

A DEADLY TRAGEDY

ALEXANDER
MCNABB

SHEMLAN

A DEADLY TRAGEDY

The third book of the Levant Cycle

After a lifetime of service around the Middle East, retired diplomat Jason Hartmoor is dying of cancer. He embarks on a last journey back to Lebanon where he studied Arabic as a young man at the Middle East Centre for Arabic Studies, the infamous 'British spy school' in the village of Shemlan far up in the hills overlooking Beirut.

Jason wants to rediscover the love he lost when the civil war forced him to flee Lebanon. Instead his past catches up with him with such speed and violence, it threatens to kill him before the disease does. The only man who can keep him alive long enough to face that past is Gerald Lynch.

Available on all ebook platforms and in paperback online or from your local bookstore by quoting ISBN-13: 978-1477586594.

Made in the USA
Middletown, DE
09 June 2023

32338924R00209